DANAE PENN

A MYSTERY

OF BLOOD

AND DUST

Cover design: JD Smith

Published by Nichol Press

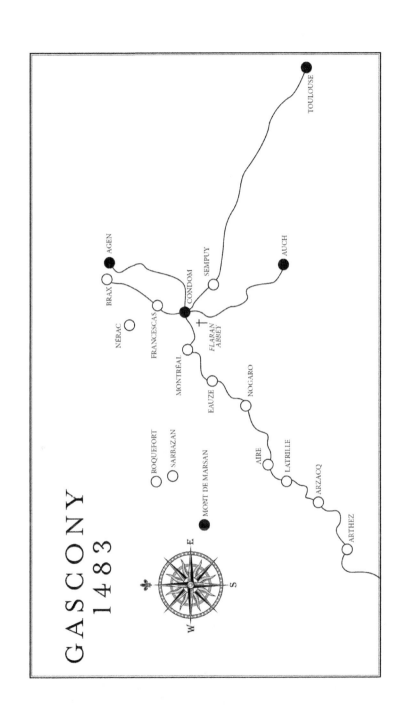

GLOSSARY

abbesse - keeper of public baths (and brothels)

adischatz - good morning / hello (Gascon)

adiu - goodbye (Gascon)

Ave Maria - Hail Mary / prayer to the Virgin

aygue ardente - firewater (now called armagnac)

babioles - trinkets

bourret - new white wine

cantigas - canticles / hymns (Spanish)

Capitoul (Toulouse) - municipal magistrate

chai - wine storehouse

chasuble - ecclesiastical vestment / sleeveless mantle

Consul (Condom) - town councillor

conversos - Jews converted to Christianity (Spanish)

coursier - courser / steed

Credo - the Creed (time taken to say)

crestian, crestiane (f.), crestias (pl.) - originally, returned Crusaders with skin diseases, feared to be lepers; valued craftsmen but discriminated against, especially in XVI-XVII centuries and called *cagots*

destrier – warhorse

étuves – public bath houses, sometimes used as brothels

hamín – Jewish dish of vegetables, eggs, meat and spices

host – wafer used in celebrating Mass

hypocras – sweetened, spiced wine

mercés – thank you (Gascon)

molieròta – miller's wife or daughter (Gascon)

notaire – notary / solicitor

Pair – Father / Daddy (Gascon)

Paternoster – Our Father (time taken to say)

schaum – double-reed musical instrument

Seneschal – governor of a city or province

spokeshave – two-handed plane

tio – yes (Gascon)

Ultreia ! – cry of Santiago pilgrims : 'Ever onwards !'

vendange – grapeharvest

vignerons – vine growers

CHAPTER ONE

Monday 9 September 1483

Belina squeezed Guillaume's leg as a warning, but he continued to shout at her brother Jordi, banging the table so that his trencher jumped. Catalina snatched it away and threw it at the cats. Geraud tried to reach his beaker but his bandaged hand overturned it and cider flowed across the table.

"I'm so sorry," he whispered.

"Never mind, it's because of your wounded arm," his brother replied, mopping up the cider.

The girl beside Geraud put her arm round him and muttered something that made him smile. The others wondered what it was that she'd said. So far no one had been able to speak to the new arrival, and they wished that Geraud would explain who she was and where he had found her.

The couple had arrived at the mill two days ago, with Geraud unable to dismount without Jordi's help and the girl astride a mule with two saddle-bags which she had unhooked and carried into the house, spreading dust everywhere. That was the first reason Catalina found it hard to accept her. Plenty more were to follow.

Guillaume and Jordi continued their argument about the Spanish Inquisition, each accusing the other of ignorance, while Belina watched the cats fighting over the remains of her husband's trencher and her cousin Christau helped himself to more of Catalina's delicious chicken with fennel.

No one noticed that the door had been pulled open until the visitor touched Guillaume's shoulder.

"Messire Guillaume," his groom said, "you must come at once to the Sainte Eulalie chapel."

"Whatever for?" said Guillaume, scowling at him. "Antoni, you know very well that I told you not to disturb me when I am seeing my family."

"It's urgent, Messire. There's been a murder, and there's blood everywhere."

"Who would fight in a chapel?" Guillaume got off the bench and stretched.

"Don't know. A watchman was sent to find you and it took him ages. He was out of breath when he managed to track me down in your absence."

Belina wondered if Antoni had been in his favourite tavern instead of the cathedral stables, but she kept her thoughts to herself. Best not to annoy Guillaume. He was already in a dangerous temper.

"Antoni," Geraud said as loudly as he could, "please could you look at my horse sometime. She has carried me for hundreds of leagues right through Spain and over the Pyrenees and she's worn out."

But Antoni was already out of the house, helping Guillaume mount his own horse.

"Don't worry, Geraud," said Christau, wiping his hands on the tablecloth and taking no notice of Catalina's scowls, "I will ask Sansas to look at your horse and deal with any sores or other problems. He is a groom and will know exactly what to do."

Guillaume and Antoni rode into the town of Condom in silence until they reached the cathedral staff residence, where Guillaume dismounted and rushed up the stairs to his chamber.

When he came back he was carrying his investigation bag. He had calmed down and put himself into observation mode, ready to start finding out what had happened in the chapel and why.

They rode down rue Jean-Baptiste past the leper colony and soon reached the chapel. Antoni's horse pushed its way through the crowd near the chapel door, followed by Guillaume, who was watching the faces in the crowd for any telltale signs. He assumed that some of them were crestias from the leper colony, but there were several pilgrims too at the chapel door asking the watchman guarding it to let them in.

Guillaume dismounted and shouldered his way through. He gave his reins to Antoni, who was still on his horse. "Look around carefully and remember what and who you see."

Antoni touched his cap in acknowledgment. The crowd retreated a few feet, scared of being trampled by the two horses.

Guillaume had not been inside the Sainte Eulalie chapel for many months. It was outside his normal area of Condom, and when he went to Mass – which was not often – he joined Belina and their friends in the cathedral.

He looked around him, expecting to see the blood that Antoni had told him about. But all he saw was an altar, a dusty floor, walls with peeling paint, two large chests and another smaller one in the darkest corner.

He walked to the far end of the chapel, looked at the dust on the altar and pushed open the door to the vestry. It was there that he saw the blood – on the floor, on a green chasuble and on the body of a young woman who was lying on her back. Insects were buzzing around the blood which oozed out of her throat and on to the many jewels around her neck.

Guillaume knelt down beside the corpse, trying to stop his clothes touching the pools of blood, and noticed the flies laying their eggs in the mouth, nose and open eyes of the victim. This horrible sight told him that the death had happened that morning. He checked the eyelids and then peered at the left hand. The right one still held a needle and thread. The young woman's skin was translucent, her lips and nails pale. Her hands were blue and her eyes were flattened.

He stood up and glowered at the man near the window. "Move away from the window so that I have more light!"

"I don't take orders from young men."

"Oh yes you do." Guillaume's bad temper had returned. "I am in charge. Who are you and what are you doing here?"

"I am Messire" – he stressed the word – "Chezelle, tooth-physician of Dame Senclar."

"Dead women don't need their teeth pulled. I repeat, what are you doing inside this chapel?"

"Dame Senclar requested me to keep a close eye on this young man here," he pointed to the prisoner, who was pinned to the wall by a watchman.

"Why is Dame Senclar interested in his welfare?"

"Because she disapproved of him very strongly indeed."

"Why," Guillaume repeated as he walked towards the watchman and the prisoner.

"He has had the boldness to press his suit upon Dame Viola, the daughter of Consul Lussan." Chezelle pointed to the corpse.

Guillaume bit his lip. So the dead young woman was Viola Lussan. He wondered why she should have been in such a small chapel near the leper colony. And why she had been sewing something.

"How does Dame Edith know that?" Guillaume looked at the prisoner, who stared back, expressionless.

"Dame Edith is absolutely certain this man is a murderer."

"Why?"

"What do you mean why?" Chezelle pulled the prisoner sideways. "He has been working in Consul Lussan's mansion, making furniture there in preparation for Viola's marriage."

"When was that due to take place?" said Guillaume.

"Before Christmas. At Martinmas, perchance. Depends on the dowry I expect."

"Consul Lussan is a rich man," Guillaume observed. "Who's the lucky bridegroom?"

"Not so lucky now. The girl is dead, as you can see."

Guillaume turned round and shuddered in spite of his experience at dealing with dead bodies. He remembered that Belina used to talk about Viola Lussan. They'd been at school together. That meant the corpse was twenty-two years old, give or take.

He returned to questioning Chezelle. "I asked you who Dame Viola was going to marry."

"That's my secret."

"Don't be stupid. This is no time for secrets." Guillaume turned to the watchman. "Bring the young man out of the vestry – and don't let him escape."

"He seems too docile to try that, Messire."

"I agree, but it could be just a ruse to catch us off guard."

The watchman tightened his hold on the man and pushed him through the doorway into the chapel, while Chezelle began to rummage among the chasubles in the big wide chest that lay against the wall.

"Take your hands off those holy vestments." Guillaume pulled the tooth-drawer away. "Get out of here. You're not in your rightful place and you know it."

"And where is my rightful place, young man?"

"Pulling Dame Edith's teeth as if she were a horse, I'm sure," Guillaume pushed the older man through the doorway, removed the key to it from the vestry side and locked it behind him.

"You will suffer for your bad manners," said Chezelle.

"I doubt it. Just get out of the chapel before I get the watchman to sling you out."

Guillaume thought of Belina and how much she loathed the Senclar family. Perchance she was right to hate them, and perhaps he was wrong to tease her about that hatred.

He brought himself back to the present and led Chezelle

from the chapel. He could go to Dame Edith like a puppy if he wanted to, but he needed to get away from the scene of the crime right now.

Guillaume, the watchman and the prisoner followed the tooth-drawer out and Guillaume locked the door behind him, putting the long, heavy key in the purse attached to his belt. He waited until Chezelle had climbed into a carriage and been driven towards the town, then told the two watchmen to take the prisoner to the cathedral prison nearby.

"Normally we put prisoners in the Seneschal's gaol, Messire Lansac."

"I know you do. But this one has been found inside a religious building so he needs to be kept in the cathedral prison."

The watchmen did not object – the cathedral prison was nearer. They set off with the docile prisoner, followed by Guillaume and Antoni on their horses, with Antoni telling Guillaume about the pilgrims and the musical instruments they had been carrying. "They all wore the same badge on their hats, Messire Guillaume. They bore an enamel Compostela shell above a pewter carving of four people."

As they passed the leper colony Guillaume noticed that his prisoner looked straight ahead of him. No one called out from the cottages on his right, because they had formed a procession of their own, heading towards their tiny lepers' cemetery carrying a dead child wrapped in sacking. Guillaume tried to block out the mournful singing and the sobbing of a young woman.

"They have funerals every week, Messire," said the watchman in front of Guillaume. "Unhealthy crowd."

"Perchance they would be healthier if they were to get enough to eat," Guillaume suggested.

"Leprosy, that's what it is. And that's what we shall get if this prisoner is a leper."

Guillaume told him to keep his grip on the prisoner, but he checked the young man's face for telltale signs of the disease, of which there were none.

They came to the massive door of the cathedral prison and greeted the guards.

"What's this, Messire Lansac, a thief of pilgrims' clothes?"

"Not this time. Much worse. Perchance he is a murderer."

One of the guards took the prisoner and removed the satchel that was slung across his shoulder. Guillaume told him to put the prisoner in the strongest cell and to lock the satchel inside the guardroom chest. He dismounted and told Antoni to take the horses back to the stables.

The guard pushed his prisoner in front of him down the steps to the dungeon. He asked Guillaume to carry the lantern at the bottom of the stairs and they walked slowly to the end of the dusty passage. Rats scuttled away from them and cobwebs brushed Guillaume's face. He covered his nose and mouth with his free hand as the stench worsened.

The guard stopped suddenly and Guillaume almost dropped the lantern. "I'll put him in here." He turned a key in a massive iron lock and pushed the prisoner inside.

"I will question him straight away," said Guillaume, "and then return to the guardroom to sign the register. May I keep the lantern please?"

"I suppose so, but it makes it hard for me to walk back through the passage."

"In that case, wait here while I do my first interrogation," said Guillaume.

The guard looked shifty. In the background rats scurried. "He doesn't look that dangerous," he said finally. "I'll leave you to it and go back to the guardroom." He gave Guillaume his key, telling him to lock the door immediately after him.

Guillaume put the key in the purse hanging from his belt and listened to the guard's footsteps fading. Then he picked up the lantern and held it near the prisoner's face. His first impression was one of great sadness. The man's eyes stared vacantly over Guillaume's shoulder, his mouth was turned down and a tear leaked from his left eye. Yet he was clean shaven and carefully dressed.

"What's your name?"

"Josep, Messire."

"Where is your home?"

The prisoner shook his head and the tear dropped to the dirty floor.

"Answer my question. Do you live in the leper colony?"

"Yes. That's why I sometimes go inside the chapel."

"Are you a crestian?"

He nodded. "Yes."

"Did you kill the young lady?"

The crestian turned away and sobbed.

Guillaume grabbed his shoulder. "Answer my question, Josep."

The man shook his head and continued sobbing.

Guillaume gave up, unlocked the door, went through it quickly, and turned the key in the lock. He went carefully back to the foot of the stairs. Was the man a murderer? Was his sorrow an act or was the grief genuine?

He climbed the steps and ducked his head through the low doorway into the guardroom.He returned the dungeon cell key and said, "All I have been able to discover is that his name is Josep and he lives in the leper colony near here."

The senior guard tensed and sucked in his next breath. "A leper? You bring us a man from the colony?" He pushed the prison register to Guillaume at arms length with his fingertips and Guillaume wrote the prisoner's details down.

"Yet he is a Christian, like you and me. And he seems very miserable. Treat him gently, I don't want him to die on us."

"He could be putting on an act, Messire Lansac."

"He could indeed, but somehow I think his unhappiness is genuine. Don't give him anything which he could use to kill himself. Keep his satchel safely in your chest. I will be back on the morrow and question him properly."

He signed the register and went outside into the sunshine and fresh air.

CHAPTER TWO

Guillaume walked back along rue Jean-Baptiste towards the cathedral. Deep in thought, he collided with a mule turning into rue Barlet. "Look where you're going," snarled the mule-driver. "You lazy town folk spend your days dreaming." He pressed his goad into the mule's rump and swore.

Guillaume took no notice. He had just remembered that he'd left his investigation bag inside the vestry. Should he retrace his steps and fetch it, or should he go to Consul Lussan's mansion and break the news of his daughter's death to him? He decided on the latter, and walked on as far as the door of the cathedral's staff residence.

As he was crossing the courtyard he heard a shout. His English neighbour, Sir John Keyham, was waving and beckoning him to come over to the table at which he was sitting. Although he was reluctant to waste any more time before visiting the consul, Guillaume did not want to upset his crippled neighbour. He walked over to greet him.

Sir John signed to Alain, his manservant, to pour out some *hypocras* for Guillaume to drink.

"Thanks. I need it." Guillaume gulped the liquid down rather than sip it.

Sir John made a question mark in the air with his left hand.

"I have just come from the Sainte Eulalie chapel where there has been a horrible murder. It's upset me."

Sir John made another question mark.

"A schoolfriend of Belina's. Viola Lussan, with her throat cut. Blood everywhere." Guillaume held out his glass to Alain for another drink. "I don't understand why she was there. It is near the leper colony and it looks as if the murderer is a crestian." He drank the *hypocras* but declined a further refill.

"Why do you think that, Messire Guillaume?" Alain asked.

Guillaume told him how he had found the tooth-drawer in the chapel, and a young man pinned against the vestry wall by a watchman. He put his glass down and told them he had to go and change his clothes and then visit the Lussan mansion to break the bad news to the Consul that his daughter was dead.

He went up the stairs to his chamber and removed the clothes that had been made dirty in the prison and the chapel. He noticed several bloodstains and cursed. Belina was always cross with him for getting blood from corpses on his clothes. It was hard to get out, she said. He had a quick wash and put on his best doublet and hose, stroked the cat, and made sure she did not go out with him.

He strode to the Place Lion d'Or, turned right down rue des Armuriers, and banged on the front door of the Lussan mansion.

"Yes Messire?" a doorkeeper in the Lussan livery asked him.

"I need to talk urgently to Consul Lussan please."

"He is not at home, Messire."

"This is not a casual visit," Guillaume snapped. "I have important news for him which cannot be delayed."

The doorkeeper told him to come in and wait inside while he fetched the steward. Guillaume looked at the paintings and tapestries that adorned the walls of the splendid room. There were chairs instead of stools, and a table with a silver plate on it, as befitted the abode of a wealthy consul.

The steward bustled into the hall accompanied by three small dogs which jumped up on to Guillaume. "Who are you and why do you request to see the Consul?" he asked.

Guillaume explained that he was the Bishop's Inquirer and that he had an urgent and important message for the Consul.

The steward hesitated and frowned. "The Consul is not here today. He is at a betrothal banquet in the Prelet mansion."

"A betrothal banquet?"

"Yes. At least, that was what we were told."

"Who are the happy couple?" Guillaume asked.

"Dame Viola and the son of Consul Prelet."

Guillaume gasped. The steward stared at him.

"How long have they been away?" Guillaume asked.

"That's complicated to answer. The Consul and his wife left mid-morning, but Dame Viola's maid said that her mistress had a difficulty with her gown and would be leaving the mansion as soon as possible."

"So when did she leave it?" Guillaume asked.

"She didn't." The steward sighed. "Consul Prelet sent his steward's assistant down here to fetch her but Mounette – who is Dame Viola's maid – explained that there was still a problem with the gown."

"What was this problem?" Guillaume asked.

"I don't know. I'm just telling you what Mounette told me."

"How could they have a betrothal banquet without the lady to be betrothed?" Guillaume asked.

"Presumably the banquet did not take place." The steward went over to the door and shut it. "Consul Lussan came here himself in a furious temper, and insisted on seeing Dame Viola in her bedchamber."

"I understand the anger," said Guillaume, "but surely it is not seemly for him to enter his daughter's bedchamber?"

"Definitely not, and Mounette refused to let him inside it. There was much shouting, but in the end he left here alone and returned to the Prelet mansion."

"Well, that means I must go to see Consul Lussan there," Guillaume said. "Thank you for your information."

He left the mansion abruptly, giving the steward no

opportunity to ask him why he had wanted to talk to the Consul in the first place. He hurried through the Place Lion d'Or, past the cathedral, but found his way blocked by people and horses in the rue Royale. He passed children to one side and a mule and cart to the other. Oblivious to shouts, he walked up to the very imposing door of the Prelet mansion.

Fortunately, Guillaume knew the doorkeeper, Bernard Baylac, from when he had worked in the cathedral. "Good to see you, Bernard. You are just the person to help me, because I need to talk to Consul Lussan urgently. I was at his mansion, but his steward told me that his master was here."

"Indeed he is, Messire Lansac, and he is in the most awful temper. Don't say I didn't warn you." He grinned, brought Guillaume inside the mansion and told a servant that the Bishop's Inquirer needed to speak to Consul Lussan.

Guillaume was led through a magnificent room and into a dining-hall. The servant approached a portly man with grey hair and a very red face. "Messire Consul, the Bishop's Inquirer is here to see you," he said, indicating Guillaume.

"I've no time to see Bishop's Inquirers. The only person I want to see here is my daughter, as well you know." He waved his arm in Guillaume's direction. "Tell this man to take himself off immediately."

The servant looked at Guillaume. "Do you wish to leave, Messire Lansac?"

"I cannot do so until I have spoken to Consul Lussan, either here in front of everyone or privately, but speak to him I must."

Guillaume approached the Consul, but stopped before he came within arm's reach. The man's temper was extreme, and he wondered how best to deliver the appalling message about his daughter.

An elderly lady with many jewels round her neck scowled at Guillaume. "Who are you? What do you want?"

Guillaume bowed and approached her. "I am the Bishop's Inquirer and–" he began.

"I know that," the lady snapped.

"I have an important message for Consul Lussan." Guillaume wondered whether the stately lady in front of him was the wife of Consul Prelet, or of Consul Lussan, or indeed someone else entirely. The closed world of Condom's consuls and their families was not one he shared.

"Do you want to deliver it here in front of us, or to the Consul in private?"

"That is for him to decide."

"Is it about his daughter? Does the Bishop know why she is not here?"

"He does not know yet, but I know why she is missing and where she is now."

Everyone in the room shouted at once, "Where? Tell us where?"

Guillaume had no idea what to say. He had been rehearsing his speech for Consul Lussan while he walked to rue Royale, but he had not anticipated an audience as large as the one that faced him now.

Consul Lussan stood up. "Answer our question at once, you wretched man."

"Here? Or in private?"

"Here of course, you fool." The consul approached Guillaume. "When next I see the Bishop I will insist that he removes you from his staff."

Guillaume made no reply. The Bishop of Condom was so seldom in the town that the threat was meaningless.

"It is with great sadness that I must tell you Dame Viola has died. That is why she is not here."

The atmosphere changed and the consul appeared to diminish in stature in front of Guillaume. One lady searched for the cloth in her alms-bag, wiped her tears and blew her nose.

Guillaume looked at them all, wishing he knew who they were. The oldest man, wearing beautifully cut clothes and a large ring on his hand, spoke first. "Why have Consul Lussan's servants not informed us of this?"

Guillaume told him that the servants were not yet aware of Dame Viola's death.

This surprising statement kept them all quiet for a few seconds, until they found their voices and began to question him.

Guillaume waited until they had calmed down and stopped shouting at him and each other. He explained as gently as possible that Dame Viola had been found this morning by Messire Chezelle, Dame Senclar's tooth-drawer, in the vestry of the Sainte Eulalie chapel. Her throat had been cut. He had not yet discovered why she had been in such a place, who had murdered her, or what Chezelle was doing there.

"Was she wearing her betrothal gown?" asked one of the ladies who was being comforted by the people beside her. Guillaume wondered if she was Dame Lussan, Viola's mother.

"No, she was wearing everyday clothes," he replied.

"Did she have jewels on her?"

"Yes."

"How did she get to the chapel? I don't understand it."

Guillaume nodded. "I don't understand that either but I will find out. I have only just begun my investigation into her death."

"What have you discovered?"

"Only what I have just told you. I wanted to inform Consul Lussan and his wife before I started investigating."

"Of course. Thank you for your consideration."

Guillaume tried to see who had uttered those words. The voice was calm, polite and sensible. He looked at the back of the room where the voice had come from and saw a young man sitting on a stool and reading a document. Beside him was a young woman who was trying to catch the man's attention, leaning over to look at the document, her breasts almost falling out of the low-cut gown. The effect was spoilt by the fact that the breasts were rather insignificant, apparently too small to attract the young man's attention, or so Guillaume thought.

"Answer my question," snapped Consul Lussan.

Guillaume looked away from the couple. "I am sorry, Consul, I did not hear your question."

"Are you deaf like Viola?"

"I did not know she was deaf, Consul."

"Not completely, just enough to make her unaware if someone came into her room unexpectedly," said Consul Lussan.

A few comments were muttered about Viola's deafness, and two of the ladies began to cry again.

Guillaume decided to take back control. "In due course I will need to ask each of you about Dame Viola so that I can piece together how her life was, who her enemies were, and so on. But first of all I would like to question your steward, Consul Prelet."

"Why?"

"Because that is part of my method of working. The Bishop insists upon it," Guillaume replied smoothly.

The Consul stood up with some difficulty, Guillaume noticed, and walked slowly towards the door leaning on a silver-topped cane. "Follow me, young man."

A servant was ordered to take the Bishop's Inquirer to the steward.

Guillaume followed the servant into the steward's room, where he told him that Dame Viola Lussan had died and asked him who all the guests were. The steward did not invite Guillaume to take a seat, and stood up, indicating that his reply would be brief.

The steward reeled off the names of those who had been present at the betrothal banquet: Consul Prelet and his wife and his son, Messire Charles; Consul Lussan and his wife – but without their daughter; Consul Senclar, his mother and his wife; Consuls Courial, Volpato, Gaudé, Ardit, Toupié and their wives; Messire Galerne and his wife, Dame Pauline,who was the elder daughter of Consul Prelet; Notaire Corloni and his wife, the *notaire's* eldest son and his wife and the *notaire's* eldest daughter.The list was delivered in a rapid monotone, the steward expecting Guillaume to forget most of the names. Consul Prelet's younger daughter and her husband lived in Auch and had not been able to travel to Condom for the banquet. Neither had the younger son, who was a priest in Auch.

Guillaume regretted that he had no wax tablets with him so that he could list all the names. He concentrated on memorising them. Most were familiar, including Notaire Corloni, who according to Belina was a crooked lawyer from Montreal who had forged her father's testament so that her stepmother would inherit money and property which Belina and her brother Jordi should have received. And Geraud too, Guillaume remembered, now that her soldier brother had returned from Spain.

"I understand why the consuls and their wives were guests," he said to the steward, "but why are Notaire Corloni and his family present?"

"I do not know."

"Is he Consul Prelet's *notaire*?"

"I do not know that either."

Guillaume changed direction and asked how long ago the steward had been told to organise the betrothal banquet.

"Several weeks at least. Soon after the Consul's health worsened."

"The limp?" Guillaume prompted and waited for more information. The steward was silent. The clock on his table chimed into the silence. "When was the wedding planned for?" he asked.

"Christmas, or even Martinmas. The Consul was anxious not to delay it any longer than that."

"Was that for health reasons?"

"I am not at liberty to answer such questions." The steward walked to the door and held it open for Guillaume to leave the room, asking one of the servants to show the Bishop's Inquirer out.

Guillaume followed the servant slowly, giving himself time to savour the splendid decor of the mansion.

Bernard Baylac greeted him with a broad smile, the first smile Guillaume had seen since he'd been at the Moulié mill. No, not even there, he realised. The atmosphere had been too bitter, what with his argument with Belina's brother Jordi about the Spanish Inquisition and Catalina's obvious dislike of the mysterious girl who was with Geraud.

"Bernard, I need your help," said Guillaume, leaning against the wall of the doorkeeper's little room.

"Of course. Anything to help you, Messire Guillaume."

"Can you tell me please when each person arrived for the banquet and who they were? And do you have a wax tablet I could use, please? I will bring it back as soon as I have transcribed the information."

"Well now, let me think." The doorkeeper scratched his head and rearranged his cap. He gave Guillaume a much-used wax tablet and a stylus and scratched his head again. "The first two arrived very early. Notaire Corloni and his wife. But they came no distance; they live in the mansion next door."

"I thought they lived in Montreal," Guillaume said.

"In theory, yes they do, but the *notaire* and his family are often next door. The mansion belongs to the Widow Créon, the *notaire's* sister, but she is usually in Bordeaux."

"So how many of the family came with the *notaire*?" Guillaume asked.

"His eldest son and his wife, and his eldest daughter," said Bernard, "but they came much later, after Dame Pauline, Consul Prelet's eldest daughter, had arrived with her husband. They live further down rue Royale."

"Perchance the *notaire* needed to show documents to the Consul," Guillaume suggested.

"It's possible. He had papers with him."

"Who else arrived?"

"Several consuls and their wives all together, as if they had met up earlier somewhere." He paused and scratched his head again. They were talking and laughing until they saw me watching them."

"What about Consul Senclar, was he among them?"

"No. He's not popular, so I've heard. The others say he's lazy and that he wouldn't even be a consul if his mother hadn't bought his position for him."

"Really?" Guillaume tried to sound surprised, just in case other Prelet servants were within earshot. "Did he come alone?"

"No, not him. He trailed behind his tiny mother and his big-bosomed wife." Bernard Baylac carved Jeanne Senclar's bosom in the air with his hands, raising both eyebrows towards Guillaume.

The gesture reminded Guillaume of the flat-chested young woman he had seen in the main room. "There was a girl among the consuls and their wives. Not at all Jeanne Senclar's shape. Not much more than bee-stings."

Bernard laughed. "That would be Dame Ana Corloni, the *notaire's* daughter. She often stays in the mansion next door."

"She was trying to attract a young man," said Guillaume. "Who would that be? He wasn't Consul Senclar"

"That was Consul Prelet's son, Messire Charles, the future bridegroom. He arrived here last week, first time I'd seen him in months. He left Condom for Toulouse ten years ago, but when he was just a student in Toulouse he used to spend his holidays here. He would slip into the mansion next door and stay there all night with Ana Corloni. She was far too young to behave like that, really. Only just fifteen, she was."

"Did his parents know?"

"I doubt it. I think they might have had something to say about it."

"Had Charles Prelet met Dame Viola before today?" Guillaume asked.

"No idea. He spends most of his days here going riding, usually alone. I don't know where he goes – or why."

"Perchance he was meeting Dame Viola," Guillaume suggested. "Maybe they wanted a chance to get to know each other. That would be a wise idea."

"He wasn't dressed for love-making, if that's what you mean," said Bernard. "He was in a mess when he came back from his ride this morning, apparently. Went straight to the stables of course, not here."

"So how do you know he went riding this morning?"

"I've just come back from the stables." He smiled at Guillaume. "The lads were very annoyed because he threw his dusty clothes at them, saying he was in a hurry because of the banquet."

"He doesn't sound as if he was that keen on the banquet, or perhaps even the marriage itself," Guillaume observed.

"Who knows? Consuls marry for money, so they say. Consul Prelet certainly did. His wife is fabulously rich."

"Is that the lady who was wearing lots of jewels round her neck?" Guillaume asked.

Bernard gave him a detailed reply about Dame Prelet that included her background, her wealth, her looks, her behaviour, her health. "She's a better lady than Consul Lussan's wife, who comes from Agen and she doesn't fit in here. She too wears lots of jewellery, but her style is more modern."

Guillaume asked if Consul Lussan and his wife had arrived at the same time as the group of consuls, or with Consul Senclar.

"They arrived soon after the *notaire*. They looked really cross. They were riding along rue Royale arguing. I could see it from here."

"Could you hear the argument?"

"Oh no. When they arrived here they told me that their daughter would arrive later, escorted by their steward. She had a problem with her gown and did not want to delay her parents carrying precious documents and the betrothal gift."

"Did they leave their horses by this main entrance?"

"Yes, and one of the lads took them round to the stables." He paused. "That's the funny thing. I learned just now when I was in the stables myself that Consul Lussan came out of the mansion shortly after he arrived and got them to saddle up his horse. He left at a furious pace."

"Perchance he went back to his mansion to fetch some forgotten document or other," said Guillaume.

"I have no idea where he went. But he came back all dusty, like Messire Charles Prelet had done."

Guillaume asked who had left first, who had come back first, and whether anyone else had gone out riding.

It took time to fit all Bernard's information together, but he learned that Charles Prelet had left early and Consul Lussan had left soon after his arrival mid-morning in rue Royale. He was back before Messire Charles and had gone into the mansion. Soon afterwards, the steward's assistant had taken a horse and ridden it to rue des Armuriers to fetch Dame Viola, but had come back without her. After that, Consul Lussan had stormed into the stables, ordered his horse to be re-saddled and said he was going to rue des Armuriers. He cursed the steward's assistant for his stupidity. He was thoroughly nasty and the Prelet stable staff despise him.

Bernard's story was interrupted by Notaire Corloni coming out of the door. "Do not criticise your betters, doorkeeper."

The fat *notaire* and his family walked silently down the steps to the street and then up the steps of the mansion next door. All five of them looked as if they had swallowed vinegar.

Guillaume commented on their sour faces. He sat down on a stool, put Bernard's wax tablet on his knee and began to write down everything that he had heard. His mind was racing. He presumed that the crestian had killed Viola, but was he alone when he did it? Who had supplied the knife? How was Chezelle involved? He was a tooth-drawer, so he must have sharp tools. But the crestian would have been a carpenter– all crestias were carpenters – and he too must possess sharp tools.

CHAPTER THREE

The cathedral clock struck five times, reminding Guillaume that he should return to the chapel, have the body taken to the cathedral corpse room and examine the crime scene in the vestry. He thanked Bernard and told him he would return the wax tablet as soon as he had copied the names on to a tablet of his own.

Rue Royale was still full of people and animals, and he pushed his way through the crowds holding the tablet very tightly. He strode into the cathedral guardroom, disturbing the dice players, and told them he needed a couple of them to accompany him to the Sainte Eulalie chapel, bringing a stretcher with them.

"Is someone ill?" One of the guards said.

"No, someone is dead," Guillaume replied, "and I need to get the body safely into the corpse room as soon as possible."

"Is the chapel locked up?" Guillaume nodded and patted the purse fastened to his belt. "Then what's the hurry?" The guard looked back at his game of dice.

"Because the body has had its throat slit, that's why," Guillaume snapped. "Hurry up and get the stretcher. Your dice game can wait."

"Of course, Messire Guillaume."

The two youngest guards were told to get the stretcher and

accompany the Inquirer to the chapel. The others went back to their dice playing.

Guillaume led the two guards along the street to the Sainte Eulalie chapel. He unlocked the door and strode through the chapel towards the vestry.

"Where's the body?" asked the guards together.

"In here. Be prepared for a great deal of blood." Guillaume took the vestry key out of his purse and unlocked the door. As he had expected, an awful smell made him gulp and feel sick. Flies were crawling over the corpse and buzzing above her head and in the wound. The younger guard threw up, adding to the smell.

Guillaume showed the guards where to put the stretcher and the three of them lifted the corpse on to it and fixed it in place with ropes. They looked for a cloth large enough to cover the whole body, and one of the guards picked up an altar cloth lying in the open chest beside the wall.

"There doesn't seem to be anything else, Messire Guillaume."

"Never mind. Getting the body into the corpse room is much more important than an altar cloth in a chapel used by crestias."

The guard jumped as if stung by a wasp. "Crestias! I don't want to catch leprosy." He turned towards the door.

"Don't be stupid. You won't catch leprosy. Nobody has been a leper in Gascony for at least two hundred years."

"Then why do the crestias have to live outside the town?"

"Because people like you are frightened of them." Guillaume regretted his scornful words, but it was too late to take them back. He spread the altar cloth on top of Viola's body.

"Have you got another rope?" They shook their heads. "Then we must use something from here." He looked at the contents of the chest but could only find old cloths of various sizes.

"Here's a rope around a curtain," said the older guard. He unhooked it and drew the curtain back. "Here are some steps, Messire."

Guillaume looked at the wooden steps descending into darkness. "Probably leads to a crypt. I will look at that later." He took the rope and fastened the altar cloth as securely as possible while the younger guard turned and threw up again.

They carried the stretcher out of the vestry and through the chapel while Guillaume locked the vestry door, and then out of the chapel door into the sunshine. The younger guard's face lost its green colour as all three of them breathed the fresh air once more.

They walked along rue Jean-Baptiste to the cathedral corpse room followed by a crowd of crestias.

"Who has died, Messire?" one of them asked Guillaume.

"I don't know yet," he lied.

"All sorts of people use that chapel, Messire. Not just crestias. We mostly stay well away from it, except for Mass, and even then we don't enter the chapel. They give us the host on the end of a long wooden spoon."

Guillaume had heard about this practice, but he had never seen it happen. He had been brought up in Bordeaux, a big city, and when he was very young he had lived in England near Southampton. He was half English, although the only person in Condom who knew that was Belina. She had explained to all her friends and family that many Bordeaux people were tall and fair like Guillaume because it had been an English city until forty years ago. Belina had never travelled as far as Bordeaux, and did not want to. It was a frequent source of argument between her and Guillaume.

The guards reached the corpse room and untied the body, laying it on a set of flat stones. Guillaume removed the clothes very carefully and folded them. Then he removed all the jewels from round Dame Viola's neck and wrists and put them in his purse, even though the blood would stain it. He crossed himself, picked up Viola's clothes and shut the door behind him carrying the clothes rolled up inside the kirtle.

The guards were hovering near the door leading to the

monks' cemetery. Guillaume fished four coins out of his purse, gave two to each guard and thanked them for carrying out the unpleasant task. "Once you have put the stretcher back in its place, have a drink and put it all out of your minds." He turned away and asked for the corpse room register.

He signed the register and informed the clerk that the body was that of Dame Viola Lussan, of rue des Armuriers, Condom. He ordered him not to reveal the identity of the body to anyone.

"Why not, Messire Guillaume?"

"Because she has been murdered. Her throat has been slit. I don't know for certain yet who did it, but I think I have found the murderer and shut him up in the cathedral prison."

"Why not in the Seneschal's prison?"

"Because she was found in the Sainte Eulalie chapel."

The clerk gasped and crossed himself. "A murder in a holy place, how dreadful."

"I agree," said Guillaume. "I'm going back there now to find out when she was killed and how."

"A sharp knife, I suppose," said the clerk. "Probably one of those ghastly crestias did it."

Guillaume did not tell him that the prisoner was a crestian. Instead, he picked up the bundle of Viola's clothes and walked back to the chapel, let himself in again and locked the door behind him. He looked around for candles because it was beginning to get dark. He helped himself to the ones on the altar and lit them using the metal flint and the silex beside the altar. Then he unlocked the vestry door and locked it up behind him.

The smell had become a stench, but at least the body had gone. He put the bundle of Viola's clothes near the door and searched the little room carefully.

She must have been embroidering the green chasuble, because when he had seen her body earlier there was a needle and green thread in her hand and the chasuble was hanging from the thread. He picked this up and noticed a wooden object that had been hidden under the garment.

Guillaume picked two cloths from the open chest and wrapped them round his hands. He picked up the object and scrutinised it in the light of the window. It was about twelve inches long, with two wooden handles and a blade between them. It was definitely not an object which would normally be found in a vestry. The blade was stained. Guillaume sniffed it very carefully. As he expected, it smelled of blood. He laid it on top of Viola's bundle of clothes.

He pulled a wax tablet out of his investigation bag and his best stylus and put them on a table beside a dusty crucifix. He scratched down what he had seen so far, beginning with his examination of the corpse and his estimate of time of death, and then the chasuble and the presumed weapon. He fished out a second tablet and sketched the layout of the room, showing where Viola's corpse had been found, on her back facing the window.

Halfway through his drawing he paused. When he had arrived with his groom earlier that afternoon, both doors had been unlocked and their keys had been on the inside. So Viola must have felt safe if she was facing the street instead of the door. Perchance she was hoping to see somebody passing the window. Of course, she would have heard anybody coming into the chapel and then the vestry. Then he remembered that Consul Lussan had said that his daughter was deaf, which meant that the murderer could have entered the vestry carrying the weapon and have attacked Viola from behind, slitting her throat as he pulled her backwards.

Guillaume shuddered. It was getting too dark to investigate anything else. He snuffed out the two candles, picked up the weapon and tucked it very carefully into the centre of the bundle of clothes.

He glanced at the curtain beside the flight of steps down to the crypt but decided to leave that for another day. He had enough to do as it was – more than enough. He locked up the vestry and the chapel behind him and walked back to the cathedral staff residence. He wondered whether any pilgrims and crestias had seen people enter the chapel early that morning. He must remember to ask Antoni what more he had discovered when he was waiting outside the chapel with the horses. So far, all he had mentioned to Guillaume was a group of pilgrims who were musicians. But Guillaume remembered that there were more people hanging around the chapel door when he arrived from the mill. Antoni's advice was usually reliable, provided he was in a good mood. Guillaume regretted his own ill-temper when they were riding from the mill to the chapel.

It was too late for any pilgrims to still be in the street, but the crestias watched him stride past their leper colony. The door to the cathedral prison was shut and he wondered how the murderer was surviving in his dungeon cell. Still snivelling, perchance. Guillaume could imagine him curled up on a piece of matting on the earth floor, sobbing. Or was his sorrow just pretence? Perchance the crestian was disguising his guilt.

Belina was frying eggs when he reached his chamber, so there was only Minet to greet him in her usual joyous way, rubbing her fur against his dusty legs and sneezing. She stalked across the room waving her tail.

Guillaume took his investigation bag and the bundle of Viola's clothes into his workroom. He hoped Belina would not scold him for his late return. He should perchance have found someone to take a message to her when she was still in the shop. He put on his most contrite expression and waited for her to slide the eggs on to the trencher.

"Where have you been? Why are you so late?" She placed the frying pan in the sink and poured some water onto it.

"I have been to the Sainte Eulalie chapel, to the cathedral prison, to the Lussan mansion in rue des Armuriers, the Prelet mansion in rue Royale, and then back to the Sainte Eulalie chapel." He kissed her and stroked her hair. "It was dusty there. That's why Minet sneezed just now. Didn't you hear her?"

"No I didn't. Can't you see I'm cooking?"

He gave her another kiss. "Why bother to cook anything when we had such a big meal at the mill? Catalina is really a very good cook – it makes up for her bad temper, I suppose."

Belina poured some cider into a beaker and put it and the egg-topped trencher on the table. Guillaume fetched the stools from the corner and sat on the one facing the window and the moonlit courtyard. Belina cut the trencher in half and they ate their eggs. Guillaume picked up the beaker and drank all the cider.

"Why are you so thirsty?" She picked up the beaker and poured more cider into it.

"Partly the dust in the chapel, I suppose." He left a little bit of cider for her this time, but she put the beaker down and stared at him.

"And partly what else?"

"As I have just told you, going to the Sainte–"

She snatched the beaker. "Why don't you tell me what you have been doing?"

"I am trying to, but you keep interrupting me."

"Just get on with your story."

Guillaume recounted his busy afternoon, avoiding any details about the bloody corpse in the chapel vestry, and telling her about his interrogation of the consuls in the Prelet mansion and his quick visit to the Lussan mansion.

"Why the Lussan mansion?"

Guillaume had been waiting for this question, and he offered Belina his carefully prepared answer. "The person who found the dead body in the chapel told me that it was Dame Viola Lussan."

Belina stared at him in surprise and crossed herself.

Guillaume continued. "I think you were at school with her." He took Belina's hand in his.

"Yes." A tear dropped into her lap. "But I haven't seen much of her for the last few years."

"She never came into the shop?" he asked, wiping her tears with his other hand.

"Don't think so," Belina whispered.

"What sort of person was she?"

"She was kind, gentle and friendly." She paused and sniffed. Guillaume gave her his pouch-cloth and she blew her nose. "She came from a much better family than me, of course, but she never showed it. She was kind to all of us. Quite different from that nasty, thin, ugly Ana Corloni."

Guillaume waited for more memories while he clasped Belina's hand in both of his.

"She always seemed a little sad," Belina said. "As if she lacked confidence in spite of her wealthy and important parents."

"Perchance her parents caused her lack of confidence," Guillaume suggested.

"I don't know."

He tried again. "Did she dress very well?"

Belina closed her eyes, and thought. "Yes, of course she was better dressed than me with my clothes full of flour."

"Did she have any brothers or sisters?"

"Only one. He was called Mathurin, I think, same as his father."

"Was? Is he dead?"

"About four years ago, from the plague." Belina blew her nose again. "But they weren't that close."

"Did she study hard at school?"

"Yes."

"What was she especially good at?"

Belina thought for quite a while, screwing up her face. "Drawing and painting. She was very good at that."

"Anything else?"

"Not that I remember."

"Did she have many friends?"

"I don't remember. I'm sorry, Guillaume, but I lost touch with her. School friends don't always last."

"Did she get on well with boys like Jordi and Christau?"

Belina was silent for several minutes, frowning and sniffing. "She liked coming in our boat."

"Didn't her own father have a boat?"

"He probably had several, but they would have been for transporting goods or things for his properties. Wait, it's coming back to me. Her father had lots of land, and lots of men working in his fields and vineyards."

"When she was at school with you did she fall in love?"

Belina shook her head. "She was too sad and withdrawn for that. In any case, she would be destined to marry a consul's son like they all do."

Guillaume kissed her. "Much better to marry a bishop's inquirer."

Belina smiled through her tears. "It's funny that she hadn't already been married off by now."

"Yes, she waited a few years, but today was supposed to be her betrothal day."

"How do you know?"

"That was why I had to go to the Prelet mansion," Guillaume said, "to break the news to Consul Prelet and a dozen other people who were there." He paused. "More like twenty people, I suppose, including the son who lives in Toulouse and had travelled to Condom for his betrothal banquet."

"*His* betrothal banquet?"

"Yes, Charles Prelet was to be betrothed to Viola Lussan," Guillaume replied.

"Did they know each other?"

"I was hoping you could tell me that, Belina."

She shook her head and told him she hadn't heard from Viola for several years. She got up, put her beaker and the remains of the trencher in the sink and washed her hands.

Guillaume got up too and put his arm round Belina's shoulders as she began to sob.

Her sobbing lasted for nearly an hour, by which time they were in bed and he was still trying to comfort her.

CHAPTER FOUR

Tuesday

Early the next morning Guillaume picked up his interrogation bag and walked along the street past the bishop's palace, where gardeners were working among the rose bushes. He stopped to look at them for a moment and breathe in fresh air and the scent in preparation for a long time below ground in the cathedral prison interrogating the murderer.

The guard led Guillaume down the uneven steps to the dungeon and along the passage to the crestian's cell. Other prisoners eyed him and growled. He tried to recall which criminal had stolen money from the cathedral alms box, which one had hit Rocca the Treasurer last year and which one had set fire to wheat stacked ready to be delivered to Rocca's old warehouse. But the light was too dim to recognise their faces, and the smell of urine was horrible.

The guard unlocked the gate to the crestian's cell and stood aside to let Guillaume enter. To his surprise and relief the smell was less bad than the ones that were coming from the other three cells.

The prisoner was sitting on a piece of matting covering the earth floor and with his back against the cleanest part of the wall. On seeing Guillaume, he got up slowly and stared at the floor. Guillaume resigned himself to an extended period of questioning the suspected murderer. He took a tablet and stylus out of his interrogation bag and stood facing his prisoner.

"Is Josep your only name?"

"No. My other name is Sarbazan."

"And you live in the leper colony?"

"Yes."

"What is your work?"

"Carpentry, Messire."

Guillaume had expected this reply. The only work permitted for crestias was woodwork so that they would not infect everyone else. "What sort of carpentry? Building? Roof scaffolding? Oxcarts? Wine barrels?"

"None of those, Messire." He finally looked up at Guillaume instead of down at the floor.

"Then what sort of carpentry do you do?"

"I make furniture, Messire."

Guillaume scratched the word on his tablet. "What sort of furniture?"

"Whatever I am asked to make, Messire."

"A bed, a dresser, a chest, a stool?" Guillaume persisted.

The crestian did not reply.

"Answer my question."

He shook his head. To Guillaume's surprise, a tear crept down the prisoner's dirty face. "All kinds of things, Messire," he muttered.

Guillaume thought about the wooden object found next to the dead body and wondered whether it was used for carpentry. "How many tools do you have?"

The crestian opened his arms. "The guards took my satchel when I came here. My tools were in that satchel. I hope they still are."

"I will check that with them," Guillaume replied. "What time did you arrive in the chapel?"

"I would think about two hours after dawn, Messire. At least two hours."

"Why were you in the chapel?"

Silence. The crestian looked at the floor again.

"Did you have work to do in the chapel?"

Silence. The crestian shifted his weight to the other foot.

"Answer my question?" Guillaume snapped.

"No, Messire." The crestian hesitated, still gazing at the floor. "No Messire," he repeated. "I had already worked for about two hours that morning."

"Where?"

"In the mansion of Widow Créon in rue Royale."

"What were you doing there?"

"Mending a casket."

"Who had broken it and why was it broken?"

"I don't know. I was told that the *notaire* had ordered it to be mended so that he could present it to somebody that morning. It was an intricate job and took me a long time to get it right."

"Where were you working on Saturday?" Guillaume asked.

"Same place, making a linen chest. I had almost finished the carcass, and I was using my spokeshave to remove imperfections from the outside edges."

Guillaume asked him to describe his spokeshave.

"It is about twelve inches long, with two wooden handles and a flat blade screwed on between them. I push the blade away from me. For example, if I am smoothing the edge of a piece of furniture I do it like this." He grasped an imaginary object and moved it very slowly away from himself.

"Always away from yourself?" Guillaume asked.

"Yes, Messire."

"Did you ever leave your satchel of tools unattended?"

"Sometimes, but only to go to the latrine."

"Did anyone watch you working?" Guillaume asked.

"Not really."

"What do you mean? Did anyone watch you or not?"

"I concentrate on my work, Messire," the crestian replied. "I don't always notice if I am alone or being watched."

It was the first, and last, direct statement that the crestian made. Everything else was muttered or whispered. Guillaume questioned him relentlessly for a long time, but learnt nothing further. There were many protestations of innocence, but Guillaume was unconvinced by them.

The crestian's face was expressionless apart from his eyes, which were watery. They filled with tears whenever Guillaume mentioned the victim and her slashed throat.

Finally the crestian turned his back on Guillaume and faced the rear wall of his damp and dirty cell.

Guillaume took the gate key from his belt, unlocked the gate, and locked it up again when he was in the passage. He went back to the guard room and returned the key. Then he walked back to the staff residence deep in thought. What had Viola Lussan been doing in a small chapel near the leper colony instead of in her rightful place at the centre of a betrothal ceremony? The carpentry tool which he had found under the chasuble fitted the crestian's description of his spokeshave and which he had used last Saturday, but it seemed that the murderer had attacked his victim from behind as she sat on a stool looking out of the vestry window. Nothing made sense —at least, not yet.

He went across the courtyard of the cathedral staff residence and climbed the stairs leading to his chamber. Still deep in thought he walked into his neighbour, the choirmaster. "I'm so sorry, Brother Charles," he said.

"Don't mention it, Guillaume. I expect you are solving one of your investigations."

"Far from solving it. I am only at the very beginning." Guillaume unlocked the door to his chamber.

Brother Charles smiled. "You and your wife will soon solve it, just like you did the last murder." He paused. "I hope it is not a murder this time?"

"Alas it is, with blood everywhere." Guillaume stopped any further discussion by bidding Brother Charles *adiu* and shutting the door behind him. He added two tablets to his investigation bag and hurried out again.

He walked along to the Place Lion d'Or and down rue des Armuriers to the Lussan mansion. Consul Lussan was reputed to own a lot of land as well as other valuable property. Guillaume wondered vaguely what Viola's dowry would have been. Had Charles Prelet and his father been deprived of money, or of property, or of both following her death? He needed to find that out – discreetly.

Guillaume explained to the doorkeeper that he needed to speak to the steward.

"He is in the hall speaking to Messire Chezelle."

Damn, thought Guillaume. Dame Edith Senclar's tooth-drawer was a confounded nuisance. He had no business being here.

The doorkeeper showed Guillaume into the hall and announced that "Messire Lansac wishes to see you."

The steward came to meet Guillaume accompanied by three small dogs, all barking. "Why didn't you tell us the dreadful news of Dame Viola's death when you were here yesterday?"

"It was essential that I told her parents first, and they were not here."

Chezelle strode towards him, displaying his splendid teeth. "I have been informing the steward of the murder – and of the murderer. I trust he is safely in the Seneschal's prison."

Guillaume did not reply. He would prefer to keep Chezelle as ignorant as possible. He turned to the steward and asked to be taken to Dame Viola's bedchamber and to speak to her maid there.

Chezelle tried to follow them but the steward told the doorkeeper to show the tooth-drawer out.

They went through a large room and the steward pointed to a dresser. "The crestian had been working on this, smoothing some of it and carving Dame Viola's initial on it." He pointed to the V in the centre of the dresser back.

"What is the other initial?" Guillaume asked.

"C for Charles, the son of Messire Prelet. The crestian didn't like carving it.

"Why not? C is not very difficult to carve, surely?"

"It was very difficult for a man who was so deeply in love with Dame Viola."

"Was that love returned?" Guillaume asked very quietly. He wondered how many servants were nearby listening to the conversation.

"We in the servants' hall thought that it was, although of course it could have been kindness or politeness on the part of Dame Viola. She's a very gentle young lady."

"She was, you mean", said Guillaume.

The steward turned away and led Guillaume to the stairs. Guillaume picked up his bag of tablets and followed the steward up the stairs and down a long passage to more stairs which were almost hidden by a green curtain.

"Are those the servants' stairs?" he asked.

"No – I mean yes." The Steward opened the door on his left and Guillaume walked into a bedchamber.

He studied the room for several minutes, trying to get an impression of Dame Viola from its contents. The red curtains around the bed had been looped up, displaying a cream bed-cover with a white silk gown laid on it. An elegant pale-green head-cloth was on the pillow and a pair of satin shoes lay beside an empty jewel casket on a clean white cloth to the other side of the gown.

A large chest stood open to Guillaume's left. He peered inside and saw ordinary clothes which had been heaped up.

"It's my fault, Messire."

Guillaume looked in the direction of the voice. An old woman was sitting on a stool in the corner, her head in her hands.

"It's my fault," she repeated, sobbing. "I was trying to see if something was missing."

"What would be missing?" Guillaume asked her.

"I don't know. I don't know." The woman got up and walked to the door.

Guillaume took her arm gently. "Stay here please. I need to ask you some questions."

She looked at the steward.

"I expect you have so many things to see to, steward," said Guillaume. "Please don't let me delay you here."

The steward took the hint, offered Guillaume a slight bow and closed the bedchamber door behind him.

Guillaume led the maid back to the stool in the corner, fetched one for himself and sat near her. He touched her arm gently. "I am so sorry that you heard the news about Dame Viola from someone other than myself." He took her hand before she could cover her face with it. "I had hoped to break the bad news to you gently. Instead you must have heard it from that horrible foreign tooth-drawer who works for Dame Senclar."

She nodded. Guillaume continued, still speaking very softly in case people were listening outside. "Have you worked for Dame Viola a long time?"

"Since she was a babe," the maid sniffed. "She was always so kind and gentle."

"I suppose she took after her mother in that respect," said Guillaume.

"Not at all. Definitely not. Her mother is a selfish old witch."

Guillaume was not surprised. Dame Lussan's reputation in Condom was not good, and the question had been intended to sound out the maid. He waited for her to continue.

"Dame Viola's mother only thinks of herself, her clothes, her appearance, her jewels. Especially the jewels. She is always getting the Consul to buy her more jewellery."

"But the Consul is rich. He can afford it," said Guillaume.

"Last year he lost money, so they say," replied the maid.

"Bad land purchases somewhere, but I don't know any more than that."

"Perchance the Consul didn't tell his wife he had lost money," Guillaume suggested.

"He'd be too scared to tell her."

"Do all of you think that?" Guillaume asked.

"Yes we do."

"So all of you would have supported Dame Viola against her mother?" Guillaume suggested.

"Oh yes. Definitely." The maid sniffed. Guillaume gave her his pouch-cloth and asked her what her name was.

"Mounette." She dabbed her eyes with Guillaume's pouch-cloth. "We all believe that Dame Lussan doesn't love Dame Viola like a mother should. She's only thinking of herself."

"But she and her husband had negotiated a good marriage for Dame Viola," Guillaume pointed out.

"It depends what you mean by 'good'," said the maid. She launched into a long and convoluted story of how Dame Lussan had insisted that her daughter marry well so that the family's reputation in Condom would be maintained, and how that would in turn enhance her position in her own family in Agen, which was why it had taken so long to find a sufficiently worthy husband for Dame Viola.

Guillaume let her carry on about family importance, wondering why Viola had not worn the beautiful gown stretched out on her bed, even though the excuse which she had given to her parents had been that it needed to be mended. Was that just an excuse to avoid the betrothal banquet? A desperate excuse, no doubt, but it had worked. Her parents had left the mansion before her. Perchance they had business to discuss with Consul Prelet which their daughter did not know about. Guillaume reflected for a moment, glad that his marriage to Belina was a love match with no calculating parents involved.

"We liked Dame Viola's crestian," said the maid, bringing Guillaume back into his investigation.

"Why?"

"He was very skilled. He smiled a lot at her. He couldn't stop looking at her. They were so in love."

"I have heard it said that children of nobility don't get to choose who to marry," Guillaume said.

As he expected, the answer was quick and forthright. "The Lussan family are not nobility. He is a consul and Dame Lussan's father is a consul in Agen. That doesn't make them nobility."

"But it would be enough to make them *want* to be nobility," said Guillaume.

She shook her head, dislodging her head-cloth. "Consul Lussan just wants a quiet life. It's his wife who enjoys all the important events where she is the centre of attention."

"She would find it hard to displace Dame Edith Senclar's position in Condom," said Guillaume. He smiled, realising that he was saying something which Belina would have said. Belina hated Edith Senclar, and had always done so. He still hadn't got to the bottom of the reason for that hatred, but he wondered if it was something to do with Belina's stepmother.

The maid was telling him about everybody's opinion of Dame Viola and what a good artist she was. Guillaume realised that he had probably missed some important information. He took three wax tablets from his bag and made a drawing of the room on one, the bed and its contents on another, and the open chest of ordinary clothes on the third. Then he got up and looked at those clothes. They seemed dusty, especially at the hems. Yet the bedchamber floor was clean. He sniffed one of the hems and sneezed, scattering the dust.

The maid tried to take the kirtle and put it back in the chest, but he would not let her.

"I need this for my investigation." He put it inside his bag of tablets. "Does Dame Viola do her painting in that kirtle?" he asked Mounette.

"No, Messire. She paints in the room above and keeps a smock there."

"Please could you show me that room."

Guillaume pulled open the bedchamber door very quickly and four servants fled down the passage. Mounette tugged at one of the green curtains and indicated that Guillaume should go up the narrow wooden stairs.

He found himself in a large room with a wide window. There was a stand with a half-finished drawing of a tree. Brushes and paints were stacked neatly nearby and a tray of garance, charcoal and the leaves of a Judas tree was on the floor beside them. A paint-spattered smock hung from a hook near the door.

He stepped back and almost fell over a wooden bucket of water. Very dirty water, much to Guillaume's surprise. He put his thumb in it and examined the dust, which was the same colour as the dust on the clothes inside the chest in the bedchamber below. He bit his lip and frowned.

"When was Dame Viola last in this room?" he asked Mounette.

"Sunday, I think." She picked up the bucket and put it carefully beside the window while Guillaume made a drawing of the room on another wax tablet.

He looked round the room again, picked up his bag of tablets and pulled the door open. This time there were no servants listening behind it.

At the bottom of the stairs he saw another flight going down, but in darkness.

"Where do the stairs lead?" he asked Mounette.

"Nowhere special. Just the servants' quarters."

"Do you sleep down there?"

"No, Messire. I sleep in here next to Dame Viola's room." She opened a door and Guillaume saw a mattress and a stool crammed into a tiny room.

"I think I will go down these stairs," he said. "Is there a lamp or a candle?"

"No, Messire."

Guillaume put down his bag of tablets and searched for a light.

"There's no lamp because no one uses those stairs," Mounette informed him.

Guillaume sniffed the curtain at the top of the dark stairs. It had the same scent as Viola's dusty clothes in the chest.

"Are you sure no one goes down these stairs?"

Mounette nodded, but she refused to meet his eye. He picked up his bag of tablets again and she started to lead the way back to the front of the mansion. But he did not follow her. Instead, he went back inside Viola's bedchamber and looked for a lantern.

It took quite a long time to find where the lantern should have stood. Instead, he found three candles, a metal flint and a silex, a dusty, blackened cloth and some slippers. Guillaume picked them up and Mounette, who had returned to the chamber, started to cry. He examined the slippers. They were clean outside, but dusty inside. He put them in his tablet bag, while Mounette leant against the wall, sobbing.

He decided to abandon her to her grief and explore the dark stairs, taking the three candles and the tall candlestick on the table beside the bed with him. Outside the door he lit one of the candles with the flint and the silex. It was difficult to manage the candlestick as well as his bulging tablet bag, and he went slowly down the stairs in almost total darkness, feeling the stone wall with his left hand.

In due course the stairs became wider and changed from wood to stone. The passage smelled of rat droppings and he hoped he would not fall down on them. It was not as airless as the cathedral staff residence cellars, and Guillaume wondered how soon he would reach the outside. Would he find a tunnel leading down to the river? He knew that many mansions in Condom had such tunnels.

The steps came to an end and he raised the candle to look around him. To his left was a tunnel sloping steeply down, presumably to the river. Straight ahead was a tunnel on level ground. To his right were several barrels.

He bent down to examine the floor of the level tunnel and saw footmarks in the dust going away from him. His foot was larger than the dusty footprints, and wider. The footsteps in the disturbed dust were roughly the same size and shape as Belina's feet.

Guillaume walked carefully beside the footprints, down the long tunnel until he came to a steep flight of wooden steps with a glimmer of light at the top.

The steps were difficult, and he almost dropped the candlestick. There was no wall to either side and the bag swung dangerously. It took all of Guillaume's concentration to reach the opening at the top of the steps.

He pulled a curtain aside and gasped. He had found himself in the vestry of the Sainte Eulalie chapel, looking at the mess and the bloodstains he had seen yesterday.

He remembered seeing those wooden steps from above. He had assumed that they led to a crypt, and that he would need to examine it in due course for clues that would show where the crestian had hidden before attacking Viola.

Now he realised that there was no crypt and that Viola would have walked through the dusty tunnel to the vestry. But why?

Guillaume stared at the vestry, but saw again Viola's body and the flies lapping at the blood which oozed from her throat. Then his mind returned to the present and he watched a mouse scamper along the edge of the far wall and disappear behind the curtain. He lit the lantern with the flint and silex beside the candles and wondered whether to retrace his steps through the tunnel and stairs leading into the Lussan mansion or walk home from the chapel. He went over to the window and examined the keys hanging from his belt, but it was difficult in the dusk to distinguish between the large key to his chamber, the even larger one that would unlock the courtyard door and several other long keys. Smaller keys belonging to the various chests which he kept in the cathedral treasury got in the way.

He untied the bunch from the leather strap on his belt and examined each key. They were similar, and Guillaume supposed that they had all been made by the cathedral locksmith. He sniffed each one and sneezed from the dust of only two of them. He put the dustiest of those two in the lock leading to the chapel and turned it gently. But the door stayed shut. He tried the second dusty key and it worked after a bit of pushing.

Guillaume drew the curtain in order to conceal the steps leading to the tunnel, took a last look at the vestry, trying not to remember the sight of Viola's body and the flies, and went into the main room of the chapel, locking the vestry door behind him. The putrid smell of death was less strong than it had been in the vestry, but he gulped at the blend of death, dirt and moisture as he reached the main door and bent down to unlock it with the other dusty key.

He had to pull the door open and found it difficult to shut it tightly behind him. He locked it, fastened the bunch of keys to his belt, took several deep breaths and set off towards the cathedral staff residence.

CHAPTER FIVE

Quiteira was already in the shop when Belina arrived, and was putting trays on to the display table and puffing as she heaved a large tray full of metal statues and St Peter's keys. Belina fetched some phials of *aygue ardente* from the inner room and placed them on the edge of the display table, too far to be snatched away by a passing pilgrim.

"How was your dinner yesterday?" Quiteira asked, mopping her brow.

Belina sighed and pulled out another tray of *babioles*.

"What's the matter?" Quiteira insisted.

Belina told her about the family meal at the Moulié mill, Catalina's anger, Jordi's worried face, Geraud suffering from his painful wounds and being comforted by his girl.

"Girl?" asked Quiteira.

"I'm sure she must be no more than sixteen," Belina replied.

"Why not ask her?"

"Because she hardly speaks any Gascon."

"Then speak to her in French."

"No use," said Belina. "She knows no French at all."

"What does she speak, then?" Quiteira put another tray of *babioles* on the display table.

"Geraud says she speaks Spanish some of the time."

"And the rest of the time?"

"Geraud says her mother tongue is Arabic, and that he has learned to speak it himself."

Quiteira re-arranged two of the trays. "And that's the reason she lives with him, is it? Teaching Geraud Arabic." She sneered.

Belina flew to her brother's defence. "She looks after him. And he loves that."

"How was he wounded?"

"Fighting at the siege of Lucena."

"Where's that?"

"Near Granada."

"Where's that?"

Belina looked at her in astonishment. "Surely you know that, Quiteira? Granada is in southern Spain. The king of Aragon is trying to conquer it."

"Is it bigger than Condom?"

Belina laughed, for the first time in two days.

"Don't you dare laugh at me," Quiteira shouted, forgetting that there might be potential customers nearby.

A pilgrim waved his staff at Quiteira. "They say it is the biggest city in Spain," he said. "They say that everyone there is clothed in silk. They say that the Moors have discovered how to move water uphill."

"I don't believe you," Quiteira retorted. "If everyone wears silk, why are you wearing homespun?"

"Silly woman." The pilgrim waved his stick at her again. "I am a pilgrim, not a soldier or a merchant. I have not been to Granada."

"Then how do you know what it's like?" Quiteira demanded.

"Because I listen to what travellers say." He strode off towards the cathedral.

"You silly fool," Belina hissed at Quiteira. "You've lost us a customer."

"Only one client lost, Dame-never-here," came the immediate reply. "You lose far more clients than I do."

"No I don't." Belina went into the inner room to calm down and work out the best excuse for being absent while she found something to give to Jordi and Catalina to cover the extra cost of looking after two people, their horse and their mule. Geraud had apparently used up all his booty on the long, slow journey across Spain and the Pyrenees.

She adjusted her head-cloth as she approached Quiteira, and waited while she wrapped up a tiny statue of St James for a customer and placed the money for it in the shop's money-box. Belina took the coins out of the box, held them out and smiled at Quiteira. She said they were a gift to make up for Belina having to go to the Pradau hospice straight away.

Quiteira snatched the coins and stowed them in the leather purse hanging from her belt. "Thanks. How long will you be away?"

"Don't know yet. Perchance most of the morning."

"In that case I will need more persuasion money."

"Perchance I said, but I am not promising it," Belina said as she went out into the street.

Rue Jean-Baptiste was filled with people, mules, dogs and pigs. Belina picked up her skirt and threaded her way between them all, her eyes fixed on the cobbles and the mess lying on them. The woman in front of her was carrying a basket containing a duck which kept dropping a foul-smelling mess onto the street. Belina tried to get past the duck and was almost hit by urine being poured out of a window from a chamber-pot.

She arrived at the Pradau hospice feeling sour and cross, and asked to see Brother Pierre.

"Stay here, Dame Moulié," said the hospice doorkeeper. "I will have to find him."

Belina sat in the shade of a mulberry tree near the Recteur's office and waited while she rehearsed her request to Brother Pierre. She would appeal to his sense of charity and follow that up by reminding him how she had solved the case of the poisoned pilgrim last Wednesday.

Meanwhile, she stroked his dog and practised her speech on the animal. He looked at her with his head to one side.

At long last the dog got up and greeted his master. Brother Pierre was carrying several parchments and kept them out of the way of the dog. "*Adischatz*, Dame Belina," he greeted her, laying the parchments on his desk. "I hope you haven't got a difficult message for me because, as you see, I am very occupied this morning."

"*Adischatz*, Brother Pierre." Belina said. "I have come to ask you for some help for my brothers, Jordi and Geraud."

"I heard that young Geraud has returned from Spain," said Brother Pierre, unrolling one of the parchments.

"Yes, three days ago, but he is in a bad way, Brother Pierre, because he has been wounded in a battle fighting the infidels near Granada."

"So I have heard, but as you know this hospice does not look after soldiers. You will have to get help from the Cardinal Teste hospice." He paused and looked at the unrolled parchment. "In any case, that hospice is nearer the mill than this one." He unrolled another parchment and looked at it in the light of the doorway.

"Brother Pierre, I don't think he ought to be moved," Belina persisted.

"Then the Cardinal Teste hospice will have to send one of their physician assistants to tend to his injuries."

"His girl is already doing that," Belina said.

"His what?" Brother Pierre dropped the parchment on to the floor and stooped to pick it up.

"He has brought back a Moorish girl with him," Belina replied, regretting that she had revealed the existence of Wasila.

"Then he will have to decide his priorities," said Brother Pierre crisply, unrolling yet another parchment.

"*My* priority, Brother Pierre, is not my brother Geraud or his Moorish girl." Belina went down on her knees and pressed her fingers together, as in a prayer. "My priority is to give – or to lend – some money to my brother Jordi and to his very hard-working wife Catalina." She stressed the word 'wife'.

"I had already assumed that, Dame Belina, but I have a very big problem to solve before the end of today. I regret that I do not have any time to spend on any other issues." He paused. "Not even for you." He pulled Belina gently up from the floor. "*Adiu*, Dame Belina, and my very kind regards to Guillaume."

He sat down at his desk and unrolled the last parchment, peering at it through his spectacles.

Belina left the room forlornly. She walked slowly back into the centre of the town, past the cathedral and the pilgrims coming out of it after seeing the relics from the Cross and the Crown of Thorns. She crossed the Place Lion d'Or, turned into rue des Argentiers and reached the house of her former employer, Messire Benasse.

She lifted the heavy brass knocker and brought it down against the nail-studded door. While she waited to be let in she rehearsed her request to the goldsmith: Jordi and Catalina were already short of money as a result of the spoiled harvest reducing the quantity of wheat for their mill; Rocca had taxed them far too highly and they were pleased he had been killed last week; Catalina was expecting their third child, which meant that their normal expenses would increase; and on top of all these worries had come the surprise arrival three days ago of her younger brother Geraud back from the war against the Moors. To make things worse, he was wounded and none of them knew how best to look after him.

Thinking about these significant problems meant that Belina did not hear the bolts being drawn back on the other side of the door.

"*Adischatz*, Belina."

"*Adischatz*, Messire. I'm so sorry to disturb you but I have an important request for you."

The goldsmith smiled, beckoned her inside and bolted the heavy door behind her. He led Belina up the stairs away from the delicious smell of *hamín* coming from the kitchen and showed her into his main room, where she saw a couple she didn't recognise playing chess.

Belina went over to watch their game but the man put back his knight and stood up. "Please don't interrupt your game because of me, Messire," she said. "I am here to ask Messire Benasse something and I won't stay long."

"My dear Belina," said the goldsmith, "you will drink some wine, and while I fetch it from the cellar you can watch the game. It is getting very interesting." He disappeared down the stairs.

The woman pointed to the chessboard and made a question mark in the air. Belina nodded.

Dame Benasse came into the room with a bowl of hemp-seed sweets. "*Adischatz,* Belina. Are you going to play chess with our guest Dr Benj?"

"I would not presume to do that, Dame Benasse. I have come here to ask your husband for some help."

"He will be back soon. He is in the cellar fetching wine." She smiled at Belina, touched her arm and said to the chess players, "Dame Belina Moulié is a very competent chess player, taught by her husband. They often play chess together."

Messire Benasse came in carrying a pitcher of wine and some beakers. He put them on to a table and said something in a language Belina could not understand.

The unknown couple pointed to each other, smiling.

"Belina," said Messire Benasse, drawing Belina closer to the chessboard, "tell me whether white is winning over black, or vice versa. My friends refuse to tell me."

Belina stared at the board, estimating the state of the play and counting how many pieces had already been taken and were lined up beside the board. She bit her lip and wondered if she should say that the unknown woman looked in the better position. She made up her mind and pointed to the woman.

"Splendid, Belina." They all laughed and Messire Benasse poured out the wine.

Belina wondered who the couple were. The man had glossy black curly hair which he wore rather long. He was younger than Messire Benasse but with a similar facial structure, especially the prominent nose. His wife's hair was hidden by her head-cloth. She too had a rather prominent nose, and Belina thought that the couple might be Jewish.

"Are your guests your cousins?" she asked Dame Benasse.

"No, better than that. They are great friends of mine, from Toledo in central Spain. They arrived here a few days ago after a very difficult journey and with very little baggage because most of it had been stolen in Navarra."

"How dreadful for them," Belina said. She launched into a description of Geraud's arrival at the mill three days ago and that he was a wounded soldier.

"I didn't know that, Belina," said Messire Benasse. "Which physician is looking after your brother?"

"None of them, and that is what I am worried about." Belina chose not to talk yet about money.

"What about a barber-surgeon?" Dame Benasse suggested. "They know about treating wounds."

"Treating most of the wounds is already happening. Geraud's companion is taking care of that. She seems very calm and competent."

"She?"

"Yes, Dame Benasse. Geraud's companion is a young woman, a very young woman in fact. I can't understand what she says most of the time because she speaks Spanish instead of Gascon or French. But sometimes she and Geraud use a secret language of their own."

"What language is that?"

"Geraud says it is Arabic, and that he found Wasila – that's her name, apparently– at the siege of Lucena. I gather he had to pay a Swiss sergeant quite a lot of money for her." She paused. "I wish he hadn't bought her like that because Geraud has so little money."

There was an awkward silence. Messire Benasse refilled the beakers, and while his wife returned to the kitchen he talked to the couple in a language Belina could not understand, occasionally pointing at her and mentioning Geraud's name. To hide her discomfort she stared at the chessboard and moved the black knight to where she supposed the man had wanted to place it.

He pointed to the stool, smiling, indicating that she should take his place at the board.

"Oh no," said Belina, stepping backwards. "I would not presume to do that. Please continue your game."

The man looked at her and then said something to Messire Benasse.

"Belina, my dear, I am sorry that you and my guests do not know each other's languages, but if you speak in Gascon slowly they will understand most of what you are saying."

"Because they live in Spain, in Toledo?" Belina asked.

"Yes. They speak Spanish but they also know Hebrew, which is the language they use with my wife and me, and Arabic because that is a major language in Toledo."

"So they could ask Wasila about herself," Belina suggested.

"I think what is much more important is for Dr Benj and me to go to the mill with you and bring your young brother back here to be looked after properly and healed of his wounds."

"Thank you so much, but I don't think Geraud would agree to leaving Wasila alone with Catalina."

"What's Catalina got to do with it?"

"She hates Wasila."

"Too bad. Just tell her to keep control of her thoughts and her temper."

Belina explained how difficult that was now that Catalina was pregnant again. She took the opportunity to steer the conversation around to Jordi and why he needed money.

"Why didn't you tell me this before, Belina?" the goldsmith asked.

"I didn't like to. And then I became interested in the game of chess."

"How much does Jordi need?"

"I don't know. I haven't asked him."

Messire Benasse went to a box on a table near the hearth, and fiddled with something inside it. He returned with a purse of coins and told her to fasten it immediately to her belt. "I will tell my groom to get my carriage ready so that you, Dr Benj and I can go to the mill, put Geraud into it and bring him back here. There will not be room for you as well as Geraud on the way back, so we will leave you at the mill and you can give Jordi your coins."

Belina protested that if Geraud was no longer in the mill there would be less need for the coins.

"No, Belina my dear, Jordi is bound to need the money. You told me that just now." He went down the stairs to his stables.

CHAPTER SIX

Belina had never ridden in a carriage before. She hoped she would not feel sick with the motion like she did every time she had travelled in the mill's cart. Dr Benj handed Belina up into the carriage and got in beside her, and Messire Benasse told his groom to go to the Moulié mill.

"Where's that?"

"You go out of Condom on the Auch road, and at the second stone cross you turn west and drive down to the river," Belina told him.

The carriage travelled slowly along the street while Belina looked around her, trying to ignore the rocking from the well-sprung carriage. They passed the first stone cross, from where she could see the Goalard chateau and church in the distance. When they reached the second stone cross the groom turned the carriage carefully to the right and drove it down a narrow lane until they arrived at the mill, where he turned it so that the rear was nearest the mill door. Messire Benasse helped Belina down, followed by Dr Benj, who was carrying a large leather bag.

Belina led the way inside the mill. Catalina was busy cooking something in a cauldron. It smelled like stewed lamb and garlic, and the logs burning under the cauldron made the room hot and smoky. Belina peered through the smoke to see where Geraud was while Catalina put a small pot on a trivet.

Her son ran towards Belina, calling out "Belee," and Catalina turned round.

"Belina, what are you doing here? What do you want?"

It wasn't the best of welcomes, but Belina calmly introduced Messire Benasse, and Messire Benasse introduced Dr Benj.

"Who is he?" asked Catalina, giving the cauldron a stir.

"He is Dr Benj, Dame Moulié," Messire Benasse said. "He has come to see your brother-in-law."

"Why?" Catalina stood glaring at him, her hands on her hips.

"Because Belina has told me that Geraud Moulié is wounded and needs medical help."

"He's getting that already from his Moorish girl."

"Of course he is, but a physician's knowledge might help him, Dame Moulié."

Catalina sniffed, and poured hot milk into beaten egg yolks.

Belina led the way through to the little room which had been taken over by Geraud and his Moorish girl.

Geraud was half lying on a couch while Wasila rubbed some strong smelling ointment into his shoulders, oblivious of Belina's arrival with the two men.

"Belina," Geraud croaked. "Good to see you. What happened to Guillaume? Did he really need to be called away hastily yesterday?"

"Yes." She decided to say nothing about the reason Guillaume had rushed off the day before. Instead, she introduced Dr Benj as a physician to examine Geraud's wounds.

"Please do that, physician. They are hurting me very much."

Wasila backed into a corner of the room, covering her face with her head-cloth. Belina took no notice of her and suggested that she and Messire Benasse went back into the kitchen while Dr Benj approached Geraud and looked at him very intently. Then he took his pulse, counting in Spanish.

"Are you Spanish?" Geraud asked in the same language.

Dr Benj raised his index finger and continued counting. He

made sure not to look in Wasila's direction, then he examined Geraud very thoroughly, asking him questions in Spanish.

"I am going to take you into Condom so that I can look after you properly there."

Geraud drew in his breath. "No. You can't do that. It's not necessary. Wasila here," he looked around for Wasila, who was still cowering in the corner, "is looking after me very well. All that I need is something to lessen the pain."

"No. You need more than that, and you need to be kept under observation."

"Can she come with me?" Geraud pointed at Wasila again.

"That depends on Señor Benasse, not me, because my wife and I are guests in his house."

"Is he the man who came in here with Belina? The gold-smith she used to work for?"

"Yes. We will take you back in his carriage. The road from here into Condom is smooth and Señor Benasse has a calm and excellent groom."

"But I need Wasila to go with me."

"I understand," replied Dr Benj, as he turned to fetch Messire Benasse from the kitchen.

Dr Benj interrupted a quarrel between Belina and Catalina which Messire Benasse was watching from the safety of the front door. The two children had disappeared.

"I won't have that foreign girl in my house any longer." Catalina leaned forward, her fisted hands on her hips.

"It's not your house," Belina replied. "It belongs to me and to Jordi. Not to you."

"I'm the one who looks after it and it was my father's money that paid for the water-wheel to be repaired."

"So what?" Belina backed towards the door of Geraud's room out of reach of Catalina, who was waving a heavy pan.

Dr Benj took Belina's hand and took her to the settle near the hearth.

"Don't you dare touch my sister-in-law," Catalina yelled at him.

The physician pretended not to understand, although Gascon and Spanish were similar languages. He beckoned Messire Benasse and spoke to him in a language which Belina could not understand. Messire Benasse replied in the same unknown language but mentioned Geraud several times, and Belina and Catalina twice. Dr Benj said 'Wasila' at least four times.

Belina tried to stand up but Dr Benj put his hand on her shoulder. She asked Messire Benasse what they were discussing.

"What I have already told you, Belina. Dr Benj and I will put Geraud very carefully into my carriage and take him to Condom. You will stay here for half an hour or so and calm Jordi's wife down. Better still, stay here for dinner. That lamb haricot smells good. Afterwards, you can return to Condom and your shop.

"But what about the Moorish girl?"

"She stays here."

"Why can't she go with Geraud? Surely you have seen how much Catalina hates her?"

"It's hard not to, Belina." He smiled. "But that girl is probably a lot tougher than she looks, and she will take care of herself."

"But Geraud wants her near him," Belina persisted.

"Geraud has made that very clear, but it will not be possible."

"Why not?"

"Because, Belina, the only room in my house available for your wounded brother is much too small for two people."

"I don't believe you. Wasila is thin."

"Do not argue with me, Belina. I am helping your younger brother stay alive. I have given you money. *Given*, not loaned."

Belina unhooked the bag of coins from her belt.

"Don't be silly, Belina. Keep it for Jordi. I know he needs it badly. Perchance his money worries have had a bad effect on his wife. A small bag of coins may even make her smile again. How pregnant is she, do you know?"

"About four months, I think."

"Just put up with her anger, Belina. That will help Jordi."

He opened the front door and then the door into Geraud's room. "Geraud, we are going to take you into my house. You will be much better there."

Geraud put his hand out to Wasila who grasped it very tightly while they whispered together. He turned towards Belina and asked her to find a place somewhere in the mill to hide his crossbow and bag of bolts as well as his armour. He asked her to remind Christau to bring the groom he knows to look at his horse and also check that Wasila's mule was comfortable after the long journey from Lucena.

"Of course. I will do all these things for you, Geraud," said Belina, touching his good shoulder. "Don't worry."

Messire Benasse helped Dr Benj carry Geraud out of the house with Wasila still clutching Geraud's hand. Messire Benasse prized open her fingers and she began to wail and recite some words over and over again.

"What is she saying?" Belina asked Geraud as he was settled into the carriage.

"Moslem prayers," he muttered, gritting his teeth against the pain.

"Isn't she a Christian?" Belina was horrified.

"Of course not. I thought you knew that," said Geraud.

"Of course I did not. How dare you bring an infidel into my house?"

"It hasn't bothered Jordi."

"And what about Catalina?" Belina said.

"Everything bothers Catalina, as you have seen. She is a shrew, which is something Wasila will never be." He settled back inside the carriage and the groom shut the door.

"What about you?" Belina asked Messire Benasse.

"I will sit in the front with my groom. Look after Geraud's girl. Keep her safe from Catalina. Speak slowly to her in Gascon and she will probably understand. Make sure Catalina understands that any harm she does to Wasila will be reported to Jordi and Geraud, who will punish her." He grasped the hand of his groom and climbed up on to the driving seat of the carriage. "*Adiu.*"

"*Adiu,*" Belina mumbled.

Wasila called out something in her language, tears streaming down her face and gazed at the departing carriage until it was out of sight.

CHAPTER SEVEN

Belina put her arm round Wasila's shoulders and wondered how to soothe her sorrow. She did not understand why Messire Benasse had refused to take Wasila into Condom. He had shown Belina kindness and generosity, yet he denied much-needed hospitality to the Moorish girl. Belina wondered whether it was a religious problem, and cursed it.

They returned to the mill and Wasila ran crying into the little room where she and Geraud had been living.

"Get out of there!" Catalina yelled, waving a soup ladle.

Belina shut the door to Geraud's room and turned towards Catalina. "Leave the girl there. She will be out of your way if she stays inside the room."

"And I have to listen to her crying for hours on end," Catalina replied, while she helped her younger child eat his dinner.

Belina picked up one of the cats and took it over to the window, rubbing its ears until it began to purr. She watched Christau unloading empty sacks from his boat and carrying them into the mill's storehouse.

"Christau is here, Catalina," she said, "with some empty flour sacks."

"Just as well," Catalina grunted.

"Why?"

"Because we haven't got enough good sacks. People don't return them. Jordi keeps on telling me to mend the old ones, and I don't have time." She wiped the child's face so roughly that he cried out. "Your brother only thinks of himself. He assumes that I have time to mend his flour sacks. Having two more people to feed is the last straw." She walked over to the sink and poured some water into the metal bowl.

"Now you will have only one more person to feed," said Belina.

"I don't know about that. She is too choosy."

"Really?"

"Yes, she is. I have been trying to get Geraud to eat more, so I cooked a leg of pork in spiced wine yesterday. That Moorish girl leapt from the table and ran into their room."

"Maybe Moors are like Jews," said Belina, "and never eat pork."

"She will eat what I give her or starve," Catalina replied. She poured some water into a pan and began to clean it with ash.

Belina turned round and looked out of the window again. Christau had finished carrying sacks and was heaving two barrels out of his boat. They looked heavy and Belina decided to escape from Catalina and help her cousin Christau with them.

She put the cat down and walked out of the kitchen. It was very hot in the yard and Christau was sweating profusely. He gave her a quick grin and continued to roll one of the barrels towards the storehouse.

"What's inside it?" Belina asked.

"*Bourret*. It won't last long but Jordi will need plenty of it while he deals with the two problem women in there."

Belina helped push the barrel into the storehouse and then examined the flour sacks. "Catalina has just been telling me that Jordi wants her to mend them."

"That shrew of his should have mended them all by now," Christau said, rubbing his back.

"Perchance she doesn't have time," Belina suggested.

Christau shook his head. "Catalina chooses not to have time. She uses far too much of her time sitting around gossiping with her mother."

"Does her mother know about Geraud?"

"Of course she does," Christau replied, "which means that she will have told her sister in Montréal about him."

"I didn't know that Catalina had an aunt in Montréal," Belina said.

"Her husband has new work there, looking after the *notaire's* horses." Christau set the barrel upright in the far corner of the storehouse and went to fetch the second one. Belina followed him. They rolled the barrel into the storehouse and Christau sat down on a stool, wiping his face.

Belina went over to a large pile of empty flour sacks and picked one up, trying to prevent it from leaving white dust on her clothes. The seam had come apart. She looked at three more sacks and saw that they were in an even worse condition. She wondered if Catalina kept sewing materials in the storehouse. Last time Belina had seen her sister-in-law sewing it was for baby clothes. Belina remembered having offered to make some too. She had not yet found the time to do that. Which was more important? The new baby or the flour sacks? She decided on the flour sacks. That would help her brother. The new baby's needs were not yet urgent.

Belina told Christau she was going into the mill house to look for a needle and thread so that she could make a start on mending the flour sacks.

He blew her a kiss. "Keep away from Catalina. She's dangerous with her cooking pots."

Belina opened the mill house door slightly and listened. The dogs were growling. One of the children was crying.

Catalina snatched the door open. "What are you doing there?"

"Where do you keep your sewing things, Catalina?"

"Why do you want to know?"

"So that I can do your job for you with the flour sacks."

"All my threads and my needles are in the room Geraud used."

"Why?"

"Because Geraud said his Moorish girl would mend his clothes."

"Did she?"

"I don't know. I hardly saw her doing anything other than helping Geraud eat his meals."

Belina opened the door into Geraud's room. Wasila was on the floor, kneeling beside the bed, still howling. Belina took no notice of her and began to search for Catalina's sewing things.

She picked up an embroidered piece of cloth and began to admire its colours and its geometric pattern, not noticing that the wailing had stopped.

A hand grasped Belina's arm and there was a fierce hissing sound.

Belina turned round and saw Wasila's wet face partly covered by her long black hair. She looked furious.

Belina handed her the embroidered cloth and went back to her search for sewing thread. Wasila shouted at her in a language that Belina could not understand.

It took Belina another five minutes to locate the sewing threads beneath Wasila's clothes. She picked them up, together with the needle, and pushed past Wasila into the kitchen and then outside.

She could hear Wasila behind her, calling out in what Belina supposed was Arabic, but she walked steadily to the storehouse, where she sat down on a stool beside the pile of old flour sacks and tried to thread the needle. She was unable to thread it because her hand was shaking so much with anger, and then she heard Wasila laugh, which made threading the needle even more difficult. Belina kept on trying to thread it, and Wasila kept on laughing, a high and musical sound. She put her hand out for the needle and thread, took it from Belina and threaded the needle in a swift, confident movement. Her eyes shone.

Belina tried to take the needle back but Wasila moved away with it and smiled this time. They looked at each other, realising that their situations had changed. Instead of the miserable foreign girl, Belina saw a confident, smiling young woman.

Belina picked up an old flour sack and examined the broken seam. Then she reached out to Wasila for the needle.

Wasila held on to the needle but took the sack, went to where Christau had left the stool and sat down. She smoothed out the sack and began mending it.

Belina picked up the pile of sacks and put them beside the stool. "Could you mend these too please, Wasila?" she asked slowly in Gascon.

"*Si, desde luego.*"

Belina thought that the words meant 'of course'. The tone certainly implied that. She touched Wasila's arm very lightly, smiled at her and went back to the mill house. She told Catalina that she had left Wasila in the storehouse, mending the old flour sacks.

"That's the first useful thing she's done since she got here." Catalina knocked her broom on the flour and dust flew out of it.

Belina sneezed, and stopped herself from pointing out that Wasila had spent her time looking after Geraud. She went outside to look for Christau and found him unloading a bulging sack from his boat.

"Can I help you, Christau?"

"Yes please. Take this end, it's cleaner."

"What's in it?"

"Oats for Geraud's horse. Sansas had a look at him yesterday evening and put some ointment on his legs. He said the animal was half-starved because it's been in Spain, where there is not enough food for horses."

"What about the mule?" Belina asked him.

"Mules are tougher, but it needs to rest too. I was given firm instructions not to use it."

They carried the bag of oats into the stable and Belina asked him where they could hide Geraud's crossbow. Christau looked around the dark building and suggested the hay loft. "Where's the crossbow?"

"In Geraud's room. I'll go and fetch it."

Luckily Wasila was still in the storehouse mending the flour sacks, and Belina found the crossbow and its bag of bolts hidden behind Geraud's saddle-bags. She picked it up very carefully and covered the curved wood at one end before returning to the kitchen. Catalina was still busy with her cooking, so Belina tiptoed through the rushes on the floor and went back to the stable.

Christau had climbed halfway up the ladder to the hay loft and reached down for the weapon. "No Belina, take that bag off first and then turn the thing around so that I can hold its base."

She unfastened the bag of bolts and put it on a clean part of the floor, before she tucked the cloth back around the curve of wood. "Here it is, Christau. Be careful. Don't point it at me."

"Don't be silly, Belina. I've got no idea how to use a crossbow. I'm a boatman, not a soldier." He reached down for the weapon and the cloth fell off. "Leave that on the ground and hold the ladder. It's swaying too much."

She did as she was told, turning her head away and whispering half an *Ave Maria* while she clutched the ladder.

Christau interrupted her and asked for the bag of bolts, which meant that she had to climb part-way up the ladder before she could reach him. The darkness of the stable made the whole activity more dangerous and she was glad when Christau took the bag and hid it next to the crossbow.

As he came down the ladder he said, "I hope that's all he wants us to hide, Belina."

"It isn't. He wants his armour hidden too. But that will get dirty in the hay."

They thought for a while. The storehouse was full of flour dust, the mill was open to visitors, the kitchen was Catalina's territory and where she talked with her mother.

"Stay for lunch," Christau said. "Catalina is bound to have cooked too much. Jordi is always complaining about her wasting food. And then while you are eating and talking with her about the children and the cats I will slip away and find the armour in Geraud's old room, wrap it in something and take it into Jordi's office."

"She will stop you doing that, Christau."

"Just make sure she concentrates on her cooking and keep her talking."

They crossed the courtyard and went into the mill house. Catalina was sitting at the table helping the children eat their apple mousse. Christau picked up a bench from near the fireplace and put it at the end of the table, saying "Catalina, we have been smelling your delicious cooking all morning. Please could we have some of it?" He patted the bench for Belina to join him on it.

"How dare you demand my food?"

"Catalina, we have managed to get Wasila into the storehouse and mending Jordi's flour sacks," Belina said. "You should be grateful to us."

"I don't believe in gratitude."

"That is obvious to one and all, but it's never too late to learn, Catalina," said Christau, fetching a beaker for him and Belina to share. He poured some cider into it and gave it to her, saying, "that will wash down all that flour dust." He emphasized the word 'flour', even though they were covered in hay dust. Catalina had been too preoccupied with her own problems, and had not noticed their dishevelled appearance.

Belina handed the beaker to Christau and offered to heat up some food for herself and Christau.

"Not in my kitchen, you won't," Catalina growled. She got up, sighed loudly and went to the fire. Christau patted Belina's arm and finished the cider. They watched Catalina stir the cauldron, ladle the mixture in a bowl and search for two spoons.

"Here you are, you greedy pair." She dumped the bowl on to the table, almost spilling the contents, and gave them each a horn spoon.

Christau began eating while he waited for Catalina to sit down and for Belina to distract her with talk about the children and the new baby. Then he got up.

"Don't you want my food after all, Christau?" Catalina glared at him.

"Of course I do, but I need to make room for it. I won't be away long." He went towards the door while Belina asked Catalina about the baby's progress and received detailed replies. She concentrated on eating the delicious stewed lamb instead of imagining Catalina seeing Christau come out of Geraud's room with a bundle of armour and take it into Jordi's office.

It seemed a long time before Christau returned to the bench to finish his meal.

"That will be cold by now, you stupid man," Catalina grumbled.

"Never mind, it still tastes delicious." Christau wiped his fingers on the tablecloth and poured out some more cider for himself. "How I envy Jordi eating like a duke every day."

Belina added her thanks, said *adiu* to Catalina, Christau and the children, stroked the cat and left the mill house. She patted the purse of coins which Messire Benasse had given her for Jordi. Catalina's anger had prevented Belina from telling her about the money, and Belina decided to find an opportunity away from Catalina's furious glares to give her brother the money.

As she walked steadily up the hill into Condom she thought about Viola Lussan. She tried not to picture her lying dead on the chapel floor covered in blood. Instead, she tried to focus on the time when she knew Viola as a schoolfriend. Sometimes Viola had invited Belina into her mansion on the rue des Armuriers. There were many rooms and many servants. Small dogs darted about, barking and getting under people's feet while Viola tried to stop them. She told Belina that her mother adored the dogs, but everybody else disliked them. Every time she visited, Viola would pour out her problems to Belina, saying that her mother gave all her love and attention to her dogs instead of to Viola and her brother.

Belina imagined that when Viola's brother had died of the plague the mansion had become even more severe and joyless. Her father was busy with his properties, her mother was always moody and taking every excuse to complain about her neighbours, her servants and her 'dreary' daughter. Belina wondered if Viola's beautiful clothes had made up for some internal misery or other? Had Viola been unhappy with such unaffectionate parents? One day she had confessed to Belina that she was scared of being forced by her mother to marry a rich consul. She could not hide her envy when she learned that Belina was betrothed to the tall, fair-haired messenger from Bordeaux.

"Are you going to live in Bordeaux, Belina?" Viola had asked.

"Certainly not. I want to be near my family, not Guillaume's brothers."

"And are they all as handsome as he is?"

"I don't know, I have never met them," Belina had replied, "and I don't want to. I would much rather be near Jordi and Christau."

Belina sighed and almost tripped over a pile of stones. She brought herself back to the present. She had taken a wrong turning and was now in rue Cadeot instead of near the cathedral staff residence. "Quiteira!" she cried.

The woman trying to pass Belina scowled at her. "Are you talking to me?" she asked.

Belina stood to one side and told the woman that she was looking for the house of her friend, the Widow Nabias.

"Over there," the woman grunted and walked away.

Belina approached Quiteira's house slowly, staring at it. She knew that it had belonged to Quiteira's dead husband, and had been left to him by his aunt. Quiteira was proud of living in a bigger house than the one she had grown up in. It even had two bedchambers – one for the couple and a smaller one for their two sons. Now that they were both married and living in Nérac, Quiteira had been thinking of taking a lodger. She could talk of little else recently, and Belina had found it difficult to stop the flow of words describing the sort of tenant she would prefer.

She gazed at the narrow door and supposed that Quiteira had to go through it sidewards. Wasila was thin, and would have found it much easier.

"Of course," said Belina out loud, "Wasila should become Quiteira's tenant." She stood looking at the door while she thought about how to rescue Wasila from Catalina's bad temper. If Wasila could mend flour sacks for Catalina, she could do sewing for Quiteira. Belina's assistant talked for hours about how much mending and sewing she had to do. Belina decided to use Wasila's sewing ability as a means of persuasion.

CHAPTER EIGHT

While Belina was helping Christau hide the crossbow, Guillaume had been in his workroom reading through what he had scratched onto several wax tablets. He could not understand why Viola had walked through the long tunnel from her house to the chapel. Or why she had mended a chasuble when she had got there. He needed to ask Belina if she remembered Viola for her religious devotion. Had she wanted to become a nun? Was that why she'd avoided her betrothal banquet? He wondered where Belina was, instead of being at home and having dinner with him. The most likely place was the mill, where she would give money to Jordi. And then she would stay to eat Catalina's dinner.

He got up and went into his bedchamber. Belina grumbled sometimes that it was difficult to cook in it. The room became too hot in summer for her to keep the fire alight all day, and she never cooked until the evening. Guillaume found half a loaf of bread and some cheese and made himself a quick meal, finishing with two overripe pears while Minet sat on his lap and purred.

He had still not decided why Viola had defied her parents so bravely and he needed to ask Belina to think back to her schooldays and tell him everything she remembered about her. It would not be easy because it had been a sad time for Belina with her mother dying in childbed and then the arrival of her young stepmother from Montreal. He decided to go down to the shop and wait there for Belina to appear. Perchance she might be there already?

Guillaume put the cat down, washed his hands and went down to the shop. Quiteira greeted him curtly and started at once to complain about Belina's absence yesterday and again today.

He interrupted her flow of words. "Where is my wife, Quiteira?"

"Don't know. She never tells me where she's going, or how long she'll be away."

"When did you last see her?"

Quiteira shifted a tray of *babioles* on the display table and rubbed her back. "Soon after we opened the shop." She rubbed her left knee. "At least, after I had opened the shop. Your wife turned up after that. Is she ill in the mornings, Guillaume?"

"Not that I know of," he replied, arranging some of the St Peter's keys and badges.

"Does she ever vomit in the mornings, Guillaume?"

"I've just told you, Quiteira, my wife is in good health." He pursed his lips and walked into the street. He had asked Belina to try to get a loan from Brother Pierre, but she would not still be in the Pradau hospice. Where else would she go for money? The goldsmith, probably, who had taught and employed her when she had fled from her new stepmother in the mill. And after Messire Benasse had given her money, where would Belina go? Down to the mill with it, he supposed. He hoped no one had seen her emerge from Messire Benasse's house and had assumed that she was carrying jewellery. He strode up and down the street while people got out of his way.

He felt a hand on his arm and spun round. It was Belina, smiling at him. They kissed, oblivious of others in the street.

"Where have you been all morning? I've been worrying about you." He put his arm round her shoulders and steered her towards the shop.

"I'll tell you when we are somewhere more private."

Once inside the shop and out of Quiteira's hearing, Belina recounted her day. She had borrowed money from Messire Benasse, where she had met Dr Benj and his wife who were living with the goldsmith.

"Who are they?"

"A Jewish physician from Toledo in Spain," she said, "escaping the Inquisition."

She told Guillaume how she had gone with Dr Benj and Messire Benasse in his carriage to the Moulié mill. The physician had decided that Geraud should be brought back to Messire Benasse's house in the carriage.

"And the slave girl?" Guillaume interrupted.

"What slave girl?"

"The Moorish girl that Geraud has brought back from Spain, of course," he replied.

"I didn't know she was a slave," Belina replied. "Geraud never said she was."

"I think she must be, and it's dangerous for Jordi to have a slave in his house."

"He hasn't told me that."

"We will have to find another place for her," said Guillaume. "Why isn't she with Messire Benasse?"

"He said he had no room for her."

"Probably being prudent," Guillaume muttered.

Belina took him into the store-room and shut the door. She told him about her plan to move Wasila into Quiteira's house, and why it was important to get Wasila out of Catalina's way as soon as possible.

Guillaume frowned. "I don't like the idea of that Montréal *notaire* learning about Geraud's return from Granada and bringing a Moorish girl with him."

"He will make trouble when he learns that," said Belina.

Guillaume swore in words Belina did not understand. She supposed they were English.

"We need to pay Quiteira for housing Wasila," Belina said.

"Of course. Some of the money you got from Messire Benasse will have to go to Quiteira."

"How much?"

Guillaume did some calculations in his head, and leant against the store-room wall. "I'm not sure yet."

"But Guillaume, I need to know before I start talking to Quiteira."

"I will tell you as soon as I can. Don't say anything to her just now. She's in a bad mood."

"She's always in a bad mood."

"I know, but I haven't dared tell her yet that you are going to help me with my investigation."

"You haven't told me that either," she hissed.

"I'm telling you now," he replied calmly. "I would like you to go to the Prelet mansion and interrogate all the servants there."

"Why?" Belina fiddled with the footbalm pots on the shelf in front of her so that her husband could not see her angry face.

"Because I didn't have time to do that yesterday, and in any case you are better at talking to household servants then I am."

"What makes you think that?"

"Because you probably already know some of them."

She swung round, nearly dropping a footbalm pot. "Do you consider me a household servant, Messire Inquirer?"

"Of course not." He kissed her nose and replaced the pot of foot balm on its shelf. "You know so many people in Condom. Some of them were at school with you. Some of them saw you at the mill. Some of them are friends of Jordi and Christau."

She smiled. "What do I need to find out?"

"Where each person in the mansion was yesterday, and when. Get each person you are questioning to say what others were doing too."

"They might not want to tell tales on their friends."

"Perchance not," Guillaume replied, "but encourage them to tell you where Consul Prelet and his family and his guests were. Only the doorkeeper would talk freely to me and his information was limited to telling me when the guests came and left."

Belina began to fiddle the phials of *aygue ardente* on the top shelf.

"Stop playing with those things," Guillaume said, "and listen to me."

"I am counting up how many hours I shall be stuck in the Prelet mansion, and how to cope with Quiteira's anger when I return here."

"A soft answer turns away wrath," Guillaume replied.

"You know very well that I am used to dealing with Quiteira's short temper, but how can I ask her to agree to share her house with Wasila?"

"By offering her an enticing sum of money of course."

"Then you had better tell me how much I need to offer." She turned back to the shelves.

"Leave those things alone. You might break them."

The store-room door was opened wide. They stared at Quiteira.

"If you have quite finished enjoying yourselves I would be obliged to have your help, Belina."

Belina pushed past Guillaume and walked to the display table, where five pilgrims were waiting.

"Can I help you, Messires?"

"About time," the oldest one grunted. "I am going to complain about this shop."

"Why?" Belina asked him.

"We have been waiting nearly an hour to buy some carvings of St Peter. Your assistant has been rushing around, having to serve many customers." He sniffed. "You seem to have been enjoying yourself with that yellow-haired man there." He pointed his staff at Guillaume, who strode towards him.

"Put that staff down."

"I will put it down when I am ready to," the pilgrim shouted.

Guillaume snatched the long stick and went out into the street, where he made as if to break it over his knee. The pilgrim came out of the shop quickly, seized it back and walked towards the cathedral.

"Oh Guillaume," said Belina. "Now look what you've done. He'll make a complaint about me, and the Archdeacon will not know that it's your fault that I will be away from the shop again."

"Don't worry, dear, I will tell him the reason for your absence."

"What's that?" Quiteira interrupted wrapping up a foot-balm pot.

"I am sorry to inform you, Quiteira, that my wife must assist me in my new investigation."

"I guessed that already. She's been away for hours." She glared at him. "And yet she didn't carry any tablets with her. That's the first time I've known her not take tablets with her on an investigation."

"She needed to walk too far to carry heavy tablets with her," he said smoothly.

"I don't believe you. Stop telling me lies." Quiteira went to the other end of the display table, turning her back on Guillaume, and asked a patient pilgrim if he wanted to buy anything.

"Yes, I am looking for a recorder."

Guillaume fetched a box from the store-room and showed its contents to the potential customer, who asked him if he played the recorder himself.

"No, I have never learnt to play it. I wish I had."

"It's quite easy to learn, but difficult to play well, Messire."

"Why do you need to buy a new one?" Guillaume asked. "I hope your recorder has not been stolen."

The pilgrim explained that it was for a member of his group

whose recorder had indeed been stolen on Monday when he was playing on his schaum during their music practice.

"Where was that?" Guillaume asked, wondering if it was the same group of pilgrims who Antoni had watched near the chapel. "I could send somebody to look for it."

The pilgrim began to explain, with his companions joining in. Guillaume gathered that the man had lost his recorder near the Sainte Eulalie chapel at the time of the discovery of Viola's murder. He began to question the pilgrims, asking them if they had seen a dubious looking person in the area yesterday morning.

"Here is the man who snatched my staff." The pilgrim whose staff Guillaume had seized pushed the others to one side and put his hand on Guillaume's shoulder.

"Aha. I'm not surprised," said a voice behind him. "That's Lansac, that is."

Guillaume peered over the pilgrims' hats and saw Loupmont, former assistant to the Treasurer of the cathedral.

Loupmont stabbed his finger on Guillaume's chest. "I have been informed that you stole this pilgrim's staff."

"I certainly did not," Guillaume replied. "I simply prevented him from attacking my wife with it."

"Liar," said the pilgrim.

"Don't you dare accuse me of lying," said Guillaume, brushing away Loupmont's thrusting finger.

"You are lying," the pilgrim repeated.

The other pilgrims said something to him in another language and left the shop in a hurry.

Guillaume wondered whether he should run after them to ask what, if anything, they had noticed near the Sainte Eulalie chapel. His argument with the elderly pilgrim had prevented him from taking the opportunity to question useful witnesses.

Loupmont told him that the Archdeacon had ordered Guillaume to go and see him at once. He simpered.

"If you are really going to see the Archdeacon, please tell

him that I need an assistant working here all day." Quiteira put back a tray full of St Peter's keys.

"Don't keep the Archdeacon waiting." Loupmont said, "You're in a bad enough spot with him already."

"I will come as soon as I have helped Quiteira with the display table."

"You will come now, at once."

"Go back to the Archdeacon and tell him that I will be with him in the time it takes to say two *Credos*." Guillaume put the trays of *babioles* back and greeted a couple of pilgrims walking along the street.

"Don't you dare start selling again," Loupmont shouted.

"The cathedral's revenue will increase because of my sales to the pilgrims."

"I repeat, the Archdeacon has ordered me to bring you to him."

Guillaume took the box of musical instruments into the store-room. He checked his face and hair in the tin mirror and put his cap on, pulling it down to hide as much of his fair hair as possible.

He locked the store-room door and gave the key to Quiteira. "Belina will be back in the shop soon. She has only gone for a few minutes to our chamber. Sorry about my absence now, Quiteira, at this busy time. It's not my fault. It's this stupid, greedy accounts clerk here who is being a nuisance." He pointed to Loupmont and added, "as usual."

But Quiteira took no notice and continued talking to a new customer.

Guillaume strode past Loupmont in the street and reached the room next to the Archdeacon's office a little out of breath.

"*Adischatz*, Brother Jacques, Loupmont has just told me that the Archdeacon wishes to see me."

"Yes Guillaume," the monk stopped writing in a ledger, "Loupmont has declared that you attacked a pilgrim in the shop. Did you really do that?"

"Of course not. The pilgrim was waving his staff at Belina because she had not served him."

"Why not? Dame Belina is always helpful to everybody. We all know that."

Guillaume saw Loupmont scowl in spite of his breathlessness from trying to keep up with Guillaume's pace "Thank you for the compliment. It wasn't Belina's fault that he was kept waiting. I had taken her into the store-room to give her instructions on how to help me with my new investigation."

The monk stood up and went into the Archdeacon's office, shutting the door behind him. Guillaume turned his back on Loupmont and waited. He was on good terms with the Archdeacon, but he needed to be careful. His real employer was Bishop Montbrun, but he was so seldom in Condom that Guillaume regarded the Archdeacon as his employer. He walked up and down the room, refusing to look at Loupmont who had replaced the scowl with his usual smirk.

At last the monk returned and held the door open for Guillaume to go into the Archdeacon's office. Loupmont tried to follow and Guillaume shut the door in his face, knocking his cap off.

The Archdeacon greeted Guillaume and asked him what had happened in the shop. Guillaume gave him an accurate account and waited anxiously.

"Fetch that stool," the Archdeacon replied, pointing to a corner of the room, "and sit down in front of me."

Guillaume obeyed and waited.

"Loupmont is a fool, and I am not going to waste any time on his nonsense. But I have been wanting to see you anyway, Guillaume. Please tell me how your investigation is going. The murder of a consul's daughter is a very serious matter. I regret that it happened in a religious building. Otherwise, the Seneschal would be in charge of the investigation. Are you absolutely sure that the poor young lady was killed in the chapel? Could her body have been brought inside it afterwards, perchance?"

Guillaume explained his reasons for knowing that Dame Viola had indeed been killed inside the chapel vestry.

"How did she get into the room, and why?"

"I don't yet know why, but this morning I discovered how she got there. It was very surprising."

"Well? Surely the vestry door should have been locked. Did she break a window and climb through the broken glass? Was she running away from her attacker?" He paused. "Do you think the killer will attack other young women too?"

"I hope the killer is not a madman who is out to cut as many throats as possible," Guillaume replied. "At the moment I am thinking it might have been personal hatred of Dame Viola, but it is difficult to know more. Perchance the consuls could help me if they wanted to, but it is difficult for me to compel them to answer my questions."

"That is what I fear too," said the Archdeacon. "I am going to take you with me into the consuls' meeting tomorrow morning and tell them to answer your questions."

"Thank you so much, Father Joachim. Your authority would be of great use. Perchance one or more of them will reveal something."

"We can but hope so. Even consuls will not be able to hide things from you," the Archdeacon smiled, and moved a parchment to one side. "But you haven't yet told me how Dame Viola reached the vestry." He put his hands together and waited.

Guillaume explained his discovery of the tunnel leading from Viola's bedchamber to the vestry of the chapel beyond the leper colony, a long way away from rue des Armuriers. "She was found sewing a green chasuble, but I cannot understand why she was doing that in such a place." He told the Archdeacon that he had arrested a young man found in the vestry and put him in the cathedral prison.

"Yes, I know that. Is he really a crestian?"

"He is. He told me so himself. He is a carpenter and I found a carpentry tool in the vestry when the body was moved. But I do not yet know why the crestian was in the chapel and he is difficult to interrogate."

"Why? I thought you were always successful in your interrogations."

"Thank you. This crestian weeps all the time. It might be an act, but even if it is, it has not yet been possible for me to learn much. I spent a long time with him this morning, for very little result."

"Did the crestian have any accomplices?"

"That's the funny thing. When I arrived at the chapel yesterday afternoon Chezelle was there pretending that he had found the killer and had brought two watchmen with him. One of them was pinning the crestian to the vestry wall while the other was guarding the chapel door."

The Archdeacon frowned. "Dame Senclar's tooth-drawer is a mysterious stranger. But I would not have considered him a killer. However, with Edith the Poisoner it's difficult to tell why she employs him and how." The Archdeacon moved the parchment back in front of him. "Thank you Guillaume. Meet me here early tomorrow morning and we will go together to the Town Hall. Don't tell anybody, though. Those consuls can be a difficult bunch when they feel inclined. Best we surprise them, eh?"

Guillaume grinned and stood up. He returned the stool to its place in the corner and thanked the Archdeacon.

"Don't mention it, *adiu*."

Guillaume walked into the clerk's room and looked for Loupmont. "He got impatient and tried to crash into the Archdeacon's office," said the monk with his usual tranquillity. "I told him to go away. I had to tell him three times before he complied."

Guillaume smiled as he left the room and returned to his chamber, where he concentrated on what to ask the consuls tomorrow morning. He scratched his ideas onto a couple of wax tablets, changing his mind several times. Who would gain from Viola's death? Was it some revenge against Consul Prelet or Consul Lussan or their wives? What did the rest of the Prelet family think about acquiring a new member? He wished Belina would come back from the shop so that he could try to jog her memory about Viola.

Guillaume stood up and fetched the bundle of Viola's clothes, which were covered in bloodstains. It was just as well that Belina could not see them or she would burst into tears again. He picked up the two-handed plane and looked at the dried blood on its blade. Then he held the tool and pretended to cut somebody's throat with it. It would be hard for somebody like him, who never handled carpentry tools, but a tooth-drawer like Chezelle might find it easier to use. Obviously a crestian could hold a plane with confidence. In Guillaume's view Josep Sarbazan in the dungeon prison still seemed the likeliest killer.

The door opened and Belina and Minet came in together. He turned round, forgetting that he was still holding the murder weapon, and Belina had to sit on the bed to stop herself falling. The cat promptly leapt onto Belina's knees and began to purr.

Guillaume put the plane in the sink and washed the blood from his hands. "Sorry you saw me holding that." He sat on the bed and kissed her.

"How did it go with the Archdeacon?" she asked him. "Was he angry with you?"

"Not at all. He knows what Loupmont's like. It turned out that he wanted to see me anyway to discuss the murder. He is going to take me with him to the Town Hall tomorrow to question all the consuls, but don't tell anybody about that."

"Ah good. That means that I don't need to question their wives and servants," Belina stroked the cat and listened to it purring.

"Yes you do. Like I said in the shop, start with the Prelets' servants tomorrow. But for the rest of today I suggest we don't even think about the murder. I think we should talk about Geraud and his slave girl. The murderer will want to make us anxious so that we are too worried to discover who he is. I foresee difficulties ahead."

"I hope not."

"I hope not too, but we need to be prepared. We need to get the girl into Quiteira's house."

"If you want me to do that, I cannot spend my time talking to consuls' wives and servants," Belina said.

"You can do both, you're very good at combining tasks." Guillaume put his arm round her and kissed her neck. Then he picked up the cat and carried her over to her empty milk bowl. He removed the cover of the duck preserving pot, picked up the milk pitcher inside it and sniffed it. "I think the milk is still all right," he told Belina.

"Minet won't drink it if it's gone off. You know she won't."

Guillaume poured a few drops of milk into the bowl and watched Minet sniff it and then lap it up. "All right, here you are Minet," he muttered, pouring more milk into the bowl.

He left the cat and returned to the bed, taking off his clothes at the same time. "As I said, we will forget about the murder for now. Making love is much better."

CHAPTER NINE

Wednesday

After a quick breakfast next morning Guillaume gave Belina a stylus and three wax tablets in a bag and put his best clothes on for his visit to the Town Hall.

It was too early for Quiteira to have arrived and opened the shop, and Belina walked past its closed shutters and joined the market day crowd, pushing her way to the Place Saint Pierre. The street was noisy with all the animals moving in it, and smelled terrible. A cart nearly ran over her foot and a donkey nearly ate her head-cloth. The cobbles were already slippery with mess, and she bumped into a pie-seller as she dodged the contents of a chamber-pot being poured on to her from a window above. The pie-seller was furious with her because three of his pies fell off his tray but she pushed her way past three goats and left the pie-seller shouting curses at her back.

It took her some time to reach the far end of the Place Saint Pierre and go down the hill to rue Deserte, the street behind rue Royale. She asked a group of women where the back entrance for the Prelet mansion was, and they pointed to an open doorway. Belina walked through it, past the herb garden and up some steps.

A kitchen maid stood at the top of the steps, staring down at Belina with her heavy bag of wax tablets.

"If you are trying to sell something, you've come to the wrong mansion."

Belina explained that her bag carried her wax tablets which were certainly not for sale. "I would like to talk to the steward for a few minutes please."

"He doesn't see anybody without an appointment," the maid told her.

"Yes, I understand that," said Belina politely. "I am the wife of the Bishop's Inquirer, and my husband has asked me to talk to the household staff here about what happened on the day of the banquet."

"The betrothal banquet that wasn't?" said the kitchen maid. "Is that what you mean?" Belina nodded. "It was so much work for us, and hardly any food was eaten."

"Well, that would probably have meant that you could eat it instead," said Belina. "Please have me shown to the steward's room."

Another maid who had been listening to the conversation took Belina's arm and led her to a room full of sellers and craftsmen.

"Wait here while I tell the steward that you are here," she told Belina. "I need to know why he should see you."

"As I am sure you have just heard," said Belina, less sharply than she wanted to, "I am the wife of the Bishop's Inquirer. I am here to ask all the servants about what they did yesterday, and what they saw."

"I will do my best," the maid told Belina. She knocked on the door and went in. Belina waited, clutching her bag of tablets.

After about three *Credos* the maid came out and beckoned to Belina. "The steward will see you for no longer than one *Paternoster*," she said.

Several men got up and said that they were before the *molieròta*, and that she would have to wait her turn.

"She is more important than any of you," the maid declared. "She is the wife of the Bishop's Inquirer."

"I don't care who she is," said a craftsman, who was holding a large pair of pincers, "she has to take her turn." He pushed Belina towards the wall and stood in front of the door that led to the steward's room.

An ink-spotted clerk told him to let the visitor through, and turned towards Belina saying, "please come this way."

Belina walked towards the steward's table and smiled at him. "*Adischatz*," she said. "I need to ask your servants what they were doing on Monday morning and where they were."

"Do you really think anybody employed in this household has killed Dame Viola Lussan?" The steward was scornful.

"My husband is always very thorough in his investigations," Belina replied. "He takes great care to build up a full picture of what was going on in all households."

"Then he should be investigating the Lussan servants, not the Prelet staff," said the Steward.

"He is doing that himself," said Belina. "That is why he has told me to question your staff."

The steward relented and told the maid to introduce Dame Moulié to all the kitchen servants. After that she could meet the household staff, but on no account was she to waste anybody's time. Monday's sad experiences had upset the whole household, and Dame Moulié must remember that at all times. The maid bustled Belina past several craftsmen, who glared at her.

"You are being so helpful to me," Belina told the maid. "What is your name?"

"Minga."

"What a pretty name," Belina said.

"I was named after my grandmother," said the maid, leading Belina into the kitchen and introducing her to the head cook. After a brief conversation with him, Minga showed Belina round the kitchen so that she could ask all the kitchen servants to tell her about what they had done yesterday morning.

"We had to work very hard, and then the precious banquet

was a misery," Minga said. "The bride never arrived and a lot of our efforts were wasted. The meal was delayed far too long because of her absence. The carefully prepared hot food was cooked for too long and the cold food went off in the heat so it had to be thrown away."

The kitchen staff told her similar stories and she made a summary of them on her wax tablets.

"When did you know there would be a banquet?"

"About a week ago."

"Did you know it was for a betrothal?"

"News of it got around."

"Did you meet any of the guests?"

"Not really."

"But you served them at table," Belina said half a dozen times.

Replies to this were unhelpful. The servants were tired, angry and not disposed to chatter except about the food that had been served and the drinks provided.

"Did any of the guests drink too much?" Belina asked.

"Not really. Except for Consul Senclar, when he wasn't playing with his wife's bosom."

No surprises there as far as Belina was concerned. "He was one of the few young people present, was he?" she asked. "Or were there other young people there?"

The servants mentioned Messire Charles, Dame Pauline and her husband Messire Galerne, Dame Jeanne Senclar, the son and daughter-in-law of Notaire Corloni and one of his daughters.

"Why were they present at the banquet?" Belina asked.

Nobody knew nor cared.

"Tell me more about Consul Prelet's children."

The servants agreed that Dame Pauline and her husband were often in the mansion. The consul and his son-in-law got on well together, even though Messire Galerne came from Bordeaux and traded in ever so many things. His family had bought English trading businesses cheaply when the English left Bordeaux thirty years ago, and they had done very well.

Belina was not interested in the story of Bordeaux traders and asked about the bridegroom, Messire Charles Prelet, the son who lived in Toulouse. "When did he arrive in Condom?"

"Last Friday, but he had been expected several days earlier than that."

"Why was he delayed?" Belina asked.

"Don't know. Weather perchance, or bad roads or problems with his horse."

"Does he have a good horse?" Belina asked.

Several servants thought he must have because he spent most of his time out riding alone. Consul Prelet had become angry about his son's absence because he was supposed to read lots of documents.

"Perchance he's the sort of man who doesn't like reading documents," Belina suggested. "Maybe he is not a scribe."

Her suggestion was firmly rejected. Messire Charles was a lawyer. That was why he had trained in Toulouse and lived in Toulouse.

"So, after her wedding Dame Viola Lussan would have left Condom and gone to live in Toulouse," said Belina.

Some servants agreed. Others said that the intention was for him to live in Condom and take over his father's position as Consul.

"Did the other consuls approve of that?" Belina asked.

Nobody would say. They all turned away and went back to their work. Only Minga remained. "Messire Charles did not want to live here," she told Belina." He intended to take Dame Viola to Toulouse. They were madly in love. He used to give her presents whenever he came to Condom."

"How often was that?" Belina asked.

"As often as he could. They were a loving couple."

Belina noted all this down on her wax tablets and asked Minga to take her to the bedchamber servants. She was shown into the servants' room and introduced, but unfortunately the servants were very discreet and Belina did not learn anything new. There were a few expressions of sorrow at Dame Viola's death, but nothing deeply felt.

Belina thanked them politely, and a junior maid escorted her down the back stairs and out into the herb garden. She walked wearily back through the jostling market day crowd of buyers and sellers to the cathedral shop with her heavy bag of wax tablets. Quiteira greeted her with a sigh and handed her a message from Jordi. 'We have been summoned to the lawcourt on Saturday morning. It is about flour measures. I will answer the judge's questions. You just have to be there, and on time please. Don't forget and go off somewhere instead on Guillaume's orders. Our mill is more important than he is, and it's about time you remembered that.'

Quiteira told her that Christau had called into the shop with the message but said he was in too much of a hurry to wait for Belina's return. "What does it say, Belina?" she asked.

"That Jordi and I are summoned to the lawcourt on Saturday morning."

"Oh no! It's bad enough that you leave me alone in the shop and do Guillaume's work. Now you are going to leave me alone because your brother has committed a crime."

"Don't be silly, Quiteira. It's only for some questioning about the mill. It won't take long." Belina hoped that was true, but she was worried, nevertheless.

"Make sure you are back quickly then," Quiteira replied, moving some medallions to another tray.

CHAPTER TEN

As soon as Belina had left that morning with her tablet bag, Guillaume put on his cap and checked his appearance. Like Belina, he found his walk to the Place Saint Pierre hindered by the market day animals, buyers and sellers, and he was glad to reach the Archdeacon's office next to the bishop's palace.

They discussed the likely reasons for killing a consul's daughter until they reached the door of the Town Hall, where they were welcomed inside with much bowing to the Archdeacon and none to Guillaume. They were shown through into the Council room, where consuls sat on benches at a table with the Town Clerk at the far end. Two council scribes stood at their lecterns beyond the Town Clerk and stared at Guillaume. The consuls, on the other hand, looked at the Archdeacon. Consul Prelet told the scribes to bring two stools to the table for the visitors. He greeted the Archdeacon formally and nodded to Guillaume.

The Archdeacon told them that he authorized the Bishop's Inquirer to question each consul about the sad death yesterday of Consul Lussan's daughter, Dame Viola. "Please answer the Inquirer's questions as fully as possible," he concluded.

There was silence as Guillaume took a wax tablet and a stylus out of his investigation bag and looked around the table at eight stony faces. It was going to be difficult to get these men to talk, and he was glad of the Archdeacon's presence.

"Please start your questions," the Archdeacon said very clearly.

Guillaume looked at Consul Prelet. His lined face had somehow acquired more wrinkles overnight and he looked to be in pain. "Consul Prelet," Guillaume began, "I will start with you, if I may, because you are the most senior consul," he paused, "as well as being the host at yesterday's banquet."

"Go ahead with your questions."

"When did you announce that you were going to hold a banquet?"

"In the middle of last month."

"Was it immediately known to be a betrothal banquet?"

"Yes, of course."

"Had a formal betrothal taken place already?"

The consul shook his head.

"When were you arranging for the actual marriage to take place?"

He made a gesture towards Consul Lussan who frowned and examined his fingernails. "As soon as possible. We were in the process of agreeing the terms and conditions of the marriage contract."

"And did the young couple agree to these arrangements?"

"They were not involved."

"Not involved?" Guillaume repeated. "Surely they should have been involved, or at the very least informed?"

"My son was aware of my wish for him to be married to Viola Lussan, a young lady whom he has known for many years."

"Would marriage entail your son coming to live in Condom?" Guillaume asked, "or were the couple intending to live in Toulouse?"

"In Condom, of course." The answer was very quick.

"Did your son agree to that?"

"Of course he did," the consul assured Guillaume. "My son is going to take my consul's place because of my growing health problems. He is needed here."

Guillaume tried a new line of questions. "When did he arrive here?"

"Last Friday."

"Has he been helping you with the preparations?"

"Not as much as I would have liked." The consul sighed.

"Does he know about your health problems?"

"He does, and he has done for some time."

"Could he have prepared the banquet for you?" Guillaume asked and shifted his wax tablet.

"My servants did that," the consul corrected the Inquirer. "What I would have liked was for my son to study the marriage contract and other documents very thoroughly." He paused. "Instead of doing that, Charles borrowed my best horse and went out riding,"

"Perchance he might have been meeting Dame Viola." Guillaume said.

"No, he did not," Consul Lussan said. "Viola was at home and received no visitors."

"Does she have a place in your mansion where she can receive visitors?" Guillaume asked. He wondered how much privacy Viola had had. The Lussan mansion was large, but full of servants and barking dogs. Guillaume decided to question Consul Lussan and hoped to get more co-operation from him than from Consul Prelet.

"Consul Lussan, I do not understand why your daughter was unable to accompany you to Consul Prelet's mansion," he began. "Why was there a delay? Did you intend her to make a splendent entrance?"

"Indeed not," the consul snorted. "Viola would have hated that."

"So why was there a delay?" Guillaume repeated his question.

"There was a difficulty with her betrothal gown."

"With the gown itself, or with her maidservant?"

"I assume that it was with the gown. She's had the same servant all her life."

"Why did your wife not come and help her and solve the problem?"

"My wife was occupied with her own gown."

The consul sitting nearest to Guillaume smiled and lifted his arms to show that Dame Lussan was rather fat. The consul beside him smiled too, but Consul Lussan frowned. It spoiled his handsome face.

Guillaume took his stylus and drew a corpulent woman on the wax tablet while he thought about what to ask next.

"What time did you and your wife leave your mansion to go to the betrothal banquet?"

"Just after ten."

"Did you walk there?"

"Of course not. We had too many important documents to carry. We rode there on our horses."

"So you left your mansion from your stables, instead of from the rue des Armuriers?"

"Of course not, young man. The horses were brought to our front door."

Guillaume wondered how the servants heaved Dame Lussan up on to her horse. He scratched something on his wax tablet.

"I still do not understand why you did not wait for your daughter, Consul Lussan."

"We needed time to discuss the marriage contract with Consul Prelet and his son."

Guillaume asked why this discussion had not already taken place, and was told that the finance and other aspects had been agreed some time before. However, it was necessary for Charles Prelet to read through the documents and give his legal assent.

"Were they to his disadvantage, Consul Lussan?"

"No, they were not."

"So why the delay in letting him see his marriage contract?"

Consul Lussan coughed and told Guillaume that he and

his wife had asked Charles Prelet to visit them the day before the betrothal banquet. During this visit he could look at the contract – and at Viola.

"How long did his visit last?"

"He didn't come." Consul Lussan growled. "He didn't even send an apology. When I sent my steward's assistant to inquire when he would arrive, he was told that Messire Charles had gone out riding two hours previously and was still absent."

Consul Prelet pursed his lips and shifted the papers in front of him.

"So Charles Prelet missed an opportunity to meet his be-trothed?" Guillaume asked gently. "Your daughter must have been distressed."

"Of course she was."

Guillaume nodded. "Did she burst into tears at his absence, or was she stoical, or perchance they had already met some-where and she had only just returned home."

"My daughter was not absent that day. She took his absence calmly. A consul's daughter does not show her emotions."

Guillaume moved the questioning on to the next stage of Monday morning, and Consul Lussan confirmed what Bernard Baylac had already told Guillaume. Consul Prelet's steward's assistant had been sent to rue des Armuriers to fetch Viola, but had returned without her. He had therefore ridden back to his mansion himself to fetch his daughter. But he too returned without her. Naturally, he did not say that he had lost his temper in the Prelet stables. Guillaume made a note on his wax tablet to check with the Lussan servants about what their master's behaviour had been like in front of them.

He looked at the stern faces around the table and wondered how long they and the Archdeacon would let him continue asking his questions. He asked each consul when he and his wife had arrived for the betrothal banquet and when they had left, how well they knew the young couple, whether they were thinking of hosting a dinner for them and whether they or their family had gone out riding with Charles Prelet.

The arrival and departure times tallied with what Bernard Baylac had already told Guillaume. No one admitted to knowing the young couple very well or to having hosted a dinner for them. They did not think that anybody in their families had gone riding with Charles Prelet.

Henri Senclar had not deigned to join in this conversation. Instead, he tapped his fingers on the table. Guillaume asked him pointedly about his use of time yesterday. There were gaps in the times. Senclar maintained that he had arrived with his mother and his wife much earlier than Bernard had told Guillaume. He denied knowing Charles Prelet well. He did not say that he had left the Prelet mansion while they were waiting for Viola to arrive and that he had returned later with dirty shoes.

Guillaume reminded himself that the most likely cause of these discrepancies was meeting a young woman for an assignation. He wondered if that would have been Aralha, the Senclar kitchen-maid who had helped Belina in her investigation over the pilgrim's death the previous week.

He turned to the Archdeacon and asked for his permission to continue his investigation by visiting the mansion of each consul and questioning their wives. "Ladies are very observant," said Guillaume, "and I am sure they can tell me more about the young couple, for example."

The Archdeacon stood up, so Guillaume did too. They bade their farewells to the consuls and were shown out.

On the way back to the cathedral, the Archdeacon asked Guillaume if he had found out anything much.

"Not enough, but I was unlikely to get to the bottom of why the Lussans had gone to the betrothal banquet earlier than their daughter. I will check their servants' stories about that very carefully. And I need to question the Prelet stable staff. I expect my groom knows some of them and can help me encourage them to talk."

"What about Henri Senclar?" said the Archdeacon. "I thought he looked guilty; not just a little bit, like he usually does, but *very* guilty."

"I thought so too, but it might have been some young woman he'd been pursuing."

"Like father, like son," said the Archdeacon.

"Did you know Dame Edith Senclar's husband?" Guillaume asked him.

"Not really. He was as thin as his wife, and son and spent most of his time and energy sleeping with women, including married ones. Worse still, he negotiated with Dame Edith's mother in Lectoure to marry her young daughter, even though she was only just thirteen. As soon as he married her he set about getting her pregnant so that he could make use of her great wealth very quickly. He probably regretted that his tiny young wife survived the birth of their son, Henri."

"Wasn't his own wealth sufficient?" Guillaume asked.

"Yes, but his is new wealth. Three generations ago the Senclars were modest people. They are said to be descended from a Bishop's butler."

"Really?" Guillaume replied. "Just like Henry Tudor's ancestors. He is descended from the Bishop of Bangor's butler."

"Where is the diocese of Bangor?" the Archdeacon asked.

"It's in Wales, not France."

They went into the cathedral discussing Consul Prelet's bad health.

CHAPTER ELEVEN

Sir John Keyham was in the cathedral staff residence court-yard having his right arm massaged by Alain, his manservant. He lay back in his specially built long chair and shut his eyes, enjoying the smooth movements of Alain's hand on his nearly paralysed arm. It was one of the few parts of his day that he could enjoy, sitting in the shade of the mulberry tree.

Alain picked up the ointment pot so that he could scrape more out of it, and as he did so he heard someone walking across the courtyard. His view was hidden by the tree, but he peered through the leaves and watched a man carrying sad-dle-bags go into the chamber that had been shared by Rocca, the dead Treasurer, and his Flemish friend, Barvaux.

Putting a finger to his lips, he placed the ointment pot on the table beside Sir John and tiptoed out from the shade of the tree. He wondered who could be going into a chamber the cathedral guards had sealed up following Rocca's death in Condom and the drowning of Barvaux in the Beauregard mill-race.

Alain moved into the shadow of the residence wall and waited for the man to appear again. He could hear him inside Rocca's chamber and the sound of something heavy being moved. He hoped the thief was not violent. He would have a knife, of course, everybody carried a knife. The thief had not been carrying a staff or a stick, so he would not be a pilgrim.

But all sorts of craftsmen carried sharp objects, and there was much talk about crestias carrying a range of fearfully sharp tools because they were carpenters. And then there were tanners and butchers and fishmongers, all of whom had especially sharp knives. Alain knew that vineyard workers also used knives for pruning. His legs began to shake as he waited for the thief to emerge.

The door opened and two swollen saddle-bags were placed outside it by someone wearing gloves. Alain wondered whether the thief was a groom, although Rocca had not possessed a groom and had rarely ridden a horse. He was a clerk for the counting-house, not a man who was at home in the open fields or hunting forests. Alain tried to remember if Barvaux had possessed a groom and realised that he must have done because he had ridden across France from Flanders in his pursuit of the two English princes.

Alain watched the owner of the gloves step out into the courtyard, lock the door with a key hanging from his belt, and fiddle with the seals that had been put in place by the cathedral guards. The thief picked up the two saddle-bags, putting one of them on his shoulder and walked slowly towards the outer door while Alain slipped back into the cover of the mulberry tree and told Sir John that he was very sorry but that he needed to follow the thief. He ran to the outside door and saw that the thief was going down towards the river. Alain kept his distance and wondered what he should do. Guillaume had examined the chamber after Rocca's death and Alain had watched him accompany the cathedral guard when they carried the Treasurer's documents and other possessions to the cathedral treasury. Barvaux's possessions had been left in the chamber.

Alain knew that Barvaux had drowned when the river Baïse was in a dangerous and turbulent condition. He was a discreet manservant and hardly ever left Sir John alone for long. His was a pleasant life and he had no intention of upsetting it by involving himself in other people's problems, but he couldn't let a thief vanish with a load of stuff stolen from a locked room.

He watched the thief turn into the cathedral stables with the saddle-bags, and ran down the hill and into the stables, knowing that there would be plenty of stable lads there and possibly an idle groom or two. Alain tried to tell the first person he saw that a thief had just walked into the stables, but he was so out of breath from running down the street and from being frightened that he was unable to make the stable lad understand him. Instead, he continued to polish a saddle.

Alain grunted at him and went through the room and into the main stable where there was very little light and he saw nothing but horses' bottoms and their tails swishing. He wrinkled his nose at the smell. It was not Alain's sort of place and he regretted his impulse to follow the thief.

"*Adischatz*, Alain," said a young voice behind him, and he turned and saw Miqueu, a stable lad he knew quite well because he would bring asses' milk to the residence for Alain to give to Sir John.

"*Adischatz*, Miqueu. I'm so happy to see you. Please help me." He brushed the sweat from his forehead, sighed and looked for somewhere clean to sit.

"Of course I will help you, but what do you want me to do? Is Sir John ill? Is he dead?"

"No, no." Alain gulped. "It's a thief. He's just come in here with two big bags which he has stolen. At least I'm sure that he's stolen them."

"Follow me and we'll look for him then." Miqueu took Alain past all the horses' bottoms, past the flies and stamping hooves and into a better room. "Has anybody seen a thief?" he yelled.

Various stable lads and two grooms stopped what they were doing and stared. "That foreign fellow has just come back with two bags," said one of the grooms. "He went that way." He pointed to an outside door.

Alain walked towards it, but the stable lads reached it sooner and everybody pushed to get outside before Alain could do so. The energy and exuberance were wearing him out.

"Hey, hey," Alain heard somebody shouting. "You! Leave that horse alone."

By the time Alain had discovered where the thief was, the man was surrounded by a crowd of youths clinging to his legs and trying to remove the saddle-bags from a tall and angry horse. The animal was neighing loudly and stamping its hooves, but when Alain got closer he saw that there were socks covering the hooves. A new fashion for horses, perchance.

"What's all this noise?" A grey-haired man pushed past Alain and reached the prancing horse, calming it down.

A chorus tried to explain what had happened as Miqueu took Alain's arm and introduced him to the head groom. Alain pointed to the thief and explained why he knew he was a thief.

"He's put socks on the hooves so that nobody would hear the horse walking on the cobbles outside," the head groom said. "Well done! That's the proof of a thief." He grabbed the thief's arm and twisted it.

"Let me go!" the man cried.

The head groom told a lad to fetch the Watch. "Be quick, Janticot."

"I am not a thief, and this is my horse," the man said.

"No it isn't. It's the horse that belongs to that foreigner who we haven't seen for a week. You're only his groom."

"That's right," said another lad. "We know you, you're always spying on us. I bet you've stolen from us too."

"Rubbish. I repeat, this is my horse."

"No it isn't," said one of the grooms. "Your horse is that poor creature in the corner." He pointed to a bay horse munching at some hay.

The thief denied this and was still arguing when three men of the Watch arrived with Janticot. The head groom told them what had happened and introduced Alain to them, saying that he was the hero who had caught 'this here thief'. Alain felt better at hearing this. Being a hero wasn't his usual way of life, although sometimes Guillaume would praise him for the way he cared for his crippled master, Sir John.

The stable lads tried to remove the two large saddle-bags from the horse.

"Oh no you don't," cried the thief. "You leave my property alone, damn you."

"Are those bags yours?" asked the senior watchman.

"Of course they are."

"Then take them off yourself and open them up."

"No." The thief kept close to the horse, preventing anyone from removing the saddle-bags.

"Do as I order."

"I will not. I don't take orders from watchmen."

The senior watchman said something in Gascon to his men and they pulled the thief from the horse. More Gascon orders were given and the stable lads removed the saddle-bags, groaning at their weight.

"Messire watchman," said one of the lads, still panting, "this fine horse belongs to a friend of the Treasurer. It has been here for some weeks now, and we all know it."

"Where is its owner?"

"We don't know. We haven't seen him for a while." He pointed to the thief. "That is his groom."

"Are you sure?"

All the lads said, "*Tio*, yes, they were completely sure." They offered a negative opinion of the foreign groom, who spoke a peculiar language with his master.

"Who owns this horse?"

"Barvaux," said Alain. "He lived in the cathedral staff residence and shared the Treasurer's chamber."

"Rocca is dead," said the senior watchman, "thanks be to God." He crossed himself.

Alain crossed himself too and continued. "Barvaux has not been seen for a week in the staff residence."

One of the stable lads said that the groom had spent last week hanging around the stables, looking after his master's horse and his own. He pointed to where an ordinary horse was standing in a corner of the stables.

"Early this morning," said the lad, "a messenger arrived for this foreign groom with a piece of paper and a token. He refused money, saying that he had already been paid by a foreign merchant."

"And then?"

"This man put socks on this horse's hooves. I've never seen that done before. And then he left the stables on foot with two saddle-bags."

"Which way did he go?"

"Up the hill."

"That's right." Alain smiled at the stable lad and took up the story, telling the watchmen how he had seen the groom walk into the cathedral staff residence courtyard, unlock the door leading to Rocca's chamber and after quite a long time come out of it with the saddle-bags filled to bursting.

"And very heavy," said Miqueu, moving his arm up and down.

"They certainly looked heavy," said Alain, "And he had to carry one of them on his shoulder when he walked back here," said Alain.

The head groom put an end to the discussion by telling Miqueu and Janticot to go with Alain, the Watch and the thief to the cathedral guard room. They should make a declaration there of what had happened and who the thief was.

"Yes, Messire."

"Wait a moment," said the senior watchman, "why the cathedral? Why not the Cadeot Fort?"

"Because these are the diocesan stables. They belong to the Bishop. The thief must be questioned by the Bishop's Inquirer, Messire Lansac."

"All right. If you insist," said the senior watchman. He

led his watchmen, Miqueu, Janticot and the thief out of the stables and up the hill to the cathedral.

CHAPTER TWELVE

Guillaume was sitting in his Inquirer's work room, scratching his thoughts on to his wax tablets, when the door was flung open.

"Messire Lansac, you are needed in the guard room."

"Why?" Guillaume smoothed the tablet and closed it.

"The Watch have arrived with a horse thief."

"I do not chase after horse thieves," said Guillaume.

"That's what the Watch are saying, Messire Lansac, but there are two diocesan stable lads with them, and they tell me that the head groom of their stables has ordered that this thief be questioned by you personally."

Guillaume put his wax tablets back in their bag and put the bag in the chest. He locked it carefully and stretched his back. The interruption was annoying. He had been considering the behaviour and movements of Charles Prelet, who had taken many rides out instead of preparing himself for his betrothal ceremony and banquet. Were the young couple in love? Were they strangers? Belina had told him during their midday meal about her visit to the Prelet mansion, and that she had not been able to find out much from the Prelet servants except for one maid who insisted that Messire Charles was madly in love with his bride-to-be.

Guillaume knew that it would have been a difficult interrogation if he had done most of it, as he had originally planned to do. For Belina to tackle it alone, it would have been like walking up one of the mountain passes in the Pyrenees.

He walked to the guard room where he saw a man sitting on the floor with a leg tied to a ring in the wall. The man looked a little familiar to Guillaume. Then he noticed Miqueu standing proudly next to the cathedral's senior guard.

"Messire Guillaume," said Miqueu, "look what I have found." He pointed to the prisoner. "A horse thief."

"Where did you catch him, Miqueu?" Guillaume asked.

"He didn't catch the thief, Messire Guillaume. I did."

Guillaume peered at the corner where this declaration had come from and saw Alain, Sir John Keyham's manservant. That was a surprise.

"Well done, Alain." Guillaume went up to him and touched his shoulder. "Where did you find him?"

Alain told Guillaume how he had seen the thief go in and out of Rocca's sealed chamber.

Guillaume frowned. "But the Treasurer's chamber was locked and sealed after his death. I watched them doing it."

"That man there," said Alain, pointing to the prisoner, "had a key, and he was able to get into the chamber after he had fiddled with the seals. He locked the door again and moved the seals back into place when he left."

The senior guard pointed to one of the keys on the table among other objects which Guillaume presumed had been removed from the prisoner's belt. A large number of coins lay there too.

"What did you do next Alain?" Guillaume asked.

Alain continued his story, again at great length, about how he had followed the thief with his saddle-bags down the hill towards the Barlet Bridge. He had wondered how far he was going to walk with such a heavy load. But the man turned into the cathedral stables, which gave Alain time to get there too. He gave a detailed description of how he, with much help from Miqueu and Janticot and all their colleagues, had managed to stop the thief from escaping on a stolen horse.

Miqueu took up the story, telling Guillaume about the unknown messenger who had given the thief a message earlier that morning, before the thief had fetched two empty saddle-bags and disappeared.

Guillaume tried not to smile at Miqueu's excited tone.

"I am *not* a thief," the prisoner interrupted.

"Yes, you are," Miqueu shouted back at him.

"How do you know that the horse does not belong to the prisoner, Miqueu?" Guillaume asked.

"Because I have seen the Flemish visitor ride it nearly every day."

"Lately?" Guillaume asked.

"No. Not since Rocca's death. But I am sure that the horse belongs to the Fleming and not to this man here on the floor." He pointed to the prisoner.

"He's dressed like a groom," said Guillaume. "Does he have a horse in the diocesan stables?"

"Yes, but not as good as the one he was trying to steal."

Janticot supported Miqueu's declaration, adding that the foreign groom was a crafty fellow. Nobody liked him.

"Have you both given your declarations to the Guard?" Guillaume asked.

They nodded. They could not read or write, but they were Gascons. They could certainly make clear enough declarations for a guard to write down in the register.

"What about you, Alain? Have you made your declaration too?" Guillaume asked.

"I have put my name on the register, but there hasn't been time for anything else yet."

"That's all right. I will talk to you myself in the staff residence. But now I think you should go back to Sir John. It's not good to leave him for too long."

"Thank you, Messire Guillaume." Alain moved towards the door. "I didn't like leaving him, but I thought I should follow the thief."

"You acted correctly and bravely, Alain," said Guillaume.

Alain smiled and went outside.

"Can Janticot and I go back to the stables now?" Miqueu asked Guillaume.

"Yes, provided the guard agrees," Guillaume replied.

"All right," the senior guard said, "but be prepared to give more evidence later." He touched Miqueu's shoulder. "Well done, lad."

The guards untied the prisoner's leg and pulled him upright. "Where do we put him?" they asked the senior guard.

"In the day cell so that Messire Lansac can interrogate him."

Guillaume followed them down a passage and into a dark and pungent room. The guards pushed the prisoner to the ground and tied his leg to the ring in the wall.

Guillaume was surprised at the quality of the prisoner's boots. He stared at him for several minutes while he considered his line of questioning. He remembered that Sir George Harliston had told him that Barvaux's groom had spied on Belina, and he wondered why. Belina had been indifferent about this when he asked her. According to her, the groom had never watched her – or at least she had never seen him. She couldn't remember what he looked like. Guillaume was not so sure.

"Your name?" he asked the groom. The man turned his head away and refused to answer. "Don't be silly, and don't be childish," Guillaume told him. "I will check the cathedral staff residence register. You arrived with that Flemish friend of Rocca's. His name was Barvaux. So your name will be known. In the meantime I will call you Barvaux's dog."

"I am not a dog."

"To me, you are a dog." Guillaume kicked the man's leg. "Where are you from?"

"Brugge."

"Where's that?"

"Flanders."

"Same as Barvaux?" Guillaume asked. "How long have you worked for him?"

The man scowled and turned away. Guillaume decided to change the subject. He said he would examine everything that was in the saddle-bags and the prisoner would be charged with stealing it all. "The bags were very heavy," Guillaume continued, "far heavier than a groom's possessions should be. I will establish their value and you will be punished in accordance with that sum. Punished by lashes and weeks of imprisonment."

"No!"

"Yes," said Guillaume, "I repeat, lashes and weeks of imprisonment. Possibly months," he added, "depending on how uncooperative you are."

"What do you want to know?"

"Who was the messenger you saw this morning and what was the message?" Guillaume moved nearer, hovering above him.

"I don't know who the messenger was. Honestly, I don't know. He gave me a token and a piece of paper. I offered to pay him but he said he had already been paid."

"What was he dressed like?" Guillaume asked. "What language did he speak?"

"Ordinary travelling clothes. I don't remember much about them. He spoke in a sort of French, a bit like the people here do."

"What did the message say?" The man did not reply. "Answer my questions!" Guillaume snarled, kicking his leg.

"To collect my clothes and go to Bordeaux."

"I don't believe you," Guillaume declared and gave the man another kick.

"It's true, Messire," the man whimpered.

"It's a lie, and you know it," said Guillaume, putting his foot on the man's knee. "What did the message say?"

"To collect my clothes and travel west."

"Where to?"

"Until we meet up."

"Who is 'we'?" Guillaume pushed his foot hard against the prisoner's knee.

"My master," the man whispered.

"How do you know that?"

"Because the token came from my master."

"Barvaux?" The man nodded, and turned his face away. "Give me that token." Guillaume ordered.

"The guards took it. It was in my belt."

"How are you sure it was from your master?" Guillaume asked.

The man told him about the code system his master had set up, and the words that would be included in any message.

"Where is that message?"

"I threw it away."

"Then tell me what it said."

"I've already told you, Messire. To collect my clothes and travel to the west."

"Your master's clothes?" Guillaume demanded, pressing the prisoner's knee against the floor.

"Yes," he gulped.

"So you believe that your master is alive?" Guillaume asked.

"Yes."

"Are you sure?"

"Yes."

"How are you sure?" Guillaume asked.

"The token and the message could only have come from my master. I am absolutely sure of it." The man looked up at Guillaume for the first time. "Messire, I am telling you the truth."

Guillaume believed him. But how could Barvaux be sending a message and a token? He had been drowned in the Beauregard mill-race with Guillaume watching. The planks from Barvaux's boat had tumbled down the river, together with heads and limbs. Barvaux had drowned, his death witnessed by Guillaume, Jordi, Christau and the two princes. If Barvaux had managed to survive he would be chasing after the princes, still determined to capture and kill them. He would not let them escape a third time.

Guillaume told the guard to keep the prisoner in the cell for at least two weeks, with little food. "He has stolen his master's horse, money and clothes. It will do him good to repent at leisure for that crime."

They walked back to the guard room with Guillaume deep in thought. He signed the register, declaring that he had made an initial interrogation of the horse thief, and went up the stairs to see the monk who kept the cathedral treasury to ask him for help in unsealing and unlocking Rocca's chamber.

"But Guillaume he's dead, and that Flemish friend of his hasn't been seen for a week. Rumours have it that he must be dead too."

"I certainly thought he was," said Guillaume. "Indeed, I watched what I thought were parts of his dead body flow over Beauregard weir."

"So why do you suddenly want to see inside Rocca's room?"

Guillaume told the monk what he had heard from Sir John Keyham's manservant. "He is a servant I have known for more than three years. He cannot have made up such a story. I know him too well to doubt his honesty."

The monk got up and pressed a hand to his back, wincing. He put on his spectacles and went inside his keyroom. Guillaume waited, trying not to see again the drowning of Barvaux and the Senclar boatmen.

"Here you are, Guillaume." The monk put a large key into Guillaume's hand and called out for his assistant to get his seal-breaking tools and accompany the Inquirer to the staff residence.

They walked along rue Jean-Baptiste and into the residence

courtyard. Guillaume told the locksmith that the dead Treasurer had had a Flemish visitor who had also been presumed
dead until now. Guillaume was sure that the Treasurer's chamber had not been opened up since his death, when Guillaume
himself had searched the room and all Rocca's possessions
had been taken to the cathedral treasury. His money and
documents had been put in a casket and placed in the safe
room. The only things left in Rocca's chamber had been the
Fleming's fine clothes and a pair of boots, together with a
heavy locked box.

"Was this horse thief wearing the boots?"

"Well spotted," replied Guillaume. "Yes, he was."

The man removed the seals from Rocca's door and Guillaume handed over the large key which the treasury keeper
had given him. He unlocked the door and they went into the
chamber. It smelt mouldy and dusty. The floor was strewn with
clothes. Guillaume pointed to the shoes near a stool. "You
were right. The horse thief would have sat on that stool, pulled
on the Fleming's boots."

"Did the Fleming have big feet, Messire Lansac?"

"I don't remember. He wasn't especially tall, though." Guillaume stroked his chin. "About the same height as his groom,
I think."

"So the horse thief is also a boot thief."

Guillaume smiled, and touched the man's shoulder. "You
should be an inquirer."

"I would love to work with you, Messire Lansac."

But Guillaume was surveying the condition of the room,
trying to establish if the objects which were now in a chest in
the cathedral guard room would have belonged to Barvaux
rather than to his groom.

"Would you like me to tidy this room, Messire Lansac?"

Guillaume hesitated, still seeing the dead bodies tumbling
over the weir in his mind. He pulled himself together. "No,
don't bother. I will keep the key, if I may."

"Of course, Messire Lansac, but please keep it very safe or I will get into a lot of trouble."

"I promise you I will look after it very carefully."

They left the room. Guillaume locked the door, hung the key on his belt and accompanied the man to the courtyard door. "Many thanks for your help," he said, putting his arm round the locksmith's shoulders.

CHAPTER THIRTEEN

Guillaume crossed the courtyard trying to decide whether he should go up the stairs to his chamber or go to the cathedral shop. He started to climb the stairs, but halfway up he paused. Belina had told him last week that she had been selling lots of *babioles* because so many of the pilgrims were returning from Compostela.He turned round, rushed down the steep stairs and went through to the shop by the back entrance. Belina was selling foot balm and Quiteira was putting a tray of St Peter's keys on the display table while a pilgrim was examining a phial of *aygue ardente*.

Guillaume approached him and told him what was in the phial and that it helped pilgrims relax at the end of the day and made their tired feet ache less. He smiled at the pilgrim. "Where have you come from today?" he asked as he wrapped the phial in a piece of cloth.

"Mouchan." The man put his purchase in his satchel.

"And before that?"

The answer took several minutes, with descriptions of places, good and bad people met, muddy tracks . . .

Guillaume waited patiently and then turned the conversation back to people the pilgrim had met who had been going towards Spain.

"Someone smartly dressed," said Guillaume, "with rather long black curly hair."

"Not a pilgrim, in other words."

"No, a merchant perchance, but travelling without his groom."

Another pilgrim interrupted Guillaume's questions. "Messire, smartly dressed merchants always travel with a groom."

"I know," Guillaume replied, "which is why I am hoping that this particular merchant would have been noticed."

Neither pilgrim remembered meeting anyone resembling Barvaux, and they left the shop in a hurry to visit the cathedral and see its famous relics brought back from the Holy Land as well as those given by Pope Leo III.

Guillaume served some more pilgrims, plying them with his questions and not receiving any useful answers. Quiteira complained that he was 'all-talk-and-no-sales'.

"Sorry Quiteira." Guillaume gave her his best smile. "It's important for my investigation that I find out who has been going westwards recently." He started to serve a pilgrim's wife who was asking for a pot of foot balm.

"Don't tell me any of your lies, Guillaume."

"Quiteira, you know very well that I do not tell lies."

She put a metal statue of St Peter on the display table and turned her back on him.

He continued selling and questioning, but felt that he was making no progress until two couples passed by the shop chatting. Guillaume noticed the good quality of their clothes, the absence of the broad-brimmed hats that all pilgrims wore and the fact that only one of the four walked with a stick. He pushed past Quiteira and went out into the street.

Three long strides later he overtook the couples and turned to face them. "Excuse me," Guillaume said while he tried to think of how to stop the couples' progress down the street.

The man with the walking stick poked at the paving stones and scowled.

Guillaume seized his opportunity and touched the stick saying, "Messire, your stick needs mending."

"No it doesn't."

Guillaume put his foot near the base of the walking stick and said that the point was damaged and the man was in danger of falling.

"I've been telling you that all morning," said the other man.

Guillaume recognised his Flemish accent so he asked the man very politely which part of Flanders he came from.

"Brugge."

"Dirk," said one of the ladies, "please refer to it as Bruges. Otherwise, this Frenchman will not understand."

"Actually, I know the Flemish names for Bruges," Guillaume said, "because until recently a friend of mine has been sharing his house with someone from Brugge. Perchance you met him on your way here. He set out for Compostela a few days ago."

"Most people on the Way of St James are pilgrims."

"But you are not pilgrims, I think," said Guillaume. "Are you merchants?" They nodded. Guillaume told them about Barvaux's appearance and his musical voice.

"A man with rather long, gleaming, curled black hair?" both ladies said.

"Yes," Guillaume agreed, "and often not wearing a cap or a hat. He's very proud of his hair. My wife wondered if he might be partly Greek." Belina had found Barvaux very attractive, Guillaume remembered.

Guillaume asked if he was riding a horse.

"No, but we saw him inside an inn so his horse could have been in the stables, like ours were."

"Where was that?"

The four discussed together where the inn might have been and then said that they could not remember.

"What sort of inn was it?" Guillaume asked. "It is always good to know which ones are good and which ones should be avoided."

Another discussion while Guillaume waited patiently. "I think it was the Deux Faucons," said the older lady.

"No, that was only two days ago."

"Perchance it was the Singe, the other lady suggested. "The one with the bad service."

"That's it, the one which was almost as bad as the inns in Spain."

All four travellers told Guillaume how awful Spanish inns were, and that they had to bring their food with them, including for their horses.

"Oh dear," said Guillaume, "which inn was that? I need to know so that I can advise people to avoid it."

"A poor sort of place, and with girls for hire. I didn't like my wife staying in it but it was the only inn in the village. Even the pilgrims had to use it."

"Did this black-haired Fleming find a girl?" Guillaume asked.

"Indeed he did. Very quickly, but didn't wait to give her any food." The merchant scratched his chin. "Just took her up the stairs without eating supper first."

"That's odd," said Guillaume. "He was fond of his food here. And he dressed well, too."

"He certainly wasn't dressed well when we saw him. I thought he looked down on his luck, and had perchance been robbed."

Guillaume thought that if the Fleming was Barvaux, it would have been he who had been the thief, not the victim. "Did you talk to him?" he asked.

"Yes, we did. We asked him to recommend an inn in Condom for us."

"And?" Guillaume prompted.

"He looked at our clothes and our signet rings and said that he had stayed with a friend but that he could recommend a mansion owned by Consul Senclar."

Guillaume only just avoided showing his excitement. "Are you staying there?"

"Yes, we sent a messenger to reserve rooms there in advance.

We spent such a comfortable night there that we have decided to stay there another two days. To rest the horses."

"Dirk, our rooms are comfortable, the cooking is excellent, but the younger Dame Senclar is a boastful, intrusive nuisance."

Guillaume smiled. "She has that reputation in Condom, and my wife and I are among many who do not like her." He tried to bring the conversation back to where they had met Barvaux. He needed to know how far west he had travelled.

"How many days ago were you in this bad inn?" They thought it was Saturday.

Guillaume suggested it had perchance been in Aire.

"No, it was before that. The weather was bad and we couldn't reach the town of Aire. We had to put up at this bad inn at Latrille. After that we took care to stay in towns, in Nogaro and in Eauze."

Guillaume thanked them for their help and turned back towards the shop where he would need to convince Quiteira that he was leaving Condom in a hurry and that Belina would have to take over his investigation of the death in the Sainte Eulalie chapel. Quiteira would be furious, and Belina would be even angrier.

He started to rehearse what he would say to his wife and her assistant when the man with the stick pulled his arm. "Not so fast. You said that my stick needs mending. But you never told me where I can get it mended."

"Just continue down this street, Messire, towards the Sainte Eulalie chapel on your right. Before you reach it you will pass a group of cottages on your left where crestias live. They are the carpenters of Condom and can repair your stick."

"By crestias do you mean lepers?"

"Not really," Guillaume assured them. Their very distant ancestors came back from the Crusades and some of them – a very few – were lepers. But no crestian is a leper now. There has been no leprosy here for the last hundred years."

"I don't want to go near lepers," said the older lady.

"You heard what this man has just said. They are not lepers."

"I don't care. You can go by yourself. I'm staying here."

The younger lady agreed and suggested they go back to that nice shop they had just passed.

Guillaume was delighted and told them he would help them choose whatever they wanted to buy, and that his wife kept the cathedral shop. It stocked many fine things to buy, more than just standard *babioles* for pilgrims. He led the two ladies back to the shop and left their husbands to cope alone with the crestias.

Belina was rubbing foot balm onto the feet of a farmer's wife, so Guillaume introduced the two Flemish ladies to Quiteira, telling her that they would like to see the very best things she has for sale.

"That means jewellery, Guillaume. I'll get some from the store-room." She went into the inner room and returned with three wooden boxes which she put on a chest instead of on the display table. "Please come and look at them here, dames, it will be easier than near the street."

"And safer too," Guillaume said, bringing two stools for the ladies to sit on. "Do please take your time, dames, and ask Quiteira for her advice if you want to. She knows all there is to know about jewellery."

He went out into the street without telling Belina or Quiteira and walked very quickly, pushing slow-moving people and animals out of his way, so that he could reach the Cadeot Fort as soon as possible and talk to the Seneschal.

When he saw Guillaume, the Cadeot Fort guard stood to attention and greeted him courteously.

"*Adischatz*," Guillaume replied, "I would like to see the Lord Seneschal, if you please."

"What reason should I give, Messire Lansac?"

"My new investigation into the death of Consul Lussan's daughter."

"I didn't know she had died. Was it murder?"

"It was indeed."

The guard waited for more information but Guillaume kept silent. "Do you need our help in arresting the murderer?"

"I have already arrested a suspect," Guillaume replied, "and put him in the cathedral prison."

"But Messire Lansac," the guard spluttered, "the Seneschal insists that all murderers should be locked up in here. It is much safer."

"That's why I need to talk to the Seneschal."

The guard whistled, as if summoning a dog, but it was a young soldier who appeared, chewing a piece of bread. "Take the Bishop's Inquirer to see the Lord Seneschal," he ordered, "And be sure not to be chewing in his presence."

Guillaume followed the soldier into the fort and up the wooden stairs to the room next to the Seneschal's office. The soldier told the clerks there that the Bishop's Inquirer wished to see the Seneschal. The chief clerk got off his chair slowly. "*Adischatz*, Messire Guillaume. The Seneschal is very busy today. Could you come back tomorrow?"

"Regrettably not. I have to leave Condom very early in the morning and it is most urgent that I speak to the Seneschal about my journey."

"Perchance I could help you instead, Messire Guillaume? If it is travel information which you need, we here can give you the situation on roads and bridges." He paused and then added quietly, "and brigands."

"I am going to need that too, thank you, but I do need to discuss the reason for my journey with the Seneschal."

Guillaume walked towards the door to the Seneschal's office. The chief clerk gave a signal to an underling to open it and let Guillaume through the doorway.

The Seneschal was alone at his desk. His hound got up, growled at Guillaume and walked towards him, the hair on his back rising. Guillaume looked away from the dog and waited for the Seneschal to notice his presence.

"What do you want, Lansac? I am very busy today and had ordered no interruptions."

"Your staff made that very clear to me, Lord Seneschal, and if my request had been less important to you, and less urgent to me, I would have agreed to come back tomorrow."

"Well?" The Seneschal leant back in his chair and crossed his arms.

Guillaume told him about the murder in the Sainte Eulalie chapel, that he had arrested a crestian found near the body, and that he had put him into the cathedral prison close to the chapel.

"Lansac, you know very well that murderers are always kept here in this Fort."

"Yes, of course I do, Lord Seneschal, but as he is a crestian I thought he might spread his leprosy to your people here." Guillaume hoped that the Seneschal would not see through such a groundless excuse. Surely he knew that crestias no longer were lepers.

"I don't believe that, and neither do you, Lansac."

"Your soldiers will, though," Guillaume pointed out.

The Seneschal sat still for a long time while Guillaume waited. Then he looked at the papers on his desk and came to a decision.

"All right, Lansac. Keep the murderer in your cathedral prison if you want to. But make absolutely sure that he is well guarded, much better than your prisoners normally are." He picked up a paper from the pile on his desk.

"There are two more requests I need to make, Lord Seneschal," said Guillaume.

"What are they? Can't you see that you have already taken up too much of my time?"

"I need written authority from you that my wife can question people about the murder of Consul Lussan's daughter."

"That's your work, Lansac."

"She is from Condom and people speak much more readily to her than to strangers like me, or indeed your own staff."

"True. Dame Lansac is very competent. I was most impressed with the way she discovered who had poisoned that pilgrim in the Pradau hospice last week." He smiled. "You are a lucky man, Lansac."

"I know, Lord Seneschal." Guillaume waited while the Seneschal wrote an authority for Belina and signed it.

"Give my best regards to your wife, Lansac, and thank her for the work she does. I wish more women were as competent as she is." He sighed, and said, "And the other request?"

Guillaume told him as succinctly as possible about the dangers Barvaux's survival at the Beauregard weir last week posed to the princes and how he, Guillaume, absolutely must catch Barvaux before he reached the princes and killed them.

The Seneschal frowned and tapped his fingers on his desk while Guillaume waited and looked at the rushes on the floor.

"All right, Lansac. I will give you an authority to go after the rascal and when – or rather, if – you find him and overpower him you can use the document I am writing now to get any soldiers nearby to arrest him and bring him back here."

"Thank you very much, Lord Seneschal."

"Don't waste too much of your time on chasing Barvaux. Be back here as soon as possible. You need to finish investigating the murder of Consul Lussan's daughter."

Guillaume assured him he would be back as soon as he could. He put the precious document in his purse and left the room before the Seneschal could change his mind. He made his way to the bishop's palace behind the cathedral, where he was relieved to see that the room next to the Archdeacon's office was still open, with people coming out of it. That meant that the Archdeacon had not yet left for Vespers. Guillaume found him putting a pack of documents into a chest and locking it up with difficulty with an immense brass padlock.

"Allow me to help you Father Joachim," said Guillaume, cupping the heavy padlock in his right hand.

"Thanks Guillaume. As each year goes by, this lock becomes more difficult for me. I really need to get it changed."

"The locksmith could make you something lighter and easier."

"Yes, I suppose so." The Archdeacon went into to his office and frowned. Guillaume saw that his desk was even more covered with papers than the Seneschal's had been. He rehearsed his request to Father Joachim while waiting for him to speak first.

"How do you think your questioning of Consul Prelet and all the others went? Did the crestian have any accomplices?"

"I am making progress, but I think that the crestian might have been paid to do the murder. Belina questioned the staff at the Prelet mansion this morning because Charles Prelet might have paid the crestian, or even paid somebody in Condom to find and pay a crestian."

"It's taking up a lot of your time, I suppose," said the Archdeacon.

"Yes, up until now." Guillaume paused while he thought how best to tell the Archdeacon that he needed to absent himself, borrow a diocesan horse and receive funds for his journey to the west."

"Well?"

"The problem is," Guillaume began, "that I have found out that the Fleming who I thought had drowned at the Beauregard weir last week has somehow survived – I can't think how – and is riding west towards Spain."

"How is that a problem for us here in Condom?"

"It's not a problem for us, but it's a danger – a mortal danger – for the two English princes Belina and I saved the day that Barvaux drowned."

"How and why is there a danger?"

"The princes are on their way to Spain and thence to Lisbon in Portugal, and Barvaux will try again to kill them."

"Why?"

"He has been ordered to do so by the enemies of the English King Richard."

"Why should anyone, even enemies of a king, wish to kill two young princes?"

"The enemies of the king are conspiring to overthrow him so that the son of one of the conspirators can become king.

"Guillaume, what happens in far-away England is not of much interest to us here in Gascony. Why should we be involved?" The Archdeacon shuffled his papers.

"It would damage the Bordeaux wine trade."

"Are you sure?"

"Yes. My family in Bordeaux are certain of this danger. Keeping King Richard alive, and the two princes also, is essential to trade – as well as the citizens of England."

The Archdeacon took off his spectacles and stared at Guillaume. "What are you asking me to do? Come to the point."

Guillaume told him that he would need to absent himself, maybe for a few weeks, to borrow a diocesan horse and groom, and be given money for his journey.

"All that is a nuisance just now," the Archdeacon replied, "and you know that we don't have much money because of the way Rocca sent it to Paris."

"The two young princes need my protection, Father Joachim."

"Well, you will do that without a horse or a groom. You will travel light. But I will give you money, even though we cannot really afford it. Nor can we afford your absence when there is an investigation into a murder inside a religious building."

Guillaume pointed out the advantages of travelling with a horse and groom, but the Archdeacon cut him short.

"I repeat, I will give you money. If Dame Belina also needs some she can ask me for help too. Go to the Accountant's chief clerk, tell him what money you need, give him the written authority which I will write out for you now, and return from your travels as soon as possible."

He sat down at his desk, put his spectacles on and wrote the authority.

"Thank you for your help, Father Joachim," Guillaume said through clenched teeth, taking the document. He walked out of the room and went straight to the Accounts room to get the money which the Archdeacon had grudgingly allowed him to be given for his journey. Guillaume was well aware that the Accountant would be angry.

CHAPTER FOURTEEN

The Accountant was just about to leave his office when Guillaume arrived and was furious at his request. He flung the bag of coins on to the table and told Guillaume to get out. As he walked to the staff residence, he rehearsed his speech to Belina. It was not going to be easy. She was bound to be at least as angry as the Accountant had been just now.

He went to his chamber and found Belina putting away her wax tablets.

"Have you finished writing about your visit to the Prelet mansion?" he asked her.

"I have only used two tablets, then there were too many customers for Quiteira to serve by herself."

"Oh dear. I always find it is easier to scratch a report down as soon as possible after questioning witnesses."

"But you, Messire Inquirer, do not have to work in a cathedral shop. You. . ."

He interrupted her. "It should be less stressful for you now that Rocca is dead."

"There's still Loupmont. And the arrogant Accountant."

"Yes, I agree with you about them. In fact, I have just come back from a meeting with the Accountant."

"I hope he hasn't reduced the money the cathedral pays us," Belina said.

"No. It was not that. In fact it was to give me money on the orders of the Archdeacon."

"Ah, good. How kind of Father Joachim," Belina looked at herself in the tin mirror on the wall and touched her head-cloth.

"Not really," Guillaume replied. "Even he was being difficult."

"Why?"

"Because I had asked him not only for money but also for permission to take my horse, my groom and my groom's horse to Spain."

"Spain?" Belina leaped up, eyes flashing.

"Yes, possibly as far as Spain. Béarn certainly, Navarra perchance."

"I don't believe it. You're teasing me."

He pushed her gently down on to the stool. "Belina, my love, it is true. I have to leave tomorrow morning and travel as far west as I can."

"You have forgotten how long it will take you to find Antoni and get two horses ready for such a long journey."

"I am not taking Antoni. The Archdeacon refused to let Antoni and two diocesan horses leave Condom."

"So you are going to walk to Navarra," she replied. "You had better dress up like a pilgrim and carry a staff. I will give you three pots of foot balm."

"I am not going to waste my time walking. I will travel 'change', and it is for that reason that the Archdeacon has authorized quite a large sum of money for my journey. The Accountant was most unwilling."

"And why are you going on this sudden journey?"

"To catch Barvaux before he reaches the Princes."

"What?" she hissed. "Barvaux drowned at the Beauregard weir. You watched him drown."

"Apparently he is such a strong swimmer that he survived what I thought was certain death. All the others drowned. I remember very well seeing parts of their bodies tumbling over the weir."

"How can you possibly know that Barvaux survived?" she asked, raising her voice.

"Shhh. Brother Charles might hear you."

"I don't see how you can know that Barvaux is alive," she whispered.

Guillaume told her as succinctly as possible how Alain had seen Barvaux's groom behaving suspiciously in Rocca's chamber before going down to the stables to steal Barvaux's fine horse. But thanks to Alain, and Miqueu too, the thief had been discovered and the head groom had summoned the Watch to arrest him.

"I'd never have thought Alain would have been so bold as to do that," Belina said.

"Me neither." He smiled at her, but she continued to glare at him. "He walked up with the Watch and their prisoner to the cathedral guard room and they have put him into a cell there."

"But that still doesn't show that Barvaux is alive," Belina pointed out. "It's more likely that the groom had decided to steal his master's horse and escape from Condom."

"That is what I thought at first, but I was able to get him to confess that Barvaux had sent him a message, ordering him to bring his master's clothes and boots and horse westwards.'

"Did you hurt this groom, Guillaume, in order to make him confess?"

"A little, but he deserved it. I hadn't forgotten how he had spied on you."

"He did no such thing," Belina said with great indignation.

"Oh yes he did. Sir George told me so."

"I don't believe you," Belina shouted.

"Shhh."

"I will not be quiet."

She got up from the stool but he pushed her firmly back on to it, keeping his hand on her shoulder.

"Even if Barvaux is alive and does travel westwards that doesn't mean that you personally have to chase him," said Belina.

"Yes it does."

"Why?"

"Because the groom told me that Barvaux was chasing the princes in order to kill them."

"The princes didn't travel westwards, Guillaume. They went south. I remember you explaining the route to Sir George."

"Yes, but he will catch up with them at Puente de la Reina. And he will kill them as soon as he can. Heave them over the side of the bridge or something."

"And if somebody sees him?" Belina asked, wiping a tear from her cheek.

"He would murder them too."

"He could bribe them," she suggested.

"No. He will not have enough money on him, especially now that his groom is in a cell in Condom and his money casket is safely stored in the cathedral guard-room. Barvaux will be missing his clothes and his coins."

Tears were streaming down her face. "Take my pouch-cloth. It's bigger than yours." He wiped her face and put his arm round her shoulders.

"How long will it take you to catch up with Barvaux?" she asked him.

Guillaume told her about his calculations of where Barvaux had been when the two Flemish couples had seen him, how far he would have got by the time they had reached Condom yesterday. So if he left Condom tomorrow, riding light, he would reach Barvaux somewhere between Arzacq and Arthez.

"And then what will you do?" she asked.

"Not sure yet. I have papers signed by the Seneschal authorizing me to arrest Barvaux and to hand him over to French troops."

"And if he gets as far as Béarn? What will you do then?"

"I have thought of that. I will use the Seneschal's authority to take a couple of French soldiers into Béarn and find Barvaux there."

"And then?"

"I don't know yet." He kissed her moist cheek.

She clutched his hand. "All this will take many days. I will read through what I have put on my tablets this afternoon about my investigation at the Prelet mansion, and the rest of the investigation will have to wait until you return to Condom in triumph."

"Oh no. The investigation cannot wait that long. The death of a consul's daughter has priority. You must take over all the questioning. It's something you do very well."

She stood up and shouted "No!"

"Shhh."

"I will not keep quiet. I will not obey your orders like that. I will not beg entry into consuls' mansions. I will not try to question powerful consuls, and their wives and their servants, and waste my time and patience. I will…"

He interrupted her. "Stop shouting, Belina, and listen to me."

She stamped her foot. "No."

"Yes, you will listen to me," he replied, with his hands on her shoulders, "and carefully." He gave her complete instructions about who she should question – all the powerful consuls, and their wives and their servants – and what she should be looking for. She must assume that each person is telling a lie until it is clear that their answer is the truth. "Make sure that Antoni goes to the Prelet stables and finds out who went in and out of them during the last four days. Take my investigation bag and go into the vestry of the Sainte Eulalie chapel and do your usual crime scene check there." He took two dusty keys from his belt and put them on the table. "Be sure to bring these keys back with you. After that, you must question the crestian in the cathedral prison. Wear your oldest clothes for going there. It's very dirty."

"Will he attack me?"

"It's unlikely. He seemed very docile to me, but make sure you are accompanied by one of the prison guards, just in case."

"And Barvaux's groom?"

"You don't need to see him. I've extracted all I can from him. After you have done all that questioning and made a summary of your findings, you must make a start on questioning the crestias near the Sainte Eulalie chapel and the pilgrims in the area."

"What pilgrims, and why?"

"When I first went to the chapel there was a group of pilgrims nearby with musical instruments. They may be useful witnesses. Antoni told me that they all had a special badge on their hats with an enamel Compostela shell on top of a pewter carving of the Virgin Mary holding the baby Jesus on the left, a bell-ringer and a bishop in the centre and an angel on the right."

"I don't care what the badges look like. I can't, and I won't, do what you are ordering me to do." She looked at the mirror and fiddled with her head-cloth.

"Of course you can. And you will. It will keep you busy in my absence." He smiled, looking at her sad face.

"I am busy enough running the shop. You know very well that I am."

He smiled again.

"And as well as being busy I will have to deal with all the nasty comments about being abandoned by my husband, about not having babies, about my marriage being in danger. You never think of that when you ride off to Bordeaux, leaving me all alone to be laughed at. The people of Condom think you are a bad husband."

"Don't listen to them."

"How am I going to question Jeanne Senclar, for example, when she is too busy scoffing that I have not yet started a family?"

"If she makes you really angry then just accuse her of having to marry because she was pregnant."

"I wouldn't dare to talk to her like that," Belina gasped.

"Why not? Everybody knows that's how she trapped Consul Senclar."

"True," she admitted. "But it will not help my investigation if I accuse her of that."

"She will not help you anyway. You know she won't," he said. "So question her servants instead like you did last time."

She stared at him, her teeth clenched, her left hand tugging at the skirt of her kirtle. Guillaume thought she looked like a very stubborn mule. He made her repeat his instructions twice over and helped her up from the stool.

She started to prepare their evening meal, having difficulty in getting the fire to light with the flint and the silex and then banging the frying pan against the sink. Her behaviour reminded Guillaume of Catalina's last Monday.

He realised that she was moving too close to the fire and risked falling into it, so he pulled her away from it and dragged her to the bed. "Stay there. I will get the meal." He put the pillow under her head and brushed her tears away.

Between her sobs Belina asked him why he thought that the princes were more important to him than she was.

It was a difficult question for Guillaume. He remembered the attitude of the Archdeacon earlier that evening when he'd said that what happened in far-away England was of little interest to the people of Gascony. Belina would agree with him. Of course she would.

Instead of answering her question Guillaume cut a slice of the stale bread to use as a trencher. He put some oil in the frying pan and placed it on a trivet over the fire. He broke four eggs into the pan and let them cook slowly while he fetched a pitcher of wine, put a beaker on the table and poured a little wine into it.

"That wine will be sour by now," Belina said.

"It isn't, and it will be much better for you than warm, flat cider. Come and sit down. The eggs are ready."

He filled the beaker with wine and slid the fried eggs onto the trencher, took out his knife and cut squares of bread and eggs. Belina sniffed the beaker and drank some of the wine. "*Mercés*," she said. She picked up one of the squares of bread and eggs and chewed it while he put his arm round her shoulders.

When they had finished the eggs and most of the trencher, Guillaume put the rest of it in Minet's bowl and picked up a phial of *aygue ardente* from the top shelf. He poured half of it into a little pottery cup and made Belina drink it, saying "You need this medicine. You need to be brave. I will be back as soon as I can, I promise you."

She grunted and sipped the liquid. "*Mercés*." She refused to say anything else for the rest of the evening, and sat on the bed while he washed the beaker and his knife and put some water in the frying pan to soak overnight. By the time Guillaume had returned from the latrine she had undressed, put on her nightcap and was under the coverlet.

He went into his work room, picked up his saddle-bags, frowned, and returned them to their place in the corner. He pulled out his chest of riding clothes and assembled the clothes he needed for a long journey, added his cap and belt and everything hanging from it. Then he drew the satchel which had been used by the poisoned pilgrim out of another chest and filled it with the clothes.

He slept badly and was woken by Minet miaowing in his ear. He gave her some milk and stroked her until she purred. He cleaned his teeth with his tooth scraper, washed it and put it in its tiny hemp bag and put his comb in its own little bag.

"What about your shaving things?" Belina asked him from the bed.

"I'll grow a beard. It will save time."

"It will grow yellow and everyone will see you're a foreigner."

"I don't care." He picked up his riding boots and sat on the bed.

"Why don't you care?" she demanded. "You always try to hide the fact that you are English."

"Half English," he corrected her, pulling on his left boot.

"And half Bordelais," she said, "which is still almost the same as English."

"It is not," he replied. "You know it isn't."

"I don't know, and I don't want to know. I hate Bordeaux."

"Don't be stupid, Belina," he grunted as he struggled with the boot, "you've never been to Bordeaux."

"I don't want to either."

"Belina, my love, don't let's quarrel." He put his hand on her breast and kissed her neck whilst she stayed still.

"If you didn't go away so often and so suddenly we wouldn't need to quarrel."

"When I come back we will start a family, I promise you." He kissed her again, but she still didn't move, so he picked up the satchel, opened the door and went out, slamming it behind him.

CHAPTER FIFTEEN

Thursday

Belina cried for what seemed like a very long time, then she turned over on the bed and almost crushed the cat which was curled up beside her. Minet was furious, scratched Belina's arm, leapt off the bed and began to wash herself.

Belina stretched and went over to the sink to dab water over the scratch and dry it with the towel that was hanging on the rail over the sink. She tried to find a clean pouch-cloth in her clothes chest without leaving blood on the garments piled inside it. It took a long time and Belina began to cry again as she sat on the bed and pressed the cloth to her wound. Minet leapt back on the bed, curled up beside Belina and purred so loudly that Belina was able to recover her spirits and look ahead to the morning's tasks instead of going over and over Guillaume's sudden absence and their quarrel in her mind.

She got dressed and ate breakfast standing up, drinking cider with the last of the stale bread, followed by two pears. She fetched Guillaume's investigation bag and the tablets in their bag from his work room, added the two keys from the chapel to her tablets, put on her head-cloth and shoes, stroked Minet and walked to the top of the stairs. She thought about the first time she had met Barvaux coming down these stairs with Rocca. In spite of herself, she still remembered his hair, the clothes he wore, his voice and rosemary scent, and most of all his fine dark eyes.

She went down the stairs slowly, her mind still on Barvaux. A wicked man who she had supposed to have drowned. For a moment she wondered whether it was just an excuse thought up by her husband to cover his absence. It was unlikely, but not impossible. They had been married for three years but she still did not know him very well, and he had not told her much about the missions he took to Bordeaux, which he said involved a plot for King Richard to invade Gascony.

She opened the door of the shop and saw that Quiteira was in deep conversation with Anne Labadie, one of the cathedral's seamstresses, who was showing Quiteira some coloured threads.

"I think this blue one would be best," Quiteira was saying, "even though I don't have enough time any more to do embroidery."

"Why not?"

"Because Belina is never here. She's always off doing Guillaume's work. I'm fed up with looking after this big shop by myself."

"But Quiteira, Belina is just behind you."

Quiteira spun round and saw Belina with her two heavy bags. "Going somewhere with those, Belina?" she asked.

"Yes. I have to go to the Sainte Eulalie chapel, where there has been a murder."

"Who's been killed?" Anne asked.

Before Belina could reply, Quiteira said, "Dame Viola Lussan, the daughter of Consul Lussan."

"Oh no! How dreadful! Such a good artist too." Anne pulled out her pouch-cloth and wiped her face.

"I know," said Belina, "and a lovely person. I was at school with her and she would confide in me about her parents. At first, I thought that she was just comforting me because of my mother's death, but later I realised that Viola really was unhappy at home. Nobody loved her."

"Didn't she have any brothers or sisters?" Quiteira asked.

"One brother, a few years older, but he died of the plague."

Quiteira handed the coloured threads back to Anne and stood with her legs apart, staring at Belina. "Wasn't she supposed to be deaf?"

Belina nodded. "Hard of hearing, not really deaf."

"That means that the murderer could have crept up behind her and hit her over the head with a paving stone," Anne said. "My husband and his friends used to talk about doing that to Rocca."

"I can understand anyone wanting to kill Rocca," Quiteira said, "but who would want to kill a gentle young dame?"

"I don't know, Quiteira," said Belina, "but I am going to find out."

"How?"

"By going first to the scene of her death, and then by asking all the consuls, their wives and their servants what they were doing last Monday, the day of the murder."

"Why can't Guillaume do that?" Quiteira asked, bringing her fist down onto the display table and making the ornaments jump.

"Because he is questioning the man who is suspected of being the killer, and who he has put in prison," Belina replied.

"In that case," said Quiteira, "*you* don't need to question anybody." She paused and sighed. "And you can get on with your own work – which is here, inside this shop – and leave Guillaume to do his work."

Belina decided it was safer not to reply. She picked up the two bags and went out into the street.

She had a hot, uncomfortable walk carrying the bags to the Sainte Eulalie chapel. She pretended not to see the door to the cathedral prison on her right, trying instead to avoid the mess on the paving stones. Soon afterwards she found herself walking past the leper colony with its wretched cottages with chickens and pigs going in and out of the tiny doorways. A slightly better building was being re-thatched and the workmen whistled at Belina. She tried to comfort herself that they were not shouting '*molieròta*' at her, but their whistling did not bode well for the discussion she needed to have with the imprisoned crestian. She decided to postpone that for as long as possible.

A group of pilgrims were standing in the shade of a cedar tree opposite the leper colony, sharing a gourd of cider and wiping their faces with their hat brims. She hoped they would not whistle at her as she passed them, and she whispered two *Ave Marias* to herself.

The Virgin answered her prayers. The pilgrims put their hats in a pile, picked up their musical instruments and stood together in the shade of the tree. They began to play and sing, with one of them waving his arm at them to keep time. Belina turned to watch the performance. The music soothed her and she felt for a coin in the purse hanging from her belt. Three crestias joined her and she kept a close eye on her bag of tablets while she hooked the investigation bag over her shoulder. Two farmers and a sheep joined the crestias and then a group of women.

The pilgrims began with a song about St Bernard and then one by him. *"Jesus, the very thought of thee, fills my heart with joy."* Then they sang some Spanish *cantigas* composed by King Alfonso X which Belina had often heard Brother Charles singing, and finished with a hymn for Vespers, *"Let the heavens resound with praise."*

After this song one of the pilgrims picked up his hat and approached the audience. Everybody put a coin in it until he came to the crestias, who shook their heads. Belina knew that they would be too poor, but would the pilgrim realise that? He muttered something in a language unknown to Belina and returned to the shade of the tree, putting the coins into a little box.

Belina picked up her bags and walked down the street to the chapel where she was glad to see that a cathedral guard was at the door, preventing people from going in.

"*Adischatz*," Belina greeted him. "My husband has asked me to examine the room where the murder happened. Can you let me go inside?"

"Of course I can, Dame Lansac, but it's not a pleasant sight for a lady. Your husband should have remembered that. I would not dream of letting my wife see a bloody mess."

"I quite understand, Guard," Belina told him, "but I have become used to seeing places where murders have happened."

She walked through the door and across the dusty chapel to the vestry door. She picked out one of the keys from her tablets bag and unlocked the vestry door. She sneezed from the dust as she turned the key and let herself into the room. She locked herself inside the vestry and put the key in her purse. This was an action which Guillaume had made her learn two years ago when she began to help him investigate crimes in religious buildings. If she had the key, nobody could lock her inside a room full of blood, insects – and ghosts.

She looked around the vestry. The body had been removed, thank goodness, but the floor was covered in congealed blood and bloated insects. It smelt horrible and Belina had to cover her nose with her pouch-cloth.

She took a tablet and a stylus out of their bag and sat down on a stool next to the window. She saw an upturned chair lying partly in the blood. Beside the chair was a large green silk cloth, partly blood-stained. A chest was on Belina's left with long, narrow drawers that would contain chasubles and altar cloths. An open chest was beside it, containing a heap of cloths and a smaller chest sat against a wall with two books and some candlesticks on it. A crucifix hung above the chest, covered with cobwebs. In a far corner was a long curtain, although the window beside her had no curtains. Next to the stool was a sink, a brass bowl and a dirty towel. A small lantern was on the floor under the sink.

Belina made drawings of all this on a tablet. She could not understand how Viola had come to be in such an unattractive place. She remembered her as a gentle, kind person and as a young girl who was also nicely dressed and clean – not that that would have been a difficult achievement for the daughter of a wealthy consul. Belina tried to remember what property Viola's father owned. But property and landholdings were not interesting subjects for Belina even now, and certainly hadn't been when she was a schoolgirl. She would have to find out, but from whom? A *notaire* would be the best source of information. She hoped that Consul Lussan owned nothing in Montreal because Belina was loath to talk to the *notaire* in Montreal. She agreed with Jordi that he had fraudulently given much of their inheritance to their stepmother, his cousin, when he had drawn up their father's testament.

"Blood is thicker than water," she said out loud. There was real blood in this room, and it was her job to examine it and decide what had happened. Viola's blood. But was all the blood Viola's? Had there been a fight?

Belina could not understand why the chair had been facing the window instead of the door. She stood looking out of the window and saw a path that led to the green area where the pilgrims had been singing. She wondered whether a pilgrim, for example, could have walked along the path and looked through the vestry window. But why would they want to do that? And were these pilgrims in the area early Monday morning?

The window was cleaner than the rest of the room, which made Belina think that perchance Viola had looked out of the window. Belina felt the window itself to check that it could not be opened. There was no damage to it, which meant that the murderer had entered the room by the door. But if it had been locked and Viola had been sitting on the now-upturned chair, she would have had to get up and unlock it. Could she have been expecting someone and therefore left the door unlocked?

But why would Viola, who lived in rue des Armuriers, meet someone in this decrepit chapel beyond the leper colony?

Belina measured the room by counting her paces in each direction. She scratched the numbers on her tablet. She noted the location of the blood puddle and the contents of the vestry and then picked up one of the cloths and examined it. It was a chasuble made of dark green silk and covered with pale green embroidery. A needle and thread were hanging from the blood-stained edge, and she nearly pricked her finger on the needle.

She frowned. Why would Viola have been sitting in this vestry embroidering a chasuble? It made no sense, and she would need to question Viola's servants. She hoped they would be less difficult than the Prelet staff had been yesterday morning.

She put the chasuble with its needle and thread into her investigation bag and walked round the room again. The long curtain concealed some steps which must have been the ones Guillaume had used when he walked through the tunnel from the Lussan mansion in the centre of Condom. Had Viola walked through that long tunnel? And if so, why? Did she do that every day? Or just the once, on the morning of her betrothal banquet?

Belina tugged the curtain back into place and saw a cloak hanging from a hook. She removed the cloak very carefully and held it against herself. It was a woman's garment, good quality but very dusty. The hood too was dusty.

She stuffed the cloak into the investigation bag and bit her lip. It looked as if Viola had worn this cloak with the hood covering her hair, and had walked through the tunnel guided by the lantern which was now under the sink.

She took one last look at the little room, searching for another weapon. Guillaume had shown her the one he had found, a carpentry tool called a spokeshave. It was, she supposed, something that crestias used, since they were the people who worked with wood. The only people who worked with wood, as far as she knew.

In any case, a crestian had been found at the scene of the murder. He was now in the cathedral prison and had told Guillaume almost nothing. It was unusual for Guillaume to have learnt so little in an interrogation. She did not think she was likely to learn much either.

She wondered what Chezelle had been doing in, or near, the chapel yesterday morning. A tooth-drawer like him would surely not have been dealing with crestias' teeth problems. Nor pilgrims' teeth problems for that matter. His medicinal work was limited to caring for Dame Edith Senclar's teeth. Were they so bad? Nobody had ever seen her smile. Chezelle's daily work was spying on people and reporting all that he had seen and heard back to Dame Edith. Belina always took care to avoid him.

She picked up the investigation bag and found that it was now too swollen to hang on her shoulder. The tablet bag was even heavier, weighed down by several tablets with her drawings scratched on them together with her list of objects and measurements.

She struggled with the bags through the door into the chapel and put them down again while she locked the vestry door and hung the key on her belt. The outer door was open and there a second guard had joined the first one. Belina decided to ask him to carry her two heavy bags to the shop. She walked slowly through the dusty chapel and greeted the guards.

"*Adischatz*, Dame Lansac," said the new arrival, "whatever are you carrying?"

"My husband's investigation bag and lots of wax tablets. They are heavy."

"They look it. Here, let me carry them for you. Where are you going?"

"To the cathedral shop please."

The guard put the tablet bag on his shoulder and carried the investigation bag in his left hand. Belina followed the guard and her two precious bags along the street to the shop.

The guard was ahead of her and it was difficult to keep up with him because she was so tired physically and mentally. When they reached the shop, Belina asked the guard to go right inside it and leave the bags in the far corner.

Quiteira interrupted her sales patter to a pilgrim. "So you are here at last, Belina. I've missed out on several sales."

Belina shrugged her tired shoulders and turned her back on Quiteira, choosing to thank the guard instead. Then she put the bag of tablets in the store-room and locked it.

"Don't do that," Quiteira snapped.

"It's only for a few minutes, just enough time for me to take this other bag up the stairs."

"What's in it?"

"Clothes." Belina avoided any more unwelcome questions by picking the bag up and going into the courtyard with it. She waved to Sir John Keyham whose right arm Alain was stroking with ointment and went very slowly up the steep stairs to Guillaume's chamber, her mind full of Viola's death.

"Dame Belina, let me carry that for you."

She turned round carefully. It was Alain, Sir John's man-servant and the man who had discovered Barvaux's groom stealing his master's horse. Belina regretted his heroic action. Her husband had gone she knew not where, perchance for a considerable time, and left her to solve a murder by herself again.

Alain took the bag and led the way up the rest of the stairs and along the passage to the door to Guillaume's chamber.

Belina followed more slowly, almost in tears. She took her door key from the group of keys hanging from her belt and put it in the lock. A loud miaow and a scratching sound came from inside.

"All right, Minet," Belina called out, "please be patient."

"Don't worry, Dame Belina," said Alain, "I'll catch the cat when you open the door. Unless you want her to stay out."

"No thanks Alain. I prefer her to be inside." She opened the door and Alain struggled with Minet until Belina took the cat from him and pushed the door shut with her shoulder.

She gave the cat some milk, stroked her and breathed in the smell of ointment from her fur which been on Alain's hand when he held the cat. She went down the stairs again to the shop to fetch the bag of tablets from the store-room.

Quiteira was standing in the middle of the shop, hands on hips. "Oh, there you are at last. These customers wish to buy some large phials of *aygue ardente* and you have locked the store-room."

"Sorry Quiteira, but my tablet bag is not supposed to be left alone." Belina unlocked the store-room and reached for some large phials. "How many?" she called out.

"Three."

Belina took down four phials from the top shelf and brought them to the display table near the customers. "I have added another phial because you have had to wait so long for me."

"Thank you, Dame. How much do you want for them?"

Belina told them and began to wrap the phials up separately, each in its own piece of cloth. She took the money and tried to smile at the customers. Instead, she began crying and she was glad when they left.

"What's the matter with you?" Quiteira asked.

"I'm tired." Belina fetched the tablet bag from the store-room and left the shop with no further explanation.

There was no sign of Sir John or Alain in the courtyard, and Belina had to struggle up the stairs with the bag of tablets by herself. She dumped the heavy bag in the inner room, removed her head-cloth and lay on the bed until Minet started to purr in her ear.

Belina gave the cat some milk and glanced at her face in

the mirror. She did not like what she saw. Lank hair, wrinkled forehead, red eyes. She washed her face, unplaited her hair and brushed it before plaiting it again. She opened her phial of lavender scent and dabbed some behind her ears.

Guillaume had used the last four eggs the evening before, and she could only find two bits of cheese and some pears. She knew she had not eaten enough food since the two dinners cooked by Catalina. However, she could easily solve that problem by buying a chicken pie or two, in the Place Lion d'Or on her way to rue des Armuriers.

She went into the inner room, took the used wax tablets from their bag and put them in Guillaume's work chest. Then she added two clean tablets to those still in the bag, along with another stylus.

Belina lifted the bag to check its weight because she would be carrying it when she visited the wives of the first two consuls to ask them about the betrothal banquet. She bit her lip as she worked out how much information she was likely to be able to scratch on to the tablets. She could not do that in front of the ladies being questioned, and she would not need to draw any room or its contents like she had done in the crime scene at the Sainte Eulalie chapel.

Her hand hesitated inside the tablet bag. Then she pulled out all the wax tablets to examine their condition and put the messiest one back against the wall. She placed two tablets into the bag and put on her head-cloth. She was ready to start on the next stage of her investigation.

CHAPTER SIXTEEN

Belina left Minet curled up asleep on the bed, closed the door softly and left the courtyard by the outer door instead of going through the shop as she usually did. Another altercation with Quiteira would take up too much time and try her patience further.

She walked to the Place Lion d'Or and bought two chicken pies from the tray of a pie-seller standing in the shade opposite the inn. To save time she ate the pies standing up and brushed the crumbs from her kirtle. Then she walked down to the end of rue des Armuriers to the pottery workshop of Consul Toupié. The consul's wife was showing some large green beakers to three young men. Belina could see through the shop to the kiln in the yard where more young men shovelled charcoal into the base. She waited outside in spite of the sunshine while she decided what she would say to Dame Toupié.

"*Adischatz*, Belina," the potter's wife greeted her. "Are you checking the way I display *my* objects for sale and comparing it with how you set out your stall?"

"No, Dame Toupié, I am here to check your memory about the betrothal banquet last Monday."

"Come up the stairs where we can talk in comfort." Dame Toupié gave instructions to her assistants and led Belina up a ladder.

"My husband is busy watching the kiln being loaded, Belina. Do you need to speak to him too?"

"No thank you. I would not want to disturb him. I suppose that the banquet took up enough of his precious time yesterday."

"Indeed it did. And of course what was worse was that there was no betrothal."

"But you ate the banquet, I hope," said Belina.

"Yes, but in almost silence."

"Did everybody stay for the meal?"

"Of course they did. Consul Prelet's cook is famous for his banquets."

"Do they have banquets often?" Belina asked.

"All their meals are very formal. They show the importance of Consul Prelet. Of course, they are not as lavish as yesterday's meal was." She paused. "But they are usually full of cheerful chatter." She picked up a pottery pitcher and poured some cider into a green beaker. "Drink this Belina. You are looking hot and thirsty."

Belina gulped down the very welcome liquid and handed the beaker back. "*Mercés*. You were right, Dame Toupié, I needed that drink. Did anybody on Monday say what they thought had happened to Viola Lussan?"

"We didn't dare to do so in front of her parents, but after they had left we women talked about it while the consuls muttered at the far end of the room where we couldn't overhear what they said."

"That's a pity," said Belina. "My husband has to investigate the death of Viola. That's why he has asked me to talk to you and the wives of the other consuls."

"Good luck with some of them, Belina."

"That is why I have started my inquiries with you, Dame Toupié. You pay attention to other people. I remember Viola telling me that her mother only pays attention to herself."

Belina asked about the behaviour and actions of Consul

Lussan and his wife, but did not learn much, except that Dame Toupié did not like either of them. On the other hand, Belina did learn that Consul Prelet had been ill quite often during the last twelve months – forcing banquets to be cancelled – and that he had wanted his son Charles to return to Condom and take over the administration of very substantial properties as well as taking over as consul.

"How easy would it be for him to become the most senior consul?" Belina asked.

"My husband and the other three lesser consuls would not agree to it. They don't want to be ordered around by a younger man and an inexperienced one at that."

"How old is he?"

Dame Toupié did some sums in her head. "I would think at least twenty-nine," she said. "Quite a bit older than gentle Viola."

"Did the young couple know each other?" Belina asked.

"Probably not, because Charles Prelet is seldom in Condom. He prefers Toulouse. I don't blame him really."

"What does he do in Toulouse?" Belina asked.

"He is a lawyer. I don't suppose he would want to give that up."

"He could be a lawyer in Condom," Belina pointed out.

"Not the same thing at all. He'd be cock of his own dunghill here of course, and everybody would flatter him. His sleeves would shine with everybody stroking them."

Belina smiled. "If I understand you correctly, you would not be among those stroking his sleeve."

"No. I never do that. Not even the Bishop gets flattery from me. I pride myself in never being obsequious."

"What was Charles Prelet's reaction when he heard his betrothed was dead?"

"I don't know. I wasn't looking in his direction. We all avoided looking at each other. It was such a surprise."

"Did you or anyone else have a feeling that Viola's life was in danger last Monday?"

"To tell you the truth, I haven't thought about Viola Lussan for a long time. My sons are married, their wives are busy bearing and rearing children and I have two god-daughters to think about as well."

"But you went to the banquet," said Belina.

"That was not just to eat the food. It would have been considered bad manners if we had not been there for the betrothal or to be introduced to a soon-to-be-consul."

Belina asked after Consul Prelet's daughter and son-in-law. Had they been present at the banquet and did Dame Toupié think they were against the favours granted to their absent brother? Or were against the idea of money being spent on him?

Dame Toupié poured herself some cider and looked at the beaker while Belina waited, trying not to show her impatience.

"Hugues Galerne is a successful merchant here. He trades in many things, including gold from Bordeaux, which arrives there in Portuguese ships from Africa. His mansion has wonderful tiles on the walls that he told me came from Portugal, but he refused to tell my husband how the Portuguese make them."

Dame Toupié took another sip of her cider. "Pauline Prelet married him several years ago and has borne him three sons, I think. Perchance four. All of them will be brought up to be merchants, no doubt. There has been some talk that her husband visits the *étuves* too often, especially when she is pregnant. She has the reputation of being quick-tempered with him, and their sons and their servants."

"Was she angry during the banquet?" Belina asked.

"Yes. She walked out of the room, almost knocking over a servant carrying wine glasses." Dame Toupié sipped some more cider. "She must have been away at least half an hour."

"So she could have met a killer and paid him a fee?" Belina asked, surprising herself at the boldness of her question.

"Belina, my dear, I don't think Pauline Galerne is that bad. She may be short-tempered, but why would she want to kill Viola Lussan?"

"Why would anybody want to kill Viola Lussan?" Belina sighed. While she was working out what to say next, a curtain was pulled aside and a small boy walked in carrying a puppy.

"Look Mamie," he cried, "here's the biggest puppy. Can I keep him?"

Dame Toupié got up, took the dog from him and smiled at it. "I say you can have it, Titot, but ask your father and mother first. Let's go and find them."

Belina got up, not noticing that the boy's mother was hiding behind the curtain. "Thank you for your help, Dame Toupié. If you think of anything else please let me know."

She went very carefully down the ladder with her bag of wax tablets, through the airless shop and out into rue des Armuriers. It was a hot walk up the hill to Consul Ardit's mansion, two doors away from the Lussan mansion. She knocked on the nail-studded door and waited.

A window opened above her and a maid called down, "What do you want?"

"I am the wife of the Bishop's Inquirer, and the Lord Seneschal has ordered me to question everyone who was present at the banquet on Monday in the Prelet mansion."

"All right. I will come down and open the door for you."

Belina waited close to the door so that the animals going up and down the rue des Armuriers did not bump into her.

She heard bolts being drawn back from the door and saw it open a few inches.

A man's voice said, "Bruna, who is there?"

"Dame Lansac, Messire, the wife of the Bishop's Inquirer."

"What does she want?"

Belina could hear the maid describing the Seneschal's orders.

The door was flung open and Belina found herself facing Consul Ardit, the wine merchant.

"Come in, Dame Lansac." He shut the door behind her. "I don't have time to talk to you because I need to go to my *chai*. We are preparing for the new *vendange*."

"I understand that, Messire, but I have come here to speak to your wife rather than yourself." Belina took the Seneschal's document out of the purse hanging from her belt. "This is the Lord Seneschal's written authority for me to question people following the death last Monday of Consul Lussan's daughter."

She crossed herself, as did Consul Ardit and the maid.

"Show Dame Lansac up the stairs into the parlour," the consul told the maid. "Do you know who committed this terrible crime?" he asked Belina.

"My husband has already put the main suspect into prison," Belina told him, "but he needs to find out why Viola was killed and if anybody else was involved."

"I don't understand why anybody would want to kill a sweet girl like Viola," Consul Ardit replied.

"Nor do I, Messire. I knew her when we were at school together and she was a good friend of mine. I am so sad she has died." Belina brushed away a tear.

The consul did not reply. He frowned before turning round and going down the passage. Belina followed the maid up the wooden stairs and was shown into a large room with several windows. A tabby cat was looking through the glass panes and waving its tail, just like Minet did when she watched birds.

The maid announced Belina's arrival and the purpose of her visit and the lady reclining on the couch greeted Belina and pointed to the stool beside her.

Belina sat down and began her explanation that she had been a school friend of Viola Lussan and that she was very sad about her death.

"Yes. It seems a very violent way of avoiding a betrothal," said Dame Ardit.

"Do you think Viola didn't want to marry Consul Prelet's son?" Belina asked.

"I don't know what she thought, but it was very odd that she didn't arrive at the Prelet mansion at the same time as her parents. My husband and I were surprised at the behaviour of Consul Lussan when she didn't arrive soon after them."

Belina waited for more comments while she studied Dame Ardit's appearance, looking at her unplaited lank hair framing a thin face. She was in the last stages of pregnancy.

"He snarled at his wife for not helping Viola with her preparations for the betrothal ceremony. Apparently, they had left their mansion while their daughter was still being dressed in her new gown."

"What did Dame Lussan say?" Belina asked.

"I don't remember the exact words, but she maintained that she had been very occupied with her own gown and head-cloth."

"What was she wearing?" Belina asked, trying to test the lady's powers of observation and memory.

"A blue gown with matching head-cloth. Too many jewels."

"Were they old jewels," Belina asked. "Ones she had inherited, perchance."

"No, not at all. She wore new jewellery. Must have cost her husband a lot."

"But Consul Lussan is known to be a rich man," Belina pointed out.

"He might have been originally, but my husband says he owes a considerable sum for wine purchases from us."

"Oh?" said Belina.

"The marriage is – or rather was – expected to take place near Christmas when many people make large purchases of wine. My husband does not like having to wait until Our Lady Day to be paid, unless he knows that a customer has a true money problem."

"So if I understand you correctly, Dame Ardit, Consul Lussan's wife spends money on herself and her jewels rather than letting her husband pay for his wine."

"Correct." Dame Ardit shifted her heavy body uncomfortably on the couch. "But she is very self-willed, you know. Always talking about herself and her grand family mansion."

"Where's that?"

"Agen. She's not Gascon. She doesn't fit in here at all."

"I wonder why Consul Lussan married her then," Belina said.

"They say that some of her family lands were next to some of his property."

"So how did she behave when she heard that her daughter was dead in the Sainte Eulalie chapel?" Belina asked.

"She was angry. She told her husband that it was his fault that they had not waited until Viola's gown was ready."

"But she could have waited," Belina said, "while her husband went by himself to the Prelet mansion."

"That is what we had been saying all morning."

"So people had little compassion?" Belina asked.

"Oh yes, of course they had compassion. The death of a child is a terrible thing. And who knows how bad news affects a person?"

"What was the behaviour of Consul Prelet and his wife?"

"Surprise and annoyance, I think," Dame Ardit replied, "but they hid their views quite well. They are both descended from very good lineage."

"What are they going to do about their son's marriage?" Belina asked.

"They did not say. Probably they haven't had time to decide."

"What was their son's reaction when he heard that his betrothal had been cancelled?"

"He showed no feelings whatsoever," replied Dame Ardit. "He sat apart from the rest of us reading documents."

"That sounds very odd to me," said Belina.

"Dame Prelet told us that Charles had been delayed in Toulouse and had arrived in Condom two days later than planned."

"So he had not had time to read documents about the dowry and donations?"

"I suppose so," Dame Ardit replied.

Belina began to ask about the young woman who Guillaume had seen standing near Charles Prelet, but Dame Ardit sighed and asked Belina in a weak voice to go to the door and call out for her maid.

Belina got up from the stool and went to the door. She opened it quickly and found herself very close to the maid, with two other servants nearby looking sheepish, as if they had been listening to the conversation.

"Please see to your mistress's needs," Belina told the maid. "I hope she has not taken ill."

The maid pushed past Belina and ran to the couch. "Dame Ardit, you asked to see me."

"Yes, I need a drink. I feel a bit faint. Then ask this woman to leave me be." She sighed again.

Belina picked up her tablet bag, thanked Dame Ardit for her help, and hoped her health would recover quickly.

She went down the stairs and out of the mansion, regretting the sudden end to her questioning, and walked up the hill to the Place Lion d'Or and back to the staff residence, stopping on the way to buy more eggs, milk and cheese, together with a loaf of bread and some pears.

Belina spent the rest of the afternoon writing on her wax tablets, regretting that she had carried them to the two mansions that afternoon without using them. She decided not to carry anything tomorrow when she was visiting the other consuls' wives. There was not much to record really. The odd behaviour of Consul Lussan and his wife contrasted with the casual disdain of Charles Prelet.

She spent a long time scrubbing the frying pan with ash. She swept both rooms, which made Minet sneeze and insist on going out, then she unplaited her hair and washed it. While it was drying she washed some clothes and a head-cloth. By the time all that was done it was evening and too late to go down to the shop and help Quiteira. Belina did not look forward to telling her tomorrow morning that she would be away all day.

CHAPTER SEVENTEEN

Friday

Belina's worries were justified next morning. Quiteira scolded her for her absence and hinted that she should receive more money for having to work alone.

Belina opened her purse and took out a dozen coins.

"Oooh! As many as that? You and Guillaume must be feeling guilty." Quiteira snatched the coins.

Belina smiled, hooked her purse back on to her belt and left the shop. She crossed Place Saint Pierre and entered Consul Gaudé's furshop. She was pleased to see that one of the saleswomen was someone she knew. "*Adischatz*, Mariotte, please may I speak to Dame Gaudé?"

"*Adischatz*, Belina. I think she is resting in her chamber because of the hot weather. I will ask one of the maids. Can I tell her why you have come to see her?"

"Of course you can." Belina took out the written authority from the Seneschal and told Mariotte about her investigation task.

The maid was soon back, and led Belina up stone stairs and into a large, darkened bedchamber.

"*Adischatz*, Dame Lansac," said an elderly woman beside the tall window. Belina could hardly see her in the gloom because of the tapestry covering most of the window. "Come and sit beside me here."

Belina crossed the bedchamber carefully and sat down on a couch covered with satin cushions.

"Welcome, Dame Lansac. I am sorry to receive you in my bedchamber but I don't like going down the stairs any more than necessary because of my bad knees. All the rain this year has made them very painful. And my shoulders hurt too." She continued in her quavering voice. "That's why this room is rather airless."

Belina smiled and launched into her speech about investigating the death of Viola Lussan.

Dame Gaudé interrupted her. "Such a pretty girl, and she was so much in love with Consul Prelet's son."

"Was she?" Belina asked.

"Indeed she was. It would have been a perfect match. Charles Prelet was returning from Toulouse to marry his childhood sweetheart. They had known each other all their lives." Dame Gaudé picked up a cloth from her lap and wiped away the tears on her face. "It's such a shame that they didn't even have time to get betrothed."

"When did you learn that the banquet was for their betrothal?"

"Oh, a long time ago, my dear." She wiped her face again. "But I was expecting it, of course."

"Charles Prelet must have been very upset when he learned of her death," Belina said.

"Indeed he was. I looked at him immediately and he was close to tears. I thought he would leap up and rush out of the room in his misery, but he very nobly stayed there to comfort his parents."

"Did he say anything?" Belina asked.

"I don't remember. That nasty Corloni girl would have interrupted if he had."

"Why?"

"Because she is nasty, like I said." Dame Gaudé sniffed and blew her nose. "Always trying to hook a man. I made sure that she was never alone with my sons."

"I hardly know her, Dame Gaudé, but I don't find her pretty."

"She is far too thin, but very sexy."

Belina brought the conversation back to the betrothal banquet and asked if everyone had arrived at the same time. Dame Gaudé took a long time to tell Belina that most of them had arrived together but that Consul Lussan and his wife had been there before them.

"Did anybody leave at any time?" Belina asked.

Dame Gaudé told her about Consul Lussan leaving in an angry mood and returning in an even worse temper.

"Was Dame Lussan annoyed too?" Belina asked.

"If she was she didn't show it. But she is too vain to show her emotions, my dear. Viola takes, or rather took, after her father. Mathurin Lussan is a fine person, but too reserved in my opinion. All his wife thinks about is her appearance, her beautiful clothes – because she is always beautifully dressed – and her jewellery." She paused for breath.

"Was she wearing many jewels for the betrothal banquet?"

"She was covered with them." Dame Gaudé grinned. "Expensive new jewellery. But then the furs which she wears in winter are also expensive. Nothing but the best for Dame Lussan. She must cost her husband a mint of money." She grinned again. "She is our best customer."

"I suppose Consul Lussan would have also spent a lot of money on Viola's gown and jewels for the betrothal banquet," Belina suggested.

"Probably more than he could afford."

"Do you really think so?" Belina asked, feigning her surprise.

"My husband suspects that for the last year or so Consul Lussan has been a bit short of money."

"I had always supposed that he owned a lot of property," Belina said.

"My husband has heard that some of his land has been spoiled by two years of bad harvests because of the storms, frosts and rain."

"That has happened to many people," Belina pointed out. "My brother's mill has ground less wheat for the last two years."

Dame Gaudé took no notice. She carried on talking about the decline in Consul Lussan's fortunes. "The death of his only son hit him hard too. My husband said that he had invested badly." She talked at great length about these mistakes while Belina regretted the waste of her time in having to be shut up in an airless bedchamber listening to an old woman discussing finance and the fur trade.

"If Consul Lussan has become as poor as you think, Dame Gaudé, why would Consul Prelet choose Viola to be married to his son?"

"For love, my dear. For the great affection they had for each other for so many years." She blew her nose again. "It's just like my youngest son's marriage, too. He married for love, just like Viola was going to. My husband was not keen on his choice at first, but now we are both very happy for them. They have six lovely children and three of them have children themselves. I am a great-grandmother."

The door opened and Consul Gaudé walked into his bedchamber and had almost reached the couch before he noticed Belina.

She stood up and told Consul Gaudé why she was there.

"My wife and I are very distressed at the news," Consul Gaudé told Belina. "I was surprised, though, that Consul Lussan was more angry than sad. And his wife was annoyed too. I would have expected her to dissolve into tears, but she controlled herself completely."

"She's not Gascon," Dame Gaudé interrupted him. "She's from Agen. Women from there are cold and arrogant. They are not loving mothers . . ."

Consul Gaudé interrupted her, "or loving grandmothers or great-grandmothers like you." He kissed her forehead.

Belina took the opportunity to escape from the airless room. She thanked Dame Gaudé and found her way to the stairs and out the front door.

She screwed her eyes up against the harsh sunlight and sniffed the dusty air. A faint smell of decay reached her from the market hall, but she preferred it to Dame Gaudé's airless bedchamber, which had been made even more horrible by the stench of a very full chamber-pot.

Belina went into the market hall and sat on a bench near some chicken legs that were being cooked on a grill. She was soon served with two legs and a chunk of bread, and she asked for a beaker of cider.

"I have some *bourret* which has just arrived," the cook told her. "Would you like some?"

"Yes please." Belina drank the new wine too quickly and almost choked. However, she needed the liquid. She paid for the hasty meal, taking care that the cook did not spill chicken grease on the precious document in her purse, and left the market hall.

She walked down rue Royale, looking for the mansion of Consul Volpato. She remembered the sour comments Guillaume had made about him: too young to become a consul, ambitious wine shipper, became rich because he sent his wine to Bayonne via Mont de Marsan instead of shipping it down the Baïse to the Garonne and then to Bordeaux. Her suggestion that Bordeaux wine dealers charge too much to ship Gascon wines was rejected by Guillaume so fiercely that she did not talk about the Bordeaux law banning trade in Gascon wine until after Christmas, which meant that it would be too rough and dangerous for ships to sail across the Bay of Biscay to England.

She stopped outside Consul Volpato's mansion and lifted the brass knocker on the new front door. But before she could knock, a man behind her said, "who are you?"

Belina turned round and saw a youth in new livery.

"I said, Dame, who are you?"

"Why do you presume to ask?" she replied.

"Because I am doorkeeper to Consul Volpato."

Belina took the Seneschal's written authority out of her tablet bag and passed it to him.

The youth held it upside down and pretended to read it until Belina took it back. "It is an order from the Seneschal for everybody to see me and tell me about the banquet last Monday in Consul Prelet's mansion."

"Ah yes, when the girl didn't show up. I bet the consuls were angry, wasting their time like that."

"That is what the Seneschal wants me to find out," Belina told him. "Is Dame Volpato in please?"

"I'll let you inside and we'll see if she agrees to see you." He pushed the heavy door open and stood aside for her to go into the hall.

It was difficult for Belina to walk past him with her tablet bag and she could smell the sour wine on his breath.

The hall was newly painted and guarded by two grey-hounds. One of them stood up, walked towards Belina and sniffed her shoes. Belina presumed that chicken grease had fallen on them.

The youth put his arm round her waist and told her that if she wanted him to tell Dame Volpato that she was here she would have to give him a kiss first.

Belina trod on the greyhound's foot and it made a dreadful noise. Two doors opened and the hallway filled with people. The greyhound limped towards the oldest person present and whined.

"What's the matter, Vidau?" he said to the dog.

"He is right to complain," Belina said, "because I trod on his foot."

"Why?"

"To warn you all that I was being annoyed by this boy

here," Belina pointed to the youth, "who said I must give him a kiss because I am asking to see Dame Volpato."

The man frowned. "Is that true, Menjou?"

"No, she's telling a lie," came the smooth reply.

"I don't think so," said a maid, "he's always trying to kiss girls."

Belina liked being called a girl by somebody younger than herself. She waited while Consul Volpato's servants decided whether or not to allow her to see Dame Volpato.

"What are you all doing in the hall?"

Belina tried to see who the speaker was, but he was hidden behind a tall servant.

"It's a lady to see Dame Marguerite," said one of the maids.

"Why?"

Belina explained the reason and flourished the Seneschal's written authority.

A very well dressed, youngish man pushed everybody aside and took the document. He read it carefully and gave it back to her.

"I see. I don't have much time just now," he began.

"I understand that, Messire. I have come to speak to Dame Volpato."

"No. You will speak to both of us. Come this way." He led her into a room at the end of the hall. Belina looked at an ink-stained clerk writing on a ledger, and assumed she was in Consul Volpato's office.

"Enric, would you please ask one of the maids to fetch Dame Volpato here. She has a visitor." The clerk sidled out of the room.

"It is good of you to give me your time, Consul Volpato," Belina said.

"Hmmm. Thank you. Especially after I wasted several hours last Monday at the betrothal banquet."

"Did you know in advance that the banquet was for a betrothal?" Belina asked him.

"One week beforehand. Maybe less."

"Did you know Consul Prelet's son well?"

"Not recently. Charles Prelet is younger than me so we didn't really know each other at school."

Belina suggested they went riding together in the past.

"Yes, hunting mostly. Hawking too when he could borrow two hawks from the Keeper of his father's birds of prey."

"Did you have a hawk of your own?" Belina asked.

The consul smiled. "No. They are very expensive to buy and to keep." He scratched his ear. "But I am thinking of getting one soon. I know somebody who needs to sell his birds."

"Who is that?" Belina asked, to keep the conversation going while they waited for Dame Volpato to appear.

"Consul Lussan. He has fallen on bad times, and needs money quickly."

"Oh," Belina said, "though perchance now that there is no wedding and no dowry he will be less worried about money."

"You mean that he had his daughter murdered in order to be able to repay his debts?"

"Certainly not," Belina replied quickly. "I wouldn't dream of saying such a thing."

"Nor would I, but Dame Lussan might. She's never got over the death of her son, and my sister – who lives in Agen – tells me that she is angry that her son died of the plague instead of her daughter."

"I hope you are not suggesting that Dame Lussan murdered her daughter," Belina said.

"I wouldn't put it past her. I wouldn't put anything past her."

Fortunately for Belina's peace of mind, the door opened and Dame Volpato wafted into the room, accompanied by the scent of lavender and a greyhound puppy. She kissed her husband and smiled at Belina.

"You are the *molieròta* who married the Bishop's Inquirer, I think?"

Belina pursed her lips. "Yes, I am Dame Lansac."

"Of the *babioles* shop in rue Jean-Baptiste." Dame Volpato sat on her husband's chair and offered Belina a thin smile. "Are you here to sell us some *babioles*?"

Belina stared at her, but kept her temper.

"My dear, she is here to ask us about the betrothal banquet last Monday."

"Ghastly day." Dame Volpato picked a document off her husband's desk and fanned herself with it.

"Did you think that Consul Prelet thought that Viola Lussan would not accompany her parents to the banquet?"

"I don't know," Dame Volpato replied. "He's an old man in poor health. He is thinking about his own death, in my opinion."

"I would not put it as strongly as that, my dear, but these last few months he has certainly aged and become more infirm." Consul Volpato stroked his ear. "Dame Prelet has taken over quite a lot of her husband's work, sorted out tenants' problems, hired servants, seen that rents are collected. All those things – even though she too is aged."

"They say she is older than her husband," said Dame Volpato.

"True. But it's reputed to be a fairly happy marriage. The great wealth she brought with her would have helped, of course."

"My husband noticed the calm way she dealt with his declaration of Viola's death," Belina said.

"I was looking at Charles Prelet to see how he took it," Dame Volpato said. "Was he a cast-off lover, or relieved unwilling bridegroom?"

"Which was he?" Belina asked.

"Impossible to know, or even guess." Dame Volpato stroked the greyhound puppy. "The girl beside Charles Prelet had a totally expressionless face too."

"Who was she?" Belina asked. "A Prelet relative?"

"Notaire Corloni's daughter."

"Why would she have been at the banquet? Or were all Notaire Corloni's children there?"

"No, they can't have been," said Consul Volpato. "There are far too many of them."

"If I understand it correctly," Belina said, "Notaire Corloni and his family live in Montreal, not Condom. How could they have attended a banquet?"

"They would have stayed in the mansion next door to the Prelets."

"Do they own that?" Belina wondered if her and Jordi's inheritance had been stolen in order to buy a mansion in the rue Royale.

"No, or at least not yet. It belongs to the *notaire's* sister, who is a rich widow living in Bordeaux. She lets her brother and his wife and children stay in her mansion whenever they want to."

Belina continued with her questions about the Prelet family. Were Charles Prelet's sisters angry or pleased or surprised at the death of Viola?

"I don't know about the younger sister," Consul Volpato replied, "She lives in Auch with her husband, who is a lawyer. Neither of them was at the betrothal banquet because he was working on an important property case. And the younger son is a priest in Auch. He wasn't at the banquet either."

"And the older sister?" Belina asked.

Consul Volpato told her the same information that she had already heard from Dame Toupié and added that he did not envy Hugues Galerne at all. He omitted any comment about going to the *étuves*, of course.

"Is Charles Prelet a lawyer?" Belina asked.

Consul Volpato nodded, and said, "In Toulouse. Doing rather well, apparently."

"Has he been in Toulouse long?" Belina asked.

"You should be asking Consul Prelet that sort of question, not me."

"I will in due course," Belina replied, "but it is too soon after the shock of Viola's death for me to do that."

"I think he's been there for about ten years," said Dame Volpato, "and he's likely to stay there now."

"Because of Viola's death?" Belina asked.

"Yes."

She was about to say something else when she looked at her husband's face and closed her mouth again. Belina looked at Consul Volpato. He was frowning and tapping his desk with a forefinger.

"You must excuse us, Dame Lansac, but we both have important work to do. Please give my kind regards to your husband. I would like to talk with him not only about the banquet but also about the Bordeaux wine trade. He has interests in that, doesn't he?"

"Yes, or at least his family does."

Belina thanked them and went towards the door. Consul Volpato opened it for her and told the servants near the door to show Dame Lansac out. Belina wondered how much of the conversation they had heard through the door, or even if they had left it slightly open on purpose.

CHAPTER EIGHTEEN

Belina walked down rue Royale to the final mansion of her afternoon, and stood outside the door leading to the court-yard of Consul Courial, leading lawyer of Condom and the surrounding area. He was famous for having acquired much money from successful claims over testaments, land sales, inheritance challenges, marriage contracts and other family battles. His fees were too high for Jordi and Belina to have even considered asking for his advice, let alone his help over their father's testament. Belina wondered if she could take advantage of having to question his wife about Viola's death to introduce the subject of Notaire Corloni.

She showed the Seneschal's written authority to the door-keeper, who glanced at it and gave it back to her. "Come in, Dame Lansac, and I will summon a maid."

Belina waited for several minutes while she looked at the large hall, hung with tapestries and iron sconces for torches. At the far end was a dresser with metal plates on its shelves. Belina wondered whether they were pewter or silver. If the latter, that showed that Consul Courial was a very wealthy man.

A maid came up to her and said, "My mistress will see you, Dame Lansac. Please follow me up the stairs."

Belina walked up the stone stairs and was shown into a small room where another maid took her through to a much larger room, with more tapestries on the walls and three more dressers. The one nearest to Belina gleamed with silver plates and other objects.

"*Adischatz*, Dame Lansac." A small, rather stout middle-aged lady smiled at her and pointed to a chair for Belina to sit on. It was a welcome treat to sit down on a chair after her day of walking and talking.

"Carine, pour some *hypocras* for Dame Lansac, please."

Belina was very grateful. She was thirsty and tired, and this was the first person she'd visited since Dame Toupié who had offered her a drink. She sipped the sweetened and spiced wine with great pleasure.

Belina made her usual speech about her investigation.

"I was surprised at the death of Viola Lussan," Dame Courial said, "and of course very sad that she died and the means of her passing. Have I heard correctly that the poor girl's throat was cut?" Belina nodded. "But what did not surprise me so much was the anger of her parents."

"Why not, Dame Courial?"

"Consul Lussan is reputed to be in debt." The lady stopped for a moment, and then said, "Please promise me not to talk about this, Dame Lansac."

"Of course, I promise you. I will only tell my husband."

"And the Seneschal?"

"Not yet. My husband will decide when to report our findings to the Lord Seneschal, and what to tell him."

"Good, so I can continue in safety. Consul Prelet had originally negotiated with Consul Lussan for a rather substantial dowry to be paid on the day of the betrothal. The contracts had taken time, in the usual way of such documents, to be drawn up and sent to Charles Prelet in Toulouse for his acceptance. However, a few days before the day of the betrothal banquet Consul Lussan had confessed that he could not include most of the land stipulated in the marriage contract."

Dame Courial sipped some *hypocras* and continued, "This

land was part of Dame Lussan's dowry, valuable territory in Agen itself and farmland adjacent to Consul Lussan's own fields. When she discovered that those lands had been included in her daughter's dowry Dame Lussan was furious, and so were her family in Agen. Dame Lussan insisted that only Lussan land should be included in Viola's dowry. The problem with this change was that the Lussan lands have lost much value in the last two years because of the bad harvests and flooding."

"I had always supposed that Consul Lussan was a wealthy man," said Belina.

"And so he was, Dame Lansac. However, he has made bad investment decisions that have forced him to survive on less money than before. But Consul Prelet was unaware of this during the dowry negotiations. He felt very let down by the day of the betrothal banquet."

"Did his son feel let down too?" Belina asked.

"Yes, of course he did. His mother confided in me that she had wondered whether they should cancel the betrothal banquet and the betrothal itself. However, Consul Prelet's health is deteriorating rather quickly, and he is determined to go ahead with the arrangements for his son to settle in Condom. That involves being married to a young woman who until recently was known to be the most eligible bride here."

"Did Charles Prelet agree with his father or his mother about his betrothal to Viola?" Belina asked.

"I don't know. I am not sure how keen he was on the marriage in the first place. He's been in Toulouse a long time now, studying to be a lawyer and then setting himself up. Everybody tells me – or rather they tell my husband – that Charles Prelet is successful in Toulouse."

"In that case," Belina said, "he could marry a girl from Toulouse rather than one living in Condom."

"He already has a girl, as you put it, in Toulouse, but he is not married to her."

Belina put on her no-expression face. "Why can he not marry her? Is she married to somebody else?"

"I don't know. Indeed, I know nothing about her, other than her existence."

"Do they have children?"

"I don't know that either." Dame Courial picked up a piece of embroidery and began stitching.

"What reason did Consul Lussan give for Viola not accompanying them to the banquet?" Belina asked in order to change the subject entirely.

"That she had a problem with her betrothal gown. I did not really believe that, but none of us said anything. We all know that Dame Lussan is a difficult woman and best not argued with."

"Did you know Viola?"

"Not very well. I have always helped my husband with his work, studying documents for his cases and running the household so smoothly that there is nothing for him to waste his time on. I don't spend much of my time on sociability." She smiled at Belina and continued her stitching.

"I knew Viola when we were at school together," said Belina. "Did your daughters know her at all?"

"They were at school in Auch, in the convent there. I hardly saw much of them myself at the time." she sighed and continued, "I am not sure whether Viola was prepared – in every sense of the word – to live in Toulouse."

"But I understand that Consul Prelet was determined that his son should return to live in Condom," Belina said.

"Yes, he made that known. But personally I don't think there would be enough interesting legal work for an ambitious and successful young lawyer like Charles Prelet to settle here in Condom."

Belina wondered whether she should ask if Consul Courial's sons were also lawyers and working for him. Such a question would be too pointed. She would make a note on her tablet to ask somebody else. The Archdeacon perchance.

"Would his sister, Dame Pauline, welcome his return to Condom?" Belina asked. "Perchance her husband, Messire Galerne, would have found it useful to have a well-trained lawyer to help his trading activities?"

"Difficult to know," Dame Courial replied. "In any event, the younger Prelet daughter is married to a lawyer who lives in Auch, which is not that far away." She paused and continued stitching. "Although they are very seldom seen here in Condom. I don't know why that should be."

Belina continued her questions. "Do you remember what Charles Prelet's behaviour was when my husband told everybody that Viola was dead?"

"Why do you ask? Hasn't your husband told you?"

"No, because he was facing Consul Prelet and Consul Lussan."

Dame Courial smiled. "I remember that he had no expression on his face, rather like you didn't just now." She smiled.

"My husband told me that there was a young woman standing near Charles Prelet. Who would she have been?"

"Ana Corloni."

"But I thought she lived in Montreal," Belina said.

"Sometimes there, sometimes in her aunt's mansion next door to the Prelet mansion, sometimes also in the Senclar mansion, I believe."

Belina was surprised. "Does she know the Senclar family that well?"

"Oh yes, she's a great friend of Jeanne Senclar." There was a long pause while she continued stitching and frowning. "I think I prefer Ana Corloni to Jeanne Senclar, but I don't care much for either of them."

Belina wanted to ask about the behaviour of Edith Senclar and her son Henri at the news of Viola's death, but the door opened and the best-dressed man in Condom walked in. She stood up. Dame Courial told her husband why she and Belina had been talking about the death of Viola Lussan.

"Indeed, it is very sad. Although neither of us knew the young woman well, the manner of her death was dreadful. I hope your husband can solve the murder – I understand it was a murder."

"Yes Consul Courial," Belina replied. "My husband has imprisoned the crestian who was found in the chapel beside Viola's body, but he needs to find out much more – whether other people were involved, why Viola was killed and so on. We are only just at the start of our investigation."

"I would like to help you, Dame Lansac, but at the moment I am very busy with three important court cases and do not have the time. Indeed, this is why I have come in here, to ask my wife to look through some documents provided by the defence. She is very good at this sort of thing." He smiled, and continued, "I understand that your husband gets you to help him for very similar reasons. A lady sees things differently. She can see the relationships between pieces of evidence that a man misses."

Belina smiled at him and began to thank him.

"That's all right, Dame Lansac, but now I really must ask you to leave us because these documents are private. I will ask Carine to show you out."

He went to the door while Belina thanked Dame Courial for her help.

"I wish you and your husband good fortune in your investigation. I am sorry our discussion has been cut short, but that is the inconvenience of being married to a lawyer."

She put away her embroidery and reached for one of her husband's papers, nodding to Belina.

CHAPTER NINETEEN

Belina returned to the staff residence, regretting that her interesting conversation with Dame Courial had been cut short. She changed into her oldest clothes and head-cloth. She decided not to burden herself with a bag of tablets and went down the stairs and into the shop to explain to Quiteira where she had been all day.

"Good gracious, Belina, why were you wearing such ragged clothes to visit consuls' wives? I don't believe you saw any of them. You look worse than you do when you've been in the mill and got covered with flour."

Belina told her that she had changed from her good clothes into her oldest ones because she was going inside the cathedral prison to question the prisoner there.

"What prisoner?"

"The young man found beside the body of Viola Lussan."

"That's Guillaume's job. How dare he expect you to go inside a prison, even if you are wearing your worst clothes?"

"Because Guillaume has already questioned the prisoner and got nowhere," Belina replied.

"I thought he was supposed to be an experienced interrogator."

"He is. Of course he is. But he wondered if I could succeed where he could not."

Belina left the shop without bidding Quiteira farewell and walked along rue Jean-Baptiste to the prison.

"*Adischatz*," she greeted the guard on the door.

"*Adischatz*, Dame Lansac, how are you this fine day?"

"Determined to get my husband's prisoner to answer my questions."

"Good luck with that. Messire Guillaume couldn't get anything out of him." The guard spat into the street. "And he usually gets every prisoner to speak one way or another."

"I know," Belina replied. "But he thinks I might succeed where he hasn't."

The guard took her into the guardroom, where two more guards stood up and greeted her politely. She told them that she needed to question the crestian in his cell with one of them present "just in case he gets violent."

"I don't think he's violent, Dame Lansac. He's very docile."

"I'm relieved to hear it," said Belina. "That way I can discover more about him." She turned towards the older guard and asked him whether the crestian had confessed to the murder in the Sainte Eulalie chapel.

"No. He won't talk at all, just sits staring at the wall of his cell." He unhooked a key from his belt and gave it to the younger guard. "Take Dame Lansac to the crestian's cell," he said, "and stay there until she has finished and wants to come back. Make sure the prisoner is not violent."

"You said just now that he is not violent," Belina told him.

"Not so far, but I'm taking no chances with your safety, Dame Lansac."

Belina followed the young guard down some stairs and along a dirty dark passage, past a cell with an old man in it sitting on a bucket. The smell was appalling.

The guard stopped near the end of the passage and unlocked the bars of a cell containing a young man sitting on a piece of matting on the floor and staring at the wall. The guard led Belina gently inside and shut the door behind her.

Belina stood inside the cell trying to ignore the smell of urine. The prisoner had turned his head when he heard the door opening but now he was back to staring at the wall.

"*Adischatz*," Belina began. "I have come here to check if you are being treated correctly." No reply. "My husband had you placed in here because you were found next to a dead body. He needs to know why you were there and who you are."

Still no reply. Belina tried more persuasion and said, "My husband usually compels suspected murderers to confess. He is giving you this one chance to avoid being hurt. It is in your interest to reply to my questions."

The prisoner stood up and turned round.

"What is your name?" Belina asked him.

"Josep."

"And your other name?"

"Sarbazan."

"Where do you live?"

"In the leper colony."

"Were you born there?"

The prisoner shook his head.

"Where were you born?"

He shook his head again.

"Please answer my question."

He stared straight through her, as if he was staring at the wall once more.

"Do you know where you were born?" she asked gently.

No reply. He rubbed a tear from his dirty face.

Belina tried another approach. "If you live in a leper colony that means that you are a crestian. Am I right?"

He nodded.

"Do you do carpentry?"

"Yes."

"What sort?"

"What do you mean?" he asked.

"Roofing, furniture, beds, plates, beakers, buckets, wine barrels? Which is it?"

"Furniture." This time the stare was at her instead of through her.

"Big furniture like beds, or little pieces like stools?"

"Mostly in between. Tables and dressers."

"Was that why you were in the Sainte Eulalie chapel?" Belina asked.

He bit his lip and then decided to say no.

Belina tried to remember the furniture in the vestry and in the main room of the chapel. It had all looked old to her. So if he said he was in the chapel because of its furniture it would have been a lie, although saying it would have been a temptation.

"Why were you in the chapel?" she asked him again.

No reply.

"Please answer my question," Belina told him. "If not, you risk my husband forcing you to answer it. Or him ordering the guards to hurt you."

He stared at her, with tears rolling down his cheeks.

"Tears are not an answer," Belina said. "My question is very reasonable, and it is in your interest to answer it."

She waited while he wiped his face with his hand and began to sniff.

"How long were you in the chapel before you were discovered there?"

He stared at her, still sniffing and she gave him her pouch-cloth. He blew his nose and tried to give the cloth back to her.

"Keep it," Belina said. "Your need is greater."

He blew his nose again and gulped.

"Please tell me how long you were in the chapel before you were discovered there."

"Not long, but I don't know how long."

"Did you know the people who discovered you?"

"No."

"Why were you in the chapel?"

He burst into tears and refused to reply.

Belina asked him where he did his carpentry, and he told her it was in several different buildings but often in Consul Lussan's mansion more recently.

"Did you know Dame Viola Lussan, his daughter?"

The prisoner burst into tears again, while the guard jangled his keys and cleared his throat.

Belina took no notice of either of them as she thought what she should ask next. "Where did you learn to make furniture?"

No reply, just tears streaming down his face.

"Please answer my question."

He shook his head.

"When were you last in Consul Lussan's mansion?"

He stared through her again, not even trying to wipe away his tears, while the guard cleared his throat again.

Belina walked towards the guard and asked him if he thought the man would continue to act the way he was doing.

"Yes. He cries for hours, Dame Lansac. He's a waterfall of tears. Very uncooperative. A miserable man."

"I think I will leave him to his grief then," Belina said. "Please let me out and lock him up again."

She sidled out of the cell and waited for the guard to lock the bars. The crestian was still standing in the middle of his cell, wiping his nose on her pouch-cloth. She followed the guard along the passage and up the stairs, frustrated by her lack of success with the crestian.

"Did you get him to talk?" the senior guard asked her.

"A bit, but not enough. He seemed lost in his sorrow."

"In grief perchance," the guard suggested.

"Yes, but I don't see how he would have known Consul Lussan's daughter," Belina replied.

"Dame Lansac, I suspect that he saw her somewhere, fell in love and when she spurned him – which she would have done, of course – he killed her."

Belina thought about his suggestion. It was unlikely but not impossible, given that he had told her he had worked in the Lussan mansion. If Viola had been found dead in her own home he could have been a suspect, but her body was found some distance away in the Sainte Eulalie chapel. Had he dragged it there through the tunnel?

The guard interrupted her thoughts by asking when Guillaume would begin his second interrogation session.

"I don't know yet," Belina replied. "I wish I did. He's welcome to the task."

"He should not have passed the job to you, Dame Lansac."

"I agree, but he did give it to me." Belina said *'adiu'* to the guards and walked into the clean air of rue Jean-Baptiste and back into the staff residence via the courtyard door. She needed to change her old clothes and head-cloth and wash away all the dirt and smell of the prison.

As she was crossing the courtyard she heard Sir John call a greeting to her so she turned round, wondering whether she should approach him while she was still dirty and smelly from the prison.

Then she saw Antoni near Sir John, drinking. Guillaume would not approve of him doing that, and she wondered if she should tell him so.

"*Adischatz* Dame Belina." Antoni finished his drink and put the beaker on the table. "I have been waiting for you. Quiteira told me that you were in the prison. You shouldn't have been there. I'm glad you are back safely."

Belina approached the table and said "So am I. But I am glad to see you too, Antoni, because my husband asked me to ask you two things."

Antoni put his feet together and waited.

"Firstly, what were the badges that the group of musical pilgrims wore near the chapel on Monday morning?"

"I have already described them to Messire Guillaume, Dame Belina."

"Yes, but I need to know them too in case I meet the same pilgrims and ask them if they saw somebody going in and out of the chapel."

Antoni described the specific badges on the hats of those pilgrims. "And your second question?"

"It is more of a task than a question. Please go to the Prelet stables and discover who went in and out of them during the last few days, at least since Charles Prelet arrived from Toulouse. After that, please could you ask the same questions in the Lussan stables."

"Of course I will do that for you, Dame Belina." Antoni smiled. "What I can tell you already is that the people in the Lussan stables have seldom even seen Dame Viola, and they don't like her parents. Charles Prelet is using his father's best horse too much and the horse and his groom don't like him doing that. His sister, Dame Pauline – I forget her married name – is not liked at all by her husband's stables staff."

"Why not? Does she hurt the horses?"

"Perchance. She is always in a temper and she tries to take her sons riding, which stops the grooms doing their normal work."

Belina did not suggest that taking time to help children ride a horse might stop the grooms from drinking in the Cheval Blanc. Instead, she said, "Does her husband annoy them too?"

"He works them too hard, with too many journeys to Bordeaux and back. And he is too tight with his money, although he has plenty of it."

"What about the Courial stables?" Belina asked.

"Very different. Everybody has worked there for years. They have great respect for Consul and Dame Courial. Tomas would love to move there from the Senclar stables, but nobody ever leaves the Courial stables."

"Could you ask Tomas the same questions about who went in and out during the last few days and let me know what he says."

Antoni told her how boastful Miqueu had become after he had helped in the arrest of Barvaux's groom and left the courtyard.

Sir John moved his left hand up and down. Then he pointed at his table with a glass and a jar on it. That gesture meant that he was offering some *hypocras* to Belina. Sir John's manservant appeared, picked up the jar of *hypocras* and looked at her.

"Yes please, Alain, but just a little."

Alain poured out some of the sweetened spiced wine into a second glass and gave it to her. "You need sustenance, Dame Belina. Nothing like *hypocras* for restoring strength."

"True, but I have already drunk *hypocras* today."

"Really. Not in some tavern, I hope."

"Indeed not, Alain. I was in Consul Courial's mansion, drinking with Dame Courial." Belina paused. "She was nice and friendly until right at the end when she suddenly dismissed me."

"Perchance she wanted to go to the latrine. Old ladies are like that sometimes."

"No. It was because her husband came into the room."

"Ah. The great man himself."

Sir John waved his left arm to show that he too would like to drink some *hypocras*. Alain filled his glass and gave it to him. Then he fetched a stool for Belina and left them.

Belina sat down and sipped her *hypocras* while she told Sir John how she had spent the last two days. Since Sir John could no longer speak or write, he could not betray her through indiscreet talk. She told him that everybody had liked Viola, nobody had liked her mother, that several people thought that her father had become poor. She had not discovered whether Viola had known Charles Prelet and that they wanted to marry each other. Consul Gaudé's wife was adamant that they were in love – childhood sweethearts in fact. Nobody seemed to know much about Charles Prelet except that he lived in Toulouse and was a lawyer there. Belina did not mention that he had a mistress, according to Dame Courial, or that Dame Volpato might have said the same thing if her husband not suddenly ended the conversation.

Sir John put his *hypocras* glass on the table and drew two question marks in the air with his left hand.

"You mean that there are two theories about Charles Prelet and Viola. One that she was madly in love and the other than they hardly knew each other and that it was an arranged match?"

Sir John pointed his finger at the sky. That meant 'Yes'.

"But which is more likely?" Belina asked him.

He shrugged his left shoulder.

Belina talked about Notaire Corloni and how she distrusted him. She mentioned that the mansion next to the Prelet mansion belonged to the *notaire's* sister and that the Corloni family stayed in it so she would need to visit it sometime. Sir John pointed his finger at the sky.

"To question the servants?" Belina asked.

His finger moved upwards quickly.

"And tomorrow I need to visit the Senclar mansion and question everybody there," Belina told him. Sir John smiled. "Even though they will not help me."

Sir John made a question mark in the air.

"The two Senclar dames despise me," Belina said.

Sir John shook his head and reached for his glass.

Belina finished her *hypocras* and stood up. "Thank you so much, Sir John. Talking to you has really helped me." She went up the stairs to Guillaume's chamber.

She wrote her thoughts down on two of her wax tablets. It was difficult to know whether Dame Gaudé, the furrier's wife, knew more than the others about Viola being deeply in love with Charles Prelet. None of the other ladies had said such a thing, and the last two had known about a girl in Toulouse. Dame Gaudé did not like the *notaire's* daughter, but none of the others had paid any attention to her. So Dame Gaudé might have imagined the faults of the *notaire's* daughter. Perchance she thought that she had seduced one of Dame Gaudé's sons.

Belina decided to take Sir John's advice to visit Widow Créon's mansion in rue Royale, but not yet. The Senclar mansion visit took precedence, and in the morning she would be meeting Jordi and Christau in the lawcourt because Loupmont had accused Jordi of cheating. Then she would call in at the Senclar mansion.

Belina had a much better evening and night than the day before, and she woke refreshed and ready to go to the lawcourt.

CHAPTER TWENTY

Saturday

Belina rose early, washed her face and hands and had the last piece of bread for breakfast. She hoped Jordi would give her one of his good loaves later. She put on her best head-cloth, stroked the cat, left the residence through the courtyard door and walked to the lawcourt in rue de la Monnaie.

Jordi was waiting for her. She kissed his cheek and decided not to tell him that Guillaume was not in Condom. Instead, she asked him about the case that Loupmont had brought against him.

"Does it involve me too, Jordi?" she asked.

"Yes, but only because you are a tenant of the mill too. Loupmont maintains that I cheat the Bishop on the weight of flour declared to be ground from his wheat."

"*His* wheat? His personal wheat or that given to him as part of the tithe?

"Both." He cursed Loupmont, using several words which were new to Belina.

"Have you cheated him, Jordi?" Belina asked him.

"No, of course I haven't. I'm not stupid."

"Then we have nothing to fear," Belina said as they entered the lawcourt together and sat near the front waiting for the judge to arrive.

They kept up a harmless conversation about Catalina and the children, plus the new baby that was expected in a few months' time. They never mentioned their young brother Geraud or the Moorish girl. They assumed that the people in the lawcourt were keen to hear chatter about the accused miller. Prudence in such a place was essential.

The judge was announced and everybody stood up. He was a member of the Seneschal's staff, and Belina knew him slightly. He was a reasonable man, to the best of her knowledge.

"Please be seated. I call Loupmont, now resident in Condom but formerly of St Mihiel."

Loupmont puffed himself up and walked up to the plaintiff's place in an overconfident swagger. He swore an oath on the bible that he was telling the truth, the whole truth, and nothing but the truth.

"Declare your case," said the judge.

Loupmont launched into an account of how Moulié cheated all his customers over flour weight, and how the Bishop was being defrauded by this dishonesty.

"Do you have proof of this?" the judge asked.

Loupmont produced a sheaf of papers which he said were people who denounced Moulié.

The judge looked through them and pointed out that there was nothing from the Bishop himself.

"As my Lord Judge surely knows," said Loupmont, "the Lord Bishop is not in Condom. He is in Tours at the Court of the new King."

"I will wait until he returns to Condom and discuss your complaint with him then," said the judge. "Case postponed."

Jordi pressed Belina's hand and they smiled at each other. But their relief did not last long.

Loupmont stayed in his plaintiff place and told the judge that he had a second case against Moulié.

"Also about weights and measures?" the judge asked.

"No, even more serious," Loupmont replied. "I call attention to the suffering caused to the Widow Moulié of Montreal by Moulié Jordi and Lansac Belina, her stepchildren."

"What have they done?" the judge asked.

"Defrauded her of her rightful inheritance from her late husband, their father."

"This is a new case," said the judge, "and must wait until the next hearing. No documents have been submitted."

"They are being assembled," said Loupmont. "What is important is that you and the court should learn that the dishonesty of Moulié is not only by cheating by a miller but also by the cheating of a widow."

Jordi leapt to his feet and shouted, "He's lying."

"Sit down, Moulié," the judge said. "I am not here to judge this new case but since Loupmont has brought up this new accusation against you I will hear his declaration."

"Loupmont is nothing to do with my stepmother," said Jordi, "at least as far as I know. His position as newcomer to the cathedral staff only gives him a small link regarding the Bishop's tithe. It gives him no right at all to talk about my inheritance."

"The Moulié mill belongs to the Bishop," Loupmont said. "Therefore, I have every right to declare that the Bishop is being defrauded by Moulié." He told the judge how Widow Moulié had married the Widower Moulié when she was Dame Corloni and had every right to expect an inheritance.

"She got much more than she was entitled to," Jordi shouted.

"Sit down, Moulié. I am listening to the plaintiff," said the judge.

Loupmont explained that Notaire Corloni of Montreal had examined the real testament made by the father of the two in this courtroom, and that the bulk had 'very naturally' been left to Dame Moulié, his beloved widow. Notaire Corloni had always suspected the stepchildren of having altered the testament so that they could continue to profit from the mill.

Belina stood up and said that was a lie.

"Dame Lansac, sit down at once," the judge ordered. "Do not interrupt Messire Loupmont's declaration."

Belina remained on her feet, scowling.

"I repeat, Dame Lansac, sit down," said the judge. "I do not like declarations to be interrupted."

"It is not a declaration," Belina said, "It is a collection of lies."

"I repeat for the third time, Dame Lansac. Sit down."

Loupmont smirked and continued with a long list of complaints that had been told to him by Notaire Corloni about the great suffering and sorrow felt by Widow Moulié. Belina and Jordi tried to contain their anger at this totally unexpected accusation coming on top of the one about the miller's measures of flour.

Belina stopped listening to Loupmont. Instead, her mind returned to her childhood and the death of her mother in childbed. The arrival of the young stepmother had been a bitter blow. None of them had supported it and life had become a battle of wills. As soon as their father had died the stepmother had returned to her family home in Montreal and then bought herself a fine large mansion, filling it with a couple of expensive greyhounds and many of the contents of the Moulié mill. The three orphans had coped as best as they could, with Jordi remaining in the mill and marrying Catalina, Belina working for Messire Benasse and then marrying Guillaume, and Geraud becoming a soldier and going to southern Spain. In Belina's view, the three of them were the victims, not their stepmother.

Belina's thoughts returned to the present with the sound of the Clerk of the Court telling everybody to rise. Belina had missed the judge's decision.

"Let's get out of here," Jordi whispered to Belina. He took her arm and steered her out into the street and made sure nobody could hear their conversation. "I am sure that our stepmother has put Notaire Corloni up to this. After all, we know they are cousins. Blood is thicker than water."

"Yes," said Belina, and her thoughts turned at once to the sight of the bloody chasuble and the puddle of blood in the Sainte Eulalie chapel. She missed Jordi's reply and looked at the position of the sun. Time was getting on and she needed to visit the Senclar mansion and question people there, even though she dreaded meeting them.

"Jordi," she said, "I have to go to the Senclar mansion because Guillaume has asked me to question the wives of all the consuls about the betrothal banquet last Monday when Viola was killed."

But Jordi was much more interested in solving his own problems. "How long will that take you? I need to talk to you about Loupmont's accusations."

"Of course you do," she replied, touching his arm, "I imagine I will be less than an hour." She thought for a moment. "Let's meet again outside the Senclar stables and walk from there along the path to the mill. Is that all right with you?"

"It will have to be. Don't be late, Belina. I'm in no mood to be kept waiting." He kissed her cheek and walked towards the Place St Pierre while she went down to rue Sainte Luce and the Senclar mansion.

CHAPTER TWENTY-ONE

When Belina and Jordi were in the lawcourt, Guillaume's groom Antoni and his brother Tomas were at the Condom forge near the Saint Esprit Gate. Tomas was very envious of his brother, because with Guillaume away somewhere and for an unknown length of time, Antoni had nothing much to do except chatter and drink in the Cheval Blanc. Tomas, on the other hand, was overworked as usual, as were all the Senclar servants. Antoni had never told him that he helped Guillaume with his investigations by listening to people gossiping in the Cheval Blanc and other inns and taverns.

They were waiting their turn to have one of Dame Edith's carriage horses re-shod, and Antoni could not understand why the horse had travelled so much recently.

"The old dame doesn't often go out," Tomas replied, "but her tooth-drawer uses the carriage every day."

"Whatever for?"

"It varies. Sometimes it is for going to Lectoure or to one of her other properties – she owns dozens – but mostly he just prowls around Condom spying on people," Tomas said.

"For himself, or for Dame Edith?"

"Don't know really. I never drive the carriage, so I only get to hear about what people say."

"Which is what?"

"Chezelle will order the carriage without saying how many

hours he will need it for. It's only after they have left the rue Sainte Luce that he deigns to let the driver know. It's very unfair."

"Who has he been spying on recently?"

"A crestian."

"A crestian? Whatever for?" Antoni looked at the sun and estimated how long they have been waiting at the forge already.

"It's been going on for several weeks."

"What has?"

"Spying on the crestian, like I've told you," Tomas replied, "and last night we discovered more about the crestian."

"Such as?" Antoni asked.

"He's been put in prison."

"Because Chezelle caught him stealing?" Antoni asked.

"No, worse than that," said Tomas. "He caught him cutting someone's throat."

"You mean the girl in the Sainte Eulalie chapel?" Antoni asked.

"Yes, the girl you told me about, the one who had had her throat cut. You had to fetch Messire Guillaume to see her – and disturb your drinking in the Cheval Blanc."

"I wondered why Chezelle was there," Antoni said, still looking at the position of the sun and thinking about an early drink in the Cheval Blanc, after which he would walk to the Prelet stables and talk to the grooms and lads there as Belina had asked him to do.

"Did Messire Guillaume ask him?"

"Don't remember."

"But it was an odd place for the girl to be found," said Tomas, "and that is why we all got talking about it in the stables."

"Maybe Chezelle killed her," Antoni suggested.

"That's what we are wondering," Tomas admitted.

"Why would Dame Edith order a consul's daughter to be killed?"

"Envy of her youth and innocence. At least that's what the oldest groom says."

"Of course, it could have been the younger Dame Senclar," Antoni suggested.

"It's certainly well within her ability."

"Or Consul Senclar himself, perchance? For repelling him."

"Probably not," Tomas replied. "The Consul has lots of girls, but they're mostly head-cloth makers or their sisters. I don't think he would be interested in a young lady."

They turned their attention to another *coursier*, which was having shoes fitted. Two grooms were talking to the blacksmith while his assistant stood by with the pincers. The blacksmith manoeuvred the horse into a better position which meant that the two grooms turned round. Antoni and Tomas realised that one of them was a Prelet groom. "*Adischatz*, what are you two doing here?" The groom asked them.

"Waiting our turn to have our horse re-shod, Halip," Tomas said. "I hope you'll not be long."

"I don't mind how long we'll be here," Halip replied, "I'm hearing all about Toulouse and the girls there." He introduced the new groom to them, and said that Jean had arrived last Friday from Toulouse.

"Why are you in Condom?" Antoni asked him.

"Because I am the groom of the steward of the sister of the friend of Messire Charles."

"Who's he?"

"Messire Charles Prelet, whose parents live here in Condom."

"You mean, Consul Prelet?" Antoni asked, "The father of the bride."

"Bride-to-be, if I understand it correctly. Although she has just died," said Jean.

"Yes," the three Condom grooms said together.

"She had her throat cut, is that right?" Jean asked.

Halip and Antoni told him what they knew about the betrothal banquet and the murder in the Sainte Eulalie chapel.

"Messire Charles won't be sorry," Jean said at the end of their story.

"She was a pretty girl," said Antoni.

"Messire Charles already has a pretty girl – a very pretty girl."

"How do you know?" Tomas asked.

"Because her sister is the wife of my master in Toulouse."

"So why would Messire Charles agree to marry somebody else?" Halip asked.

"That's what my steward and my master do not understand. They suspect some bad reason."

"Let's get this straight," said Antoni. "Is Messire Charles Prelet married to the very pretty girl in Toulouse or not?"

"Not yet, but they live as if they are married to each other." He paused and smiled. "And they already have two children."

"Does Consul Prelet know that?" Tomas asked Halip.

"I very much doubt it," he replied. "At least, I've never heard any rumour about such a thing." He paused. "Of course, Messire Charles has been living in Toulouse for several years now, so we don't know much about him here in the stables."

"In Toulouse he rides every day, even though he is busy working as a lawyer," said Jean.

"He has been riding here too," Halip said, and described the way in which Charles Prelet had not given them much notice when ordering them to saddle his father's best horse. He had even gone riding on the morning of the betrothal banquet, which they had not expected.

"Perchance he was meeting the bride?" Tomas suggested.

"Not likely," replied Halip. "He was in the same dusty clothes he had worn the day before when he went riding, the same clothes he arrived in from Toulouse."

"You mean," Antoni asked, "that he rode from Toulouse, and didn't come in a carriage?"

"Not he. Don't blame him of course," said Halip.

"I don't either," said Antoni, "but Toulouse is several days' ride from here."

"I have done it in five days, although I rested in Sempuy for two days," Jean said.

"Why did you do that?" Tomas asked him.

"Orders received and not questioned."

"Perchance the sister paid your expenses," Antoni suggested, "the girl who is jealous of Dame Viola Lussan."

"Who's that?"

"The girl who was murdered."

The blacksmith interrupted their conversation and asked them to pay him. Tomas led Dame Edith's carriage horse towards the forge while Antoni told him he would go with Halip and Jean to the Cheval Blanc where they could all quench their thirst.

"Meet me there later if you want to," he told Tomas.

"If I want to," Tomas replied. "You mean to say, if I have time to get away from the Senclar stables and go drinking with you."

"Suit yourself," said his brother. He accompanied Halip and Jean to the Prelet stables, where they left the re-shod *coursiers* and walked down to the Cheval Blanc.

There weren't many people in the inn, and they settled themselves comfortably in a corner. Antoni called for three beakers of cider, and they drank to each other's health.

"You need to rest for several more days," Antoni told Jean. "What do you plan to do, and does Consul Prelet know that you are here in Condom?"

"No, he doesn't," said Halip. "We are keeping it quiet."

"Why?" Antoni asked.

"Least said, soonest mended."

"So who do they think you are?" Antoni asked, trying to pretend he was Guillaume investigating a crime.

"A cousin of mine," said Halip.

"What does your steward want you to find out?" Antoni asked.

"Why Messire Charles decided to return to Condom and to marry the girl."

"And what have you discovered?" Antoni tried to sound less interested in the answer than he really was.

"That Messire Prelet is feeling old and ill and wants his son to become a consul here, preferably Senior Consul, as his father is now."

"There are others here already, who would be more acceptable than a young lawyer from Toulouse," Halip said.

"I expect so, "said Jean, "but what I have discovered so far by listening to the stables chatter is that a powerful lady called Dame Edith is willing to use all sorts of tricks to get her son made Senior Consul."

"He'd be no good in that position," said Antoni.

Halip agreed, and launched into a description of Consul Senclar.

"If I understand it correctly," said Jean, "Consul Senclar's mother would gain a lot more power and money if her son was Senior Consul."

"True," said Halip and Antoni together.

"And she has a reputation for greediness as well as hard-hearted treatment of her tenants."

"That's true too," said Halip.

"And poisoning victims," Antoni added.

"Really?" Jean opened his eyes wide. "Are you sure?"

They gave him several well-known examples of Dame Edith having had people poisoned.

Antoni called for more cider and they continued their tales of Consul Senclar's pleasureful style of life which made it easier for his wicked mother to get him to do as she wanted.

"You mean she orders him around?" Jean asked.

"She's too crafty for that," said Antoni.

Jean drank his cider and frowned.

"Don't you like this cider?" Antoni asked him.

"It's fine," Jean replied.

"So why are you frowning?" Antoni asked, still pretending to himself that he was Guillaume questioning a suspect.

"I'm thinking about what you are saying about this old Dame Edith," Jean began.

"She's not that old," Halip interrupted him. "She married when she thirteen and had her son nine months later. She's not old like Messire Charles's mother is."

"So," said Jean, "she's a woman still full of ambition for herself rather than for her children. What do you think, Halip?"

"You're right," Halip agreed. "What else have you guessed about her, I wonder."

Jean drank some more of his cider. "Well, if Messire Charles returns to Condom and marries the daughter of another consul." He paused, and asked if the dead girl's father was a consul too. Halip nodded. "A vigorous, skilful lawyer like Messire Charles would push the idle young Consul Senclar out of his way," said Jean. "Messire Charles is pleasant enough if you don't annoy him, but he does not let anybody or anything stop him from doing what he wants."

"So, how was Consul Prelet able to persuade him to get married to a girl in Condom, forcing him to give up his girl in Toulouse and their two children?" Halip asked.

"As I've already told you, that's what we in Toulouse do not understand," Jean replied. "And that is why I have been sent here."

"Are you suggesting that Messire Charles is ruthless enough to have murdered the girl who his father had arranged to marry him?" Antoni asked.

Jean thought for a moment. "I wouldn't completely put it past him. But being a lawyer, he would have worked out that it would be safer to get somebody else to do the actual killing."

"A crestian, for example," said Antoni, thinking of his earlier conversation with his brother.

"Are there crestias here?" Jean asked him.

"Indeed there are, and the man who was found beside Dame Viola's body was a crestian," Antoni told him.

Jean whistled. "Why would a crestian kill the daughter of a consul?" he asked.

"Perchance if Messire Charles had paid him to do so," Antoni replied more boldly than he should have done.

Jean frowned. "Don't take my comments about Messire Charles's motives as seriously as that."

"I don't," Antoni replied immediately. "Of course I don't."

Halip asked Antoni if a crestian really had been found next to the body, and was told very firmly that Antoni himself had been there with Messire Guillaume and that the Sainte Eulalie chapel was very near the leper colony where the crestias lived. He decided not to mention Chezelle's presence.

"Who is Messire Guillaume?" Jean asked.

"I am his groom," said Antoni, "and he is the Bishop's Inquirer."

"You mean to say that he is investigating the crime?" Jean asked.

"He's already solved it," Antoni replied in his smoothest way. "He's put the crestian in prison."

"Aahh," said Jean, "thank goodness for that." He stood up, thanked Antoni for the cider and walked out of the inn.

Halip and Antoni looked at each other, surprised that Jean had left so suddenly.

"Halip," said Antoni, "I think that we should keep this conversation to ourselves."

"You're right. I don't want Jean to do us harm because he regrets talking to us. Promise me you will not tell Messire Lansac about what you've learned just now."

"I promise you," Antoni said. It was an easy promise to make because Guillaume was far from Condom, but he did not tell Halip that.

CHAPTER TWENTY-TWO

Belina walked from the lawcourt to rue Sainte Luce and approached the front door of the Senclar mansion. Her throat pricked and she clutched the skirt of her gown.

"*Adischatz*," she greeted the doorkeeper.

He looked down at her and frowned. What do you want, *molieròta?*"

"The Lord Seneschal has ordered me to visit all the consuls of Condom and question them concerning the betrothal banquet last Monday." Belina did not produce the Seneschal's written authority in case the doorkeeper snatched it from her or even tore it up.

"There was no betrothal," he replied. "Don't you know that?"

"Yes. That is why I am questioning the consuls and their wives."

"And you think a consul would kill the daughter of another consul?" he sneered.

"The Lord Seneschal needs to know who was present at the banquet and what their behaviour was on hearing the news that the daughter of Consul Lussan was dead."

The doorkeeper laughed. "They probably hid their feelings and ate the banquet."

"It is unlikely that Consul Lussan and his wife could have hidden their feelings," Belina said.

"Consuls don't have feelings, *molieròta*."

"On the contrary," Belina replied. "I questioned all of them yesterday, and their wives. I assure you that they all had feelings of sorrow."

"Why didn't you question Consul Senclar then?"

"I had no time left. All the others live close together," Belina replied. It was not strictly true, but it was the best excuse she could think of.

The doorkeeper let her into the hall and shouted for a servant. Belina looked round the room, decorated to impress rather than to welcome.

"Dame Lansac?" a servant greeted her.

"*Adischatz*," Belina replied and said that the Seneschal had sent her to question Consul Senclar and his family.

"I don't think they will consent to be questioned by a woman. Why isn't your husband here instead of you?"

"Because he is discussing the death of Consul Lussan's daughter with the Archdeacon," Belina replied. She did not show the Seneschal's written authority.

"I will tell them you are here. It is for them to decide whether they need to see you."

"Thank you." Belina followed him down the hall and into a large room before he could stop her.

Consul Senclar was seated at a long table, and his hand was playing with his wife's breasts. His mother was seated at the same table but with her head bent over a document. Belina walked up to the table and pulled the Seneschal's written authority out of her purse. She made her usual speech and gave the document to Dame Edith.

"Give that to me," Consul Senclar ordered, but his mother took no notice. Instead, she read through the document very carefully.

"Why is there no mention of Messire Chezelle in this document?" she asked Belina.

"The Seneschal gives priority to the most important witnesses."

"Messire Chezelle is the most important witness," Dame Edith rebuked her. "He found the dead body and the murderer."

"Perchance *he* was the murderer," her son interrupted, exposing his wife's left breast.

"Don't be so stupid, Henri, and stop pulling at your wife's gown like that."

"I am not interested in the gown, only in what is covered by it. Or rather, was covered by it."

Dame Jeanne leaned forward so that her right breast was exposed too.

"Messire Chezelle is not at home at present," Dame Edith told Belina. "Tell your husband to meet him here this afternoon."

Belina's face assumed its best blank expression. She proceeded to ask her usual questions about the betrothal banquet, who the other guests were, what their reactions had been when they heard of Dame Viola's death, and when they left the Prelet mansion.

"Do I understand correctly that you have spoken to all the consuls and their wives?" Dame Edith asked.

"All except Consul Prelet or Consul Lussan and their wives," Belina replied. "I think it is too early to disturb their grieving."

"What makes you think that any of them are grieving?" Consul Senclar asked.

"The Lussans have lost their daughter and the Prelets have lost the young lady they had expected to become their daughter-in-law," Belina replied.

"Personally, I think that Chezelle and Lussan arranged for the girl's death."

"Henri," Dame Edith hissed, "Don't say such things!"

"I wouldn't put it past Chezelle to kill a girl if somebody paid him to do so."

"Henri, control your tongue," Dame Edith said, still looking at the Seneschal's document instead of at the pair in front of her.

Consul Senclar seized both his wife's breasts. "Don't try to control me. You only make me angrier."

"True."

Belina asked Dame Edith if she had noticed the behaviour of Consul Prelet and his wife when they heard that Viola Lussan was dead.

"I did not look at them."

"Had Messire Chezelle been invited to the banquet?" Belina asked.

Consul Senclar snorted. "Nobody would invite him anywhere. He might start examining their teeth."

"Like they were a horse," said Belina.

"Don't be vulgar, *molieròta*," Dame Edith rebuked her.

Belina felt that she was not the vulgar woman in the room. That was Dame Jeanne, whose breasts were still outside her gown.

"Why was Messire Chezelle in the Sainte Eulalie chapel last Monday?" Belina asked Dame Edith.

"I do not know."

"Does he often go to that part of Condom?" Belina persisted.

"I do not know."

"Why were two members of the Watch with him?"

"I have told you twice already, *molieròta*. I do not know how Messire Chezelle spends his time."

"Yes, you do know. I have often told you. He spends it in the *étuves*," said Consul Senclar. "But he never gets the best girls, even though he asks for them."

"Henri, I do not wish to know such things. Please control your tongue."

Consul Senclar kissed his wife fervently. "As you can see," he told his mother, "I don't control my tongue." He got up and rushed from the room.

Belina wondered if the scene she had just witnessed happened often. On the other hand, some of the consul's wild comments about the murder might be true. She wondered what to do next. Wait and see if he came back, or take her leave?

The consul returned, holding hands with a young woman. She looked a little familiar to Belina. Tall and very thin, with a rather ugly face with two warts, piercing eyes and a strong chin. She wore a very elegant head-cloth and pale-green gown.

"Here's another visitor," said the consul.

"Ana, how lovely to see you!" Dame Jeanne got up, rushed towards the visitor, and kissed her on both cheeks. "Have you come to spend the night here?"

"No."

"But please do. We have so much to discuss."

"I don't think so."

"Of course we have," Dame Jeanne gushed. "I want to tell you all about the baby I am carrying." She patted her stomach.

"Keep that sort of conversation for women who have babies."

Dame Jeanne looked at Belina. "That certainly excludes the *molieròta* here," she said.

"*Molieròta?*" Ana Corloni asked. "The woman with no babies."

"Yes, she's been asking us about that awful betrothal banquet and what the Prelets said when they heard Viola Lussan had been found dead. But, Ana, you were there when they learned about the death of Viola Lussan."

"I don't remember much about it, other than the excellent food."

"My husband has told me that you were present," Belina said, "and that you were talking to the son of Consul Prelet."

"No I was not."

"My husband is not a liar, Ana. He has told me that he saw you talking to the son of Consul Prelet."

"Don't address me as Ana, *molieròta*."

"We were at school together, Ana," Belina replied. "Viola, you and me."

"I don't remember either of you."

"I am more interested in what you remember from the betrothal banquet last Monday," Belina insisted.

"Too bad." Ana shook her head and her elegant head-cloth shifted dangerously. "Farewell, Dame Edith, farewell Jeanne." She strode out of the room.

"Notaire Corloni's daughter needs to get married and learn to control her temper" Dame Edith said.

"Ana thinks that she isn't married yet because she doesn't have my sort of bosom," said Dame Jeanne.

"Rubbish, you silly girl. Marriage is about money, not the size of a girl's breasts." She gave the Seneschal's written authority back to Belina.

"Your marriage, perchance, but not mine," said Dame Jeanne.

Belina looked at Dame Edith. Like Ana Corloni, she was very thin. Belina remembered that Guillaume had discovered from the Archdeacon that the elder Consul Senclar had been thin. She supposed that he had been keen on money because it was well known that Dame Edith's parents in Lectoure had been very rich. Perchance he had been like his son, and Chezelle too apparently, and had got his sexual pleasures at the *étuves*.

Belina decided that she was not going to learn anything more of use to her investigation. She thanked Dame Edith for her help, and walked from the room.

There was a different doorkeeper on duty, fortunately for Belina, so she was able to leave the mansion without hindrance, walk down to the Senclar stables and meet up with Jordi and Christau.

Belina had almost reached the stables when she felt a hand tap her shoulder. She spun round, hoping that it was not Chezelle or a watchman come to take her back to the Senclar mansion. To her great relief it was Aralha, one of the Senclar kitchen-maids. Belina owed Aralha her thanks for helping when she was investigating who had poisoned the pilgrim two weeks ago.

"*Adischatz*, Aralha, you look very out of breath"

"*Adishatz*, Dame Lansac. I have been running fast to catch you up. I have important news for you."

"How lovely, Aralha. What is it?"

"It's a secret. That's why it is safest to tell you here in this lane." She looked to see if anybody was nearby.

"Do tell me your secret, Aralha. Nobody can hear us here."

"You mustn't tell anybody, or I'll get into trouble."

Belina assured her she would tell nobody.

"Not even Messire Lansac?"

"No, not even my husband."

Aralha launched into a very detailed account of how the *abbesse* who was the Keeper of the *étuves* had an expensive private room that rich customers could reserve for several hours of dining, drinking and bathing. It was a fantastic room with a wooden bath filled with warm water where she and a man would share a delicious meal with lots to drink. When they had finished they lay on an enormous bed, very comfortable with a silk pillow. The hourly wage which the *abbesse* paid Aralha for working in the private room was much higher than the usual one which she paid to girls in the *étuves*, although it could be dull being played with for hours by some rich old man who had drunk too much.

"Does your betrothed, Ramon, mind you doing this sort of work?" Belina asked.

"Not at all, because I get paid so well. That way, we can set ourselves up with an inn of our own."

Aralha continued her story by saying that yesterday afternoon she had gone to the private room at the *abbesse's* request and found herself with Dame Senclar's tooth-drawer. She had never liked him because he was always pulling at the skirts of Dame Senclar's maids.

Aralha described her passionate afternoon while Belina

waited for whatever information might of interest to her. She hoped Jordi and Christau were not getting too impatient at her late arrival. Chezelle was on her list of suspects for Viola's murder. Why had he been at the chapel last Monday? She wished Guillaume was in Condom instead of miles away looking for Barvaux. Guillaume could interrogate Chezelle whereas she, the despised *molieròta*, could not presume to question him.

She had missed some of Aralha's description of her 'work', but learnt that Chezelle had drunk much more than was good for him, Aralha had pulled him out of the bath tub when the water had become cold and had moved him on to the bed, where she had tried to get him excited.

"He kept on and on about Dame Edith having ordered him to go early morning last Monday to the Sainte Eulalie chapel and to take two watchmen with him. He never rises early and he overslept. Also, it took time to get two watchmen to go past the leper colony, and he had to pay them before they agreed to accompany him. And then when they did get there they found the poor girl dead with her throat cut and blood absolutely everywhere."

Aralha paused. Belina gulped at the memory of the chapel and the pool of congealed blood. She felt for her pouch-cloth and missed the next few sentences of Aralha's story.

"The tooth-drawer was really angry that Dame Senclar had told him off for not arriving there earlier. He didn't understand why it made a difference. After all, he had got the killer pinned down by the watchmen and he had sent for Messire Lansac, your husband, to arrest him and put him in prison. He couldn't understand why she was so unappreciative. And he had to demand that Dame Senclar paid him for his services."

"Dame Senclar doesn't like paying out money," Belina commented. "Perchance she thought it was extortion."

"At any rate, the tooth-drawer went on and on and on about her lack of appreciation. It was very dull."

"It sounds like you earned your money, though," said Belina.

"Yes." Aralha smiled and rubbed her thumb against her forefinger. "Lots and lots of lovely coins. Ramon was ever so pleased when I told him."

Belina said nothing.

"You won't tell anybody, will you Dame Lansac?"

"No one at all. Very many thanks, Aralha for your really useful information."

Aralha turned back towards the kitchen entrance of the Senclar mansion while Belina ran as fast as possible down to the stables, where both Jordi and Christau greeted her angrily, as she had feared.

CHAPTER TWENTY-THREE

Belina, Jordi and Christau walked to the mill, trying to avoid the worst of the mud on the path. The river was brown and flowing fast, bringing branches down with it. Christau kept looking at the water instead of joining in with his cousins' conversation.

Jordi was furious at the introduction of a second lawsuit. Their 'wicked stepmother', as they always called her – even to her face – had messed up their lives yet again, and Loupmont had taken advantage of it. Millers were always being accused of cheating on weights of flour and wheat, and Jordi could cope with that accusation. It was the fight for justice for their inheritance that would be really difficult. Notaire Corloni knew far more than they did about inheritance laws. Who could they ask for help?

Belina finally got a word in and suggested that she follow up her visits to consuls yesterday with a gentle request for advice on what she and Jordi should do, and could do.

"That won't work," said Jordi. "The consuls will stick together."

"What about Charles Prelet?" Belina said. "He might have a motivation to keep on the right side of me, and therefore of Guillaume."

"I doubt it. Anyway, what danger is he in? He won't have murdered his betrothed."

"I'm not so sure," Belina replied.

"You'd better keep your views to yourself and Guillaume."

"So Jordi, who do you think would have killed Viola Lussan?"

"Could have been any number of people. It could be Viola's parents because they didn't want to pay her dowry or for an expensive wedding. Consul Lussan has been losing money. His harvests have been bad for at least two years. And then there could be a maid who didn't like Viola. . ."

"That's not likely," Belina interrupted. "Viola was a sweet person."

"Only as far as you know. Anyway, I am much more interested in solving our problems than those of the consuls. Leave the murder mystery to your husband."

They continued trying to avoid the mud and talked about Geraud's wounds. What had caused them? Why wouldn't he talk about his time in Spain? Was Wasila a slave who had been given as booty, or had Geraud rescued her? They supposed that she was a Moor. Was she living unlawfully in France? Would Loupmont and Corloni have them arrested for that? So many problems. Jordi wondered whether Catalina was right to be suspicious of Wasila.

"She is horribly hostile to her, Jordi," Belina pointed out.

"She is not used to foreigners. She is not like you, seeing pilgrims in your shop, hearing different languages. She is at home all the time with her cooking and our children. You must make allowances for that."

"Yes, I suppose so."

They walked through the wood near the mill and emerged into the yard. To their great surprise, they saw a carriage. Jordi asked the driver who he was.

"The driver of Dame Senclar."

"What are you doing here?" Jordi asked him.

"Waiting for Messire Chezelle."

"What's he doing here?" Jordi asked him.

"I do not know. I never ask him why he goes anywhere," the servant of the much-feared landowner and poisoner answered.

Belina wondered if Chezelle had helped Dame Edith Senclar poison people. Then she thought about Aralha's work yesterday afternoon with Chezelle in the *étuves*.

As they turned the corner of the millhouse they found themselves confronted by Chezelle and two members of the Watch. One was brushing flour off his livery but the other shouted at them, "Halt! Stay where you are!"

"We are on my property," said Jordi, "and I will go wherever I please. What are you doing here anyway?"

Chezelle walked very close to him. "We are searching for an army fugitive."

"Then you won't find him here in my mill," said Jordi.

"Why not?"

"Because I have never been in any army. Neither has my wife, nor my children. If you are looking for fugitives, try some of the taverns. The Serpent, for example. And now, I would be obliged if you would leave my mill before I throw you out of it."

Chezelle scowled at him and the watchmen moved closer. Belina said two *Ave Marias*. Chezelle continued to stare at Jordi menacingly and Belina hoped that her brother would not call him 'tooth-drawer', or worse. The session in court had angered him and he was not always good at holding his temper.

One of the watchmen grabbed Christau. "Here's the fugitive."

"I am not a fugitive," Christau shouted and pulled himself clear of the watchman's hand. "You know damn well that I am not. I'm a boatman. Now get off our land before we throw you off it." He readied his fists for a fight.

Chezelle grabbed Christau, shouting that he was a fugitive and not wounded at all.

"Of course I'm not wounded," Christau growled. "Let go

of me or I will punch you in your ugly face and knock your gleaming teeth out."

Chezelle did not let go, so Christau punched him so hard that he fell back on to a flour sack, bursting it.

Jordi swore at Chezelle, putting the sole of his boot on the man's chest and preventing him from getting to his feet. The two watchmen stood by, not helping Chezelle at all.

"Arrest that man!" Chezelle told them.

"Which man, Messire Chezelle?"

"The rascal who has just hit me, of course. Chase him. Arrest him!"

They all looked to see where Christau had retreated to, supposing it might be to the storehouse, and left Chezelle to struggle to his feet by himself.

The younger watchman glanced at the river and pointed at someone who was swimming across it with difficulty because the water was bringing down so many branches. "There he is, Messire, in the river."

"I hope he drowns," said Chezelle. "Go after him."

"You go after him if you want him that badly. We don't want to drown. That river is in a dangerous state."

"Do as I tell you, watchmen."

"You are not our master, Messire Chezelle, and neither is Consul Senclar. We are watchmen of the City of Condom, not your servants."

"Nor anybody's servants," said the other watchman.

"In that case," said Chezelle, trying to get his dignity back in spite of being covered in flour, "we will go to the Senclar mansion and make a formal complaint."

"I shall come with you and make a formal complaint of my own," said Jordi. "You have ruined a sack of flour and you owe me for it."

Chezelle threw four coins on the ground. "Take these, you greedy bastard."

Jordi picked up the coins and put them in his purse. "Now get off my land."

"I agree, but I will take your sister with me."

"You will not," said Belina.

"Why?" Jordi asked Chezelle.

"Because I need to question her about the fugitive," Chezelle said smoothly.

"She'll not tell you anything about any fugitive," Jordi declared.

"I am not going with them," Belina said.

"Yes you are, sister," came Jordi's quick reply.

Belina looked at him, very surprised. He made a movement with his left hand which meant that he had his secret reasons and that she should obey him. It was a signal they had developed when their new stepmother had arrived at the mill and her presence had upset them.

Belina continued to stare at her brother and he wrote the letter W in the air. Of course, she realised, Chezelle might find Wasila at the mill. That would bring a load of trouble down on Jordi. She walked towards the carriage, regretting that she had not had the opportunity to be given one of Jordi's good wheat loaves, or to stay to eat the meal Catalina was no doubt preparing.

Belina sat in the Senclar carriage beside Chezelle, wondering how she would cope with being questioned about a fugitive in the mill. How would she avoid telling them that her brother Geraud was in Messire Benasse's house? How could she keep the existence of Wasila secret?

Chezelle got down from the carriage when they reached rue Sainte Luce and strode into the Senclar mansion. A servant helped Belina down, clutching her in an over-friendly fashion. His grip on her chest was annoying and Belina hoped he would not call her '*molieròta*'.

The two watchmen told the doorkeeper why they were there and that Messire Chezelle wished Dame Lansac to be interrogated inside the Senclar mansion. All three were taken to a large room with tapestries hanging on all the walls, where a man was seated at a long table near the big window.

Belina looked around her for a stool or a bench but there was nothing. She supposed that all the seats had been removed in order to make the interrogation more stressful.

"*Bonjour,*" the man said in a bored voice.

"*Adischatz,*" Belina replied, hoping to make things difficult for him. He would have prepared his questions and comments in French. She would reply in Gascon and enjoy his discomfiture.

"Your name please," the man continued in French.

Belina did not reply. Instead, she looked at the floor and the herbs strewn on it.

"Answer my question."

Belina stared at him in silence.

The man knocked his fist on the table and the ink-horn tipped over. It had been filled to the brim and most of its ink spilled on to the table, dragging the quill pen with it.

Belina tried hard not to smile, but she noticed that the younger watchman was grinning, so she grinned back at him.

The other watchman went to find a servant to clear up the mess and returned with a maid and a stool for Belina. She smiled at him and said "*mercés.*"

"Bring your stool nearer here," the man ordered. He was still talking in French, so Belina sat on the stool and stayed where she was.

A door opened to her left and a greyhound came in, sniffed Belina's muddy shoes and sat down beside her. It was followed by Chezelle. He had changed his clothes and shoes, but his temper remained as foul as ever.

"Get up when I come into the room," he said to Belina in French.

She pretended not to understand and stroked the greyhound gently.

Chezelle walked to her part of the room and repeated his order. The greyhound stood up and growled at him. Belina could not help smiling, and she was pleased to see that the watchmen were smiling too.

A servant came in bringing two elegant stools with him which he placed on either side of the man at the table, taking care to avoid the maid in her efforts to remove the ink.

Dame Senclar walked in, frowned at the ink and sat on the other side of the man.

Belina wondered who else would come in, or whether the stool was for Chezelle. To her surprise, she discovered that the stool was for Notaire Corloni, who made a grand entrance.

"Come to this table and face me," Dame Edith ordered Belina in French.

Belina hesitated for a minute and then she got to her feet, picked up the stool and approached the table, followed by the greyhound.

She sat down facing Dame Edith and stared at her. Then she adopted the tactic which the crestian had used with her yesterday evening: she looked straight through Dame Edith and at the tapestry on the wall behind her. She stroked the greyhound, relying on it to keep Chezelle away from her.

"Lansac Belina," Dame Edith began in her thin voice, "you are here to answer questions from myself and my lawyer." Belina waited and continued to stroke the greyhound. "There is an army fugitive in your mill, and that is against the law."

Dame Edith was talking in French, as she usually did, so Belina did not reply.

The lawyer whispered something to Dame Edith to which she said, "This woman can certainly speak in French, albeit with a Gascon accent. She will speak to us in French."

"Dame Senclar, you cannot require her to do that. In Gascony, witnesses and defendants have the right to speak in Gascon if they choose to do so."

Notaire Corloni turned towards him and said, "no problem, *Maître*, I will speak to her in Gascon and let you know what she says."

"Get her to admit that there is an army fugitive in her mill," Dame Edith ordered.

The *notaire* changed the words into, "*Molieròta*, stop wasting our time and admit that you are hiding an army fugitive in your mill."

Belina stared at him while she worked out what to say. "Tell Dame Senclar and her lawyer that there is no army fugitive in the Moulié mill. The only people living in it are my brother, his wife and their two children. My brother and I do not own the mill, but rent it from the Bishop. Obviously, we would not keep an army fugitive in it – but of course we do not know any army fugitives anyway."

Notaire Corloni interpreted Belina's declaration correctly. Dame Edith said that the Bishop should repossess the mill and let honest millers live there and work it.

While Notaire Corloni was interpreting this comment, which Belina had understood in any case, Belina saw that Loupmont's accusation that morning that Jordi was cheating the Bishop about flour measures could very well be linked with Dame Edith's plan to put her own workers in the mill. Belina knew that extending her landholdings and therefore her rents was Dame Edith's main occupation – apart from poisoning people.

Dame Edith's comment did not require an answer, so Belina waited. Notaire Corloni launched into another attack and questioned Belina, in Gascon, about Christau's movements during the morning of the betrothal banquet.

"My cousin is a boatman. He has nothing to do with banquets in the mansion of Consul Prelet," she said, waiting for whatever might come next.

"My information is that he was seen going into the Sainte Eulalie chapel early that morning."

"It's unlikely. He spends all his time on the river," Belina replied.

"I repeat, he was seen going into the chapel."

"Your information source presumably has bad eyesight," Belina replied.

"He has excellent eyesight, *molieròta*, and he is standing right behind you."

Belina turned round and saw Chezelle smiling.

"In my opinion," said Notaire Corloni, leaning forward on the table, "your cousin Christau Moulié murdered Consul Lussan's daughter." He paused. "And there is no use you denying it."

"It is much more likely that Messire Chezelle killed Dame Viola Lussan," Belina replied.

Chezelle clutched Belina's shoulder and shouted, "How dare you accuse me of such a crime?"

"Why shouldn't I? You are accusing my cousin of a crime," Belina replied.

"Your cousin should be locked up in prison," Chezelle said. The others agreed.

"Messire Corloni," Belina said, "where do you believe that my cousin spent the morning last Monday?"

"Hiding from the Watch and cleaning all the blood from his clothes."

"How long would that take?" Belina asked him.

"All morning, no doubt."

Belina smiled. "My cousin Christau was having dinner with me, my husband, my brother, his wife and their children in the mill last Monday. And I assure you that there was no blood on him."

"I don't believe you," Notaire Corloni replied, "and you haven't said why he has gone into hiding."

"He has not gone into hiding."

"Messire Chezelle declares that he has. He swam across the river, escaping from the watchmen."

"He was not escaping from the watchmen. He was putting a distance between himself and Dame Senclar's tooth-drawer – who was in a rage, and on my brother's property."

Notaire Corloni turned Belina's declaration into French, omitting the mention of 'tooth-drawer'.

Dame Edith instructed the *notaire* to ask questions concerning the army fugitive instead of about Christau and the death of Consul Lussan's daughter.

The *notaire* frowned and leant on the table again. "Going back to the army fugitive, *molieròta*, admit that you have two brothers in the Bishop's mill and one of those is an army fugitive."

"No."

"Dame Edith will make a request to the Seneschal to have his men extract the truth from you." The *notaire's* voice was full of menace.

"There is no need to threaten me with the Seneschal," said Belina in French, more blithely than she felt. "As you already know, the Lord Seneschal has given me written authority to question all the consuls and their wives about what they did, saw and heard during the betrothal banquet last Monday."

The lawyer looked startled and almost upset the ink-horn again. Notaire Corloni moved it to safety.

"*Molieròta*," said Dame Edith, "I insist that you tell the truth about your brother harbouring an army fugitive."

Belina replied, "I don't answer questions put to me so rudely."

"You are in my mansion and I will address you in whatever form I choose." Dame Edith's lips were as thin as the point of the goose quill on the table in front of the lawyer.

"Dame Senclar," said Belina, "I will inform the Lord Seneschal of your rude behaviour towards me." Belina's legs were shaking but she tried to look calm.

Dame Edith hissed, but Belina saw the watchmen grinning again. She hoped they would chatter about the courageous way in which she was standing up to the dreaded Dame Senclar, poisoner of Lectoure.

"I will get the Seneschal's troops to search the Moulié mill."

Belina saw the threat in that comment. It was vital that she get Wasila away from the mill as soon as possible. She was not sure how much the Seneschal liked or did not like Dame Edith, but keeping Wasila in the mill was very dangerous now. It was not only Catalina's wrath which they would have to deal with. The Seneschal might, perchance, have overlooked the presence of her brother Geraud in the mill because of his battle wounds, but the presence of a Moorish girl, presumably a slave, would require him to arrest her, and possibly Jordi too. Catalina's aunt had very likely chatted in Montreal, and Notaire Corloni would have heard not only about Geraud but also about Wasila.

"Dame Lansac," said the lawyer, "I am pleased that you have decided to speak in French with Dame Senclar, but I am annoyed that you have delayed this discussion and wasted my time by your stubborn refusal to do so earlier." He pointed his fingers together on the table, taking care to avoid the ink.

"Thank you, *Maître*," Belina replied with false demureness. "The use of the Gascon word '*molieròta*' delayed my responses."

The lawyer whispered in Notaire Corloni's ear, and Corloni grinned, saying "*Maître, molieròta* is a Gascon expression referring to a miller's wife who gives her very personal favours to any of her husband's customers to whom she takes a fancy."

"In that case," came the lawyer's stern reply, "it is not an appropriate term for the wife of the Bishop's Inquirer." He stood up. "This meeting is at an end. I will report to the Seneschal when I find the time."

Belina hoped it would take him many days before he or the Seneschal, found the time. She stood up and walked from the room.

CHAPTER TWENTY-FOUR

Belina walked to the rue des Argentiers and lifted the brass knocker on Messire Benasse's front door. She leant against the door frame and began to shake from delayed fear. How long would it take before the Seneschal searched the mill and found Wasila? Were the Benasses in danger because they were caring for Geraud? She must warn them.

The door opened and Belina greeted Dame Benasse. "Belina, my dear, what a pleasure it is to see you. Do come in."

Belina went into the hall, unaware that she had been followed by a Senclar guard, and went up the stairs behind Dame Benasse.

"My dear, I am in the middle of cooking *hamín* but Dr and Señora Benj are here and will look after you." She opened the door of the parlour. "By the way, when did you last eat today? You are looking very sickly, you know."

"I have had a difficult morning, Dame Benasse, and my last meal was a quick breakfast."

"I will bring you something to eat, my dear." Dame Benasse hurried down the stairs to the kitchen.

Dame Benj greeted Belina with a broad smile and pointed to a comfortable chair. What a difference it was from being in the Senclar mansion with nowhere to sit. Belina sighed at the memory and smiled at Dame Benj.

"*Está Vd. enferma?*"

Belina could normally understand some phrases in Spanish, but she was too weary to heed Dame Benj's inquiry about her health.

Dame Benasse came in carrying a tray of cakes and fruit which she put on a table near Belina. "I will bring you some cider, my dear. Meanwhile, make a start on these little cakes. We don't want you fainting on us."

Belina picked up a cake and said, "I hope I am not as weak as that," but Dame Benasse had already gone back down the stairs to the kitchen, returning with a pitcher and a beaker. "This cider will help you too, my dear," she said, pouring some into the beaker, "You look as if you have had a tragedy. Please tell us what the problem was, if you want to." She smiled at Belina. "We will not tell anybody if you want us to keep your secrets."

"I would like you to tell your husband, please, Dame Benasse," Belina replied.

"Is it a money problem perchance?"

"Worse, much worse." Belina told them of her experiences that morning in the Senclar mansion (twice) and at the mill. "I fear that the Seneschal will send people here, Dame Benasse, and find Geraud."

"Don't worry, my dear, we can look after ourselves. Geraud is wounded and is being cared for by a physician. What is more, it was the physician himself who insisted that Geraud should be brought here.

"How is he?" Belina asked.

"He is making good progress."

Belina finished her beaker of cider and Dame Benasse poured her some more. "Thank you. Can I see my brother please?"

"Dr Benj is with him at the moment, changing his dressings. When he comes back in here you can ask him about Geraud. Ah, here he is."

Belina got up and asked him in slow Gascon how her brother was.

He replied in slow Spanish that Geraud was making good progress and was in a lot less pain. No bones had been broken but he was full of bruises, many of them internal. His chest had been damaged and he found breathing difficult and painful.

"Oh dear," Belina replied, "May I go in and see him?"

"*Desde luego.*" He opened the door to the tiny room where Geraud was lying on several mattresses.

Belina sat on the floor beside her brother and held his hand. They stared at each other until Geraud found enough strength to thank Belina for having friends like the Benasses and Dr Benj.

She smiled and pressed his hand.

"How is Wasila?" he asked.

Belina told him that she was all right in the mill, busy mending flour sacks which helped Jordi and Christau while keeping her out of Catalina's way.

"I am sorry to have brought so much trouble to Jordi," he whispered.

"Don't worry about it," she reassured him. "I am going to move her out of the mill and she will stay in the house of my assistant Quiteira. She will be much safer there."

"Is Catalina so dangerous? Surely not?"

"No, she's just foul-tempered," Belina replied. "The danger – or possible danger – is from Dame Senclar who wants to turn Jordi out of our mill and put her own tenants in it. Finding Wasila would give her an excellent excuse."

"But we own the mill, the three of us, don't we?" Geraud asked.

"No. The Bishop of Condom owns it, but we are fixed tenants. In any case, the Bishop is not here, he's in Tours," she said.

"So we are safe from Dame Senclar."

"I hope so." She pressed his hand again and held it until his eyes closed and he drifted off to sleep. Belina got up from the floor, left the room and returned to the parlour.

"How is he?" Dame Benasse asked her.

"Sleeping. He's looking very peaceful." She turned to Dr Benj. "Thank you so much for looking after him."

He smiled and said something to Dame Benasse that included the word 'Wasila'.

"Belina," said Dame Benasse, "Dr Benj is telling me that Geraud is very keen on his Moorish girl being brought here, and Dr Benj is clear that the girl would help Geraud recover his health and his spirits more quickly." She paused. "But my husband and I know that we cannot have Wasila in our house." She smiled at Belina.

"Because Geraud is in such a small room, you mean?" Belina asked.

"That is one reason, Belina, but the main one is much more difficult to overcome. It is already a bit dangerous having Geraud here, as you and I were discussing earlier, but housing an escaped Moorish girl, very probably a slave, would bring us big problems, and she would be arrested and never seen again."

"Are you sure?" Belina asked.

"Yes. We have heard tales of that happening in other cities in France. People are so easily stirred up to hate foreigners, and Wasila presumably has dark skin."

Belina thought about this. She had supposed that Wasila's face had been darkened by the sunshine of southern Spain. Guillaume had told her once that people with very black skin were sometimes seen in Bordeaux and that they were African sailors from Portuguese ships. But Wasila certainly was not black. Far from it.

"I hadn't really noticed what colour skin she has," Belina replied.

"Does she wear a cloth over her head which covers her head and neck completely?" Dame Benasse asked. Belina nodded. "That probably indicates that she is Moslem," said Dame Benasse.

"Is that a problem for you?" Belina asked.

"No, my dear, of course it isn't. But an enemy could use it as an excuse." She paused.

"And you told me that you and your brother Jordi have enemies. That is the sort of enemy which I had in mind. Something rather dangerous seems to be happening and we must be careful."

"I am so sorry for bringing this danger to you, Dame Benasse," Belina said. "What would you like me to do?"

"Carry out your plan as soon as possible, my dear. Bring Wasila to your assistant's house." She paused. "She should have something to keep her occupied and inside the house."

"You mean mending flour sacks?" Belina asked.

"Not flour sacks, but sewing something, perchance. Something for your shop, for example."

She spoke to Dame Benj in their language and Belina waited for the reply to be translated.

"Dame Benj tells me that Moorish women are excellent at embroidery, especially of silk clothes. Apparently, they have beautiful silk gowns in Granada. That gives me an idea." She got up and went to the door. "Wait a moment."

A few moments later she returned, holding a silk gown which she showed to Belina. "This is an old gown, as you can see, but it is a good one and still fits me. I haven't worn it for at least three years because the embroidery has come unstitched and my eyesight is not good enough to repair it well."

Belina took the gown carefully and looked at the part where the blue embroidery had become unstitched. "I could at least see if Wasila could mend it. Quiteira might have silk thread in her house. I hope she has, anyway."

Dame Benasse smiled at her. "I will get something to carry it back to the staff residence in without anybody seeing it."

"I don't think there's anybody around who would be looking to see what I am carrying," Belina said.

"Well just in case there is somebody, I advise you to keep it protected from curious eyes. I will wrap it up in a cloak and take it down the stairs for you." She disappeared and returned with a cloak which she wrapped round the gown.

Belina thanked Dr Benj and his wife and followed Dame Benasse to the bottom of the stairs, where she took the cloak-covered gown. She waited while the heavy bolts were drawn back from the door.

They stepped into the street together and Belina said, "Please give my thanks again to Messire Benasse for the money he loaned to Jordi. Or would he like it back now that you are looking after my other brother?"

"Of course not, my dear. In any case, Jordi may need it if that dreadful Loupmont is giving him trouble."

"I wish the Archdeacon would get rid of Loupmont," Belina said.

"So does everybody. My husband knows of many farmers and *vignerons* who Loupmont is suing for money or produce or grapes."

"Is there still a lot of that sort of poverty here?" Belina asked.

"Yes. This afternoon, my husband is having a meeting with Consul Ardit, the wine merchant in the next street, who is owed money, and therefore he too has a money problem."

"He told me yesterday that Consul Lussan owes him quite a lot of money," Belina said.

"Consul Lussan's financial problems have resulted in other people getting problems like Consul Ardit, including Notaire Corloni's eldest son. Consul Lussan has acquired several angry enemies that way this year, including Notaire Corloni's wife and her cousins in Condom. It doesn't help that Dame Lussan is always seen wearing expensive new clothes and jewellery. I don't think Consul Lussan would have had money for a dowry for his poor dead daughter. He had not asked my husband for a loan for a dowry, nor for a wedding, and those are common reasons for people needing to borrow money."

"Would the betrothal banquet have been paid for by

Consul Prelet?" Belina asked, "or by Consul Lussan, or by both of them?"

"Presumably only by Consul Prelet, my dear. But the wedding and the dowry would have to be paid for by Consul Lussan. He should be selling his wife's jewellery, not buying her more. And I suppose he would have bought jewels for his daughter too, and gowns and head-cloths and a betrothal gift."

"With Viola's death," said Belina, "he has saved a lot of money."

"Yes, you could say that. And some of his creditors are insisting on having their bills paid, including Consul Ardit."

"I hope that doesn't point to why Viola was murdered," Belina said.

"I thought you told me that Guillaume had found the killer and put him in prison."

"Yes, but he might have been paid to kill Viola on the orders of her real enemy – or her father's enemy," Belina replied.

"Or her mother's enemy," said Dame Benasse. "She is reputed to have plenty of enemies. Getting rid of her daughter by paying a murderer would be cheaper than a wedding, the dowry and all the other expenses."

"I need to question the prisoner again," Belina admitted.

"Get Guillaume to do that, my dear."

"Yes of course. Guillaume would be much more successful than me."

Belina realised that it was high time to stop talking in the street. She thanked Dame Benasse again and walked to the cathedral shop. The Senclar guard who had been hiding behind the bend in the street followed her again.

CHAPTER TWENTY-FIVE

Belina was just about to walk into the shop when a watchman came out of it.

"Dame Lansac, I have been waiting for you for nearly an hour," he greeted her rudely.

"Then why didn't you leave a message with my assistant, Widow Nabias?" Belina grunted.

"She can't read."

"I know that, but she can be given a piece of paper and trusted to keep it carefully for me. She can certainly remember anything you say to her. I don't see why you felt you needed to waste your time waiting for my return to the shop."

The watchman took a document out of his purse and gave it to Belina. "Read this and confirm that you will do what it says."

Belina tried to stop her hand shaking as she unfolded the paper. It was a summons to the lawcourt for Tuesday morning together with Moulié Jordi and Christau. Whatever for? There was no mention of miller's wheat measures, or of her father's testament. What else had the judge found to accuse her, Jordi and Christau of doing?

She thanked the watchman, put the summons document in her purse and went inside the shop without saying "*Adiu.*"

"There you are at last," grumbled Quiteira. "You have been away all day, yet again." She put a tray of medallions back into their drawer below the display table.

"I am so sorry, Quiteira," Belina replied, trying to add as much contrition as possible into her voice, "but it is the fault of Dame Senclar and that fool Loupmont."

"Why, and which Dame Senclar?"

"The older one, Dame Edith, who sent her horrid tooth-drawer Chezelle to the mill to look for Jordi."

"Why? Does she want to buy his flour to make into face cream?"

"I wish she did. No, she is accusing Jordi and me of defrauding our stepmother."

"But I have always understood that it was the other way round," Quiteira said. "Surely, it is you two who are her victims?"

"Very true," Belina agreed. "I don't know why Dame Senclar is suddenly coming up with such an accusation after all these years."

"Perchance the younger Dame Senclar has put her up to it," Quiteira suggested. "She's a bad one.I wouldn't put any evil ruse past her."

"I agree with you absolutely," Belina replied, touching Quiteira's sleeve.

"Thank you Belina. By the way, there was a nasty watchman here for a long time waiting for you. I don't know what he wanted to tell you. He grumbled at your absence of course, and then suggested I should give him some *aygue ardente*."

"Did you?" Belina asked.

Quiteira shook her head. "You must have seen him on your way in here because he walked out of the shop just before you came in."

Belina told her that the watchman had summoned her, her brother and her cousin to the lawcourt next Tuesday morning.

"What for? Yet another absence. I am fed up with you never being here."

Belina told her that she did not know the reason for the summons and that she too was fed up with being absent so much.

It was only then that Quiteira calmed down and noticed the bundle which Belina was still carrying. "What's that? Old clothes from the mill?"

Belina made her come to the back of the shop and into the store-room where she unwrapped the cloak and showed Quiteira Dame Benasse's damaged silk gown.

"That's lovely material," said Quiteira, "And very fine embroidery, even if some of it is damaged. Is it for the Moorish girl who is hiding in your mill?"

"Whatever do you mean?" Belina asked.

"What I said. I am very well aware that your brother and his wife have a heretic living in their house."

"Who told you such a thing?" Belina asked her.

"Never mind who the source of my information is. I don't reveal secrets," Quiteira replied.

"You'd better not speak about it to anybody else."

"So it's true?" Quiteira smiled. "I knew it was. It's just like you and your brother to do something dangerous like that. Is Guillaume involved too?"

"He had no choice," Belina admitted.

"What's more," Quiteira continued, "I've heard that your young soldier brother has already left the mill."

"If you are really as sure as you are trying to appear, tell me where you think my soldier brother, as you call him, has gone."

"I'm waiting for you to tell me that, Belina."

"I'm not going to tell you anything." Belina wrapped the silk gown up again inside Dame Benasse's cloak.

"In the Pradau hospice, I suppose," Quiteira suggested, "as a reward for you solving the problem of their poisoned pilgrim."

Belina said nothing. Instead, she sent a quick prayer to the Virgin Mary, asking her to make Quiteira continue to believe that Geraud was hidden inside the hospice.

"Will Brother Pierre agree to the Moorish girl joining your brother in the hospice?" Quiteira asked.

"I haven't asked him, because he probably would not permit it."

"I'm sure he wouldn't," Quiteira laughed. "So the girl is still hidden inside the mill?"

"Yes, she is still living in the mill. Catalina is angry about it," Belina replied.

"I'm sure she is," Quiteira laughed again.

"It's not funny, Quiteira. Catalina treats the girl very badly. She's cruel."

"It is you and your brother who are being cruel," said Quiteira.

"Why?"

"Because you have left a poor young girl all alone in a strange house in a strange country under the care – or rather lack of care – of your sister-in-law."

"We don't see where else she could live."

"And if Chezelle visits the mill again and this time finds not only Jordi but also the Moorish girl, what will happen to her?"

"I dread to think," Belina replied. But she was already thinking how best to get Quiteira to agree to let Wasila lodge in her house in rue Cadeot.

"Well, you had better think, Belina, before Catalina loses her temper and denounces you all."

Belina seized her chance. "You see this gown, Quiteira," she touched it, "Wasila, the Moorish girl, is very good at sewing. I gave her a whole pile of broken flour sacks to mend for Jordi."

"Expert in mending flour sacks is one thing, Belina. Embroidery is quite another."

"Geraud is very proud of Wasila, and last Monday he said that she has a great talent for sewing. He says that Moorish women often have." Belina took care to hide the existence of Señora Benj in Condom. The family meal at the mill last Monday was far too angry for anybody to have talked about embroidery.

"What sort of clothes is she wearing?" Quiteira asked.

"Dirty and travel-stained, of course, but originally they would have been good."

"And what sort of fingers does she have? Large, fat ones or long thin ones?"

"Long and thin. She tries to keep them very clean – and free from flour." Belina wondered whether this would be the moment to ask Quiteira to lodge Wasila. She was well aware that such an action would be dangerous for Quiteira.

"Why doesn't she make herself more clothes, Belina?"

"I think that might be difficult in the mill. She is in a dark room and the main one is full of two lively children and their angry mother. Wasila mends the flour sacks in the mill storehouse but it would be impossible to cut out and sew clothes in such a flour-covered place."

"Is there nowhere else, Belina?"

"Well, yes, there could be a wonderful place for her to make clothes, mend clothes and anything else that needs mending, including the embroidery on this gown." She touched it again.

"Where's that?"

"In your house, Quiteira. You have often told me that you want to take a lodger but that you wanted to have a woman who was quiet, clean and tidy."

"I know I have, but women who are looking for a lodging are either sluts or looking for a man."

"Wasila is no slut. Very much the opposite, as I have just been telling you. And she already has a man she adores. A man for whom she left her own country to travel all the way to Gascony."

"Yes, but that would mean your wounded soldier brother would be in my house too. There's no room."

"My brother is best being looked after where he is," Belina said, "because of his wounds." She paused, trying to work out the best way to induce Quiteira to take on something dangerous that would change her life at home. "Of course, my brother would pay you for housing Wasila."

"I would insist on it," Quiteira said, "and in advance too."

Belina pulled a small purse out of her pouch, and opened it. Quiteira's eyes lit up and her lips curled upwards.

"Here is what Guillaume and I were going to give Jordi to help him get Catalina to agree to Wasila living in the mill while Geraud is recovering." She put seven coins in Quiteira's hand. "Take these as a first payment, Quiteira."

"But not the last payment I trust."

"Certainly not," said Belina.

"How and when will you get that Moorish girl to my house?"

Belina pretended to think, as if it was a completely new suggestion for her, while she put the purse back in her pouch.

"It will be dark soon, and we have to shut up the shop. Why don't I fetch Wasila early tomorrow morning from the mill and come to your house with her? It's Sunday tomorrow so you will have all day to show her the room which she can use and also give her whatever mending you want her to do."

"All right. But what if this Moorish girl takes something of value from my house and walks out with it and I never see her again?"

"Just lock your door when you are inside, Quiteira, and next week when you are going to the shop lock your house and take your key with you in the usual way."

"Of course. Very good suggestion, Belina, but a bit ruthless."

"Doesn't matter. It's much better than leaving Wasila in the mill, where Catalina could be much more ruthless."

Quiteira smiled and kissed Belina's cheek. "Let's shut the shop up now so that I have time to get home and prepare my house a bit."

"Of course." Belina went into the main room and began putting the trays of *babioles* into the drawers beneath the display table. "Don't bother with the shutters. "I will see you as early as I can tomorrow at your house, Quiteira, and thank you very much."

"Don't mention it. I'm glad to help. I might even be glad of the girl's company." They embraced quickly and Quiteira left the shop, humming.

Belina heaved a sigh of relief and she forgave Quiteira for all her scolds and sulks. She went outside to pull down the awning and saw Antoni running down the street. That's fortunate, she thought, he can help me with the awning and the shutters.

"Dame Belina," he greeted her, panting, "*Adischatz*. I have news for you. I have something really important to tell you."

"Has Guillaume returned?"

"No. It's something important for your investigation."

"Well Antoni, come through the shop and into the store-room." She led the way through to the inner room, pulled out two stools and said to him, "Have you visited the Prelet stables yet, like I asked you to?"

"That's what I need to talk to you about." He did not let on that he had not yet visited the Prelet stables. Instead, he recounted the conversation at the blacksmith's forge and later in the Cheval Blanc with one of Consul Prelet's grooms and a groom from Toulouse called Jean who worked for the sister of the mistress of Charles Prelet.

Antoni paused and looked at Belina, with his brows raised.

"Thank you, Antoni," Belina said. "I have heard that Charles Prelet has a mistress in Toulouse, although I did not know they had children. But I haven't heard anything about a sister. Tell me more."

Antoni told her that the groom had left Toulouse ten days ago and had ridden to Sempuy and spent two nights there to rest his horse. Then he had ridden to Condom, where he had stayed at an inn near the Cheval Blanc and the Galerne mansion. "He is keeping an eye on Dame Pauline and her husband, learning about their reputation."

Antoni went back to his main story about Charles Prelet. "According to Jean, the two sisters were gorgeous young women, with sparkling eyes and lovely breasts. The sister he worked for was herself the new wife of a lawyer, an older man, one of the *capitouls* of Toulouse. It was obvious to all the servants that she would help her sister become rich too, and Charles Prelet was the sort of ambitious lawyer who could become a *capitoul*. "Much better than being a consul in a little town like Condom," said Antoni. "Those were Jean's very words."

"It doesn't sound as if Charles Prelet was really interested in getting betrothed to Viola," said Belina.

"I think that it suited him nicely that she died."

"Oh Antoni, don't talk like that." Belina took out her pouch-cloth and wiped her eyes.

"He might not have killed her himself, of course. He could have got his groom to do it, or somebody in Condom who wanted money – the crestian for example." He paused. "Perchance the man who is now in the prison was paid by Charles Prelet. Or by him and his sister, Dame Pauline Galerne?"

Belina continued to wipe her eyes while she tried to pull herself together. "Thank you very much, Antoni, for this information about Charles Prelet. Please keep it to yourself. I must shut the shop now. I told Quiteira to leave early because she has had to put up with my absences. She is always so angry about them because of the extra work she has to do, but I do understand her point of view."

"That is what I like about you, Dame Belina. You understand other people's point of view."

"I try to, but I don't always succeed."

Antoni helped her pull down the awning and close the shutters.

Belina showed him out of the shop door and burst into tears. She had had a really difficult day. She sat down and sobbed for a long time before finding the physical and mental strength to go into the courtyard, up the stairs and into the chamber. She missed Guillaume so much. She had not thought that her marriage would have involved all these difficulties and absences. But once she had reached the door of the chamber she found Minet was waiting for her, purring and rubbing herself against her skirt. Belina unlocked the door, picked up the cat and went inside.

CHAPTER TWENTY-SIX

Sunday

Next morning, Belina was up, washed and dressed much earlier than usual. She had a quick breakfast of milk and bread, folded Dame Benasse's old silk gown very carefully and put it inside a clean towel. Minet looked on with such interest that Belina had to protect her parcel with one hand while she put an old kirtle on the bed, knowing that Minet was very partial to sleeping on that garment. The ruse worked. Belina smiled at the purring cat and went out of the door.

She went down the stairs carefully because it was only just light, crossed the courtyard and unbolted the door into the street, taking no notice of the cathedral bell which was ringing for early Mass. She walked to the mill, lost in thought. Who had killed Viola, when and why? If it was Chezelle, why would he have been in that part of Condom and why would he, a person from far-away Châtellerault, want to kill her? Would he kill someone at Dame Edith's request? But Dame Edith killed using poisons and he, a tooth-drawer, would have access to poisons.

The most likely murderer was still the crestian. He had been working in Viola's mansion, so maybe he knew Viola. He might have seen her in the mansion. But if he was so keen to kill her, why did he do so far away from that mansion, near where he lived in the leper colony? And what was Viola doing inside the chapel vestry? Guillaume thought she might have walked through the dusty tunnel from the cellars of her mansion to the chapel. But why would she do such a thing?

And then there were Viola's unaffectionate parents who might have wanted to kill her. They would not have done it inside their mansion because they would have been seen, either just before or just after they had killed her, and they would have had blood on their hands and their clothes. But it was not impossible that they had hired someone – the crestian, for example – to kill their daughter and then arranged for Chezelle to turn up at the chapel and find the crestian with the body.

That thought brought Belina back to the possibility of Dame Edith being the person who had ordered the killing. But what would her motive be? To take revenge against the Lussan family for something? Some land purchase which had not gone her way, perchance? Or it could be her son Henri who had ordered the murder – or even done it himself – taking vicious revenge against the Lussans. Perchance he had been trying to seduce Viola and she had refused him.

Belina tried to imagine that Viola was not as innocent as everybody supposed, and that she had been having an affair with Consul Senclar. What if Dame Jeanne had got to know about it and had paid somebody to kill Viola out of jealousy?

Belina narrowly avoided stepping into a puddle by the river-bank and clutched the parcel closer to her. She allowed her mind to wander to the Lussan servants, and then to the Prelet servants and Charles Prelet himself. After all, he had been riding a lot during the short time since his arrival in Condom, and Dame Courial had told her that he had a mistress in Toulouse. Consul and Dame Volpato probably knew that too, and yesterday Antoni had told her the same thing. Belina regretted that she had been too tired to remember to ask Antoni if he had questioned the Prelet stables staff about Charles Prelet and Consul Lussan and anybody else using the stables last Monday.

Her mind returned to Charles Prelet and searched still further. Perchance the mistress in Toulouse had wanted Viola killed and had sent somebody to do that? A person who was unknown in Condom and who perchance had got the crestian to kill Viola, or had done the deed himself and fled back home to Toulouse. Why would Charles Prelet's sister want to kill Viola? Or maybe her husband did? Perchance they were both waiting to inherit from Consul Prelet and were against having someone else to share that inheritance with? Had Messire Galerne's fruit and sugar import trade collapsed? If Guillaume were here he might know about the latest condition of Bordeaux trade with Africa where Messire Galerne's fruit came from – or so he had told the expensive grocers who sold his dates and sweets.

Another possibility would have been Prelet mansion staff, who did not want to have a young woman thrust into their midst and start ordering them about. Perchance there was a jealous maid who had her eye on Charles Prelet. Perchance he had a mistress in Condom as well as in Toulouse.

Yet another possibility was that the crestias in the leper colony had taken against Josep for some reason, so they had organised the murder and got him trapped with Viola's corpse.

The more Belina thought about the killing, the more people she thought might be responsible for it, and she was still pondering the mystery when she reached the mill. She went past the place where Christau had knocked Chezelle on to the ground, bursting a bag of flour, and then into the storehouse, hoping to find Wasila there.

The Moorish girl was indeed in the storehouse. There was a neat pile of flour sacks near her and she was stitching a sack.

"*Adischatz*, Wasila," Belina greeted her and received a big smile in return. Wasila pointed to the pile of mended flour sacks.

"Well done. Jordi will be delighted," Belina told her. The girl could probably not understand the words but their tone would have conveyed friendliness at least.

Belina fetched a stool and sat on it near Wasila who continued her sewing while Belina carefully removed the towel from around Dame Benasse's silk gown.

"Ooh," said Wasila, putting her sewing down on the pile of mended flour sacks.

Belina unfolded the gown, looking at Wasila all the time. The girl was staring at the gown, wide-eyed. Then she put out a hand to feel the silk and stroke it.

Belina pointed to the area where the embroidery had been damaged and Wasila looked at it more closely. She launched into a language unknown to Belina, pointing to the embroidery and showing how it should be repaired. Then she put the gown to her face and crooned with pleasure while Belina looked at her, delighted by the change of mood and bearing of the previously unhappy foreign girl bent over her flour sacks.

Wasila held the gown close to her body and stared at Belina.

"No, it is not for you to wear. It is for you to mend," Belina said in very slow Gascon.

Wasila's mouth turned down and her body drooped again.

Belina imitated the action of sewing in the damaged embroidery part of the gown.

"*Si.*"

Belina pointed at Wasila, who said '*si*' three times. Thus encouraged, Belina launched herself into a very slow Gascon speech, telling Wasila how she would take her into Condom to live there, away from Catalina and much closer to Geraud. "Are you ready to leave now?" she finished.

Wasila smiled, folded the gown carefully and quickly, wrapped it inside the towel and ran out of the storehouse before Belina could stop her. Belina moved the flour sack that Wasila had been mending to the pile of sacks waiting to be mended, left the storehouse, shutting the door behind her, and walked into the mill house. Catalina was busy in the kitchen and did not see her. The two children were having their breakfast and did not notice Belina either, so she was able to go unseen into the room which Geraud had used.

Wasila had assembled her clothes and was putting them into a saddle-bag on top of two pairs of shoes. She was humming as she added Dame Benasse's gown inside the towel and then she looked around the dark room, picked up a silver casket and put that in the bag too.

They walked into the kitchen, where Belina told Catalina that she was taking Wasila into the cathedral staff residence in Condom so that she would be much nearer to Geraud.

"Aah, Belina, that's wonderful. Thank you so much. I hope she is not the nuisance to you that she has been here."

"Well, she has mended the flour sacks," Belina replied. "Please tell Jordi that."

"Yes, all right." Catalina gave Belina a quick kiss and resumed her cooking.

While Wasila walked from the mill house carrying the saddle-bag, Belina watched from just outside the door. She saw Catalina put down her cauldron and dance in front of the kitchen sink waving her arms and singing at the top of her voice. Belina shut the door quietly, caught up with Wasila and helped her carry the saddle-bag.

It was a long walk up the hill but early enough for them not to suffer from the heat. On their way up the lane Belina thought about Antoni's story of Charles Prelet and Aralha's tale about Chezelle. It could be that Chezelle was the murderer, but she was unable to work out what his motive could be. Charles Prelet's motive was easier to understand; he did not want to marry Viola. But that didn't mean he had to slit her throat. And which of the two men was more likely to have paid the crestian to kill Viola? Belina felt that she was making slow progress.

They passed the Cadeot Fort, which Wasila refused to look

at, and walked up rue Cadeot to Quiteira's house. While she was knocking at the door, Belina watched Wasila's behaviour. She was glancing up and down the street and sniffing the not very clean air. Neighbours had thrown the contents of their chamber-pots on to the cobbles and animals were passing by on their way to the market hall. They made plenty of noise and added to the smell. The door opened and Belina gently pushed Wasila in front of her so that they could go in sideways, still carrying the saddle-bag.

Quiteira stood watching them, legs wide apart and hands on hips. Not very welcoming, Belina thought, but perchance she had been cleaning her house as she waited for them. "I am sorry we are later than I had expected, Quiteira, but the bag slowed us down."

Quiteira did not reply, but did at least manage a small smile at both women. She picked up the saddle bag, took it into a room at the back of the house and put it beside a bed covered with a large, fairly white cloth.

"Why is that bag so heavy?" Quiteira asked.

"It contains Geraud's possessions too."

"Why isn't he using them already?"

"Not safe to do that in the Pradau hospice." Belina hoped that Brother Pierre would forgive that lie.

"How is Geraud?"

"Getting better slowly, the last time I saw him."

"When was that?"

"Yesterday."

Wasila touched Quiteira's arm very gently, smiled and opened the saddle-bag. She pulled out the towel, unwrapped Dame Benasse's old silk gown inside it and held the gown up against herself, while muttering something which Belina could not understand.

Quiteira took the gown from her and placed it very carefully on the cleanest part of the coverlet. Wasila showed her where the embroidery had been damaged, pointing to the gaps in the stitching and then to herself.

"Belina," Quiteira said, "I'll get my sewing basket and see if I have blue thread for that gown."

Wasila took her clothes out of the saddle-bag and laid them on the coverlet. Then she sat on the bed, removed her muddy shoes and put on some lovely slippers which were in the bag. She placed the muddy shoes under a stool.

Quiteira returned with her sewing basket. "We're in luck. There's plenty of blue thread in here, underneath the needles and the scissors." She put the basket on the stool and pointed to Wasila, and then to the basket and then to the gown stretched out on the bed.

Wasila touched Quiteira's arm again and said "*mercés.*"

"Ah," Quiteira said to Belina, "so she does speak Gascon. You told me she didn't."

"She knows some words and understands a lot more if you speak slowly to her."

Quiteira took Wasila's arm and led her round the house, pointing out the latrine (which smelled ghastly), and the kitchen which looked as if Quiteira had just cleaned it. There was half a loaf of bread and a piece of cheese on the table together with three apples and some walnuts. Quiteira touched her new lodger's arm and smiled, a big warm smile this time, and received an even larger smile in return. She invited Wasila to eat them and she poured out some cider for her.

"Would you like some too Belina?"

"Yes please. It's a long walk from the mill to here."

Quiteira took another beaker off the shelf and shook two flies out of it before filling it with cider. Belina drank to her health and told her how grateful she was to her for helping Wasila.

"I need to leave now, Quiteira, because I have two more mansions to visit, and I want to take advantage of the shop being shut because it's Sunday. I feel so bad about deserting you so often last week."

Quiteira grunted and pour more cider into Wasila's beaker. "Why can't Guillaume visit those mansions?"

"He says I notice things better than he does."

"I think he's being lazy, but you know best of course."

Belina hugged her, touched Wasila's shoulder and let herself out through the narrow door.

CHAPTER TWENTY-SEVEN

Belina walked quickly back to the staff residence, still unaware that she had been observed coming out of Quiteira's house and was being followed. She was thinking about Guillaume and wondering where he had got to by now in his journey to find Barvaux. She still could not understand how Barvaux had not drowned in the Beauregard weir. Was the whole story not true, and had Guillaume gone secretly to Bordeaux instead?

When she reached her chamber, Minet was still asleep on the bed. Belina placed a stylus and two wax tablets into a bag and put on her second-best pair of shoes. She needed to visit the mansion that belonged to Widow Créon, the sister of the hated *notaire* and she hoped that she would not find herself face to face with his cousin, her wicked stepmother. The cathedral bell was ringing for High Mass and she would have to thread her way through the people going into the cathedral by the south door.

Belina left Minet inside the chamber and went slowly down the stairs carrying her bag of tablets. She walked across the Place Saint Pierre again, trying to look inconspicuous and hoping that no one would see her and delay her. She put Quiteira and Wasila out of her mind and concentrated on what she had learnt from the Prelet servants last Wednesday. Some of the servants had been scornful about the mansion next door. The mistress was seldom there because she was the widow of a Bordeaux wine merchant and lived in a mansion in the best part of the city. Her thoughts turned to Notaire Corloni. Why was he making trouble for Jordi? And how did Chezelle fit into the picture? And how well did Loupmont know the *notaire*, if at all?

She reached Widow Créon's mansion and looked at the front door, comparing it with that of the Prelet mansion beside it. It was smaller, with fewer nails studded into it. The knocker was smaller too and not polished, unlike the Prelet one. And the door was shut instead of being open and guarded by a liveried servant.

She looked up at the first and second storeys, where most of the windows were shuttered. There was a tower, like all the mansions in rue Royale, but it was shorter and thinner than that of the neighbouring Prelet mansion. Belina clutched her bag of tablets, picked up the knocker and hammered the door.

It was opened at once by a youth. "What do you want? The pedlar's entrance is in rue Deserte."

"I know it is," Belina replied calmly," But I am not a pedlar. I am the wife of the Bishop's Inquirer."

"So what?"

"My husband wishes me to talk to the servants of this mansion."

"Whatever for?"

"Because he is investigating the death of a young lady."

"There's been no deaths in this mansion."

"I did not say there had been," Belina continued calmly.

"So you can't come in," the youth smirked.

But Belina was too quick for him. She pushed past, ramming the tablet bag against his knees, and walked down the hall.

The rushes on the floor were moving because of ants and other insects crawling among them, and Belina was glad that she was not wearing sandals.

The youth called out, "there's a woman come in here without permission."

"Tell her to go away."

Belina stood still and waited for the owner of the hidden voice to appear. The youth ordered her to go away.

Belina smiled at him and said, "Please fetch the steward."

"No."

"Do as I say, or I will report the entire household to my Lord Bishop."

The youth opened a door at the far end of the hall. "She wants to see the steward."

"Who is it?"

"She doesn't say."

Belina strode toward the door and pulled it open further. She found herself facing an elderly man with a paunch.

"I am the wife of the Bishop's Inquirer, as I have already told this boy."

"Oh."

Belina waited and stared at the man's bald head.

"What does the Bishop want to know?"

Belina told him about her investigation, flourished the Seneschal's written authority but did not give it to him.

"The mistress is not here, Dame. She is staying in Bordeaux."

"I know that already," Belina told him. "I wish to speak to all the servants, starting with the steward."

"That's me." Holding his chest out and his stomach in, the man led Belina to his office, and pulled out a stool for her. "What do you want to know?"

Belina began her usual interrogation, receiving unhelpful answers while the steward looked at her as if she had taken her clothes off. She waited for the *molieròta* word, but fortunately that did not come. She asked if anybody lived in the mansion when the owner was away.

"Sometimes."

"How often? Once a week? A month? A quarter? Please give me a correct answer."

"Why?"

"Because I am asking you. The Bishop needs to know."

Belina learnt that the *notaire* of Montreal, the mistress's brother, was often in the mansion because he had more work in Condom now as a result of many sales and purchases of property. Sometimes his wife came too, for shopping for example, or to go to the apothecary.

"Does she have friends here?"

"Yes, she has many friends in Condom."

"Dame Prelet, for instance?" Belina asked.

"No."

"Even though Dame Prelet lives next door?" Belina probed.

"Dame Prelet is an older lady, a real lady."

Belina smiled and asked if she could be shown round the mansion and meet the servants.

"Why?"

"Because it is what the Bishop wishes me to do."

If the steward saw through Belina's lie he did not show it. He led Belina through the mansion and introduced the servants who answered her questions carelessly. No one could remember much about the day of the betrothal banquet except for a stable lad who happened to be in the kitchen when she was questioning people there. He told Belina that the Prelet stables servants had not liked Messire Charles Prelet, the consul's eldest son who lived in Toulouse and who hardly ever came to visit his parents. The stables staff were even more put out by the behaviour of Consul Lussan. But Belina knew that already, so she did not question the stable lad more deeply about the opinions of the Prelet stables servants because she had asked Antoni to talk to them. She wondered why he had not told her about his findings when he was telling her about the groom who had arrived in secret from Toulouse. However, his tale about Charles Prelet's private life in Toulouse was already very useful to her.

The mansion was in a mess, which surprised Belina because all the other mansions which she had visited had been clean and tidy, some richer than others but all of them in good order. The silver displayed on the dressers in this mansion was tarnished and there were some spaces as if objects had been removed.

Belina took a closer look at one of these spaces and turned to the Steward. "What has happened to the silver dish which should be here?"

"What do you mean?" The steward produced a rather sickly grin.

"There should be something here," Belina replied, "and it is missing."

The steward took his spectacles out of his purse, clipped them over his swollen nose and peered at the space.

"There has never been anything in this space, Dame," he told Belina.

The maid behind him began to say something but the steward interrupted her and told her to fetch the housekeeper.

Belina continued to look at the pieces of silver and four other gaps where silver had once stood. Then she looked at the other pieces of furniture. They were spaced round the walls, but when she looked at the walls more closely she noticed that the furniture must have been shifted as if something else had been removed. A small dresser perchance. She peered at a tapestry hanging on the wall showing a hunting scene. "This is a nice piece."

"Notaire Corloni bought it recently," said the steward.

"Where did he buy it?" Belina asked. "Tapestries like this one are not made in Condom. This could even have come from Flanders." She touched it very lightly.

"He bought it from Consul Lussan."

Ah, thought Belina, yet another sign that Viola's father was feeling poor. "How long ago did Notaire Corloni buy it?" she asked the steward.

"Can't remember." The steward introduced the housekeeper to Belina and said she would show the Bishop's Inquirer's wife the rest of the mansion, "if that is really necessary."

"Yes it is," Belina replied. She had already seen enough of the mansion, but she thought that it was the easiest way to meet more servants and question them. The housekeeper led her through the entire building, with each room looking dirtier and more untidy the further she got away from the front door. The one exception was a large, very clean room on the first floor with a wide bed and several chests near it.

Belina asked if the bedchamber was used by Widow Créon.

"Oh no. This is Dame Ana's room. She has used it for many years and she is often here for several days at a time. That's why she keeps so many clothes and shoes here." The housekeeper pointed to the chests and to the shoes lined up on trays against the wall.

"But all those shoes are for inside the house only," said Belina. "Does Dame Ana never walk in Condom?"

"Of course she does," the housekeeper replied, "to visit Dame Senclar for example. But she keeps her town clothes and shoes in a little room near the back entrance so that the mansion does not get muddy inside."

Belina thought that Ana was the only clean and tidy person in the mansion, but she did not say so. "Who is Dame Ana?" she asked, to keep the conversation flowing.

"The *notaire's* daughter. She uses the mansion quite often. She is always kind and polite to us. She knows a lot about furniture and how it should be mended."

"Where did she learn that?" Belina asked.

"From her father, I expect. A *notaire* has to value everything in a house when there has been a death."

"Does she help her father in this?"

"I don't know. How should I know what Dame Ana does with her time in Montreal?"

Back on the ground floor they approached a door near the back entrance, and Belina lifted the latch. The door would not move and Belina looked for the key. There was a keyhole under the latch, but no key.

"What is in this room?" she asked the housekeeper.

"It is the room where Dame Ana keeps her town clothes and shoes."

"So why is it locked? No other room has been locked."

"It is not usually locked, Dame."

"So why is it locked now?" Belina repeated.

"I don't know." The woman touched her head-cloth and continued, "neither do I care."

"But you are the housekeeper, aren't you?" Belina said.

"Yes, Dame, but this is a large mansion, with its owner away and her family only using it from time to time."

"Do they warn you in advance if they are coming to stay?"

"Never. They don't consider us. The only one to consider us is Dame Ana. She is always generous to us."

The housekeeper led Belina back to the steward's office and disappeared before Belina could thank her.

"The housekeeper has shown me every room except one," Belina told the steward.

"Why did she miss one out? I specifically told her to show you everything. You heard me say that."

"There was a room near the back entrance which was locked and the key was missing," Belina replied.

The steward frowned. "There is a room near the kitchen which is used as a workroom to repair furniture. But it is not locked. Nothing of value in it. Just broken furniture. That sort of thing."

"I saw that room. It had the frame of a linen box being made and several pieces of furniture waiting to be repaired. It is clearly being used as a carpentry room. When did you last look inside it?" Belina asked.

"I don't remember. Is there anything else you want to know?"

"Yes, I would like to look at the accounts ledgers."

"Whatever for?"

"Because the Bishop has asked me to do so."

"Why?"

"Because he wants me to tell him what I find in them." This was a bold lie, Belina knew, but the steward was annoying her. If she found anything amiss she would tell Guillaume to inform the Seneschal.

The steward took a ledger off a shelf and laid it on the table near his desk. "Help yourself. Take your time. Waste your time if you want to." He went to the door. "I will get one of my clerks to keep an eye on you."

He came back with a boy who limped. "This is Jeannot. He will watch you like a hawk, Dame. Don't say I haven't warned you."

Belina sat on a stool and opened the ledger. It was messy and careless, but she was used to working with accounts books, and she studied the entries carefully. Jeannot stood close by and stared at her.

It did not take her long to see that the steward was cheating Widow Créon while she was living in far-away Bordeaux. Belina took a wax tablet out of her bag and scratched her findings on it. Then she added a few observations about her tour of the mansion and her interrogation of the servants.

Belina put her second wax tablet back in the bag together with the stylus, and stood up. Jeannot was still staring at her but she took no notice and asked him to show her the way out.

"Back or front entrance?" he asked.

"The front entrance, of course."

She followed the boy through the disordered mansion and out into rue Royale. The street was crowded with people and animals, and Belina walked carefully towards the cathedral, keeping her eyes on the cobbles so that she could avoid the messier parts of the dirty street. She tried to think about what she had achieved that morning in Widow Créon's mansion, but her main thoughts were that insects had bitten her ankles when she was inside it.

When Belina returned to the chamber, Minet welcomed

her and went straight to her bowl. "All right, here you are." Belina sniffed the milk in the pitcher and half-filled the small bowl. She cut herself some bread and cheese for her own meal. She thought about Quiteira's welcome meal for Wasila and smiled. She had forgotten how kind Quiteira could be when she was not feeling overworked.

She scratched the bites on her ankles and sighed. Minet jumped on to her lap and purred. "Thank you, Minet," Belina said, stroking the cat, "you have great perception, comforting me like this."

She thought back to her tour of Widow Créon's mansion that morning and hoped that her visit to the Lussan mansion would be more useful – even if everybody was bound to be sad. Or would she find that Viola had not really been liked or respected?

Belina washed her hands and thought about how many wax tablets she would need for her visit to the Lussan mansion. In the end, she decided not to take any because Guillaume had already examined Viola's bedchamber and her painting room. She would rely on her memory.

CHAPTER TWENTY-EIGHT

Belina walked to the Place Lion d'Or and rue des Armuriers and looked at the large front door of the Lussan mansion, comparing it with the other seven front doors she had seen that week. It looked ancient but very solid, like Consul Lussan's reputation.

A servant opened the door and asked her what she wanted. Belina flourished the Seneschal's written authority and gave her usual explanation.

"I don't think either Consul or Dame Lussan will see you. They are too busy."

"I understand that," said Belina, touching his arm, "I would not want to disturb them at this difficult time. I have come here really to talk to the servants who worked for Dame Viola."

"Why?"

"Because as I have just told you, the Seneschal has ordered me to find out who killed Dame Viola and why."

"None of us know why anybody would kill such a lovely young lady as Dame Viola."

"I agree with you," said Belina. "I was at school with her, and I always found her kind and friendly."

The doorkeeper showed her into the hall and went to fetch the steward. Belina looked at the walls and realised that a large painting seemed to have been removed. Or perchance it was where the tapestry had been that she had admired in Widow

Créon's house. Belina wondered whether the Lussan servants had been paid recently.

"*Adischatz*, Dame Lansac." The steward came towards her, frowning.

"*Adischatz*." Belina explained again that she needed to speak to the servants who had looked after Dame Viola.

"I will take you to them, but please remember that they are in grief at the moment."

"Of course I will. Indeed, I am in great grief too over the death of Dame Viola. We were at school together and I have many happy memories of her."

The steward led her to the back of the mansion where the servants were preparing black cloths to put throughout the mansion. Furniture was being moved. Stagnant water was being thrown away so that Viola's soul would not drown and be unable to reach Paradise. Belina expected that a tile had already been removed from the roof to allow Viola's soul to escape. Mirrors and shiny objects were being covered with white cloths and a maid was telling one of the dogs about the death. Another maid was distributing images of St Veronica.

The steward interrupted the activity and said, "Dame Lansac is here to ask you questions. Please answer them, even if they upset you," the steward told the servants, and pulled up a stool for Belina.

She sat down and made a little speech about Viola and how much she had enjoyed her company when they were at school together, how her husband the Bishop's Inquirer had asked her to visit Viola's home and speak to the people who worked most closely with her.

Silence, except for some sniffing. Belina looked at the servants and tried to decide which one would have been Viola's maid, the woman who had told Guillaume that she had known Viola ever since she was a baby. An elderly woman at the back of the room seemed the most likely person because her eyes were the reddest of the group and her expression was the saddest.

Belina got up and approached the woman. "Please tell me, are you one of the people who looked after Dame Viola?"

The woman nodded and burst into tears. Belina put her arm round her shoulders and waited till she had stopped shaking.

The other servants told Belina that the woman was called Mounette and she had been Dame Viola's nurse. She had always looked after Dame Viola.

"Did anybody else help her?"

"I did," said three different women, as if in a chorus.

Belina stared at each one. Two were homely and clearly grieving. The third was younger, and wearing several bracelets. Belina decided to question her first.

"I like your bracelets. I used to make jewellery, and I can see that they are rather special."

The maid put her arms behind her back.

"She got them from a man," a servant said, "not from any of us."

"Were they made in Condom?" Belina asked the maid.

"I don't know. They were a present."

Belina thought about Aralha, kitchen-maid in the Senclar household who would meet Consul Senclar in his boathouse when he was feeling amorous. Aralha had received a bracelet from him, but she never wore it inside the Senclar mansion apparently.

"From Consul Lussan perchance?" Belina asked, even though it was an impertinent question.

"Certainly not."

"From your previous employer, then," Belina suggested.

The maid crossed her ankles and looked at the floor.

Belina dropped the subject and began real questions. The answers were mixed with sobs and nose-blowing but they were all similar. They had all respected Dame Viola, their hearts were broken because of her death, and they begged Belina to find the murderer.

"It must have been a terrible blow to you all," said Belina, "and to Consul and Dame Lussan too."

"The Consul was angry rather than distressed," said one of the servants.

"Dame Lussan seems in a better mood now than she was before the murder," said Mounette.

"Were mother and daughter very close?" Belina asked, although she remembered well that in her younger days Viola was distant from her mother.

"No," everyone chorused. Somebody growled that Dame Lussan was not a loving mother. The others agreed and offered many examples. Dame Lussan had loved her son, who had died of the plague four years ago, but she didn't seem to like her daughter much. They thought she would have preferred her daughter to have died instead of her son Mathurin.

"Why?" Belina asked them.

There were many reasons, and nobody was really sure. Dame Lussan was the centre of her world according to the maid who looked after her clothes and her jewellery. "Dame Lussan has beautiful jewellery," she sighed.

"Inherited from her mother and grandmother, I suppose," said Belina, choosing not to mention the goldsmith, Messire Benasse.

"Much of it was inherited," said a maid. "She comes from a rich family in Agen, an old Agen family. But she bought new jewels for the betrothal banquet."

"For Dame Viola too," said another maid, "but Dame Viola is not especially interested in jewellery."

"*Was* not," said the first maid.

Several women began to cry again and Belina decided it would be kinder to them, and more useful to her, if she spoke to Viola's nurse alone. She asked Mounette if she could be shown Viola's bedchamber. Mounette led Belina up the stairs and down a long passage and into a large room at the end.

Belina looked round the chamber, at the bed, the chests and a mirror above a sink. Everything was tidy, but a bit lacking in personality. Then Belina remembered that Viola had a second room up the stairs where she painted. Perchance that would show more about her.

She sat on the bed and patted the coverlet beside her, asking the nurse to sit there.

"Mounette," said Belina, "that is your name, isn't it?"

The elderly maid nodded.

"And have you always known Dame Viola?"

"Even before she was born. Her mother did not like being pregnant because she was proud of her figure. I did my best to look after Dame Viola even before I saw her alive."

Mounette sobbed, and Belina pulled out her pouch-cloth and gave it to her.

"*Mercés.*" Mounette wiped the tears from her face. "I am sorry to be like this, but my heart is broken."

"Please help me to understand how Dame Viola was preparing for her betrothal banquet."

There followed a disjointed description of the week before, with Consul and Dame Lussan expecting Messire Prelet, the son of Consul Prelet, to visit them and him not arriving.

"Was Consul Lussan angry about such bad manners?" Belina asked.

"Furious, as indeed he had every right to be, especially since there had been no message received from the Prelet mansion."

"And Dame Lussan?"

"Also very angry, especially since she was wearing a new gown for the visit."

"And Dame Viola?"

"She did not seem to mind."

"Did she want to marry Messire Prelet?"

Mounette shook her head.

"Why not?"

"She was deeply in love with somebody else, and had been for many weeks." Mounette blew her nose on Belina's pouch-cloth. "She had never fallen in love before, and she was so happy in his company. I am absolutely sure that she did not want to marry Messire Prelet, but I don't see how she could have married the man she loved. It was a very difficult situation for her."

"Why did her parents arrange for her to marry Messire Prelet if they knew she was in love with someone else?"

"They didn't know. They had no knowledge of it."

"But they must have known," Belina replied.

Mounette told her how the young man who Dame Viola adored was a crestian who had been working inside the mansion for the last three months making furniture in preparation for Dame Viola's marriage.

"Even if the crestian had talent, or was handsome or kind, how could he make Viola fall in love with him?" Belina asked.

"Because he was a really lovable, kind young man. Very good at carpentry which pleased Dame Viola because she is – no, was – an artist herself. And he had good looks. Not handsome, but pleasant to behold."

"So," said Belina, "you encouraged Dame Viola in her affection for the crestian?"

"Of course I did."

"Did other servants like him too?"

"Those who knew about him did. But we were very discreet of course. Consul Lussan would have been absolutely furious, and Dame Lussan would have hated the scandal."

Belina asked Mounette how the young couple managed to meet each other without her parents knowing. A long explanation of the tunnel to the Sainte Eulalie chapel was provided, with descriptions of spiders, rats and mice.

"And dust?" Belina asked.

"A lot of dust," said Mounette, "which made it difficult to clean Dame Viola's clothes. She kept a special cloak for the walk through the tunnel, but that had to be hidden of course."

"Did anyone find it?"

"Yes alas. The new young maid with the bracelets which you liked found it when she was going through Dame Viola's clothes one day when she thought I was in the garden."

"Where did she work before?" Belina asked.

"The Senclar mansion."

"Oh?"

"She told us that Dame Edith Senclar – that's the old one – had arranged with Consul Lussan to employ her because Dame Viola needed a younger maid than myself and Bonassa and Blanca. We were most offended."

"Of course you were," Belina agreed. "How long has the girl been here?"

"About a month, I think."

"Perchance the bracelets were a present from Consul Senclar," said Belina in a casual way.

"I hadn't thought of that."

"He has a reputation, I understand, for giving expensive jewellery to young girls."

Mounette understood Belina's meaning at once. "Perchance Dame Edith Senclar wanted to throw her out."

"That was what I was thinking," said Belina. "By the way, did you know that Viola was planning to avoid her betrothal banquet?"

Mounette nodded.

"Who else knew?"

"Only Bonassa."

"Could the young maid have known about it?"

Mounette thought for several minutes, biting her lip. "Only if she overhead talk between me and Bonassa."

"Could she have watched any preparations Viola was making – such as carrying things through the tunnel?"

"I didn't see her watching anything, but she might have spied on Dame Viola putting her jewels underneath her kirtle on the day of the betrothal banquet."

"And would she have told anybody? Dame Lussan or Dame Senclar, perchance?"

Mounette did not think so, but she was not sure. And then she burst into tears all over again. Belina thanked her and said she would find her own way out.

She spent the rest of the afternoon writing on her tablets about her visits to the Créon and Lussan mansions and she said prayers for Viola's soul. How terrible it was to die before she could make her confession and be pardoned. Everybody feared that more than death or dying itself. A sudden death was a bad death. Belina prayed especially to St Adrian and St Christopher. Memories came flooding back of her mother's death and she cried herself to sleep.

CHAPTER TWENTY-NINE

Monday

Belina woke up late and Quiteira scowled when she arrived in the shop, her shoes covered in dust from the unswept courtyard.

"Here you are at last, Belina. Messire Prelet needs to talk to you."

"Tell him to wait until I have changed my shoes."

"I will not wait."

She looked him up and down. "Messire Prelet, my shoes are covered in dust. I don't want that dust to settle on any *babioles.*

He frowned at the unexpected reproof and leant with his back to the display table. "Hurry up then."

Belina went into the store-room, removed her dusty shoes and put on her slippers. She patted her head-cloth and turned round to see the reflection of the back of it in the mirror before she returned to the main room.

"Well, what is your urgent request?" she asked the impatient lawyer.

"It is not a request. It is a complaint."

"What about?"

"You have been forcing your way into all the mansions of the consuls and their wives…" he began.

She interrupted him. "At the request of the Seneschal. I showed his written authority each time."

"I object to the intrusion." He stood up straight and walked towards her.

Belina took three steps to the left. "Then tell that to the Seneschal."

"I will indeed." He strode out of the shop.

"Oh," said Quiteira, "no wonder Dame Viola didn't want to marry him."

"What makes you think she didn't?" Belina asked.

"If she had wanted to marry that arrogant turd from Toulouse, she would have gone to the betrothal banquet."

Belina spent a few minutes comparing Charles Prelet with the sorrowful crestian in her mind. She felt an inclination to like the crestian more than the lawyer from Toulouse. But which one was a murderer?

"Do you agree with me?" Quiteira asked.

"I am inclined to," Belina admitted.

Belina and Quiteira spent the next half hour selling their *babioles* to pilgrims, and discovered that some of the pilgrims had only just arrived in Condom on their way home from Compostela, while others had been staying in Condom for a few days near the shop. They remembered Belina when she was near the chapel and that Guillaume had asked them if they had seen a possible murderer.

"Why are you staying so long in one town?" Quiteira interrupted them. "Hospices don't usually allow that."

They told her that they were living in a house which took in pilgrims from Einsiedeln so that they could practise their music.

"Do the neighbours mind the noise you make?" Quiteira asked. "I would."

"In the past some neighbours have complained," the oldest pilgrim told her, "so we practise further along the street, near the leper colony."

"Aren't you scared of catching leprosy?" Quiteira was obviously feeling inquisitive.

"Of course not. There haven't been lepers for ages." The pilgrims moved towards the collection of statues, perchance wanting to avoid Quiteira's questions.

Belina carried on sorting out images of the relics of Condom cathedral until she was interrupted by a soldier from the Fort.

"Dame Lansac?"

"Yes, *adischatz*." Belina hoped that she was not being ordered to go to the Fort. She dropped an image of St Laurent.

"The Seneschal gives you this message," the soldier put a piece of paper on the display table near Belina, "and you are to sign this paper to say that you have read it."

By this time, Belina's legs were shaking, but they were hidden by her kirtle. She picked up the paper and read it quickly.

"Aahh, that's interesting," she told the soldier. "Where is the paper which I have to sign?"

He took it from his glove and gave it to her, watched her sign it and put it inside his glove again. "*Adiu*."

Belina took the Seneschal's message into the store-room to read it again.

'Dame Lansac, the senior physician has examined the corpse of Viola Lussan before I can authorise the funeral and burial. He declares that the murderer attacked from behind with a sharp blade and cut the throat, with the wound being higher on the right side of the neck than on the left. This means that the murderer is left-handed, which is rather rare.'

"Belina, come out of there at once," Quiteira shouted

Cursing the interruption when she had so much to think about, Belina put the Seneschal's message in her purse and went into the main room of the shop, wondering what was irking her assistant now.

Charles Prelet was back. She looked at the couple beside him, who were middle-aged, well-gowned and both wearing jewellery, and a younger lady with the same type of chin as Charles Prelet.

Belina waited for them to introduce themselves. She wondered whether the younger lady was Dame Pauline Galerne, the wife of Messire Galerne, known for her bad temper.

The older lady spoke first. "I am Dame Lussan. My steward tells me that you forced yourself into my mansion yesterday afternoon and interrogated my servants. You had no right to do such a thing."

If she'd been feeling charitable, Belina would have thought that the woman was suffering from grief at her daughter's death. But Belina did not feel charitable. She decided to be as unhelpful as possible.

"You are a *molieròta*," Dame Lussan continued. "You should not be in a cathedral shop. Go back to your mill."

Belina remained silent.

"I will complain about you to the Bishop," said Charles Prelet.

"The Lord Bishop is absent from Condom," Belina replied.

"When will he be back?"

"I have no idea," Belina told Charles Prelet more calmly than she felt. "No one knows. He is with the Court in Tours."

"Why?" Dame Lussan asked.

"Because he is a bishop, of course." Belina tried to keep the scorn out of her voice. She thought she saw Charles Prelet trying to suppress a grin. Belina wondered if he was pleased that he had not acquired Dame Lussan as a mother-in-law. But was that a good enough reason to kill Viola?

Consul Lussan took charge of the conversation and insisted on knowing why Belina had forced her way into his mansion and questioned his servants.

Belina gave him her usual explanation, telling him that the Seneschal had given her his written authority to question all consuls and their wives.

"And the servants too?" Belina nodded. "You had no right to enter my mansion without my permission."

Belina repeated that she had the Seneschal's written authority.

"That should only have got you as far as the back door," said Charles Prelet, "which was how you entered my parents' mansion."

"Did she question your parents' servants?" Dame Lussan asked him.

"Yes she did," said the lady beside Charles Prelet. "Wasted a lot of their time and was thoroughly disagreeable."

"That's not true," said Belina with indignation. She thought it was not her who was being disagreeable, but the four people facing her.

"Don't call me a liar, *molieròta*."

"Then don't lie to me." Belina moved to the far end of the display table and, in the style of Quiteira when she was angry, she pulled out a tray of medallions.

"Come back here and answer my questions," Charles Prelet ordered her.

"Not unless you phrase them more politely."

"Don't address me like that." He moved towards her, raising his arm.

"Hey, hey," said one of the pilgrims who had been watching the scene. "Control your temper when you are talking to a lady."

"She's no lady."

"She may well be a lady, but you are no knight."

"The dame likes our music," said the youngest pilgrim. Belina was not sure whether that comment would help her or not.

Charles Prelet swore. "This is a *babioles* shop, not a song-sters' house."

The pilgrims talked amongst themselves in their own language, and then the oldest one said that anybody could dress up in a pilgrim's hat and cloak and walk with a staff. That way, they would not be noticed. He made a gesture towards the four people who were still angry with Belina, and said to her, "any one of these four could have been your murderer disguised as a pilgrim."

"Rubbish." Charles Prelet swore again.

Belina tried hard to hide her smile at his anger. Then she remembered the Seneschal's message sitting in her purse. She went over to where she kept some paper, the ink-horn and quills.

"Please come here and write your accusation on this paper," she told her four enemies.

"Why?"

"Because the Seneschal will want to see what you are accusing me of."

"That's not a good reason," Consul Lussan protested.

"All right," said Charles Prelet, seizing a quill and dipping it into the ink-horn, "I will declare my observations of your rude and criminal behaviour." He scratched several sentences on the paper. "You three will sign it, if you please." He dipped the quill in the ink-horn again and gave it and the paper to Consul Lussan, who put on his spectacles, read the paper slowly and signed it.

Belina watched him very carefully, as she had done when Charles Prelet was writing, and she watched the way Dame Lussan and Dame Galerne wrote as well. Which one was left-handed, and therefore the murderer?

She took the paper from them and said she would give it to the Seneschal.

"Aren't you going to read it first?"

"Of course, but not until you have left my shop." She walked into the store-room and counted three *Paternosters* before she came out again and found that they had gone. She thanked the pilgrims for their help.

"A pleasure to help you. Come and listen to our music sometime." They left the shop laden with phials of *aygue ardente*.

Quiteira sighed. "He really is a nasty piece of work, that one. I think he should go back to Toulouse and stay there for ever. And take his angry sister with him. That Dame Galerne treats her servants very badly." She pulled out a tray of badges and wiped her forehead. "You really got the better of them, Belina. I am full of admiration. I wish I had your courage in dealing with consuls like that."

Belina smiled. "I am admiring myself too when I think about it. By the way, how is Wasila?"

"I still can't understand what she is trying to say even though she is speaking a sort of Spanish. But she is making very good progress with that embroidered gown. In fact, she has almost finished it. She showed it to me with great pride."

"Dame Benasse will be delighted," Belina replied.

"How do I get the gown back to her?"

Belina would seize the opportunity to visit Messire and Dame Benasse and when she was there to visit Geraud in his little room. "If you like, Quiteira, I will fetch it from your house and take it to Dame Benasse."

No reply from Quiteira. Belina wondered if she had wanted the chance to meet Dame Benasse. She needed to find an excuse for her own visit. "I have to show Wasila the chasuble which Viola was embroidering when she was killed."

"Why?"

Belina had to think up an answer quickly. "Since the girl is so good at embroidery she might be able to tell me whether Viola too was good at it, or merely pretending to sew."

"All right Belina, I will lend you my key, but please make quite sure you lock the door behind you when you are inside my house as well as when you have left it."

Belina frowned. "Why when I am inside?"

"Because there are so many soldiers around, of course. I

don't want any of them following you into my house." Quiteira pulled a tray of St Peter's keys out of the drawer below the display table and put it on top of the display table.

"You are very wise and sensible, Quiteira."

"I know I am." Quiteira unhooked her door key from her belt and gave it to Belina. "Put that on your belt now."

Belina did as she was told. "I will go up the stairs and fetch the chasuble," she said and left the shop before Quiteira could change her mind.

CHAPTER THIRTY

Belina rushed up the stairs and into the inner room of the chamber. She folded the bloodstained vestment and pushed it inside one of the bags that normally held her wax tablets. She put all the tablets into Guillaume's work chest, locked it carefully and hung the key on its hook. She walked down the stairs with difficulty because of the bag and out into the street. She crossed the Place Saint Pierre and walked down rue Cadeot as far as Quiteira's house without noticing that two Senclar guards were following her.

Belina let herself into the house and locked the door from the inside. She found Wasila in Quiteira's bedchamber tidying Quiteira's sewing basket. Dame Benasse's gown was spread over the bed.

"*Buenos días.*" Wasila looked up and smiled at Belina – a friendly smile which lit up her sallow face.

"*Buenos días*, Wasila, *cómo estás?*" Belina spoke the Spanish greeting words which she had learnt from pilgrims in the shop.

Wasila went over to the bed and showed Belina where she had repaired the embroidery. It looked perfect and Belina told her so in slow Gascon, hoping the Moorish girl would understand. Belina hoped that her tone of voice would be enough. She touched Wasila's arm and said she would take the gown back to its owner. She picked up the towel to wrap it in, but Wasila took it from her very gently and folded the gown methodically and then put it inside the towel.

Belina pulled the chasuble out of her tablet bag and put it on the floor in order to avoid it staining Quiteira's bed. Wasila knelt beside it and touched the edge of the bloodstain. "*Aie!*" she said. She made a question mark in the air, in the same way as Sir John Keyham asked a question.

Belina put a fingernail to her neck and drew it across to the other side.

"Oh," said Wasila, and then ran two fingers down her face, indicating tears.

"*Si*," Belina said, and then found that real tears were flowing down her own face. She pulled out her pouch-cloth and wiped her tears away, not noticing that Wasila was examining the chasuble in the light of the window.

Belina could hear the Moorish girl muttering something but could not understand what she was saying.

Wasila beckoned to her and showed her a part of the chasuble which was not bloodstained. She pointed to the embroidery of that part and then to the embroidery of another part of the chasuble.

Belina looked, but could not understand what Wasila was saying, even though she repeated the words several times. But Wasila persevered, and after a long while Belina gathered that the girl was saying that part of the embroidery had been stitched and then undone and then re-stitched and undone again. Wasila counted thirteen instances of re-embroidering. She ended with a question mark in the air.

Belina shook her head and said she did not know.

Wasila put her fingernail from one side of her throat to the other and made another sign of a question mark.

"Yes," said Belina, "the girl who was murdered was embroidering this chasuble."

Wasila compared the re-stitched part with the embroidery in other parts of the chasuble. She made it very plain to Belina that it was not as well executed.

"No," said Belina.

Wasila said nothing for a long time while she looked at the different parts of the chasuble and then at the re-embroidered area. Then she said, "Penelope."

Belina stared at her, not understanding the word, or words.

"*Si, si*, Penelope," Wasila pretended to sew a part of the chasuble and then unpick it, and then sewing it again, and then unpicking that. "Penelope."

Belina still could not understand.

"*Griega*," said Wasila.

"Greek?" Belina asked.

"*Si, si, Griega.*"

Belina abandoned her efforts, folded up the chasuble and replaced it in her tablet bag, making sure that the blood-stained part was not visible.

She embraced Wasila and said, "Thank you so much, Wasila. You are very skilled."

The Moorish girl smiled, a radiant smile which transformed her sad face into a beautiful one. For the first time, Belina understood why Geraud had fallen for her.

She removed Quiteira's door key from the inside lock, went past the narrow door with difficulty because of the tablet bag as well as the gown inside the towel, locked the door behind her and hooked the key on to her belt. She made her way back to Place Saint Pierre and from there to rue des Argentiers and Messire Benasse's house. It was difficult carrying the gown and the bag in the street full of soldiers and Belina still did not realise that two men were following her.

Belina put the tablet bag on the doorstep and banged the brass knocker. A head appeared at the window above her, but she didn't see it, any more than she saw one of the men who had been trailing her from Quiteira's house. She waited patiently for Messire Benasse to come down the stairs and unbolt the front door.

"Ah Belina," he greeted her, "What a pleasure to see you. How are you? Come in."

He ushered her inside and slid the bolts back into place. "Is that my wife's gown inside the towel?"

Belina nodded and gave it to him. "It has been beautifully repaired," she told Messire Benasse. "At least, it looks beautiful to me."

"The Moorish girl has done it very quickly."

"I know. I was so surprised when Quiteira told me this morning that she had nearly finished."

"What is in the other bag?"

"I will show you up the stairs if I may, Messire."

They went up the stairs and into the main room, where Dame Benasse took the towel from her husband and unwrapped it. "Beautiful," she said, stroking the gown.

Dame Benj stood up and examined the embroidery, asking a question.

Dame Benasse pointed to the part of the gown which Wasila had mended. "It looks like new, Belina. No one could guess that the embroidery had been mended. That girl has a lot of talent."

"I know," Belina replied. "Up to now, I had only seen her repairing flour bags at the mill. If Dame Benj had not encouraged me, I would not have given her your lovely gown to be mended."

The two women stroked the gown and exchanged a few words in a language unknown to Belina.

"What is in the bag, Belina?" Messire Benasse asked.

Belina drew the chasuble out of the tablet bag. She supposed that the four Jews would not know it was a Christian priest's vestment, so she did not tell them about its religious significance.

Dr Benj put his finger on a part of the bloodstain and looked at Belina.

"It is the blood of Viola Lussan, the young woman who was murdered last Monday.

Messire Benasse translated the sentence and drew his

finger across his throat. Dr Benj unfolded the garment and examined it, frowning. He said something in Spanish which Belina did not completely understand.

"Belina," said Messire Benasse, "Dr Benj thinks that Viola Lussan must have been approached from behind and her head held while the murderer cut her throat. Her blood would have flowed on to her clothes and sprayed anything in front of her."

Dame Benasse said in Gascon, "but Viola Lussan would have heard the murderer approaching her, surely?"

Belina said that Viola was hard of hearing.

"That means that the murderer knew she was half deaf," said Dame Benasse. "Or he would not have tried to creep up on her. The murderer knew his victim."

Dame Benj picked up the chasuble and peered at the embroidery, saying something which Belina did not understand. Messire Benasse translated the comment as "why was Viola holding the garment?"

Belina said that the chasuble would have been kept in the chapel vestry and that a priest would have worn it to say mass.

There was a silence while they tried to understand why Viola would have been holding the garment.

"Wasila thought that Viola was embroidering this part of the garment," said Belina, pointing to the embroidery on the back of the chasuble. "She was certain that Viola would have embroidered these stitches here," she pointed to the part, "and then unpicked them. Moreover, Wasila said that Viola had done that thirteen times. She kept saying 'Penelope'."

"Ah yes. Queen Penelope undoing her weaving," said Messire Benasse.

"Waiting for Ulysses, keeping her suitors at bay," said his wife. She translated the remarks into Hebrew.

"Penelope," Dr and Dame Benj said together and smiled.

"Wasila told me that Penelope was Greek," said Belina.

Messire Benasse told Belina the story of the Greek myth. She thought for a while, trying to understand why Viola would walk through a long, dark, dusty tunnel and sit in the damp vestry of a small chapel next to a leper colony embroidering a chasuble and then unpicking her stitches and embroidering them again, thirteen times.

Messire Benasse opened a box near the hearth and took out a purse which he showed to Belina. "This is for your very clever new sister-in-law. I will give it to Geraud to keep safely for her."

"My sister-in-law?" Belina asked. "Surely you don't mean Catalina?"

"When Geraud has recovered from his wounds he wants to marry Wasila. He told me so."

Belina asked if she could see her brother. "Of course you can, my dear. I will show you in."

Geraud was sitting in a chair beside his bed reading a book. He gave Belina a smile as radiant as the one she had received from Wasila. They embraced each other and he told her how much better he was, how well Dr Benj was looking after him and how kind the Benasses were.

Belina in turn told him about her visit to Wasila in Quiteira's house and her success with the embroidery repair of Dame Benasse's gown. "What's more, Geraud, Messire Benasse showed me a purse which chinked with coins and said he would give it to you."

"Better to give it to Wasila. It was she who did the work, after all," he replied.

Belina took a deep breath. "Messire Benasse said it was for my sister-in-law, meaning Wasila."

Geraud grinned.

"Are you going to marry her?"

"Of course I am. That is why I brought her home with me."

"Has she said yes?"

"Of course she has. We adore each other."

Suddenly there was a sound of knocking, but not on the door of Geraud's room. It came from the street.

Belina stood up and said, "I don't like the sound of that beating on the door below. I had better go back to the main room." She kissed Geraud's cheek and left very quickly.

Messire Benasse was standing in the middle of the room with Dr and Dame Benj looking at him. "Belina, my wife has gone down the stairs to see who is pounding on the door. We are a bit worried."

"I am worried too," Belina replied.

"You will be all right, my dear. We will look after you."

They waited while they listened to Dame Benasse coming slowly up the stairs and into the main room. There were no sounds of anybody coming up the stairs with her, which was a relief.

Dame Benasse flung open the door and said, "Belina, there are three guards outside with orders to take you to the Seneschal."

"Oh no."

Messire Benasse asked his wife to fold up the chasuble, put it in Belina's tablet bag and hide it. He took Belina's arm and said he would accompany her to the Cadeot Fort. She followed him down the stairs and stepped out into the street.

A group of people were staring at the guards and one of them said, "Why is Dame Lansac in the house of the usurer?"

"I used to work for Messire Benasse making bracelets and pendants," said Belina as firmly as she could.

"Are you the wife of Guillaume Lansac?" the tallest guard asked her. Belina nodded. "The Seneschal orders you to present yourself to him at the Fort, and to do so immediately."

"Has he said why he wishes to see her?" Messire Benasse asked.

"No."

"Have you a paper to show that he wishes to see her?"

The guard gave him a document which he peered at and then gave to Belina, saying "read this carefully. I have left my spectacles up the stairs so I am not sure what it says."

Belina read out: "Lansac Belina is to be brought immediately to the room of the Seneschal. Signed by Chief Clerk."

"In that case, Belina, we will walk with these guards to the Fort." He took her arm.

CHAPTER THIRTY-ONE

The guards allowed Messire Benasse to accompany Belina as far as the room next to the Seneschal's office and told them to wait. Belina looked for a seat but the only stool in the room was occupied by somebody with his back to her. She waited and tried to stop herself from shaking with fear. One of her guards went into the Seneschal's office and announced that Belina had arrived.

"Show them in."

Belina hoped this meant that Messire Benasse could come in with her, but the guard prevented this and pushed her gently into the room.

"Chezelle," the guard announced.

Belina turned round in surprise and found herself face to face with Dame Edith's tooth-drawer. Whatever was he doing here?

The Seneschal pointed to two stools in front of his desk. "Sit on these." He continued writing and looking at a document in front of him.

Chezelle cleared his throat. "I have come . . ."

"Do not speak until I tell you to." The Seneschal continued to study the document.

Belina stopped shaking and almost smiled. She waited patiently.

The Seneschal looked up from his writing and put his quill to one side. Chezelle cleared his throat again.

"Dame Lansac, the tooth-drawer has informed me that you are secretly lodging your brother in rue Cadeot, in the house of Widow Nabias. Is this true?"

"Certainly not, my Lord Seneschal. My brother lives in the Moulié mill at Gauge, where he has lived since he was born."

"I'm talking about your other brother," said Chezelle, "who is a fugitive from the army."

"He is not," Belina shouted at him.

"Calm down please, Dame Lansac," said the Seneschal. "According to Chezelle, your brother is living in the house of Widow Nabias. I repeat, is this true?"

"No, my Lord Seneschal, it is a lie. I swear to you that it is not true. If you wish, I will swear to you on the bible."

Chezelle started to say something about a key but the Seneschal interrupted him. "Does Widow Nabias live in that house?"

"Yes."

"Does anyone else live in that house?"

"Yes, the old mother of a friend of Widow Nabias," lied Belina.

"Why?"

"Because the woman is losing her senses because of old age. She has to be locked inside the mansion so that she doesn't open the door and wander out into the street and get lost. It's a typical problem with old people, and Quiteira's friend . . ."

"Don't believe her, Lord Seneschal," Chezelle interrupted. "I am certain that the fugitive brother is in that house. I have seen him."

"You can't have done," said Belina. "My brother is not a fugitive. He is a wounded soldier."

"He may well be wounded, but I insist that he is a fugitive, a traitor to France, and a criminal."

"He is not," shouted Belina and stood up.

"Dame Lansac, sit down and calm down," said the Seneschal. He turned towards Chezelle, "Why do you believe that Soldier Moulié is a fugitive?"

"Because he has left his company."

"What company?" asked the Seneschal.

"The one he was serving in."

"What is the name of that company?"

Chezelle was silent, and looked at his nails.

"Who told you that Soldier Moulié is a fugitive?"

"It is common knowledge here in Condom."

"I have not heard such a thing, and I consider myself well informed."

"Dame Senclar has proof that he is a fugitive," Chezelle declared.

"Where is that proof?"

"In Dame Senclar's strong room. She will show it to you, or to your representative."

"Which Dame Senclar, the young one married to Consul Senclar, or the widow?"

"Dame Edith Senclar, the mother of Consul Senclar," Chezelle said.

The Seneschal frowned. "In that case, the old widow has to come here herself and bring the proof with her."

"She is not an old widow," said Chezelle.

"It is my understanding that she is a widow and that her son is a consul." The Seneschal's voice was very clipped.

"That is correct."

"Then she is an old widow."

"She is fifty-one years of age. She gave birth to her son when she was fourteen."

"Did she indeed? Her husband must have been desperate to get his hands on the girl's dowry," said the Seneschal.

"You are speaking badly of a respected consul," Chezelle retorted.

"His reputation is not respected, and neither is that of his son."

Chezelle scowled. He began to reply and then thought better of it.

The Seneschal continued, "if Dame Senclar is only fifty-one years old she can walk from rue Sainte Luce to this Fort with her proof. Until that happens I am not prepared to waste my time any further on your declarations." He picked up a document and studied it.

Chezelle rubbed the side of his neck and crossed one heel over the other. Belina waited, trying not to smile at Chezelle's discomfiture.

The Seneschal put his document down and looked at Chezelle. "You are dismissed."

Belina stood up.

"No, not you Dame Lansac. I wish to talk to you now that you are here about your husband's investigation of the murder last Monday. Please sit down again."

Belina sat down on the stool and refrained from looking at Chezelle standing near her.

"I was the person who found the killer and ordered the Watch to detain him," said Chezelle. "It is I who you should be talking to."

"I talk to whoever I choose. Now get out."

Chezelle had no choice. He turned round and left the room.

"Thank you, my Lord Seneschal," said Belina.

"Don't mention it, Dame Lansac." The Seneschal put his papers aside and smiled at her. "I am inclined to believe that Chezelle might be the murderer."

"He is certainly one of my prime suspects."

"Why?"

"I would prefer to hear your reasoning first, my Lord," said Belina with unusual caution. The power of the Seneschal scared her even more than Dame Edith.

"No, your reasons first, if you please."

Belina recounted the confidences given to her by Aralha, without giving the kitchen-maid's name.

"No wonder Guillaume Lansac gets you involved in his

investigations. You discover private information better than anybody else I know."

"Thank you." Belina looked up and saw the Seneschal smiling at her.

"However," he said, "when it comes to interrogating Chezelle I don't think that would be a task for you, Dame Lansac."

"Oh no, I couldn't undertake to do that."

"It is obvious to me that this murderer is too dangerous and could strike again. I have sent four of my soldiers to the west to search for your husband and bring him back."

"Thank you so much."

The Seneschal smiled again. "I know how important it is for your husband to find that dangerous Fleming and prevent him from reaching the English princes. Nevertheless, my solders can, and will, find the Fleming and bring him back to Condom as a prisoner bound on to a horse. Your husband must go back to his real work as Bishop's Inquirer and solve that murder in the chapel."

Belina repeated her thanks, and began to tell the Seneschal that her husband was not riding his own horse.

"I know that. My troops have a *destrier* with them for William."

"William?" Belina queried.

"I am well aware that your husband's real name is William, and that he is English."

"Half English," Belina corrected him.

"Yes, but the other half is Bordelais, and they are pretty much English too."

Belina did not know what to say. Perchance the Seneschal came from Bordeaux himself. It was certainly not the time to tell him what she thought of people from Bordeaux. She waited for the Seneschal to continue the conversation.

"How is your brother, Dame Lansac?"

That took Belina by surprise. Her mind was full of Guillaume.

"Jordi and I have been having problems with Loupmont and Notaire Corloni and we have to go before the judge tomorrow to be questioned. My cousin Christau too."

"I did not know that. Loupmont and Corloni are both troublous and too keen on money. I wish you well in the encounter on the morrow. Let me know if it turns nasty for you, but I don't think it will. That judge is a good and fair person. He will not let that greedy pair fool him. Don't you worry." He paused and shifted the papers on his desk. "But I was asking about your other brother, the one who has returned from Spain. The one Chezelle was accusing you of lodging in your assistant's house near here."

"He is not in Quiteira's house," Belina declared.

"I don't for one moment believe that he is. His wounds are probably so bad that he needs to be cared by a physician and not left alone all day locked inside a house."

Belina kept silent.

"However, I don't believe your story that the new lodger in the house is a senile old woman."

Belina started to tell him that Quiteira's new lodger was indeed an old woman who had lost her mind and tended to wander the streets and get lost.

The Seneschal interrupted her. "Dame Lansac, I believe that you have put your brother's Moorish girl in that house, while your brother is somewhere else. I had originally supposed that to be the Pradau hospice, but Brother Pierre denies it. I do not believe Brother Pierre is lying."

"Oh no," said Belina. "I'm sure he would never lie. But he refused to help me with money for Jordi when I asked for it. I was very disappointed."

"A pity. Perchance he did not think he could help a heretic."

"That is what Guillaume and I supposed," Belina said.

"So who has given you money?"

Belina looked at the Seneschal. His smile had vanished. She did not want to reply with the truth, but did not dare to lie to him.

"Was it Messire Benasse, the goldsmith?" Belina nodded."Was that why you were found in his house just now?"

"No, my Lord Seneschal, I was bringing back an old gown of Dame Benasse's that Wasila had mended."

"So the money depended on the provision of her sewing skills?"

"No. Messire Benasse had already given us money. Some of the embroidery on the gown had been damaged and Dame Benasse asked me to see if Wasila could repair it."

"Wasila is the name of the Moorish girl, I take it?" Belina nodded."Did she repair it well?"

"Beautifully. She is very talented."

The Seneschal launched into a description of the qualities of the Moorish girls which French soldiers had brought back from the Emirate of Granada.

"I didn't know there were any in Condom," Belina said.

"None yet, but there are some in Toulouse. Your brother's Wasila will be the first one in Condom, and she and your brother will be very welcome here."

Belina looked at him, amazed.

"As soon as your brother has recovered enough from his wounds, I will take him on to my staff and provide him and Wasila with somewhere comfortable to live."

"Thank you. Thank you so much, my Lord Seneschal. You are very kind."

"Thank you, Dame Lansac, but I hope to gain from your brother's presence."

Belina looked very surprised. "How?"

He told her that soldiers in Toulouse who had returned from Spain had been providing very useful information about the conditions in Spain. The Moors were excellent fighters, but King Fernando was a great army leader with plenty of experience. He and his wife, Queen Isabel of Castile, had decided to launch a war against the Moors as a cunning way to stop the Spanish nobility from conspiring against them, as new young monarchs in a poor country.

"Castile has no farming apart from sheep. Aragon and the coast are less poor, but Catalonia has suffered from a civil war. Getting everyone to unite against the Moors is an excellent strategy. But there is a disadvantage for the future."

The Seneschal told Belina that the Moors were superior at farming and – like the Romans – in the provision of water. "They have an elegant culture in Granada. It is such a pity that the Spanish king and queen are determined to destroy it."

All this was news to Belina. She had always supposed that the Moors were dirty peasants.

"No, on the contrary. It will take a lot of time to beat them. And money too."

"Do the Spanish mind high taxes?" Belina asked, thinking of all the suffering caused by King Louis' taxes.

"Queen Isabel and her husband have found a cunning but evil way to avoid taxing their subjects. They have created the Inquisition, so that the wealth of Jews, and in particular former Jews, known as *conversos*, can be used to finance the war against the Moors. By encouraging a fierce hatred of Jews and Moors, using totally invented religious reasons, the queen has helped herself to their wealth."

"How could people turn against somebody like Messire Benasse?" Belina asked.

"Very easily. When people are not educated they can be steered into herding together against an enemy. In Seville, especially, there are plenty of labourers in the port who have been made jealous of Jews, especially Genoese Jews."

"Perchance they owed money to them?" Belina suggested.

"Most Jews usually lend only small amounts to farmers when they need to buy seeds." The Seneschal continued his condemnation of Queen Isabel and the Inquisition. The policy of making Jews leave Spain would mean that all the physicians in Spain would have to abandon their patients. Belina did not mention Dr Benj who had already left Toledo and was in Condom, looking after Geraud.

"In France we will benefit from the arrival of so many experienced, skilful physicians. What I want to know from your brother is his judgement of the life in the Granada area, how the war is going, have the crops been destroyed and who the soldiers are. All sorts of questions to which I need answers."

"I hope Geraud can give you those answers," Belina said. "I am sure he will try to help."

The Seneschal smiled and stood up. "Thank you for your help with the murder investigation, Dame Lansac. Please continue with it. I would expect your husband to be back by tomorrow evening. But please keep very quiet about that."

"Of course I will, my Lord." Belina left the room feeling much more confident than she had when she had entered it.

Messire Benasse accompanied her most of the way back to the shop, where she found Quiteira very upset about her long absence.

"Where have you been? Is Wasila still there? I've been so worried about you. I had a premonition that you were in trouble. Have you lost my key? Answer my questions."

"I will as soon as you give me the chance to." Belina gave her the door key, sat on a stool and took her shoes off. "Please could you bring me some foot balm, my feet are swollen."

"You walked in here as if you were skipping." Quiteira took a foot balm pot off the display table and opened it.

"That's because I found Wasila full of pride and smiles and I was able to give Dame Benasse her gown. She was delighted. Wasila is very skilled, isn't she?"

"Yes, and she works so quickly too," Quiteira replied, stroking Belina's left foot with the balm. "Anyway, I left her a kirtle to mend. She will be doing that now, I expect." She started stroking Belina's right foot. "So, what have you been doing all day, Belina?"

"I took the gown to Dame Benasse and then guards knocked on the door and arrested me. I had to go at once to the Cadeot Fort and see the Seneschal."

"Oh no!" Quiteira stopped stroking Belina's foot. "How awful! Did they lock you up?"

"No," said Belina smiling, "I saw the Seneschal."

"Were you scared?"

"At first I was so scared that I was shaking."

"That's not like you," said Quiteira, resuming her stroking. "Nothing frightens you."

Belina felt like denying that, but decided not to. She told Quiteira how Chezelle had been there, accusing her brother of being an army fugitive.

"Why is the tooth-drawer inquisitive about your brother? What is he to do with him?" Quiteira asked.

"It sounds as if Dame Edith put him up to it. The Seneschal told him that if the old witch felt that way she could walk to the Fort from her mansion and show him the proof that Chezelle said she possesses that Geraud is a fugitive."

"Such a thing would be beneath her dignity. She is the proudest woman in Condom. I hate her almost as much as you do."

Belina told Quiteira what the Seneschal had said to Chezelle and she copied the way the Seneschal had told Chezelle to get out.

"And you left too, with the tooth-drawer with his teeth well covered?"

"No, I was told to stay and tell the Seneschal how far I have got with the investigation. He is a kind and intelligent man. He asked about Geraud, but he did not ask where he is. I was so relieved."

"I'm sure you were." Quiteira put the stopper on the foot balm pot and got to her feet slowly. "I forgot to tell you that there is a message for you from the prison."

"Oh dear. I hope it is not bad news."

"That's what I said, but the messenger told me that it was good news. At least for the crestian. They have been ordered by the Seneschal to move him to a better, cleaner cell."

"That is good news for me too," said Belina, "because I have to see him again and try to get him to talk."

"Did the Seneschal tell you to do that?"

"Yes, and I must obey him." Belina put her shoes on again, got up, thanked Quiteira for putting the balm on her feet and said she was hungry and needed something to eat before going to the prison in the afternoon. She walked out of the shop before Quiteira could stop her and start complaining about her absences. She was sorry to abandon Quiteira yet again, especially since she had been so friendly and kind instead of scolding her, but she felt that the Seneschal would have wanted her to continue the investigation, to which he appeared to attach more significance than she had expected.

As soon as she was safely in her chamber Belina prepared a small meal for herself: some bread and cheese, followed by two pears. She read through the scratching on her wax tablets about what she had found out yesterday in the Lussan mansion.

She wondered whether Viola had intended to run away with the crestian. It did not seem very likely. She was willing to believe that Viola had not wanted to marry Charles Prelet, even if her parents had decided that she should marry him. Only one consul's wife out of the six she had spoken to had told Belina that Viola was in love with Charles Prelet, along with one of the maids in the Prelet mansion. Consul Volpato and his wife seemed to be aware that he had a mistress in Toulouse. Dame Courial also knew he had a mistress. Antoni had learnt that he not only had a mistress but also two children.

Belina supposed that Viola had plucked up courage to absent herself from the mansion last Monday, but what would have happened afterwards? Could she have stayed more than a few hours in the chapel or even all day? She would not have hidden herself among the crestias in the leper colony nearby.

How would they have escaped Condom? On foot? That would mean carrying very few possessions with them. They could have disguised themselves as pilgrims, but that would involve each of them acquiring a pilgrim's cloak, staff and hat. And good shoes too, Belina realised. And a gourd for drinking. Walking in this weather made people very thirsty.

Belina thought about riding. Not a horse, but perchance an ass for Viola, with the crestian leading them, rather like paintings of the Virgin Mary, St Joseph and the baby Jesus. How would they have crossed the Barlet Bridge without being stopped? No, they would have travelled towards Auch or Agen.

She could not understand why anybody would have wanted to kill a gentle young woman like Viola. Perchance she was not so gentle. Perchance she was like her mother.

She finished the second pear, washed her hands and put her head-cloth on again ready to go to the prison.

CHAPTER THIRTY-TWO

Belina walked down rue Jean-Baptiste to the prison and the guards welcomed her into their room. They told her that they had put the prisoner in a cell reserved for better prisoners.

"Do you get many of those?" Belina asked.

"You'd be surprised."

A guard took her across a courtyard and unlocked a door to a cell with a window with bars on it, so she could see inside the cell with less difficulty than with the previous one. There was no damp, foul smell either.

The guard told her to go in and to beat on the door when she had finished talking to the crestian. "I will be waiting outside. If he is a nuisance to you, just yell for help, but I think he will be quiet. He seems docile enough."

Belina entered the cell and heard the door bang behind her and the key turn in the lock. She looked at the crestian. He had stood up when the door opened and he was staring at her sadly.

"*Adischatz*," Belina began, "I see that they have moved you from that horrible cell in the dungeon."

"*Adischatz*," he mumbled, and continued to stare at her.

"I need to ask you more questions. Please answer them this time, or you may be moved back to your old cell, or even worse."

"I doubt there could be a worse one," he replied.

"Why were you in the Sainte Eulalie chapel last Saturday morning?"

He hesitated for a long time. Belina thought his silence was lasting at least two *Paternosters*, but she waited patiently.

"I had gone there to meet Viola. We loved each other and we were going to run away."

Belina had not believed Viola's nurse Mounette when she was told that Viola was planning to run away. She tried to hide her surprise from the crestian. "Run away?" She said.

"Yes, Dame, Viola and I were going to leave Condom and begin a life together far from her unloving parents."

"I see," said Belina, although she did not understand. "How were you going to travel?"

The crestian gave her a long description of how he had an ass tethered nearby, beyond the chapel and near the little bridge over the river Gèle. They would go north from there towards Francescas, hiding in barns at night until they reached Brax near the river Garonne. After that they would hire a boat to take them down the river until they found a safe place to live.

"And how would you have obtained food and drink?" Belina asked.

"We would have bought it."

"Surely Consul Lussan would have sent out search-parties and you would have been caught?"

"He would have hesitated too long. We would have been safe." The crestian smiled for the first time.

"Dame Lussan might want to act more quickly," said Belina.

"Not her. She didn't like her daughter. She behaved like a stepmother even though she was Viola's real mother."

Belina clenched her teeth at the word 'stepmother' and decided to change the line of questioning.

"Where were you before you went to the chapel on Monday morning?"

"I was in rue Royale, mending a casket."

"Why?"

"On Saturday evening I was ordered to mend a casket first thing Monday morning because the *notaire* needed to take it to a banquet that morning."

"Which *notaire*?"

"The *notaire* who lives in the mansion." The crestian paused. "At least, he sometimes lives in the mansion."

"Is he Notaire Corloni?" Belina asked.

"I don't know his name."

"Who ordered you to do this, the *notaire* himself?" Belina asked.

"No. I have never seen the *notaire*. The housekeeper brought the casket to my work room and gave it to me."

Belina asked what was wrong with it and when it had become broken.

The crestian told her that one side of the casket had been damaged. He did not know how or when it had happened.

"So you went to the mansion on Monday morning to do the repair, even though you were planning to run away from the chapel?" Belina asked.

The crestian nodded.

"Did you do the repair?"

"Yes, but it took me much longer than I had supposed it would."

"Why?"

The crestian told her that he had left the mansion at curfew time on Saturday evening without checking that all his tools were in his satchel. He had taken it home with him and it was not until Monday morning in the mansion that he had noticed that the tool he needed to repair the casket was missing.

"Which tool was it?"

"My spokeshave. I wasted a lot of time because of that. First of all, I tried to find it. After that I had to do the repair with a different plane, which was not as good for that work as my spokeshave."

Belina held her breath. "Describe your spokeshave."

The crestian went to the wall and with a fairly clean finger drew a shape in the dust

"Are you quite sure that spokeshave was really missing?" Belina asked. "Perchance you had mislaid it somewhere in the room and had not noticed it."

The crestian looked straight at her and grew taller. "I am completely sure. That spokeshave was stolen from me."

Belina's heartbeat quickened, but she remained outwardly calm. "It was on the floor beside the corpse in the chapel," Belina said.

"How do you know? I did not see it there. I did not kill Viola. I loved her with all my heart, with all my soul." He burst into tears and turned his back on her.

Belina knocked on the door to be let out. The crestian's sobs could be heard even after the guard shut the door behind her.

"Did you hit him, Dame Lansac?" the guard asked her.

"No, of course not."

"Why is he crying his eyes out then?"

"Because he feels so miserable." Belina decided to say no more than that. She asked to see the crestian's satchel.

The senior guard unlocked a chest and pulled out a large bag and put it on the table. Belina opened it and took out the pieces one by one. They were tools of the highest quality and in excellent condition. And yet the owner was a crestian.

One of the guards peered at the tools, and picked one up.

"Please put that down," Belina ordered.

"Sorry." He put it back on the table. "It is of good quality, Dame Lansac."

"I know. It surprises me," said Belina.

"Perchance he stole them?"

"It's possible," she admitted.

"One tool is missing," the guard said. "I have had to watch crestian joiners at their work and I know all their tools."

Belina asked him which tool was missing.

"A spokeshave. It looks like this." He drew the shape on the table. It was exactly the same as the drawing made by the crestian on his wall.

"What do joiners do with that tool?" she asked.

He made movements right and left, and away from his body. "Or they could turn it round and slit an enemy's throat."

Everybody stood like statues, not daring to move or speak.

"You spoke more truly than you knew," said Belina. "A spokeshave was found beside the corpse in the chapel." She clasped the table, her hands shaking.

"Sit down, Dame Lansac, and we will bring you a drink."

The senior guard replaced the tools in the satchel with great care and locked it up inside the chest. He turned back to Belina. "You seem to have caught the murderer."

"And yet the crestian doesn't look to me to be a murderer," said another guard.

"Why not?" Belina asked him.

"He is not proud enough, or insolent."

Another guard maintained that the crestian was in tears much of the time.

"Yes," said Belina, "and he was sobbing when I left him just now. It is not easy to think of him as being guilty of murder, despite the fact that everything points to his guilt."

She drank the cider in the beaker the guard had given to her and stood up. "Thank you for the drink. I needed it. Please look after the prisoner. I will tell my husband about him, and how you helped me. *Adiu.*"

"*Adiu*, Dame Lansac."

CHAPTER THIRTY-THREE

Tuesday

Belina spent the rest of the day writing on her wax tablets, but could not sleep for most of the night because she was worried about the summons to the lawcourt. Then she slept heavily and was woken up by Minet miaowing for her breakfast. It was a bad start to the day.

She washed her face and hands and wondered what clothes she should wear. What would impress the judge the most? Elegant clothes or rough ones to express poverty. After spending too much time trying on all her summer clothes she chose her second-best summer gown and her best kirtle to go underneath it.

She hoped she would not have to spend all day in the lawcourt, but just in case she did she ate a substantial breakfast of half a loaf, some cheese and two hard-boiled eggs, glancing every so often at the position of the sun to make sure that she would not be late to meet Jordi and Christau outside the lawcourt.

She put on her best head-cloth and smiled at her reflection in the mirror. Would the judge treat her kindly? After all, the Seneschal had done so. And what's more he had told Belina that the judge was a fair man. She hoped he was right. The big unknown was why she, Jordi and Christau had received the summons.

They discovered the reason as soon as they got inside the lawcourt. They sat on a long bench on one side of the room. The other long bench was crowded with Notaire Corloni, his wife, his children, his cousin the 'wicked stepmother' and Loupmont.

"Who's that?" Christau asked Belina, pointing to Loupmont.

Belina told him loudly, using such hostile terms that made Loupmont clench his jaw.

They all stood for the entrance of the judge and waited until he gave them permission to sit down.

The judge looked at the papers in front of him and said, "Moulié Jordi. Which of you two is that?"

Jordi pointed to himself. The judge asked about his childhood, his marriage, and his milling business, and Jordi did his best to answer all the questions clearly. He stressed the financial difficulties he'd been faced with at his father's death because his inheritance had been stolen by his stepmother. Jordi pointed to her, sitting on the bench next to the *notaire*.

"Thank you," the judge said. "Now, Moulié Christau, tell me about your position in the mill. How much work do you do in it, for example?"

Christau replied using almost the same words as Jordi had spoken. They had obviously practised their declaration together. It sounded rather like poetry.

The judge looked at Belina. "Dame Lansac, you were not living at the mill at the time of your father's death. Is that correct?"

"Yes *Maître,* I had already left home because my stepmother was unkind to me."

"That's not true," said the stepmother, "you know it isn't, Belina."

"It is true. You were an unloving successor to our mother.

You treated us very badly, not only by stealing our inheritance but by not looking after us. I despise you."

These were strong words for Belina. Jordi and Christau whispered to her to calm down.

Loupmont stood up and began to speak, but the judge ordered him to sit down and wait his turn. Loupmont almost fell off the end of the bench in his annoyance at being silenced.

The judge wrote something on a paper in front of him and sat without moving for a long time. Belina remembered Guillaume telling her once that judges with great experience did that. No movement, as if they were a cat watching a bird.

The judge looked at the Corloni family crowded on their bench. "Notaire Corloni," he began, "In what way are you and Widow Moulié kinsfolk?"

"We are first cousins."

"Who drew up the testament of Messire Moulié, the father of these two here?"

"I did."

"In my opinion it is unacceptable for a lawyer to write a document in which his close family are involved."

"That was not considered a problem at the time," came the prompt reply.

"It was by us," Christau shouted, getting to his feet and preparing to walk over to where the *notaire* was standing.

"Moulié, return to your place on the bench, if you please," said the judge. He put his spectacles on again and looked at his papers.

"Notaire Corloni, why did you not devolve the drawing up of Messire Moulié's testament to a neutral lawyer?"

"I was not acquainted with any neutral lawyers."

The judge gave a cynical "humph" and looked at the Corloni family arrayed in front of him. They kept their eyes downcast, and the *notaire* folded his arms across his paunch. The judge whispered to a clerk who went to a shelf behind the judge and returned with a bible. "Put a stool between the two benches, and the bible on the stool, if you please."

The clerk fetched a stool from a corner of the lawcourt and placed it where the judge was pointing. He put the bible on top of the stool with great reverence.

"Now," said the judge, taking off his spectacles, "Notaire Corloni, come here and place your hand on the bible, if you please, and promise me that you will speak the truth, the whole truth and nothing but the truth."

The *notaire* got up from the bench and obeyed the judge's orders. He started to return to his place on the bench.

"Stay where you are and answer my question. Why did you not devolve the drawing up of Messire Moulié's testament to a neutral lawyer?"

"I promised Dame Moulié that I would draw up the testament, and quickly, given that her husband was dying."

"Go back to your place," said the judge, frowning. "Dame Corloni, approach this stool, if you please, and put your hand on the bible."

The plump wife of Notaire Corloni did as she was told and looked at the judge.

"Is Widow Moulié your cousin or your husband's cousin?"

"My husband's cousin."

"Thank you. Go back to your seat." The judge pointed to the young man beside her and told him to come up to the bible and place his hand on it. "Do you swear that you are a member of the Corloni family?" the judge asked him.

"I do."

"In what way are you and Widow Moulié kinsfolk?"

"She is my father's first cousin."

The judge made each member of the Corloni family do the same thing while the Moulié trio looked on and Jordi whispered with Christau.

When it was Ana Corloni's turn to swear on the bible, she walked up to the stool with confidence and placed her left hand on the bible.

"Your right hand, if you please," the judge ordered.

"Why?"

"Because I order you to. The left hand is sinister and evil. I do not recognise oaths sworn using the left hand."

"But that's silly," replied Ana Corloni.

"Do as I tell you."

Ana Corloni shrugged her thin shoulders and rather awkwardly put her right hand on the bible and declared that Widow Moulié was her father's cousin.

"I do not believe you," said the judge. Everybody in the courtroom sat up straight. "I repeat my question. Is Widow Moulié your father's cousin?"

Ana Corloni repeated her answer while the judge looked at the Corloni family in front of him. He ordered Ana Corloni to turn sideward while he stared at her thin body.

"Go back to your place," said the judge. "Dame Corloni, stand beside the bible, if you please, and then turn sideward."

She presented her bloated sideview to the judge, and kept her face expressionless.

After her, each of her children came up to the bible in turn and did the same thing.

"What's happening, Belina?" Jordi whispered. "Why does he want to see the plump shapes of the Corlonis?"

"I don't know. Best just to wait and keep quiet."

After Loupmont had presented his ugly sideview to the judge and walked back to his place on the perilous edge of the bench, the judge ordered Notaire Corloni to come up to the bible again and place his hand on it and swear that he was the father of Ana Corloni. The judge pointed to the thin young woman next to the eldest son.

"I swear I am the father of Ana Corloni. She is my daughter."

"Are you sure?" the judge asked.

"Of course I am sure."

The judge asked Dame Corloni to come up to the bible. She seemed unwilling and he had to repeat his order. She put her hand on to her head-cloth and then on to the bible.

"Are you the mother of Ana Corloni?"

"I swear that I am."

"Is Notaire Corloni the father of Ana Corloni?"

"I swear... I swear..." Dame Corloni choked and stopped speaking.

The judge repeated his question, but Dame Corloni refused to answer him. The lawcourt was silent and everybody's eyes were on the *notaire's* wife.

"Dame Corloni," said the judge, "We are waiting for you to tell us who is the father of your daughter Ana."

Dame Corloni looked at her feet and bit her lip. She took her hand off the bible and began to speak.

"Put your hand back on the bible," the judge ordered. "Your right hand."

"It is my right hand." She squeaked.

"Who is the father of your daughter Ana?" the judge asked.

"Consul Senclar," she whispered.

"Speak up so that everybody can hear you." The judge had become merciless.

"Consul Senclar was the father of my daughter Ana."

"Which Consul Senclar?" the judge asked, "the present one, Henri, or his father Arnaud?"

"His father," Dame Corloni whispered.

"Speak up, I tell you."

"Consul Arnaud Senclar, long since dead, was the father of my daughter Ana." Dame Corloni was choking with humiliation.

The judge ordered her back to her place beside her husband and waited until she had squeezed her fat body onto the bench. He collected his papers together and looked at Belina, Jordi and Christau sitting on their bench. "Dame Lansac, Jordi and Christau Moulié," the judge began, "I am not prepared to waste any more of my time on complaints by the Corloni family and Loupmont. This case is dismissed." He got up and walked out of the room carrying his papers and his spectacles.

As soon as he was gone Jordi said, "let's get out of here before that lot of cheats do," he pointed to the Corloni family who were looking rather dazed and whispering to each other, shooting sidelong glances at Ana, now known to be only their half-sister. Notaire Corloni was looking at the floor. His wife was crying. Ana, though, was looking insolent. Belina wondered if she had always known who her real father was.

It was not until she had said farewell to a joyful Jordi and a contented Christau and was on her way back to the shop that Belina remembered that Ana Corloni had tried to swear an oath with her left hand on the bible. Her sinister hand.

CHAPTER THIRTY-FOUR

Belina walked straight past the shop, hoping that Quiteira would not see her, and then almost ran to the grassy place where the musical pilgrims played on their instruments and practised their chants. There were fewer than when she had listened to them last Wednesday, but the crowd of crestias seemed larger. She joined it and tried to listen to the singing while thinking about Ana's left hand.

When the singers stopped for a drink, a young pilgrim picked up a bowl of little cakes and handed it round to everybody. Belina took two of them and ate them slowly. One of the musicians took off his pilgrim's hat and holding it upsidedown invited the audience to put a coin in it.

Belina felt her purse inside its pouch concealed under her kirtle. She planned to give several coins, not as a reward for the music, but for the information she needed from the pilgrims. Three of the crestias put in a small coin but the others just shook their heads and looked sad, reminding Belina of the crestian in the prison.

She put several coins in the hat and thanked the man for the music.

"Do you sing, Dame?" he asked.

"Oh no," Belina smiled at him. "My cat sings better than I do."

"But you can smile better than your cat," he replied. "No cat can smile, or laugh."

Belina laughed at this comment. "True, but my husband tries to get our cat to be joyous."

"More joyous, no doubt, than the visitors to your shop yesterday morning."

"The most churlish cat would be happier than that horrible foursome," Belina replied.

The pilgrim led her towards the other musicians, reminded them of who she was and asked them to think back to early morning last Monday, a week ago. Had anybody seen an unknown pilgrim going in or out of the chapel?

Some pilgrims frowned, two said that they had not reached Condom until last Friday, and others shook their head. It was frustrating for Belina.

"Marie lives in Condom, and she was here last Monday," said one of the frowners, "and here she is with the cider. Ask her."

A fair-haired woman joined the group carrying a jug of cider. Each pilgrim held out their beaker and she filled them carefully while listening to the question about the chapel last Monday.

They drank from their beakers and waited for her answer. Wrinkles appeared on her forehead, she bit her lip and looked at the sky. Several minutes passed and Belina found it hard to be as patient as the pilgrims.

"Come on, Marie, do try to remember," said one of the pilgrims.

"I am trying." She pulled her beaker out of her satchel and filled it to the brim from the cider jug.

Belina was about to say something to make the woman speed up her memories when she put her beaker on a tree stump and declared with great confidence that she had seen an unknown pilgrim going past the house they are staying in very early.

"I was about to throw the contents of the chamber-pot out of the window so I yelled 'beware' and the pilgrim looked up and shouted, 'don't you dare'. Her hat fell off and I saw that her hair had been gracefully arranged. She had sophisticated hair, but a pinched, ugly face with warts on it."

"How old do you think she was?" Belina asked her.

"Mid-twenties perchance. Very thin. No bosom. If her hat hadn't fallen off I would have mistaken her for a young man."

"Where was she going?" Belina asked.

"Towards here, where we are now. She might have been going to the chapel."

"Did you see her coming back?"

"No, but I wasn't looking to see her again."

Two of the pilgrims were chatting together, much to Belina's annoyance, but when she was about to ask them to be quiet one of them declared in a loud voice, "We saw that pilgrim, too, coming back from the chapel, walking with her staff in her left hand."

"Sinister," his companion interrupted, "Christian pilgrims always walk with their staff in their right hand."

"Are you sure she was walking like that?" Belina asked, hoping that the answer was positive.

"Yes, Dame, when I say something is true it is always true." The pilgrim puffed his chest out.

"Thank you," Belina replied. "It is very important for me that you noticed the sinister-handedness because the killer in the chapel last Monday, a week ago, is known to be left-handed."

"How is that known?"

Belina told them about the angle of the wound and asked how they were sure that it was the same pilgrim as the one whose hat had fallen off.

"The pilgrim we saw was ugly in appearance and shape. In fact, we thought it was a youth, like Marie did."

"She was walking very fast and trying not to fall over her stick, as if she was not a real pilgrim and had never walked with a stick before."

"I remember now," said his companion excitedly, "there was

a lad up a pear tree and he threw a pear at the hat. And it fell off."

"That's right, and the woman was furious with the lad. She swore at him."

"The boy said he was sorry and that the pear had fallen by itself, that he had not thrown it. But she didn't believe him. Called him a filthy crestian."

The musician who had collected donations in his hat approached the group of crestias nearby who were waiting for the music to begin again, and asked them if one of their lads had heard the woman pilgrim swearing at him last Sunday morning.

A youngling was pushed towards the musician. "Pechoun did."

The musician took his arm and led the boy up to Belina. "Here is the pear-thrower, Dame."

"Oh, how wonderful?" Belina rejoiced. The boy looked at his feet and mumbled.

Belina told him that she did not care whether it was a rotten pear that had fallen down, or whether he had thrown the pear at the pilgrim last Monday. Neither did she care that he was up a pear tree. In fact, she was delighted to meet somebody who could help her, so please could he describe the pilgrim whose hat had fallen off.

"It was a woman 'cos her hair was piled up in a plait and she wore a woman's kirtle under her pilgrim's cloak."

"What colour kirtle?" Belina asked.

"Sort of green but with lots of streaks and spots on it. Weird looking."

"What colour were the streaks and spots?"

"Red. As red as blood. And when she put her hat back on I saw that her gloves were also covered in blood."

"Are you sure it was blood?" Belina persisted.

"Yes I am. The woman looked like somebody who had been cut by a saw. I know what blood looks like. We all know that in the leper colony. The carpenters are always cutting themselves."

Belina understood the logic in this and asked the boy what the woman pilgrim did next.

"She picked up her stick with one hand and put her hat on with the other hand, swore at me again and walked off."

"In which direction?"

"Towards the town."

"Thank you so much, Pechoun," Belina said. "You have made my day." She stood up straight and thanked all the pilgrim musicians, wished them *Ultreia!* and almost ran back to the shop.

CHAPTER THIRTY-FIVE

As she hurried down rue Jean-Baptiste, Belina thought quickly. The false pilgrim fitted the description of Ana Corloni, but how was she to prove it? She remembered the secret room near the back entrance of Widow Créon's mansion which the servants had said Ana used for town clothes and shoes and which was never locked. And yet it had been locked when Belina wanted to go inside it.

She decided to ask the cathedral locksmith who had helped Guillaume break into Rocca's chamber if he could break into Ana Corloni's secret room. She did not know his name so she asked the one of the cathedral guards to take her to the treasury.

She was led up some steep stairs and down a narrow passage to a room full of chests. An old monk was sitting at his desk reading a bible. The guard introduced Belina to him and left her there.

"Yes?"

"*Adischatz*," Belina began, "my husband has asked me to ask you if your locksmith could help me urgently."

"Have you locked yourself out of your chamber, Dame Lansac?"

"No, nothing as bad as that," Belina replied, "and my husband is inside it working among his papers." She hoped the monk would not see through her lie.

"So what do you need to be opened?"

"It is a room in a mansion in rue Royale where I think there is evidence about the murder which my husband is investigating."

"And you are sure it is locked?"

"It was when I was there last Sunday, and the servants were surprised because it is not usually locked."

The monk called out for the locksmith to come into his room. A young man put his head round the door.

"Bring your tools with you and accompany Dame Lansac to a mansion in rue Royale and break into a room."

"Are you sure?" The locksmith did not sound keen to obey such an order.

Belina explained what she wanted him to do, and why.

"How will I know which mansion, Dame Lansac?"

"I am coming with you. Don't worry. But please come with me now. This is very urgent."

The locksmith disappeared and came back with a satchel. He led Belina back down the passage and the steep stairs, and they crossed Place Saint Pierre together. He walked towards rue Royale, but Belina said it would be easier to go via rue Deserte and get into the mansion by the back entrance.

"Good. Front entrances have guards, and guards are sharp-eyed. Whose mansion is it, by the way?"

Belina told him that the owner lived in Bordeaux and the mansion usually only had servants living there. Sometimes it was used by a *notaire* from Montreal and his family.

"Let's hope that today they are in Montreal, not Condom." Belina did not tell him that the family actually was in Condom that morning.

They turned into rue Deserte and walked past the stables of the mansions of rue Royale, until they reached the ones next to the Prelet stables.

Belina led the way down the track beside the stables, through the garden and up the steps to the back of the mansion. The smell of stale food made her wrinkle her nose. She found the door of the room used by Ana Corloni and lifted the latch of the door. It was still locked.

She beckoned to the locksmith. No one else was around, and she hoped they were asleep after their lunch. He set to work and soon had the door open.

They went inside a small, dark, airless room and shut the door very quietly. The locksmith put an old chair beside it so that no one could come in and take them by surprise. Belina looked round the little room, seeing a chest and two trays. The locksmith picked up a shoe from one of the trays and peered at it in the dim light coming from a small window high in the wall.

He beckoned to Belina and pointed to stains on the shoe.

"Blood?" she whispered.

"I think so." He put the shoe back on the tray and examined the lock on the chest. Then he went to a corner, picked up a lantern and lit it with his flint and silex. He gave the lantern to Belina and knelt down beside the chest while she shone the light on the lock.

It did not take him long to open it up, and he made very little noise. He held the lantern for Belina while she removed clothes from the chest.

She pulled out a winter cloak and a winter skirt. It was disappointing, but she remembered the blood on the shoe. Next she found a pilgrim's hat, crushed by the two heavy garments above it. Under the hat was a pilgrim's summer cloak with scallop shell badges fastened to it. And underneath this welcome find was a green kirtle. She held it up near the lantern and looked at the red marks on the hem and the many streaks and spots of blood on the front.

"Blood," she whispered to the locksmith.

He peered at the garments. "Rather fresh blood, I think. About a week probably."

"Monday a week ago?" Belina whispered, looking at the

messy kirtle and imagining Ana Corloni slitting Viola's throat
and poor Viola's blood sprinkling that kirtle. She felt she might
be sick if she held the clothes any longer and she dropped
them back into the chest without folding them. She added the
pilgrim's cloak, the hat and the two winter garments, and took
the lantern from the locksmith so that he could shut the chest.
She hoped he could do this quietly.

It took him a few long minutes to bring the lid down without a sound and rearrange the lock. He put his tools back into
his satchel and looked around to see that nothing had been
forgotten. Then he quenched the lantern's light and placed it
back in its corner. He removed the chair from its position and
opened the door a few inches.

Belina waited, her heart beating. Suppose somebody saw
them? Suppose that person was Ana Corloni herself? She
said half an *Ave Maria* and noticed that the locksmith was
beckoning to her. They walked out of the room and he shut the
door as quietly as possible. Nevertheless, the clink of the latch
sounded as loud as a thunderclap to Belina.

They went down the steps and through the garden, walking
calmly. Nobody shouted at them and they passed the stables
and reached the road. There were several people and horses on
the road but no one appeared to pay attention to them. Belina
finished her *Ave Maria* and added two more just in case
Charles Prelet came by on his father's horse and recognised
her.

She did not relax until they were back in the cathedral
treasury and she was thanking the locksmith and the monk
again and again.

"Glad to be of help, Dame Lansac," said the locksmith.
"Any time you want to break into a mansion, just ask me." He
smiled and left the room.

"Did you find what you were looking for?" the monk asked
Belina.

"Yes indeed we did, but please don't tell anybody about

it. And please order your clever locksmith not to tell anyone either."

"No problem for us to be discreet, Dame Lansac. We are always discreet. But you haven't brought any evidence back with you."

"No. It will be more powerful proof to leave it where I found it," Belina replied.

"You know best. So there is nothing to store here?" he asked.

"Nothing but my thanks and admiration for your locksmith and for your permission for me to borrow him." Belina smiled and left the room.

She found her way down the difficult passage and the stairs and ran home filled with joy at her discovery. The clothes belonged to Ana Corloni, the pilgrims' description of her fitted in with the time of the murder and she was left-handed. But that still left one very important question unanswered: why would she want to kill Viola? Belina was sure that Ana had found a way to murder Viola which would make the crestian a suspect and lead to his arrest. A crestian who had been employed by Widow Créon to mend furniture. But what had the crestian done to be accused of murder? What would Ana achieve from Viola's death? Or from the crestian's death when he was hanged, as he surely would be unless Belina could prove his innocence?

She had found answers to none of these questions by the time she reached the staff residence and had gone up the stairs to Guillaume's chamber. She needed to write everything down on her wax tablets while today's revelations were so fresh in her mind

She opened the door and was met with a big surprise. Guillaume was back already. His satchel was lying on the bed and she could hear him singing in the inner room. She rushed into the room and threw her arms around him. They kissed for a long time until Minet miaowed and tried to trip them up.

"Damn that cat! Is she hungry?" Guillaume asked.

"No, just jealous."

But the cat's interruption brought Belina back to the result of her investigation. She told Guillaume as briefly as she could that the killer was Ana Corloni, even if the motive was still unclear.

"Where is she now?" Guillaume asked.

"That is the problem. This morning she was in the lawcourt in Condom with all the family. But they might have gone back to Montreal already."

"If she is not really part of the family, and by now they will all know it, she might still be in Condom even if all the others have ridden back to Montreal."

"True," Belina admitted. "I hope that's what's happened."

"I must go straight away to the Seneschal and tell him to arrest her." He put his shoes on and said, "And I must thank the Seneschal for organising my return." He fastened the shoes. "And on a magnificent horse, really fast and strong. When I have time I will tell you about my journey and what I dicovered." He kissed Belina again, but quickly, avoided Minet and went out.

Belina heard him running along the passage and down the stairs. She sat on the bed and brooded until Minet interrupted her thoughts by miaowing to be let out.

Belina went back into the inner room and began to sort out the tablets which she had already used recently and those which were covered with old scratches. She scraped the writing from two tablets, sharpened a stylus and sat at Guillaume's desk. She began with a short paragraph about Ana Corloni's left-handedness and her bastardy. The rest of the tablet was taken up with a description of evidence by the musical pilgrims and the boy who had thrown the pear. She began the second tablet with the locksmith's ability to open the little room in Widow Créon's mansion and how they discovered the blood-stained clothes and shoes there. She drew the kirtle on the tablet, and the skirt and the shoe, scratching the places which had blood marks. It was hard work and her right hand began to ache.

Belina tried to decide if Ana Corloni had joined up with Charles Prelet – and his sister too perchance – because they had wanted to kill Viola. But that seemed really unlikely because Charles Prelet had a pretty mistress and two children in Toulouse. Why would he want to abandon them for a bitter ugly woman in Condom? But his sister could have taken against Viola because she would have been a sister-in-law entitled to some of large Prelet inheritance. And where did Chezelle fit in with Viola's murder? She hoped Guillaume would see the situation with fresh eyes and plenty of experience.

She retrieved her head-cloth from where Guillaume had thrown it and laid it in its usual place on the shelf. She took off the clothes which she had chosen so carefully for the session in the lawcourt and had then worn under the trees near the leper colony, in the treasury inside the crumbling cathedral, and in the dark little room at the back of Widow Créon's mansion.

Belina washed herself thoroughly and wrapped herself in a clean towel. She undid her plaits and brushed her hair so vigorously that the towel fell off. She was putting it back round herself when the door opened and Guillaume strode in.

He threw his satchel off the bed and pulled her on to the bed, where they forgot all about the murder and Guillaume's journey chasing Barvaux and made love.

CHAPTER THIRTY-SIX

Time went by in Guillaume's chamber until the door was pounded so hard that it shook. Guillaume called out, "Who's there?"

"It's Alain, Messire Guillaume. You are wanted really urgently in the courtyard. A man needs to talk to you."

"He can wait," Guillaume yelled at the closed door. "Or he can find someone else to talk to."

"He says it has to be you, Messire Guillaume."

"Who is he?"

"His name sounds like Desarrebessan. I don't know him. Never seen him before."

"Is he alone, or with a dozen other men?"

"With a guard from the cathedral prison, Messire Guillaume.

"Why didn't you say that before, you fool?" Guillaume leapt off the bed.

"I didn't know it was important. Sorry."

Guillaume went close to the door but did not open it. "Tell the man and the guard that I will be down in the courtyard in a few minutes. Thank you Alain."

He searched for some clean clothes and put his sandals on while Belina remained on the bed watching him.

"What do you think he wants?" she asked. "The name means nothing to me."

"Me neither," Guillaume replied, "But Alain might have got it wrong." He combed his hair. "Perchance it's somebody sent by the Seneschal. If so, I must not keep him waiting too long."

As he ran towards the stairs, he saw the guard and the unknown man standing in the shade not far from Sir John, who was reclining in his special chair. A tall man wearing a cap, a brown doublet and walking boots. This meant that he had walked into Condom, not ridden a horse, although he was not dressed as a pilgrim. He had a large leather satchel slung over his shoulder.

Guillaume would need to ask him several questions if he wanted to find out more. He approached the stranger and said "*adischatz*".

"*Adischatz*" came the reply. No 'Messire' added to it.

"You asked to see me, I understand," said Guillaume. "Please tell me who you are and what you want from me."

"My name is Etienne de Sarbazan and I am from the manor of Sarbazan near Roquefort."

"Which Roquefort?" Guillaume asked.

"The Roquefort on the river Douze and near Mont de Marsan"

"And your question to me?"

"I have been told that you are the Bishop's Inquirer and that it was you who put my son Josep in prison. I want to know why and I want you to release him to me. My son is not a criminal."

Guillaume looked at the stranger. He was very tall. He wore a signet ring. His clothes were well cut and of good cloth. He could have been Sir John Keyham as a younger man. A knight without a horse and claiming that the crestian in the cathedral prison was his son. It made no sense.

"The man in the prison is a crestian," Guillaume told him, "and you are evidently not one yourself. Why do you think I should believe that the crestian in the cathedral prison is your son?"

"Because I give you my word."

"That is not enough in the circumstances," Guillaume replied. "The crestian is accused of murder. The murder weapon found at the scene of the crime is his carpentry tool, a spokeshave. And he was found at the scene."

"And where was this scene?"

"The Sainte Eulalie chapel, near the leper colony where the crestian lived."

"My son was brought up a God-fearing man. Do you not think that somebody else committed the murder and that my son stumbled on the site at the wrong moment?"

"We have been investigating that possibility, of course," said Guillaume.

"And what have you decided?" The stranger's voice was still calm but firmer.

"We have concluded that somebody else committed the murder," said Guillaume, watching the expression of relief take over the stranger's face. "What we do not yet know is why the murder took place."

"Why is my son still in prison if you know that he is innocent?" The tone was even firmer and the man took a step nearer Guillaume, staring at him.

"The proof was only found this afternoon. I have informed the Seneschal and the real murderer will be arrested. Indeed, I hope she already has been arrested."

"She?"

Guillaume told him as succinctly as possible how the murder had happened, but he did not give the name of the murderer.

"So my son can be set free?"

"I am going to do that as soon as I have confirmation of the murderer's arrest and confession."

"I demand that my son be set free."

"And so he shall be." Guillaume told him that the crestian would be freed as soon as possible, but as there was no proof that he was the son of somebody unknown to Guillaume, the crestian could not be released directly to his care.

The man stared at Guillaume and said, "If you allow it, I will put my satchel on that table," he pointed to the table near Sir John, "and show you documents which prove that Josep is my son."

"Go ahead," said Guillaume.

Sir John welcomed them to his part of the courtyard. Alain bustled up with two stools and offered to bring some cider.

"Yes please, that would be very welcome."

"Have you travelled a long way today?" Guillaume asked.

"No, only from the Cardinal Teste hospice on the other side of the river, but before that I have been walking – sometimes riding – for the last four months. Often with difficulty because the rivers are swollen."

He picked out a large leather purse from the objects which he had removed from his satchel and extracted several papers. "These show you who I am, who my wife is and who my son is. Take a look." He gave the first document to Guillaume.

It was a deed for the Manor of Sarbazan and the attached land. A lot of land, Guillaume realised. The second document was a testament from Mathieu de Sarbazan leaving all his property and his title to his son Etienne (apart from several religious bequests). The third document was a certificate showing that Josep was baptised in the parish church of Roquefort and that his mother was Bertrande, a crestiane of Roquefort, and that his father was Etienne de Sarbazan of the Manor of Sarbazan.

"So," said Guillaume, "Josep is only half crestian." He read the testament again. "Did you live in the manor while Josep lived with his mother in Roquefort's leper colony?"

"No, my wife and I and Josep all lived together near the caves of the leper colony of Roquefort."

Guillaume raised his eyebrows. "A difficult way of life, surely?"

"I chose it because I loved my wife. I love her still. My parents disapproved very strongly of her and threw me out of the manor."

"But you married in a church, nevertheless?" Guillaume queried.

"Yes, but without my parents. We married on Tuesday 15 April 1455. Here is the marriage certificate."

Guillaume picked up Josep's certificate of baptism again. It was dated 9 October 1456, eighteen months after the marriage date.

"I see what you were thinking. My wife and I did not marry in a hurry. It was a marriage of love, not lust."

Guillaume did not reply. He was considering whether to believe his visitor. He had never heard of a knight's son marrying a crestiane and choosing to live with her near her leper colony. And yet the documents seemed clear. He looked at the testament again, searching for a date. It was signed on 29 January 1483. "Was this drawn up when your father was dying?"

Etienne de Sarbazan nodded.

"But nothing was left to your mother?"

"In his previous testament everything was left to my mother, but she died before him. She died a year ago."

Guillaume looked at him. He did not look sad at the mention of his mother's death. Perchance she resembled Viola Lussan's mother. "Have you brothers and sisters?"

"Originally, yes. But they died of the plague four years ago. Many crestias died too. It was a dreadful time."

Guillaume asked him what he had been doing since his father's death and why he had delayed so long in searching for his son.

"I wanted to look after my estates and get used to my new life. The land was quite well run, but it was a new life for my wife and me."

"Were you welcomed by your servants, or rejected?"

Etienne de Sarbazan told Guillaume that after some early uncertainty they had both been made very welcome. The hostility towards his wife had been engendered by his mother, and after her death life had been easier for everybody. But his wife missed Josep and he had promised her to search for him and bring him back home.

"Why did he leave?"

"I wanted him to stop being enclosed in a leper colony. He had learnt very well how to be a carpenter and I bought him the best available tools and gave him money and clothes. I advised him to travel as a carpenter for three years."

"And those three years are nearly finished?" Guillaume asked.

"They ended two months ago."

"If he had returned home with a wife, would he have been welcomed with open arms?"

"Of course." Etienne de Sarbazan paused. "Is he married? I hadn't thought about that when I was searching for him."

"No, not married, but he was very much in love, and intending to marry her."

"Will I approve of her, do you think?"

"You would have done, I'm sure, but sadly she is dead. It was her murder that he was accused of."

"That is impossible."

Guillaume told him about Viola and her death. He stressed that Viola's mother had not been affectionate.

"That sounds familiar to me, alas."

Guillaume debated with himself whether the man's story was true. The documents certainly looked authentic and his behaviour persuasible. He decided to fetch the crestian out of prison and watch how the two greeted each other.

He stood up. "I will discuss the crestian's release with the authorities and let you know. Stay here for the time being with the guard. Do not leave this area. Make sure he obeys that order," Guillaume told the guard and walked out of the courtyard, locking the door behind him.

It was still hot in the street leading to the prison but Guillaume was lost in thought about what he had just learnt about his prisoner, Josep. He decided not to tell him that his father was here in Condom. Instead, he would watch them meeting each other in the courtyard. The father could perchance make a pretence of who he was and that he had fathered a crestian. It would, Guillaume thought, be less likely that Josep could pretend to be the son of somebody he did not know.

Guillaume entered the prison and spoke to the senior guard. "I have told the Seneschal who committed the murder on Monday a week ago in the Sainte Eulalie chapel. It is not the crestian in this prison, so I have come to release him. I am taking him to the cathedral staff residence where he will be restrained, but not imprisoned. Do not tell him that he is being freed."

"Who is the real murderer, Messire Lansac?"

"It's too soon to tell you. But the evidence is there."

The senior guard opened his register and on a rather untidy page scratched the date, the name *Sarbazan, Josep, crestian*, and Guillaume's name. "Please sign here," he said to Guillaume, handing him a bent quill.

Guillaume did his best with the quill. It was not an appropriate moment to discuss bad writing equipment.

He followed a guard along a passage and across a small courtyard to the crestian's cell. He was sitting on the floor and staring at Guillaume standing in the open doorway.

"I am taking you to another place," Guillaume told him.

The crestian stood up rather stiffly. No exercise for eight days had taken its toll on his previously supple body. He was placed between Guillaume and the guard, and in the guardroom his wrist was fastened to a chain which clipped on to the leather thong around another guard's wrist.

"Is it far?" the crestian asked.

"No," said Guillaume, "but take care not to tug at your wrist."

They walked along rue Jean-Baptiste to the door of the staff residence. Guillaume unhooked the key from his belt and unlocked the door. He pushed the crestian gently through the doorway, still tied to the guard. Guillaume locked the door again and looked into the courtyard. Etienne de Sarbazan had his back to them and was talking with Sir John. Guillaume told the guard to unclip the crestian's chain. They waited to see what happened next.

The crestian looked round the courtyard and then saw Sir John waving his left arm. Etienne de Sarbazan turned round to see who Sir John was waving to, sprang to his feet and rushed towards the crestian with his arms wide open. They met in the middle of the courtyard and embraced each other. "*Pair*, I have missed you so much." The young man buried his face against his father's chest.

Etienne de Sarbazan looked at Guillaume. "Thank you so very much," he said.

CHAPTER THIRTY-SEVEN

At that moment Belina came down the stairs, having grown impatient at Guillaume's absence. She was amazed to see the crestian clutching a man unknown to her, but she decided not to interrupt. Guillaume had not seen her arrive because he was telling the three guards that they need not stay any longer, and then he asked Alain if he could organise the residence's visitors' chamber to be made ready for father and son to stay in for a few days.

"And what about the horse-thief?" Alain asked. "The one I helped to catch."

"Oh him," said Guillaume. "I've forgotten all about him. He can stay where he is for a few months. Do him some good, keep him out of any more mischief. I am still full of admiration at the way you caught him, Alain"

He turned round and saw Belina walking towards Sir John, who was smiling. He caught Belina up and told her what had been happening. Sir John called out to Alain as he was carrying bedding to the spare chamber, and made signs to him to bring some *hypocras* for everybody. They were joined by Etienne de Sarbazan who put his precious documents back in his satchel and slung it over his shoulder. Alain brought more stools and glasses, poured out the *hypocras* and they were happily pledging each other's health when there was a pounding at the door.

"Open up in the name of the Lord Seneschal!"

That was a surprise. The Seneschal never came to this part of Condom unless it was absolutely necessary because it was considered to be the bishop's territory.

Guillaume walked over to the door and put his key in the lock. He pulled the door open an inch in case it was a jest and he found himself facing a group of drunk soldiers. But it really was the Seneschal. Guillaume welcomed him in, wondering if his arrival brought good news or bad.

The Seneschal pointed to Etienne de Sarbazan and his son drinking with Sir John and Belina. "I had hoped to find you alone, Lansac, except perchance for your wife and the old English knight who lives here. Is it true that he cannot speak or write?"

"Yes, my lord, but he understands everything."

"So who are the other two?"

Guillaume told the Seneschal about the knight and the crestian.

"Let us join them," said the Seneschal, "I could do with a drink after the tiresome time I had with Ana Corloni." He approached the table and Belina got to her feet, so the Sarbazans stood up too.

Guillaume introduced them to the Seneschal, who smiled at them and sat down on what had been Guillaume's stool, while Guillaume fetched the bottle of *hypocras* and another glass, which he filled and gave to the Seneschal. "Did Ana Corloni confess?" he asked.

"Yes, and she gave me a few surprises too. Luckily, she was still in the mansion in rue Royale and she was dragged to the Fort, resisting all the way." He drank some *hypocras*. "But I think that was just for show because when she reached my room she became less difficult. She confessed to the murder, but said it had been done on the orders of Dame Edith Senclar." He drank some more *hypocras*. "Personally, I think that she worked willingly with Edith the Poisoner but that the plot was devised by Dame Edith. Ana Corloni stole the spokeshave."

He broke off, looked at Josep and said, "Your spokeshave, in fact," and Josep nodded. "She put on a pilgrim's cloak and hat very early on Monday last week, she walked to the chapel, took off the cloak and assaulted Dame Viola from behind, killing her instantly – or so she told me. I hope that was true. She left the spokeshave where it would be found, putting the blame on the crestian carpenter. After that she put the pilgrim's cloak back on again, so that it hid her bloodstained clothes, walked back into Condom and left those clothes in the room where she always stored her town clothes. Then she was able to sneak up the stairs to her bedchamber and change into a gown for the betrothal banquet next door."

The Seneschal turned to Belina. "Without you discovering that evidence of guilt in the chest in that locked room, we could not have arrested Ana Corloni so easily, and prosecuting her would have involved forcing a confession from her."

He continued with Ana Corloni's story. "She had assumed that when she met Dame Edith at the banquet she would have been fervently thanked. Instead, Dame Edith was in a ghastly temper and furious with her. Apparently, she had arranged for Chezelle, her tooth-drawer from Châtellerault, to arrive at the chapel with two watchmen in time to catch Ana Corloni with red hands – truly, because of the blood – and Chezelle would have organised the arrest. But Chezelle, being an idle man, had arrived much too late and found that there really was a crestian there."

The Seneschal sipped some more *hypocras* and looked at Josep. "I am pleased that you have been freed, very pleased."

"Why did Ana Corloni want to kill Viola?" Belina asked. "Even after I had realised that she was the murderer I couldn't understand her motive."

The Seneschal told her that years ago when Ana Corloni was only fifteen and staying in her aunt's mansion next to the Prelet mansion, Charles Prelet was a law student in Toulouse who visited his parents occasionally in Condom. To amuse himself he would spend his nights with the young girl next door. He probably thought nothing of it, but she cherished a desire to marry her lover. His betrothal to Viola Lussan killed her dream of being a lawyer's wife in Toulouse and she became very jealous of Viola Lussan. Ana Corloni's bastardy had long been suspected but no one had known who her real father was until this morning, when the judge made Dame Corloni confess that Ana's father was Edith Senclar's husband. That was presumably the reason Dame Edith wanted to get her husband's bastard daughter hanged."

"But why did Dame Edith choose Viola Lussan?" Guillaume asked.

"Edith the Poisoner is totally devoted to her appalling son Henri, and she is absolutely determined to further his career as much as possible. She was hoping he would become the most senior Consul in Condom once Consul Prelet had died – which is expected to happen rather soon. But when she heard that Consul Prelet had arranged for his son Charles to move back to Condom and marry Consul Lussan's daughter she realised that her cherished stratagem of becoming the Mother of the Senior Consul would fail. Edith the Poisoner refused to be defeated, so she made use of Ana Corloni and Chezelle. She investigated Viola Lussan by getting one of her own maids employed in the Lussan mansion to spy on Dame Viola. That way, Dame Edith found out about Viola Lussan's secret life and hopes."

The Seneschal finished his glass of *hypocras* and Alain filled it up again. "I regret that I cannot arrest Dame Edith, which means that she has got away with yet another murder." He sipped some *hypocras*. "But Ana Corloni will hang, which is no more than she deserves. A bitter ugly bastard, and we shall be well rid of her."

He put his glass down and turned towards Belina. "When your brother Geraud is well enough he and Wasila – that's her name, isn't it? – can live in one of the chambers in the Cadeot

Fort and, as I told you before, Geraud will help me with advice about the war in Granada of which I do not approve. That Spanish physician who is looking after him now – Dame Lansac, I know he's there, living in Benasse's house – he will be very welcome to stay in Condom. Spanish Jews make excellent physicians, and we are lucky to have him."

Etienne de Sarbazan raised his eyebrows at these comments but said nothing. He had suffered more than enough from superstition because he had married a crestiane. He would not add the Spanish Inquisition to his troubles. He put his arm round Josep and looked at the Seneschal. "Thank you for saving my son, Lord Seneschal."

The Seneschal picked up his glass and stood up, so the others did too. "It is time to wish you and your son a happy future together, and to thank Belina and Guillaume – I hope I can address you in such a way – for solving the mystery."

They all clinked glasses and embraced each other.